THE MAPMAKER'S WIFE

Christine E. Forth

DEDICATION

For Rupert and Beatrice
and for
Miss Cavanagh RIP

ACKNOWLEDGEMENTS

I am grateful for the enduring support of friends and family, especially my husband and two sons and their spouses. In 2014, the mentors at the week-long Sage Hill Writing Experience in Saskatchewan helped me get this novel launched, and the many distinguished writers who gave monthly workshops at the Canadian Authors Association provided a wealth of insight and information on how to be a better writer. Special thanks to Nancy MacKenzie who, through her skill and infinite patience as an editor, pulled me gently along to the finish line, and Lynne Melcombe for her excellent copy-editing and editorial suggestions. Last but not least, hearty thanks to my wonderful writer friends here in Edmonton, especially Norma, and the members of my two writing groups, who faithfully read and critique everything I write. Thank you all.

PART I

Kildean, Ireland
Somerset, England
London, England

1844-1848

ONE

A single word descended like a swooping bird. "Circus!" It came from the direction of the great oak that grew on a grassy mound at the edge of the village of Kildean. Catherine Joyce, returning from the standpipe, heard the word, dropped her full pails and looked towards the tree. Five navvies sat under the oak drinking, laughing, chatting and gesticulating. They were workers returning home from building railways and canals in England, just in time to join their families for the spring and summer sowings.

Kildean was three hours' walk from the bustling port of Waterford, where the ships sailed to and from England, and the big oak, which people called the Resting Tree, was a convenient stopping place for seasonal workers as they shuttled between England and Ireland. When she was a little girl, Catherine enjoyed listening to their tales of the fabulous land across the sea where everyone was rich and dripping in jewels. As childhood blossomed into girlhood, she even enjoyed some mild flirting and banter with them. But since her father's death two years earlier, just after her fifteenth birthday, she had avoided the navvies at the Resting Tree, for their stories reminded her of the whimsical promises her father had made.

Yet on this bright May morning in 1844, she did not walk past the tree as she usually did. She stopped and looked up. For she had heard the word "circus." No wonder the navvies were excited. There had never been a circus anywhere near Kildean. She'd heard about circuses that travelled to Dublin and Cork, but there had never been one in Waterford County. She wanted to know more. Leaving her pails on the path, she hitched up her skirts and scrambled up the mound to hide behind the great trunk of the tree. She pressed her body close to the tree, the better to hear what the navvies were saying.

"True it is, a circus," she heard. "Didn't we see their ship dock this morning?"

"They'll be setting up in that big field down by the river, just after the first Tipperary milestone."

Catherine gasped. She knew that field. It lay among the densely packed towns and villages along the river, an hour from Kildean, less at a fast walk. A shortcut to the field led right past her cottage, up the hill and down the other side. One of the men heard her and turned.

"Well, if it isn't our lovely curly-top," he said with a grin and a raised eyebrow. "Where have you been these last few seasons?"

Catherine knew the fellow. He was one Da had warned her to steer clear of. She shot him a coy smile. "Nice to see you again, too. And how's your good wife these days? And your half-dozen children?"

His companions snorted with laughter, but the man, unfazed, patted the ground beside him. "Ah, come on, Red, don't be like that. Sit with us a while."

Catherine raised her eyebrows in mock horror. "And why would I want to sit with likes of you?"

The other men guffawed.

"Whoa there!" said one.

"Careful she don't scratch you," said another.

Catherine laughed, too, but she was laughing at them, not with them.

"Yes, you'd better watch out," she said, and clawed the air with her hands. "Now, tell me about this circus. When does it begin?"

"First performance is tonight, they say, before the sun goes down."

Tonight! Catherine looked at the sky. It was already nearly noon. She and her two sisters had all the afternoon chores to complete. With any luck, Ma was gone for the day, pulling weeds at the potato patch, so they could sneak out before she got back. Catherine ran her fingers through her unruly hair. Too much to do.

She flapped a dismissive hand at the men, and slipped and slid down the mound to the road, where she picked up her pails, spilling the water, and started home.

"Bye, Red," called one of the men with a laugh.

"Maybe we'll see you later at the circus?" shouted another, also laughing.

The home in which Catherine lived with her mother and sisters, and to which she hurried that day with her water pails, was a cabin set among a huddle of similar structures at the far lower edge of the village, where the poorest people lived. The interior of the cabin had a beaten earth floor, dusty in summer, damp in winter, with a large stone fireplace around which Catherine, her mother, and her sisters slept on straw pallets. A wooden table with a candlestick and four chairs sat in the middle of the room. A crucifix was nailed to one wall, and her mother's pride and joy, a rickety dresser with a few patterned china plates, was propped against the opposite wall. Catherine and her sisters were not allowed to touch the plates. Beside the fireplace were several large cooking pots and a big wooden spoon used to stir the pots and for other less congenial jobs. To this day, Catherine remembered the sting of that spoon on her backside, wielded by her mother for some misdemeanor.

Catherine emptied the water pails into a storage vat outside the cabin door, and entered. In the dim light of the interior, the family's lumbering sow got under her feet. It grunted in protest as she kicked it aside. Ma was not home, thank goodness, but the chickens were squawking angrily and no one had bothered to bank up the fire. Where were her sisters? She found them outside at the back, cross-legged on the ground, playing with the sow's newborn piglets. Bridget was seven years old and Norah, just five. Catherine stood before them, hands on hips, and chastised them for their laziness, but she couldn't help the smile that burst through her stern expression.

When she told them the news, they crowded around her, tugging at her skirts. They knew about circuses, but, like Catherine, had never imagined one would come so close to their village.

"Shall we be able to go, Katie?" said Norah.

"Will there be white horses and trick riders? Oh, I do hope so," said Bridget, casting her eyes heavenward, as if she'd seen a herd prancing across the sky.

"I want to see a monkey on a stick. Will there be a monkey, Katie, will there?" asked Norah, jumping up and down and pulling on Catherine's sleeve.

"You will take us, won't you?" begged Bridget.

"Sure I will, and that's a promise. But we have to be careful. If Ma comes back early, we can't tell her 'cause she'll stop us from going. We have to keep it a secret. Can you do that?" The girls nodded.

"We'll have to get the chores finished before the sun goes down and then we'll slip out."

"I'll feed the chickens and collect the peat for the fire," said Bridget.

"And I'll clean up the pig's mess and sweep the floor," said Norah. She pushed a squealing piglet towards its sow with her foot.

"And both of you, keep a lookout for Ma and tell me if you see her coming."

By late afternoon the cottage was clean and tidy, and the animals fed and watered. But Bridget had not yet returned with the peat, and the potatoes still had to be peeled and cut and put in the pot.

Catherine stood at the cottage door, wiping her hands on her apron. The news had spread fast. Already in the distance she could see people filing down from the upper village towards their cluster of cabins. So soon! They had to hurry. Catherine quickly prepared the potatoes and put them to soak in the pot. Finally, Bridget arrived with the peat and banked up the fire, but there was no time now to cook the potatoes before they left. Ma would be cross about that. Nothing they could do about it. They had to leave. Supper would have to wait.

The jam jar of coins on the mantelshelf tempted, but Catherine dared not touch it; Ma would notice for sure. She ran to her pallet and reached her hand underneath, where she kept her egg money. Da had bought the hen as a day-old chick, and helped her raise it as her own. The bird was a good layer, and the eggs were hers alone to sell. She counted the coins carefully, put them in her pocket, and crossed her fingers that there would be enough to buy three tickets.

Catherine went to the door again. The line was already filing past their cabin. She saw her mother advancing towards them against the crowd. Catherine grabbed her sisters.

"Quick," she said.

They slipped in among the crowd and became part of the moving stream of people as Ma arrived at the cabin, stopped, frowned, and scanned the line. Even if she saw them now, she wouldn't make a scene here, not in front of the whole village. They were safe.

Ahead of them, the line stretched like a braid of multi-coloured ribbon, tracing the dips and rises and gentle curves of the road, until it disappeared from sight at the bend that led to the main road from Waterford City, and then appeared again as it turned onto the hill that led to the circus ground.

People wore their Sunday best, as if Easter had come again in May. Catherine smoothed her hand on her shabby grey skirt. She had no Sunday best. Since Da's death there had been no money for new clothes. Not that there was much even before he died. Only promises. But she had shoes, which hardly anybody else had. They were his birthday gift, a few months before he died, and though Ma was furious he'd spent money on something as frivolous as shoes, Catherine loved them. Having a pair of shoes, she thought, set her apart from the rest of the villagers, and made her feel special.

The shoes were for special occasions only. She took care of them and they shone like her hair. Beautiful hair. Hair to make the angels weep, her da used to say. Deep copper red, it hung in glossy ringlets down her back. On windy days, it massed in a tangle of fiery silk. Tying it up tamed it a little, but tendrils escaped and called to her fingers to twirl them 'round, and pull out wisps at her neck and temples until the bun collapsed in a ripple of curls. The hint of judgement in the glances of the village wives (and the admiration from their husbands) as she passed by with her head uncovered, didn't go unnoticed by Catherine. Curious, she thought, that her crowning glory should evoke censure from women, but visible approval from men. And sometimes the back of Ma's hand. "Cover your hair," she would hiss and yank Catherine's shawl over her head, which would make Catherine grit her teeth and shake her head away.

Father Quinn once gave a sermon on the sin of vanity. "Vanity is a sign of a restless soul, which seeks the barren path that leads to perdition," he said, staring down at Catherine the whole time. The glint in his eye made her squirm. She stared back, held his gaze, until

Ma saw her and gave her leg a little slap. At moments like that, she hated her mother even more than usual. And Father Quinn. And the whole village. She refused to be humbled. Da had told her to ignore the wagging tongues. Wasn't her hair a gift from God, he'd said, and didn't He know better than anyone on earth?

Catherine and her sisters gained the bend, and ahead of them saw other lines from neighbouring villages merge like tassels to the main braid. Michael Keane and Kevin Ryan from the next village were up ahead with their simpering brides. There had almost been a fight at one of the Saturday dances recently. All because Michael and Kevin looked at Catherine in a way that got everyone het up just a week before their weddings. They were not the first ones, either. She smiled to herself. Let them look, for that was all they would ever do, though they might hope otherwise.

The line of people was halfway up the hill, and the chatter and laughter were getting raucous. Catherine jingled the coins in her pocket. Da would not have minded her using the egg money for this. On the contrary, he would have loved a circus. In her mind, she could feel her hand buried in his, and see Norah hoisted on his shoulders, Bridget on his other hand. She could sense his lighthearted mood, the lilt in his step, his teasing laughter. She brushed her hand across her eyes.

Bridget and Norah ran ahead to join the other children. "Go and enjoy yourselves," she called. This was not a time to be sad. But, oh, how she missed her da. Two years ago, he'd got caught up in the wheels of a runaway horse and cart belonging to Mr. Johnson, the Englishman. The village men had carried his mangled body up to the Johnson's manse and were shooed away. Later, the Englishman's wife sent a boy with a sealed envelope bearing the Johnson's insignia. Inside were four crisp five-pound notes.

"Hush money," Ma had sniffed. Still, they lived well on the twenty pounds for months. Da would have laughed. "Enjoy meat while you can," he'd have said. "When the money's gone it'll be potatoes again."

Catherine would look at her mother's workworn face and straggly hair and wonder why her father, so sparkling and full of fun, had ever married a dull and bitter woman like her. He said she'd been a great beauty once, just as Catherine was now. *That's what happens,*

Catherine supposed, *to women in Ireland when they marry. They start having babies, and they lose their looks and then they lose their men.* She looked around at the crowd heading up the hill. There were quite a few of them right there—pinched faces, long thin noses, toothless grins, shapeless bodies. It wasn't going to happen to Catherine. Da might be gone, but she still felt his hand in hers. He had believed in her, stood up for her. When Ma said she was willful, Da said she was just high-spirited. "Like an Irish thoroughbred filly," he'd said, "high-stepping, brave, with a touch of the wild in its eyes." Father Quinn had reminded him that fillies had to be broken and tamed. Well, she'd rather be a prancing filly than a blinkered dray horse harnessed to a cart, face stuck in a nosebag.

The crowd's excitement rose to a crescendo, and Bridget and Norah ran back to Catherine, pulling her by the hand to the top of the hill. They looked down to the field below, where a massive tent stretched from one side to the other. Beyond the tent was a cluster of canvas shelters, wagons, and brightly painted caravans, yellow and red and green, with tethered horses munching grass nearby. Men and women in bright costumes milled around.

Catherine and her sisters ran down the hill to beat the crowd and get closer to the front. At the gate to the field, the circus announced itself with a huge placard. Bridget tugged at her skirt.

"What does it say, Katie, what does it say?"

Da had sent Catherine to the free Hedge School for a year so she could learn to read and write, and she'd been a fast learner. "It's like this," Da had said, jerking his head towards the Englishman's manse. "They can keep us living like dogs forever, but we Irish still have the best stories and the best writers and we can all learn to read and write."

The words on the placard were easy for Catherine. "Billy Mather's Amazing Circus," she read, "and look, it says there will be clowns, and horses, and, oh yes, it says, monkeys too, and lots of other things!"

Bridget and Norah hung on to Catherine's hand as they followed the crowd to the entrance, where a man in a velvet tailcoat and a tall hat with a green ribbon around it took Catherine's money and counted it carefully. Catherine bit her lip and waited. Then the man pointed them towards the tent. They were in! They scrambled through the crowd and found a spot to sit on a wooden bench near the sawdust ring. Trumpets sounded. The chattering crowd went silent. A man in a gold-braided suit entered the ring, leading a team of white horses with red and gold bridles, and the audience erupted in cheers. The circus had begun.

When it was all over, the three sisters walked out from the tent into the twilight to head home. Bridget and Norah giggled and skipped, sharing their favourite moments. Catherine was silent. The sights and sounds and smells of the show were a blur of colour and movement, a background to the one crystal image she held. The strongman.

He wore a black costume that hugged his torso and legs, leaving his arms and upper chest exposed. His hair was dark and glossy with a stray lock that fell onto his forehead. His lips were full, his cheeks slightly ruddy. Wide leather straps encased his wrists and ankles. A golden belt glistened at his waist. He stood on the podium with his feet slightly apart, his knees flexed, his arms akimbo.

A woman in a red sequined dress stalked around the man, displaying before the audience a wreath of silver chains. The man stood statue-still as she pulled the first chain taut, held it aloft, passed it under his arms and around his body, and secured it with a large padlock. The man lowered his arms to his sides and the woman took the next chain and wrapped it three times around his body. With the third chain, she tied the first two together in a large knot at his waist. The man's arms and torso were now enclosed in the thick coil of metal.

A drumroll sounded. The audience waited. Catherine watched, entranced, as the man strained muscle and sinew against the chains. His face flushed with effort. Sweat glistened on his forehead and his chest. She heard his breathing grow faster, louder as he pushed against his cage of silver chains, as he thrust his body back and forth, and she found her own breaths matched his: inhale, exhale, inhale, exhale. His body rippled and trembled as every muscle hardened, and her heart throbbed in her ears, her head, her lungs. Then one final push, a groan, a sigh, and the chains burst apart, cascading downwards and pooling at his feet. The audience, the man with the drum, and the sequined lady fell away from Catherine's eyes as the applause faded to a distant rumble. She was alone in the tent with the man on the podium.

Then Norah tugged at her arm and said something; Catherine didn't hear what. The throbbing in her head subsided, replaced by the cheering and clapping of the audience as the strongman took a bow. As he straightened his glistening torso, she saw him look directly at her. She held his gaze, feeling the blood rush to her face. Then he smiled at her, a lopsided smile, and gave a little nod and a jerk of his head towards the back of the tent. As if to say, "Meet me afterwards." It was almost imperceptible, but it happened, she was sure. She closed her eyes. When she opened them, he was gone.

As they left the tent, Catherine told Bridget and Norah to play with the other children for a while, and wait for her at the gate. She followed the sound of voices and whinnying horses to the back of the tent. Her hands shook. Her face burned. Ahead of her, a group of performers, still wearing their spangled costumes, chatted among themselves. Some called goodnight to their colleagues, while others tossed grass to the animals in the makeshift pen erected at the end of the field. A woman's laugh came from behind one of the caravans, the sound of shouting from another. In the dim light it was hard to see anyone clearly, but she would know him, even in the dark. Hadn't his meaning been clear? She could not have been mistaken. And then, she saw him, leaning against one of the painted caravans, talking with a group of acrobats. She made to go towards him, but a woman stepped in front of her and barred her way.

"Circus folk only in here."

Catherine recognized her as the sequined woman who had held the chains. Close up, her face looked hard, her mouth held a sneer. She went to grasp Catherine's arm, but Catherine shrugged her off and ran towards the strongman. "Hey, you!" the woman shouted, "You can't go in there," and pulled the ends of Catherine's shawl. Catherine tugged her shawl away from the woman and continued her course. As she entered the strongman's line of sight, he pulled languidly away from the acrobats, jerked his head at the sequined woman, and shot Catherine a lazy smile as he strolled towards her.

"You came," he said.

Catherine, stock still now, was too overwhelmed by his smile to respond. From the corner of her eye, she saw the sequined woman stomp away.

The strongman held out his hand to her, palm up. "I'm Jack. What's your name?"

"Catherine." She could muster no more than a whisper, and thought she might faint.

"Catherine, the girl with the copper locks and cornflower eyes. So where do you live, Catherine? Far from here?"

Catherine still could not speak, only shake her head.

"So come again," he said. "Come and see me tomorrow, about noon. I'll be here with the horses." He paused. "Can she talk?" he said, turning to his grinning companions. And then that smile again. She relaxed and gave him her most radiant smile back, feeling her eyes sparkle and her face burn as he looked her up and down.

"I'll see you tomorrow then," he said. It was not a question.

She fled, still flushed, collected her sisters, and started home. His name was Jack. Jack. Jack.

In the morning, she rushed through her chores, slipped out while her mother was not looking, and headed towards the circus ground, dodging behind trees and rocks along the way to keep out of sight of any nosy villagers. At the circus ground, she looked around, breathless, heart pounding. But for a few men here and there, the field was quiet. The sequined woman was nowhere to be seen. She looked to the far end of the field, where the animals were corralled, and saw Jack with the horses, as he'd said he would be. She steeled herself to approach him, moved closer, stopped, waited, moved forward again. As she grew close, he must have sensed her presence, for he turned, smiled, and held out his hands.

"Here she is," he said. "Ruby Red Catherine with her hair and her eyes."

He'd remembered! Catherine moved closer still. Her body trembled. Her hands, which longed to touch his face and his body, felt hot and damp.

"Come and help me then. Make yourself useful, girl."

He handed her a grooming brush. She began to brush the horse. He laid his hand on top of hers, moved so close she could smell the sweetness of his sweat, and feel the heat of his body against hers. As they brushed the horse together, she closed her eyes and felt again as if the world consisted only of her and Jack.

He led her to the copse behind the field and loved her, transported her with the touch of his hand on her neck, her breast, the special place between her legs. When he entered her, she felt the grey sky open and the sun stream down, filling her with heat and light.

The next day, he loved her again. And the day after that. May passed to June. The crops sprouted, green and lush, and Catherine's chores lay neglected or hived off to her sisters, while Jack took her to ecstasy in the copse each day behind the circus field.

After their lovemaking, they lay together under the trees, talking and laughing. Jack enthralled her with his stories of circus life, the thrill of performance, the risks and the tumbles, the squabbles and feuds, the fun and the laughter. She grew jealous of the bond he had with the other circus folk—the monkey man, the sequined woman, the bearded lady—because they were part of his world. When she pouted, he cupped her face in his hands, kissed her on the lips and teased her. "You're much more beautiful than the bearded lady."

"What about the sequined woman, the one who helps you? She's pretty. Do you love her?" she asked.

"Nah! She's my assistant, that's all." He gave a sly smile, and rubbed his chin, "But you're right, she's a good looker. Never thought about that before."

Catherine frowned and slapped his arm. "But I'm prettier, aren't I? Tell me I am. You love me more, don't you?"

Jack laughed, and pushed her down to the ground, kissing her neck.

TWO

On a July day in 1844, Mary Piper waved to her brother, Thomas, as his train pulled away from the station. The platform at Bath railway station was crowded with people waving, smiling, calling their goodbyes. Thomas leaned out of the open third-class carriage and shouted something, but with the screech of the train and the din of the people, Mary strained to hear what he said. *I'll see you again soon*, it might have been, or perhaps, *Don't worry, Little Sparrow.*

Little Sparrow. Her father had given her that pet name as a child. Incongruous now for such a tall, large-boned young woman. But the name had stuck. Both her father and mother were dead now. It was just her and her younger brother, Thomas, a loyal and affectionate boy of seventeen, and though Mary stood a head taller than him, he still called his sister after a little brown bird. Sweet boy, and always so grave. She blew him a kiss and watched his face disappear in the cloud of steam that rose up to the platform's timbered roof as the London-bound locomotive gathered speed along the track.

Others had left for London before Thomas, following the trend of the emptying Somerset countryside. Few came back. They found jobs in London, they settled, they thrived. No doubt Thomas would too. Someone had given him the name of a tailor's shop. No guarantee of a job, but he was hopeful. By September, he said, he'd surely be able to send for Mary to join him in London. Not because she wanted to go, but because she couldn't stay. Not after what had happened on a spring day four months ago. One single day, that had turned her life around completely.

She folded the handkerchief she'd been waving, and replaced it in the reticule tied to her waist. Folk dressed in summer finery drifted from the wooden platform into the spacious station hall and onto the street. She put up her parasol and followed the crowd, but turned off from the main street to avoid the city centre with its grand Georgian buildings, its famous Roman baths, and its fine hotels where wealthy tourists stayed. From the station it was an hour's walk back to the little village of Woolcot where she lived. The way led through a maze of narrow lanes lined with high hedgerows, the same lanes she used to wander with her mother, Elinor, to collect medicinal herbs and wild roots to dry and steep: lavender, wild raspberry, chamomile, yarrow. As she walked, she felt a catch in her throat at the memory.

A gap in the hedgerow led across a wheat field, and then to a shortcut along the river bank to the village. A pair of proud swans with three cygnets swam in a V-formation. The cygnets' antics, as they dived and splashed and fluttered their wings, made her smile. Perhaps there would be swans in London. Riverside walks. And willow trees, like the ones that dipped into the water here.

At the village, she entered the one-room cottage she'd lived in all her life. After her father died, her mother had taken in a lodger to help with the rent until Thomas gained employment as an errand boy. Now, with her mother also dead, she and Thomas lived there alone.

The cottage was modest and cosy, with a flagstone floor and leaded windows, but often cold and damp, even in the midst of summer. The big old iron bedstead she'd shared with her mother was pushed against one wall to capture some warmth from the adjoining cottage. A washstand beside it held a jug and a bowl, soap and a towel, and a table in the centre always held a cheerful vase of flowers. The cedar trunk at the foot of the bed kept the damp and mould off their clothes and bedsheets. Thomas's trundle bed was under the front window, close enough to the fireplace on the other adjoining wall to take the chill off his sheets. The third bed, where the lodger used to sleep, was still set up by the back door that led to a courtyard. When he left, Mary took down the privacy curtain and laid it along the windowsill by the back door to soak up the rain that leaked in.

Mary removed her bonnet, placed it on the hat stand by the door, and put her parasol in the umbrella stand. The fire Thomas had lit that morning to heat water for their tea had burned low. Mary went to the bunker in the courtyard and filled the coal scuttle. With the fire built up, she lit an oil lamp and settled down in a wicker chair by the fire with her knitting.

Thomas would be halfway to London by now. He must be excited, or nervous perhaps. The oil lamp fizzed. Mary's knitting needles clicked, but she found herself dropping stitches and getting the wool twisted. She had clumsy fingers. She put the knitting down. Her mother, Elinor, had been a good knitter, with hands that were slender, delicate, but strong, too, like Mary's hands. A midwife needed strong hands. Perhaps if her mother had still been alive and been with her that spring day four months ago, things might have turned out differently. For Mary and for Thomas.

As a young child, she'd trailed her mother from house to house, village to village, watching and learning: how to massage a labouring woman's belly with lavender oil, how to gauge the stages of labour and the condition of the cervix, which herbs to use to advance labour and which for pain and bleeding.

The first time she had birthed a baby, under her mother's guiding hand, she had been barely eight years old. It was a September evening, in an upstairs room, dark but for the glow of the fire. As was the custom, village women were gathered in the room, whispering gossip among themselves to pass the time. From the bed came intermittent moans, soothed by Elinor's gentle ministrations.

When the moans turned into a shriek, Elinor smiled at Mary, and nodded. While Elinor pressed down on the mother's abdomen, Mary held out her cupped hands to receive the baby's head as it crowned.

The neighbours around the bed gasped. "She's still a child," said one. "But she knows just what to do," said another. As the shoulders and torso arrived, Mary slid her right hand down to receive them, and cradled the head in her left hand. Deftly, with the baby nestled in the crook of her left arm, Mary took the proffered blanket and wrapped the baby in it, while Elinor worked to deliver the afterbirth.

"Look at the little girl. She's a natural and no mistake," one of the neighbour women said. Another remarked, "Trust the midwife. She knows when her daughter's ready."

* * *

A coal shifted in the grate, sending sparks into the chimney and startling Mary from her reverie. She got up and went to fill the kettle from the water jar by the back door. Thomas's fishing rod lay propped against the wall. Outside the window, stars were coming out. Thomas must be in London by now. Did the moon and stars shine the same way in London? She took the kettle to the fire and hefted it onto the hook to heat.

Their mother had died two years ago. Mary had been seventeen, a large girl, shy and awkward with her peers, but comfortable with older women. She was, they said, her mother's daughter, with the same sweet nature, pure heart, and quiet compassion. But though Mary had appreciated their regard for her character, she'd known that, as a midwife, she would never be as skilled or as confident as her mother. Still, she'd been grateful for every call, and thrilled when the knock on the door came. Often, on the doorstep, a little girl. "Mama says, please come." Sometimes a panicked husband. With her bag of tools and her bundle of herbs in hand, she'd be greeted with smiles of relief from the women; husbands would be banished to the tavern. "Trust the midwife," they would say. "She'll know what to do."

Trust. That was the problem. The kettle hissed. The water had boiled. Mary poured it into the teapot and placed it on the hearth to steep. From out in the street, a baby cried. It was, she knew, her neighbour's newborn. The crying rose and fell as the mother walked her baby up and down the street. Mary wished it would stop, but it didn't. It went on and on.

She went to the wooden larder box on the mantelshelf, and took out half a loaf of bread and some cheese for her supper. She had wrapped the other half in paper and put it in Thomas's haversack so he would have something to eat on the journey.

She had never told Thomas the full story of what had happened that spring day four months ago. The day had begun with such promise. An early morning call to the next village, where a woman called Harriet Pickard was in labour with her tenth child. The daffodils were in bud along the riverside as she walked to Harriet's cottage with her bag of tools and bundle of herbs. The willow trees were leafing out, and the sun was bright.

In the days that followed, Thomas heard the story from others. From the women who'd been there, who whispered it to their neighbours, who in turn whispered it to the merchants. Soon everyone in both villages had heard. They heard how Harriet Pickard had moaned and writhed and bled all day and into the night, hour after hour. They heard how the blood flowed like a river from Harriet's womb, soaking the sheets, pouring onto the floor, seeping into Mary's clothes. And how, in the early hours, as a single, ungodly shriek emanated from Harriet's throat, her womb at last gave forth its product. They heard how the women stared, white with shock, and Mary took the thing from between Harriet's legs, handed it to the women, told them to take it away, and never to tell Harriet; she must never know. And how the blood still drained from Harriet Pickard's body, on and on, without cease, and Mary with her herbs and potions couldn't stop it; and then how, before the dawn broke, Harriet Pickard slipped away, moon-white, into the night.

The next morning, Thomas had found Mary in her shift out back at the washtub, scrubbing and rinsing, rinsing and scrubbing until her hands hurt, but still the water ran red. And her tears would not cease.

Rumours abounded. People took sides. Some of Harriet's people said that what had come out of Harriet Pickard's womb that night was devil's spawn, which Mary herself had conjured. Others sprang to Mary's defence, brought her baskets of fruit or jars of honey to cheer her, or showed off the bonny, healthy babies that she had delivered.

After a few weeks, the furor died down and people got busy with spring planting. But Mary remained silent, turned in on herself, for nothing anyone said or did, whether in condemnation or sympathy, changed the fact that she, her mother's daughter, had been the attending midwife the night Harriet Pickard gave birth to something monstrous and then bled to death before her eyes.

Mary had known maternal deaths before. There had been occasional stillbirths. It was God's way. Mary knew that. But this … this was something ungodly. After this, there could be no return to normalcy for Mary. She knew, that morning as she scrubbed and rinsed at the washtub, that she would never deliver another baby, never again hold a perfect, newborn creature in her arms, never again see the love and light in a new mother's eyes as she handed her the child. "Trust the midwife," people said. But what good was a midwife who could no longer trust herself. A midwife who had lost her nerve.

She put away her tools that day and burned her herbs. When Thomas suggested a move to London, she accepted, passively, and let him make all the arrangements.

The tea had steeped. Mary rose from her chair, poured herself a cup and finished the bread and cheese. It was fully dark outside now. Her neighbour's baby had stopped crying at last and the street was quiet. She hoped Thomas had found a place to sleep.

On the mantel shelf was a glass jar with the money she'd saved from taking in laundry these last four months. Washing other people's dirty linens was her job now. Honest work, and not so bad for the time being, until Thomas sent for her. She counted the money. There was nearly enough for her ticket to London. She put the glass jar back, finished drinking her tea, and washed her plate and cup.

She went over to Thomas's trundle bed and smoothed the covers. It might be comforting to sleep in his bed tonight, the first night she had ever spent alone. Before going to sleep, she prayed, as she always did, for the souls of her parents. She added a prayer for Thomas's success in London, and another for herself, for peace and strength.

THREE

In early June, Catherine lay with Jack in the copse beyond the circus field, their favourite place. The turf beneath them was springy. She held a buttercup under his chin, and told him he must like butter because the petals shone golden on his throat. He leaned up on one elbow, took the flower from her hand and stuck it in her hair.

"Time for me to be on my way, Ruby Red."

She flung her arms tight around him, pushing him back down. "No," she said into his neck, her voice muffled.

He pried her hands away. "Hey, now. We're a touring circus. You know that. We have to leave. We've to be in Tipperary tomorrow, then Limerick and Kilkenny for August."

Jack sat up, buttoned his trousers, straightened his shirt.

Catherine fastened the buttons on her blouse, covered her bare breast, which so recently Jack had fondled, and frowned. Leaving, he'd said. How would she bear it? Jack chucked her under her chin, kissed her nose. She shrugged him away, and pulled her skirt down, drawing her hands under her knees.

"Don't be selfish now, there's other people want to see us too. But we'll be back in September, at harvest time. Wait for me. Come to this same field. I'll be here."

"And you'll stay?" She slid her hand under his open shirt and touched his shoulder. His skin was soft, still slightly damp from their recent ardour. Jack removed her hand, buttoned his shirt and tucked it into his trousers.

"A few days." He said it so quietly, Catherine could barely hear.

"Only days?"

"Just to pack up. We'll be sailing back to England. I told you that, didn't I? You knew we'd have to go back in the autumn."

Yes, she had known it, but had buried the knowledge. Since Jack, each day was stretched and had no end. What happened tomorrow, or next week, or in September might just as well be never. But now that he had said it, it was real.

England. Across the sea. Da had made that trip and had many stories to tell. He'd picked apples and hops in Kent, hammered iron and steel for the new London Bridge, dredged ditches for canals, and hewed through rock for railways. He'd been a stevedore in the Liverpool docks, unloading great bales of raw cotton from America and helping to transport it to the mills. He'd promised he'd take Catherine to England one day, and not just England, but across the world. To Galway to see the great ocean between Ireland and America. To America itself, on a steamship, where they'd live like Red Indians. Land was cheap in America, he'd said, and they'd make their fortune. Then they'd sail back to England, take a look at London town with its great river and grand buildings, and visit the new queen.

She used to sit with him on a rocky outcrop near Kildean and watch the Johnson boy's pet kestrel wheel and soar above them, and Da would make his promises. "It'll be a fine life, Katie," he'd said, "going from job to job, country to city and back again, living free like that bird up there. See how it soars. It goes wherever it wants, dips down here and there, but it doesn't stop for long. Why would it when there are so many places in this wide world to see? That's the life to lead, Katie. We'll be birds together, you and me." She'd hugged her knees. "When will we go, Da?" "Soon, soon," he'd said. "Next year, maybe, if it's a good harvest, and if the pig bears. Or the year after."

With Da dead, Ma would never leave; she was too much in the thrall of Father Quinn, who warned the congregation that England was full of heathens. Better for the Irish to stay in their own country; money, he said, was a false god. The true God made the Irish poor, he said, because he loved them more than he loved the Protestant heathen. Another time, he said they should be grateful that people here in Waterford County were not nearly as poor as those in Kerry or Mayo. Which was it, Catherine asked herself—were they to be grateful to be poor, or grateful to be not so poor? The priest talked nonsense! How she despised him, and all of them, the whole village. But Da's promise remained soldered on her soul and gave her hope.

Now Catherine sat beside Jack, hugging her knees, and her mind raced. Jack brushed leaves off his shirt. He raked his fingers through his hair, smoothing it down. How handsome he was. Every time she caught sight of his profile, her heart beat a little faster. She shifted her body closer until their shoulders touched. She leant her head against his neck. He shifted away from her, leaned forward to tie his bootlaces. She moved closer to him again and looked sideways at him through her eyelashes.

"Take me with you when you go to England." She felt her breathing quicken and waited, willing him to tell her yes, he wanted her with him on his travels, to be part of his world.

Jack stared ahead, silent. What was he thinking? Why did he not respond?

"Jack?"

He picked up his cap and placed it on the back of his head. She loved the rakish look that angle gave him. He turned to her with a slight grin and a wink.

She knelt back on her heels beside him. She wanted to touch him, but something stopped her. Instead she clasped her hands beneath her chin, as if in prayer. "I could help," she said. "I could water the horses, sew the costumes. I could cook and clean. There's lots I could do."

He stood, took Catherine's hand, and pulled her to her feet.

"Jack?" Desire gushed within her like a river. She wanted to push him down, hold him down, implore him, *Take me with you. Take me with you wherever you go!* Did he not feel how she trembled?

"Well," he said at last, "it's an idea, isn't it? We'll think on it. You'd best be getting home now. Look at you: your hair's a mess. I want you to keep those locks all shiny and new for me for when I get back, because I will be back. Here," he rummaged in his trouser pocket and took out a comb. "You can have this. A present from Jack. To remember me by. Now go, get yourself cleaned up, and I'll see you in September."

She took the comb and touched it to her hair. It was small, made of white bone, with wide teeth. It might have been made for her, the way it cleaved through her tangles without a catch. She looked up at him, her smile radiant. "Thank you."

He pulled her hands away. "Glad you like it. If there's one thing you could do with, Ruby Red, it's a comb. Now off you go. Don't forget me, mind!"

She skipped away, turning to blow him a kiss. Jack waved back and sent her his lopsided smile. *We'll think on it*, he'd said. *Don't forget me*, he'd said. *Wait for me.* She pressed the comb to her lips and slipped it into the pocket of her skirt. *September,* he'd said.

June turned to July and the potato fields turned white with blossom. Pedlars wandered through the village with their dried fish and chapbooks and trinkets, young lovers planned their weddings, and thatchers came with their ladders to repair roofs. And Catherine dreamt of Jack. Each day, she fed the pig, fetched the water, stoked the fire, stirred the pot. Every Monday she and her sisters laundered the linens and scrubbed the clothes in the washtub out back. On Sundays, the church bells rang and Catherine joined the line of worshippers. After church, she and Ma and her sisters visited Da in the churchyard and stopped by the grave of the brother and sister she hardly remembered. But she remembered Jack.

Often, when she passed the Resting Tree with her pails, she stopped. With the navvies back in their villages, the place under the tree was usually vacant. She would climb up the grassy mound, lie down under the tree, and imagine Jack swooping down like a bird, gathering her up, and flying away with her to England, to America, to all the places Da had promised. Then she would recall each smooth inch of Jack's body, the lock of dark hair that fell on his forehead, the way his taut body cleaved to hers, his hard, flat abdomen she could fit her fist into, the dark mole on his chest, and the blue veins that pulsed in his wrists as he held her face in his hands and brushed his lips to her ear.

August brought the hungry season when the food stocks were all used up and people would ache with hunger until the new crop was ready in September. But Catherine's ache became something else, something more urgent, something deep in her belly that had nothing to do with food. At first, she thought it might go away, but it didn't. She took herself each morning to a spot behind the pig pen so her mother wouldn't hear her retches. Ma began to look at her askance, checked her linen on the line, scrutinized the faces of the boys in church on Sunday. Catherine took to wearing her shawl tucked up to her neck; Father Quinn from his pulpit looked with approval at this new modest Catherine, and when he did, Catherine turned her head away.

At night, as she lay sleepless on her pallet, hope and fear and shame swirled in her head. When Jack came back, wouldn't he have to take her with him to England? She couldn't stay in Kildean now, could she? But what if Jack didn't come back? What then? Ma would have to know. The whole village would know. Father Quinn's words echoed in her head: "gone astray," "the barren path," "fires of damnation." She thought about Da in Heaven and her face burned. She stilled her trembles by taking out Jack's comb. When she ran her fingers across its smooth contours she remembered his caress. *Wait for me in September.* That's what he'd said.

September arrived. Catherine joined the women in the fields, walking the mile and a half to her family's stony potato patch to unearth the newly swelled tubers that would feed her family through the winter. The tubers heralded the end of the hungry season, but for Catherine, only Jack's promised return could ease her hunger. And her fear. For there was no sign of Jack.

She laid her basket down, put her spade to rest in the earth, and ran her hands over her belly. How much longer could she keep her secret? A week? Two? Soon she would begin to show. She looked up at the sky. She rarely prayed, but today she needed help.

A movement above her caught her eye. The Johnson boy's kestrel was out, weaving and dipping under the charcoal sky. The same bird she used to watch with Da as he made his promises to her. Da had said they would live free like that bird. But Da was dead and Jack had not returned.

The bird descended, alighting on the boy's leather gauntlet. Catherine picked up her basket, and turned to look up once more as she left the field. The bird was on the wing again, and there, where it hovered, she saw something else, a distance away in the direction of the two hills that rose beyond Kildean. She put her hand to her forehead to shade her eyes. In the space between the hills, a section of the road that led from the west and along the river was visible. Sometimes from this vantage point one could see a mail coach speeding or a horse and cart wending along the road, or sometimes a group of travellers heading on foot for Waterford. On this occasion, what Catherine saw, what she could have no doubt about, what made her momentarily weak all over, was a procession. The basket now was light on her back as she ran from the field, along the lane to the village, from the village to her cabin where she dropped her basket, and up the hill towards the circus field.

The procession had already arrived at the field. The caravans, blue and yellow and green, were lined up in a semi-circle at one end of the field. The performers were unloading carts, erecting tents, unharnessing horses, building a corral, pitching hay to the animals. A crowd of excited children from nearby villages who had run alongside the procession were now jumping and dancing around the field. Catherine ran down the hill, stopped at the gate, breathless, and scanned the field. There were the trick horse riders and the acrobats practicing cartwheels on the grass. There was the bearded lady leaning against one of the caravans guffawing with the monkey man: the monkey was on his head, scratching. And then there was Jack, ambling towards the main tent. She ran forward, and called his name.

He stopped, turned, saw her, and held out his arms to her.

"Here's my Ruby Red girl."

She ran to him, laughing, letting her shawl fall to her shoulders.

Later, under the trees, after he had loved her again, she took a deep breath and told him. He sat up and rested his head on his knees as if in thought. She hardly dared look at him. At last he spoke.

"Well now."

Well now, what? She waited. He needed time to take in the news.

"Well now," he said again, "there's a thing." Then he smiled in his usual lopsided way. "But don't you worry, Ruby Red. I'll take care of you, and the baby too."

She exhaled. "You'll take me with you in the circus, to England?"

He turned his head and looked away from her, towards the circus field. She waited for his response. It came after a pause.

"Sure, I will."

She squeezed her eyes shut, clenched her fists, and let out a sob of relief. He put his arms around her. She clung to him. Then he took the corner of her apron and dried her eyes.

"We can't let those beautiful blue eyes get all red and raw. I told you I'd take care of you and I will. Didn't I come back when I said I would?"

She nodded.

"Listen. We're only here for a couple of days. One performance, tonight only. Our ship sails in two days. Come early Thursday morning, and help us pack. We'll leave at noon to catch the afternoon tide."

"Thursday? That's the day after tomorrow."

"That's what I said."

"You will be here? You promise?"

"I promise. Now go home. I have to get ready."

He stood and pulled her up. She held on to his hand, but he patted her rear in a teasing way. "Be off with you." She laughed. As she left the field, she glanced at the line of caravans. Which one was Jack's? The yellow one, she was sure.

FOUR

Corporal Edward Harris of the Royal Engineers sat high up on a rocky outcrop near Kildean. The hungry season was over, the harvest had begun, and the fields below him, laid out like overlapping flags in multiple shades of green, were dotted with women digging for potatoes.

Distant sounds from the village behind the outcrop drifted up to where Edward sat. The squeals and bleats of pigs and sheep, a woman's laugh, a man's shout, children at play, the clang of pots and pans. Edward could feel the anticipation in the air; full bellies again, good times returning, weddings and dances. He was sorry to be leaving in a few days. The church clock struck the hour. Noon. In the gunmetal light, the grass seemed luminous and he understood why they called this land the Emerald Isle. He pulled up a tuft of grass and held it to his face, trying to commit its turfy aroma to memory.

Above him, a kestrel wheeled and dipped beneath a bank of charcoal clouds. After it had circled several times, the bird hovered and then swooped down to alight on the leather gauntlet of a boy standing on a rise across the valley. When the boy put out his right arm, hand pointing, the bird opened its wings and took flight again, returning a few minutes later at a signal from the boy.

Impressive, thought Edward, the way the lad, who could be no more than fourteen years old, commanded the bird with almost military precision. The easy self-assurance of his class was palpable in his mastery of the bird. He'd make a fine army officer one day, Edward thought.

He knew the boy to be the son of Mr. Johnson, the landowner, who visited his domain with his family every autumn to exact harvest tribute; Edward's work as a military engineer had required him to

25

gain access to the Johnson lands. The Kildean leases were the last leg of an exhilarating, four-year tramp through Ireland with his company during which he'd weathered snow and rain, sleet and storm, clambered over scrubby moorland, and waded knee-deep in peat bogs and rushing streams. The purpose: to measure and map the whole of Ireland; to identify crossing places on rivers, the gradient of hills and routes through rocky, forbidding terrain. Then, most thrilling of all, to see how the notes and measurements translated into lines on a flat sheet of paper. The whole of Ireland reduced to geometry.

Mapmaking had become his passion, and this land had been his training ground. The assignment was now finished, and in a few days his company would pack up and be off to Waterford City to board a ship home to England.

The kestrel's shadow swept over the valley, and something bright flashed at the corner of Edward's vision. He looked sideways and saw a girl standing on a rough patch of land halfway down the hillside, on one of the stony spots that the poorest tenants rented. Like other women working the lusher fields lower down into the valley, her clothes were shabby, her feet bare. But unlike the other women, her head was uncovered and unfastened and her flame hair tumbled down her back. She stood in profile with her body completely still, her face upturned, but her head followed the kestrel's course as it wheeled and glided over the terrain.

Edward watched the girl, and the girl watched the bird. Then, with a fluid movement like amber liquid pouring into a glass, she picked up her basket, hoisted it onto her back, and made her way through the stony furrows to the gate of the field. As she left, she turned and looked towards the ridge where Edward sat, then ran from the field.

In the split second that she turned, he saw that her face was as open and full of promise as a spring day, and for the first time in years, he thought of his sister, Sarah, who had raised him after their parents died, and wanted to feel the security of her guiding hand in his. He missed her. It surprised him, but he missed her. Why now? Sarah had been dead for more than half a decade. She had raised him after their parents died, and was a fine woman—everyone who knew her said so, and she thought she knew what was best for her brother.

But she didn't. Edward was grateful for her devotion to his moral upbringing and concern for his future security. She was loyal, and sweet, and generous, and pious. But on the day of her funeral, he'd stood with his Uncle George by her grave, watched as her black-shrouded coffin was lowered, and felt as if the world had opened to him. He was a free man.

Within weeks of the funeral, he left the counting house Sarah had installed him in, and where he had been sitting on a stool at a sloping desk entering numbers into a ledger since he was fifteen, and joined the Corps of Royal Engineers. Uncle George had encouraged him. The military would toughen him up, Uncle George said. And it had.

Except that right now, Edward did not feel particularly tough. A light rain began to fall, and he put his cap on. The sky grew darker, the rain heavier, and the air chillier. Edward felt confused and fragile and didn't know why. A military man like him ought not to waver like a bewildered child. Was it the bird, or the Johnson boy, strutting across the valley to his father's estate? Or had the girl unnerved him, with her uncovered head, her erect posture, her flame hair? Why her? She was just a peasant girl, one of millions across this land. Why did she make him think of Sarah?

The rain ceased, the clouds parted, and the wet turf sparkled in the sunshine. Edward heard shouts, got to his feet, and saw several of his men climbing up the hill towards him. They jostled each other, pushed and pulled, and sparred in mock fighting as they reached the top of the outcrop. They were all excited to be going home to England and wanted to spend these last few days celebrating. One of them waved a greeting to Edward.

"Ho, Corp, you coming tonight?"

"What's on?"

"Haven't you heard? There's a circus in town. One night only. Just come down from Kilkenny on its way to England."

"'Bout an hour's walk from here."

Edward shook his head. He was not in a mood to celebrate.

"Don't be a grouch, Corp. Come with us."

"It'll be a party. One thing the Irish do well is a party!"

One of the soldiers slapped him on the back. Another gave Edward's cheek an impudent pinch. "And girls," the man said, to guffaws from the company.

Edward laughed and punched the man's shoulder, whereupon the men began to march in a circle chanting, "Girls, girls, girls for the corporal, pretty ones, ugly ones, big ones, small ones ... "

This was their usual routine. They were always trying to set Edward up with girls. After he'd had a few drinks in a tavern, they'd bring one over to him. She'd sit on his lap, stroke his face, and try to sneak him out of the back door. Sometimes he went along with it. After all, he was twenty-four, and a soldier with the requisite youthful vigour. And Irish girls were pretty. Well-built, fresh-faced. Like the one he'd seen in the field. If he went with the lads tonight, he might see her again. He shook his head.

"I have things to do. I'll see you later," he said, and added with a wry smile, "Just behave yourselves, lads. You have a reputation to uphold."

The men shouted with laughter as they left. They knew their corporal's sense of humour, for a soldier's reputation was not usually something to covet. But the men of the Royal Engineers were an elite force, a cut above the common soldier, proud of their vaunted status as military engineers who mapped the land, built bridges, forded streams and constructed fortifications for the fighting men in their wake. "The finest force that ever served the king and empire," was how Edward's Uncle George, himself a veteran of the corps, described them.

Edward watched his men go, and then started down the hill behind them. The rain began to spit again. He thought about the bird, how it always came back to the Johnson boy. There was a connection between them that went beyond command and control; a love, almost, or an emotional need. No matter how far or for how long the bird flew, it always came back. It knew where it had come from and to where it needed to return. In a few days, Edward would return to London. He might take a stroll around his old neighbourhood in Soho, say hello to the poor devil who now occupied his stool in the counting house. He wondered who was renting the rooms in Rupert Street where he and Sarah had lived. Were any of his old neighbours still there? And the tavern on the corner? Four years ago, when he'd gone down there, callow and ginger in his new soldier's uniform, the locals had all cheered and slapped him on the back. The apothecary and the shoemaker next door, would they still be there? Decent folks. Their wives, good women. They'd been kind to Edward when he was left orphaned, bought him sweetmeats and little toys. Gave Sarah sympathetic looks. Their children were his playmates, all grown up now and gone their own ways. They all admired Sarah.

No doubt the formidable Mrs. Scroggs around the corner in Bedford Court still ran the boarding house that provided employment for local girls. Always the first on the scene of any neighbourhood drama, she was there within minutes of Sarah's death, with her washcloth and water, her latest girl in tow, ready to lay out the body. Edward hadn't been sorry to see the back of her. He smiled grimly at the memory, and slid the last few yards down the slippery path to the valley.

His father's modest tailor's shop in Bedford Court would still be operating, in the capable hands of his father's partner, Mr. Charles. By arrangement with Sarah, Mr. Charles still put aside a small percentage of the shop's profits each month to build a nest egg for Edward's future. Sarah had known how to look after Edward, but she had been adamant that Edward would not become a tailor like their father, whose back had grown crooked and whose sight had failed before his time. She'd determined that Edward, with his counting house experience, should eventually take over the management of the shop from Mr. Charles and employ others to do the tailoring. Poor Sarah. All her plans for her brother come to naught. Edward would not be taking over any tailor's shop, not if he could help it.

The rain became heavier as he reached the village, and he sheltered against the wall of a shop. How meagre Kildean's shops were and how quiet the streets. Such a contrast to Soho, whose streets were always bustling with people and whose shops were always bursting with all manner of products. Near to his old Rupert Street lodgings was a map shop that Edward used to visit as a boy. A Mr. Makepeace was the proprietor, and he invited Edward in one day when he saw him gazing through the window at the intricate charts displayed among strange-looking instruments of polished brass and glass. Mr. Makepeace captivated him with his stories of working on the Great Trigonometrical Survey of India under the tutelage of Sir George Everest. He showed Edward how the instruments measured angles and distances between objects, which were then translated into the contour lines on maps. Edward hoped Mr. Makepeace's shop was still there. He had fifteen years of military service left, and after that, a partnership with Mr. Makepeace might be just the thing for his latter years. He pulled his shoulders back and stepped up his pace, and by the time he got back to the village his mood had improved and he felt more settled.

He stopped on the way to his billet to buy beer and cheese for his supper. He wondered if he should join his men at the circus after all. They said the whole village would be going. It would be a merry evening. He might drop by later. But there would be hangovers tomorrow, and perhaps some regrets. Not wise for any man just days before a rough sea voyage. Best for him to remain sober. He had things to do: boots to polish, a button to sew on, a uniform to brush. Tomorrow the company would begin to pack up.

FIVE

It was still dark when Catherine rose on Thursday morning. Ma was snoring by the fireplace and her sisters lay curled asleep together. In her apron, she bundled a spare petticoat, a handkerchief, ribbons for her hair, and the feather fan Da had bought her from a pedlar. She remembered that when she had primped before him, flicking the fan, batting her eyelashes, he said she looked like a lady. She took some coins from the glass jam jar on the mantelshelf. A favour to Ma, really, for with her gone, there would be one less mouth to feed. Jack's comb she retrieved from under her pillow, and put in her pocket. She nudged Bridget awake, pulled her outside, and whispered her plan. Still half asleep, Bridget buried her face in Catherine's chest, begged her to stay.

"Be strong," Catherine said, as much to herself as to Bridget. "When Jack and I are married, I'll send for you from England. You can travel in the circus with us. You'll like that, won't you?"

Bridget said nothing, but her snuffles ceased.

"Say nothing to Ma, not yet. If you tell her I told you, she'll whip you. Wait till afternoon, say you heard it from people in the village that Catherine Joyce ran away with the circus. By that time, I'll be at sea."

With a hug and a kiss, she sent Bridget back to bed, and set out for the circus ground.

She took the usual path up the hill. Her bundle was heavy and in the dark her feet tripped on stones. The wet grass weighed down the hem of her skirt. But her mind roiled with images: a procession of painted caravans and wagons, streets lined with cheering folk; Jack striding onto his podium and she, Catherine, in a red sequined dress

31

behind him, holding the chains aloft to the audience; afterwards, Jack and her making love in the yellow-painted caravan.

At the top of the hill she stopped to look down, but it was still too dark to see the circus ground. She scrambled down the hill, and onto the track below and quickened her pace; the field was just a few yards further. But something was wrong. Surely by now there would be noise: chatter and animal sounds as the circus packed up. As she approached the field, the sun rose above the distant trees and brightened the field, and she knew even before she reached the gate the field was empty. She looked around in dismay. All that remained were piles of dung and crushed patches on the grass where the caravans and tents had been. Gone, all of them, the bearded lady, the white horses, the monkey man, the midget family. And Jack.

But this could not be. Jack had promised to be here. Something must have happened. Perhaps they'd had to leave early, in which case Jack would be waiting for her somewhere. The copse! Their special place at the far end of the field. She ran to copse, from tree to tree to tree. It was empty.

In the next field an old man in a smock watched her, grinning toothlessly, hands tucked under his armpits, fork stuck in the ground. At first, she thought he was a scarecrow.

"The circus?" she shouted at him, "where is it?" She was near to tears.

"Gone in the night, I 'spect," he said, and cackled.

"Did you see it? When did it go?"

"Who knows? Off to sea. Sailed with morning tide, I'd wager." The man hawked on the ground and laughed again.

"Halfwit," she muttered. She blinked back tears. Jack had said they were to catch the afternoon tide. They must have changed their plans, realized they needed more time to load the ship with all the caravans and horses. Of course. They would have packed up last night and left before dawn. Not long before she had arrived at the field. Jack would not have had a chance to get a message to her. If she hurried she could catch them up, meet them on the road—she could move faster than a circus parade.

She laughed aloud with relief, stuck out her tongue at the man in the field, and hurried onto the rutted track that led to the main

Waterford City road. His squawking followed her, mocking her. *Who cares? Let the old man say what he will about me. I'll be with Jack in England.*

At the end of the track she turned left onto the main road. Rain clouds moved in. Drizzle matted her hair, mud splattered her hem. She did not stop. The thought of Jack waiting at the port pushed her on, and drove away the quibble of fear that picked at her insides. The thoroughfare was now crowded with travellers. Many had bundles, families with sacks over their shoulders and babes in arms, carts full of young men, all heading towards the port, the sea, the ships. People stared at her, raised their eyebrows. A woman alone. Old men stood at doorways and leered. One reached out to grab her breast. She pulled her shawl closer.

A company of soldiers was gaining on her from behind. They hooted, waved their hands, and pointed fingers at her. English soldiers. She tried to move ahead, weaving in and out of the other walkers. Several of them caught up with her; she was in the midst of them. They jostled her, poked her, laughed at her, made lewd comments. One got close enough to pull at her hair; another tugged at her skirt. Tears of anger smarted. Jack had left her to walk alone through a town full of drunks and leering soldiers. She broke into a run. Hoots and hollers from the soldiers followed her.

"Leave her alone! All of you, get back at once."

She glanced behind her. One of the soldiers had broken away and caught up with her. It was he who had spoken. He fell into step beside her, extending his elbow.

"Here, take my arm, young lady. Stick with me."

She looked up at him. He was not a tall man, and his build was slight, but his back was straight, and his soldier's cap gave him an appearance of height. He was not handsome either, but his face was not unpleasing. Regular features, pale blue eyes, sandy brown beard, neatly clipped. He seemed younger, thinner, and less manly than her Jack. But an erect, military stance, and an open face. A good soldier? English, too. Was there such a thing?

"Where's a young girl like you off to at this time in the morning? You should know it's not safe for you in this part of town." Something sincere in his voice made her feel she could trust him.

"Sir, I'm on my way to meet my young man. He performs with Billy Mather's Amazing Circus, and we're sailing for England today.

We are betrothed." Catherine felt a thrill as she pronounced the word "betrothed"—saying it aloud made it real.

"Ah, yes. The circus. But you're alone?"

"He had to leave before me, but he'll be waiting for me at the quay."

The soldier raised his eyebrows at this, and Catherine felt slightly resentful at the implied criticism of Jack at having left her to walk alone. Again, she pushed aside the quibble of fear.

"At least allow me to escort you to the quay. You'll be safer that way."

Catherine nodded, grateful for his concern. As they walked, he shielded her from the throng, held her fast away from the shouting merchants, the pigs and cows and mangy dogs, and his rowdy soldier colleagues, who continued to press from behind.

"I should introduce myself: Corporal Edward Harris, at your service," said the soldier, "Royal Engineers."

"Catherine Joyce, your servant, sir." Still walking, she attempted a curtsy that became merely a bob. "Thank you for helping me." She glanced up at him and he gave a slight smile. Feeling bold, she asked him, "But why would you do that?"

"Why?" He seemed to ponder the question, then said, "I suppose you could thank my sister. She raised me and taught me proper respect for women. My fellow sappers are not bad men, but their manners leave something to be desired. And besides … " He paused again. "Besides, you're lovely."

Wary, she looked up at him again. Was he flirting with her? But his eyes were fixed on the road ahead.

They turned a corner and before them loomed Waterford's great Round Tower, standing guard over the quay, which seemed to stretch for miles along the River Suir. The masts of more than a dozen ships were like a scaffold of ladders that rose up to touch the sky.

A moving mass of people filled the expanse of the quay; porters carried boxes and trunks, top-hatted gentlemen shepherded bonneted ladies with small children, carriages crashed through the crowds with crop-wielding drivers, horses reared and whinnied. Rats scampered along the water's edge, dogs sniffed and poked around at stray fish carcasses, spilled grain, spoiled vegetables. How was she ever to find Jack in this throng?

She heard before she saw a band of men in cloth hats towards the end of the quay, shouting at the tops of their lungs. Weavers. Weavers, she knew, had been crossing over to London for years to work for their heathen Huguenot masters, and they always shouted, Da told her, because the noise of the looms made them deaf. There was a village of weavers not far from the circus field; if they were from there, they must have seen the circus pass by earlier, and perhaps they would even board the same ship. The men were part of a larger crowd that heaved forward, pressing to board the nearside ship anchored in the dock. She pulled the corporal by the sleeve and hurried towards them. "Come, come, over there, that's where we'll find the circus."

As they neared the crowd, one of the weavers, a sickly, spindly looking youth, caught her eye, nodded, and grinned. She looked past him, frantic now, and searched the jostling crowd for some sign of the circus.

The corporal seemed to sense her anxiety. "Wait here," he said. "I'll enquire at the ticket office about whether a circus has arrived. Don't move from this spot."

Catherine leaned against an iron mooring post, thankful for the clash and clamour of the wharf, the pervasive stench of fish and human sweat and animal dung that blocked out all thoughts. She fumbled in her pocket and fingered the bone comb Jack had given her.

She became aware of the weaver lad staring at her. He stood on the edge of the pressing crowd, slightly apart, apparently more interested in her than in assuring his place on the ship. She glared at him, and he pointed his finger.

"I seen you," he shouted. "At the circus you were. I seen you there with your strongman. No sense looking for him here. Circus gone. Already sailed. Yesterday on the morning tide."

One of the other weavers, an older man, grabbed the boy's jacket and tried to yank him back into the crowd, but the boy stood his ground, laughing. The older man smiled apologetically, but she could only hear the loathsome words echoing in her head. *Already sailed.* How would the idiot boy know? But the sick pain in the pit of her belly told her it was true.

She slid down the mooring post and sat on her heels. The weaver boy kept laughing, and her distress turned to anger. The crowd of men still pushed and shoved against the barrier to the gangplank, waiting for the gate to open. The ship was about to board. She would sail on that ship to England and she would find Jack. She could not go back to Kildean. It was unthinkable. Ma would disown her. The village would shun her; the nuns would take her and her child.

She saw the corporal hurrying back, threading his way through the crowd, and dropped her head, closed her eyes, and crossed herself. The crowd of men pressed around her. Laughter. Someone grabbed her arm, hands jostled her back and forth, someone else pushed her down, pulled at her skirt, her hair, the sleeve of her blouse. She struggled but was held fast to the ground, as cold fingers probed under her skirt, sliding between her legs.

As she opened her eyes, the weaver boy's face leered at her, and in the next moment was smashed and bloodied on the ground. She saw the corporal fall beside him, saw his head strike the ground, saw blood stream from his head as a boot kicked him onto his back, where he lay deathly still. There were shouts, men pushing and shoving, fists flying, faces distorted, feet running, then the shrill of whistles, as constables elbowed through the crowd, wielding truncheons. Then nothing but blackness.

SIX

Edward tasted blood in his mouth. He wondered how long he had been prostrate on the hard ground. He rolled over and sat up, groaning. When he put a hand to his head, blood dripped through his fingers. One of his men was at his side, dabbing Edward's lip and head with a kerchief dipped in a nearby pail of water. He dabbed until the red stain turned to pink and the bleeding subsided.

"Good as new, Corp, you'll live. T'other fella got the worst of it; they're hauling him away to the clink."

It came back to him. The girl on the road. Catherine Joyce. The same one he'd seen standing in the field the other day, looking up at the bird. He'd caught up with her, chaperoned her through the crowds, and on the way she'd told him an unlikely story about a circus lover waiting at the wharf.

He oughtn't to have left her alone by the mooring post, with rough men pressing around. But she'd been persuasive and he'd wanted to humour her. "Wait for me here," he'd said. "I'll see what I can find out about a circus." When he came back, she was on the ground, her skirt up, the idiot weaver boy's hands on her. He'd lunged at the boy, pulled him away, punched him on the chin, but then a boot had hit his head and he'd fallen to the ground.

Around him, a commotion. To his left, the idiot boy, his nose bloodied, was being loudly reprimanded by a constable, surrounded by a band of shouting men threatening their fists at him. The constable held one of the boy's arms in his grasp, and wielded his truncheon like a wagging finger at the boy. The older weaver man tugged at the constable's jacket. Snatches of conversation reached him: "assaulting a lady," "poor boy, doesn't know any better," "serious offence," "doesn't understand, not right in the head," "see what the magistrate says."

The girl had come 'round and was sitting up, pulling her skirt around her, looking stunned. No one else was paying any attention to her. The crowd seemed more interested in taking sides on who was to blame for the fray, the weavers and their supporters on one side, the soldiers and some of the other waiting passengers on the other, preferring to throw their hat in with the symbols of authority and courage. All around people were shouting, everyone it seemed, loudly voicing their opinion of what had happened.

Edward crawled over to the girl.

"Come," he said, "it's all right. Your attacker has been dispensed. The constable is taking him away." He managed to stand, still slightly wobbly, and held out his hand to help her up. He picked up her shawl and wrapped it around her shoulders for modesty. She stood blinking at the fracas. "You've had a shock. You must go home now. I'll see you back to the main road. Don't talk to anyone, just walk straight home."

The girl turned, and with an astonished look, pulled away from his comforting arm.

"I'll not go home," she said. Her eyes were fierce. "I've come to find Jack. I'm to join his circus. We're to be married. I'm going England to find him."

"I'm sorry, my dear, but the circus has sailed."

"Then I'll travel alone and meet him there."

Her eyes were defiant, her jaw set, but she couldn't disguise the slight tremble of her chin. She looked so vulnerable. He tried to be gentle but firm. "My dear young lady, you can't possibly travel alone on a ship full of soldiers and weavers and labourers. They'll eat you alive."

"I'll manage. All I have to do is get to London. That's where his circus is performing."

"London? Have you any idea how big London is? It's not Waterford. There are millions of people. Have you family or friends there?

She looked away. He noticed her chest heaving, but she stood firm, her feet planted, her hands by her side.

His voice softened. "Look, Miss Joyce, I have to leave now; the ship is about to board. Go home, back to your mother and father. Believe me, it's best for you." He turned away to join his company in the queue, which was already boarding.

She called after him. "Oh, but you don't understand. I cannot go home."

He turned back at the ferocity in her voice. She clasped her hands in prayer. Her eyes seemed ready to shoot steel shards. "My father's dead, and my mother beats me. Take me with you. I'll pay my way." She dug into her pocket and produced a handful of coins. "Please, you helped me on the road, you protected me from the weaver boy. Help me now to get to England."

She stretched her hands towards him, her brow creased. Tendrils of hair, escaped from her bun, curled around her face, lit golden by the sun. He shook his head, and with a supreme effort, averted his eyes, and once again turned his back on her.

She called again, more stridently, "Please, sir."

Slowly he turned back towards her. Her shawl had fallen away and her blouse had slipped over her shoulders, exposing the divine cleft between her breast and her arm. She seemed oblivious to its effect, of how men might stare and leer at her. He wondered how it would feel to slip his hand into that cleft and touch the pillowy softness of her breast. But he wanted, too, to cover her nakedness, retrieve her modesty, envelop her in a cloak of protection.

Her hands were clasped in prayer again; her face glowed, her lips were full and moist. She smiled beguilingly at him. Her teeth were white and even.

"Wait there," he said.

He strode over to the crowd that still surrounded the constable and the weaver boy. He pulled the older weaver man towards him and spoke to him quietly. The weaver cupped an ear to Edward, then responded with a shake of his head, waved his hand, and turned away. Edward persisted, held the man's sleeve, and took some coins from his belt pouch. The man shook his head again, and continued to remonstrate with the constable over the fate of his son. Edward took more money from his pouch. This time the man stopped, and nodded. Edward hurried back, took Catherine's arm and pulled her towards the crowd, which shuffled onto the ship's now-open gangplank.

"I must be as mad as you are, but here's your ticket. The weaver is staying behind with his son. That means two places have come free. You will have one of them."

It was madness. He should have sent her packing back to her village. This Catherine Joyce, with her wild eyes and her wild hair. She didn't belong in England. She was a child of emerald fields and rocky tarns. Barefoot, tilling fields, feeding pigs and chickens, milking a cow. Loving another man. She may have been the loveliest creature he had ever set eyes on, but everything about her suggested reckless naïveté. He ought not to have allowed her to beguile him with her eyes and her smile. But the least he could do was ensure her safety on the ship. Once they docked, she would no longer be his responsibility.

On the rocking, raging sea voyage, he kept the reaching hands and drunken grasps away from her, the accidental-on-purpose lurches that pushed and shoved her as the ship heaved through the rough sea. On the quay she had looked diaphanous, ethereal, with the sun on her hair and her skin plump and pink and glowing. She'd reminded him of a painting of a Greek myth he'd once seen at the National Gallery, all soft, half-naked skin and rosy lips. Now, here on deck, she was real, retching over the ship's side, green-gilled, bloodless, tears streaming, face red-blotched. And still she was beautiful. He cleaned her face and wiped her tears with his handkerchief.

"How is it that you are so well?" she asked.

"I'm fortunate. There are not many people who can survive crossing the Irish Sea without being seasick." It was a notoriously unforgiving journey. "For some reason I'm one of the few who are not affected. Are you feeling better?"

"Much better. The cold wind helps."

When night fell, they bedded down on the deck. He put his knapsack beneath her head, and watched as her breathing slowed and her eyes closed in slumber. Sleep eluded him. He lay on his back, on his side, on his front. He longed to touch her but kept his distance. The swell of sea subsided as the ship moved to calmer waters. The vessel rocked to the snores of the passengers. His lips tasted salty; his clothes felt damp.

He propped himself up on one elbow and looked at her. The moonlight made a triangle of white on her face. He touched it, then pulled his hand away sharply as if burned. Her hair was spread out on the knapsack pillow, slightly damp, the ringlets tangled and twisted. His breathing came fast. He turned away, then back again. He sat up, pulled his knees up, and buried his head in them. If only he could sleep. A walk might help, but he dared not leave the girl alone; she was too vulnerable, asleep with her hair like that. Her hair. He looked at her again, closed his eyes. *I must not, I must not.*

He lay back, fingered his knife in its sheath by his side. Slowly he withdrew the weapon, tested its sharpness with his thumb. He sat up, looked around. Everyone was asleep, laid out like a catch of fish on the deck. All but the duty sailors, laughing quietly over their rum at the bow. The only other sounds were the gentle snores of the sleeping passengers, the creak of the timbers, and the gently cracking bluster of the sails. He took his knife in his right hand. With his left, he stroked the girl's hair; it felt like silk. His hand crept to the nape of her neck and he tucked his fingers into the mass of hair at the back of her head. He wound a lock around his finger, pulled it clear of her lovely head, and took up his knife. The blade was sharp; it sliced through her hair with ease. He took the lock, touched it to his cheek, breathed the scent of it, then quickly replaced his weapon. The lock of hair he coiled up in his hand and secreted in his top pocket. After that, he slept.

As morning broke, they entered the Bristol Channel. People began to stir, stretch, gather their belongings. The ship was waking up. For Edward, docking and disembarking was not so much waking as falling back into a dark, dreamless sleep. On the ship, with Catherine at his side, he had existed only in the moment and had felt alive as never before.

Her smile was radiant as he helped her down the gangplank. She seemed ready to jump for joy. "England," she said, "we're truly in England! And how far is London?"

He explained London was yet more than 100 miles away.

"So how do I get there?"

His company was to board the new railway train for London, and then travel by steamboat to their garrison in Woolwich. He could not take her with him. But he could not leave her. That he had decided even before they left the ship. The idea that her Jack was waiting for her somewhere was, he knew, folly. A greater folly was to abandon her. It would not be long before she'd be one of the hundreds of sad Irish women who begged their way through Wales and the west country to London, tramping by day, sleeping in hedgerows by night, and for what? In London, poverty, disease, and unspeakable misery awaited. As long as she retained her blush, she might make a few bob from soldiers and sailors, and find a hovel to sleep in. She might, if she were lucky, be taken up by one of the grander houses of pleasure. But once toothless and diseased, only the workhouse or death would be her fate.

Edward dug into his pocket and bought her a train ticket. He forbore the jeers and lewd comments of his men, and hustled her to a third-class carriage toward the back and away from the soldiers. He sat her down beside an older woman and man with a baby, and told her to stay put. The train would take her to London, he said, and he would come back for her when they arrived.

She flashed him her brilliant smile. "Then you'll help me find the circus?"

"We'll see," he said, exasperated. "First let's get you set up in London."

He felt himself wading deeper. Her ocean beckoned him. Having helped her make passage to England, he was now planning to take her to London, promising to get her set up. If only she were less single-minded, if only she would put the useless Jack from her mind, and instead look at him, Edward, as someone more than a gallant friend. If only he could think beyond the blue of her eyes, the fall of her hair against her pale shoulders, the red bow of her mouth.

On arrival at Paddington Station, he dodged his colleagues again, and ran down the platform to the last third-class carriage. There she was; though sooty from the open carriage, her smile was broad and her eyes shone. Nothing, not the thirty-six-hour journey across the Irish Sea nor the five-hour train journey, had stilled the determination he saw in her steady gait as she stepped onto the platform. She was a spunky girl and no mistake.

"This is London?" Her eyes were like sapphire saucers.

"This is London," he said.

She grabbed his arm, snuggled her face to his shoulder. "Oh, Corporal, thank you for bringing me here. You cannot know how much this means. You will help me with just one more thing, won't you? To find Billy Mather's Amazing Circus?"

Was that all she could think about? He felt used. He sighed. So be it. He would soon be rid of her. He had a plan. "Follow me," he said.

As he'd considered what to do with Catherine in London, he realized there was one person from his old Soho neighbourhood who could help, and though he found her demeanour distasteful, he also knew she was a steadfast resource for young ladies seeking respectable employment. Edward didn't know if she was still operating her boarding house, or even if she was still alive. But it was worth a try.

Mrs. Scroggs's boarding house in Bedford Court was around the corner from his old home in Rupert Street, and was a formidable presence in the neighbourhood. Mrs. Scroggs prided herself on running a clean and respectable house. Not for her the reputation and fusty rooms of the lower sorts of boarding houses of Drury Lane. She catered to a better class of travelling salesman, a visiting family member, an occasional clergyman, and sometimes even a gentleman, and she enforced strict no-drinking, no-gambling, no-female-visitors rules.

No one could remember Mr. Scroggs. If he had ever existed, it was likely a diminished existence in her shadow, though some people conjectured he left her a small sum of money, which had enabled her to open the boarding house.

Though no longer young, she had no lack of suitors. Several elderly widowers customarily competed for her hand, and perhaps they considered her handsome, but more likely they eyed the comfortable living she made. So far, she had rejected them all. As she proclaimed to anyone who would listen, what good would a husband do for her but dispense orders, purloin her money, and occupy a bed she would prefer to sleep in alone. Her one lady tenant, Miss Everett, she said, agreed it was fortunate to be in a position to decline offers of marriage. But people thought Miss Everett unlikely to have much advice to offer Mrs. Scroggs on the subject, for that lady had retired to her room many years earlier and did not receive unaccompanied men, widowed or otherwise.

Mrs. Scroggs was often seen in the doorway of her house, arms folded over her ample bosom, her apron clean and starched, peering up and down the street. She was a large woman, with a florid, rubbery face and massive hands. In a shrill voice, with a singsong intonation that betrayed her Welsh origins, she harried her servant girls to fetch the water, sweep the steps, and clean the brass. That voice sounded like a clanging bell in Edward's memory, as regular as the church chimes on Sundays. It was not a pleasant memory, but perhaps now she could be useful to Edward.

Mrs. Scroggs liked to remind people, in case they should ever forget, that not only was she as good neighbor and a God-fearing woman, but also a dispenser of charity in accordance with the teachings of the good Lord. It was Mrs. Scroggs's vaunted charity that Edward hoped would be dispensed now. She approved of Edward and his chosen profession, and had proclaimed on several occasions that "the Royal Engineers are the finest and noblest company of men to ever serve the Empire." But he had never asked her for a favour. One rarely did. Usually the initiating of favours came from Mrs. Scroggs herself. But Edward could think of no other option.

Now, as Edward led Catherine by the elbow through the streets towards Soho, he apprised her of his plan and told her that he would do the talking and she should simply nod and smile, and say nothing. She stopped in the middle of the pavement, pulled away from his grasp, and stood with her hands on her hips.

"No," she said, "I shan't. You can't make me. I didn't come here to be a servant. I came to find Jack. You promised you'd help me find him, and if you won't help, I'll strike out on my own."

She made to walk away, but glanced behind her as she went, her eyes narrowed. She was testing him. Exasperated, he grabbed her arm and gave her a shake, a little more roughly than he had intended.

"Don't be foolish, Catherine. You're nothing in this city without a protector. Do as I say, and you'll be all right."

She scowled at him. He held out his hands to her.

"Look, this is a big city. Jack could be anywhere, and it could take a long time to find him. In the meantime, you need food and somewhere to sleep and a job. I'll help you with that. And then … " he tried to suppress the falter in his voice, "then I'll help you look for Jack. It shouldn't be too hard to find his circus."

It was a lie, of course, but it felt good to see her face relax and a reluctant trust return. *He's been good to me thus far*, her eyes seemed to say, *so I'll let him lead me*.

It was twilight when they arrived and the courtyard was quiet and empty but for the lamplighter doing his rounds. Edward pulled Catherine's shawl over her head and across her shoulders, and told her to keep her head down. He rang the doorbell. Mrs. Scroggs answered the door herself with a lighted candle in her hand. She smiled in recognition at Edward.

"Why, Mr. Edward Harris, back in your old neighbourhood. Oh, a corporal now, I see! How smart you look in your soldier's uniform. I always knew you'd do well. I told your dear sister that too, such a fine person she was. She raised you well, she did. Oh … and who's this, may I ask?"

She peered towards Catherine standing behind him, bundled in her shawl, barely visible in the dim light. She was, Edward explained, a poor young servant girl, beaten and cast out by a cruel employer, left to wander the streets of London, and in moral danger too. He'd been walking down to the river to catch a steamer to his garrison in Woolwich and found her near Chelsea, crying and hungry.

"What's to become of her, I wondered. And suddenly, who should enter my mind but my old neighbour, Mrs. Scroggs. There's a charitable, Christian lady, I thought. Mrs. Scroggs, I know you often have honest work for young ladies. Take pity on this poor child, please. She needs a place to stay and she will work hard for her keep."

Mrs. Scroggs stepped forward, lifted Catherine's chin and held the candle close to look at her face.

"Irish," she sniffed, and stepped back. "I don't take Irish. You should know that, Edward. More than enough decent English girls. Take her away." Mrs. Scroggs flapped a dismissive hand at Catherine.

"I understand," said Edward. He replaced his cap, turned to Catherine and in an audible whisper said, "I'm sorry, young lady. I was hoping this good woman would have a job for you. She is known to be kind and Godfearing, and always tries to help her neighbours. But it's not to be. Come along. I'll take you to the workhouse now."

Catherine nodded, as instructed. Edward bowed to Mrs. Scroggs, and took Catherine by the arm. "Thank you Mrs. Scroggs. We'll head to the workhouse now."

Mrs. Scroggs frowned. "Hmm," she said.

"I do understand your position, Mrs. Scroggs, and I'm sure the parish will help her," said Edward, and turned to leave.

"Wait," Mrs. Scroggs called after him. "It so happens I have a position vacant. One of my girls recently left for a cook's job up in Kensington. A very high-class family. I was able to give her an excellent character reference. I'm pleased to say she's gone right up in the world. She started here as a kitchen maid. I've hired a new girl for the vacancy, but she's not arriving for a week or so."

Edward waited. Catherine kept her head down.

"I have rules, you know. I don't usually take Irish because they're lazy and don't respect my rules. Drinking and loud singing at all hours."

Edward smiled to himself. His plan was working. How easy it was to flatter a woman like Mrs. Scroggs.

"So do you perhaps have a position for this poor child?"

"Only because it's you, young Edward, and because I knew your father and your sister, Sarah. Such a very fine woman, she was, and such a tragic loss. It was I who laid out her body, as you know. But leave the girl with me. Come here, child," she pulled Catherine towards her, held the candle high. "I'll say this for the Irish, their women are robust. I dare say this one can be useful to me until the new girl arrives. Then we'll see." To Catherine she said, "There's to be no drinking, mind, and no wandering off to those Irish shindigs in St. Giles. And it'll be Baptist or Methodist on Sundays. There's no Rome in this house. What can you do? Country, I suppose. No experience of town houses. You'll have to learn how to polish the silver, blacklead the grates. Make the beds. Have you ever made a bed? Have you ever slept in a bed?" Mrs. Scroggs scoffed and shook her head. "Irish. I must be mad."

Edward nodded to Catherine and bowed. "Goodbye, young lady," he said, "I wish you well."

Mrs. Scroggs took Catherine by the shoulder and pushed her into the hallway. "In you go. Polly will find you a bed. Polly, come down here!"

"Thank you, Madam. You have been most kind." Edward left and headed toward the river to catch his steamer. It was finished, over with. He had done his Christian duty by the girl, had gone over and above, and ensured her safety. His company was waiting for him, and his commanding officers would have a new assignment, which could be anywhere in the Empire. He no longer had to worry about Catherine Joyce and could put her out of his mind. Yet as he made his way through the darkened streets, he saw her face mirrored in the glow of the gaslights and in the candles burning in the windows of the houses he passed.

Walk fast, he told himself. The further away he got, the more the memory of her would fade. He counted his steps as he walked. One, two, three. Then right, left, right, left, as in a march. It helped. He was at the river within an hour and caught the last steamer to Woolwich. The waves licked the side of the boat like tongues of pitch. Soon he would be miles away from Catherine Joyce, out of London, out of Ireland, back at his garrison in Kent with his colleagues. He looked over the side, into the blackness of the water, and thought he saw a woman drowning, arms flailing, hair spread out in filaments of silk, mouth open in a pleading cry. He blinked, and saw that it was only the moonlight playing tricks on the water.

SEVEN

Mary took Thomas's weekly letters to Mr. Nugent, the newsagent in Woolcot's High Street, for help deciphering them, for she was not a strong reader. Thomas reported he had found a position as an apprentice tailor with a well-established firm. And having got the lay of the land, he had discovered there were some good openings for young women in domestic service. It might not be what she'd been used to, but he felt it would suit Mary admirably, since their mother had taught her how to run a household, keep a clean hearth, and cook a fine meal.

So, she thought, she was to become a servant. But, Thomas reassured her, there might be opportunities for advancement. So be it. Thomas would be there for her, but no one else would know anything about her and she could start a new life.

In early September, with Mr. Nugent's help, she read urgent news from Thomas:

I have been fortunate to make the acquaintance of a most respectable woman who employs several young ladies. And she tells me she has an opening for a housemaid. Naturally, I recommended you, dear sister. I believe the woman in question has taken something of a shine to me, hence her willingness to take you on sight unseen. But she cannot hold the opening for long.

My dear Little Sparrow, I look forward to your arrival in London as soon as you are able to make the arrangements. This is a wonderful opportunity for you, and you must not delay.

On reading Thomas's letter, Mary felt slightly faint and asked Mr. Nugent for a chair. Noticing her shaking hands, he called his wife, who brought her a glass of water. She recovered, and feeling foolish, thanked the Nugents and hurried home with Thomas's letter in her apron.

She thought she ought to be relieved at Thomas's news, but now that it was really happening, the prospect of moving to London and leaving everything she knew terrified her. Yet the thought of spending the rest of her life in Woolcot, surrounded by painful memories and eking a living as a washerwoman, was worse. If only she could be braver. It had been six months since that spring day, six months since she'd made the decision to leave Woolcot and the memory of all that had happened, yet some days she felt as if all her strength had been sapped from her body, leaving her as frightened and fragile as a wounded bird. But she could not go back on her decision. She would go to London. She had no other choice.

Less than a fortnight later, she found herself speeding through the countryside on this newfangled mode of transport they called a train, still feeling like a fragile bird despite her bulky frame, which was squeezed uncomfortably into a crowded, open-air carriage. Many people, she'd heard, found train travel exciting, but not Mary. She clutched the seat every time the train snorted, creaked, or lurched. Its noise and speed terrified her. How could a conveyance move so fast? What if it careened off its rails, hurled its passengers out onto the fields, and crushed them with its iron bulk?

The other passengers were knitting, reading newspapers, munching on bread and cheese. They might all have been sitting calmly on a bench in the village square for all the fear they showed. Watching them made her feel better. Trains were safe, people said; they were the safest form of transport. Safer, Mrs. Nugent's wife had said, than holding on to a slippery newborn baby. She'd said it with a wink and a chuckle, but then quickly gasped and covered her mouth. Mary knew she hadn't meant to be tactless in referring to Mary's abandoned career, but nevertheless her stomach lurched at the comment. Mr. Nugent had jumped in. "Don't worry, Mary, just enjoy the ride. You have more chance of being thrown from a horse or a coach than from a train."

She sat back against the wooden seat of the open train carriage and before long became accustomed to the clickety-clack of the train wheels, even finding it to be a pleasing rhythm. But still the apprehension she'd felt since receiving Thomas's letter remained. She'd been so sure that leaving Woolcot was the best thing for her, but the closer the London trip came, the more worries crept into her mind. People spoke differently in London. She knew that from the strange chatter of the well-to-do folk who visited the Roman remains in Bath. If she couldn't understand them, how would they understand her? And what about their houses? She knew how to keep house in Somerset, but would London be different? London was dirty, people said; all the buildings were covered in soot and the air was thick and foggy. She could not imagine living in a place where you could not see where you were going, like a blind man, or where it hurt every time you took a breath.

She opened her eyes and looked onto the countryside as the train clattered along. Contented cattle grazed in the fields. The trees and hedgerows were tipped with copper and gold. At each halt along the way, she was tempted to step down from the train and lose herself in the solitude of the September countryside, forget about London, and give up this venture. But there was no going back. She would begin a new life in the Modern Babylon. She suppressed the catch in her throat with a cough. A large woman sitting opposite her looked concerned and inclined her head towards her.

"Are you feeling unwell, dear?"

Mary recovered herself and smiled at the woman. "No, I'm all right, thank you."

"Off the big city and all? Bit anxious, are you?" Mary nodded. "You'll be all right, dear." The woman patted Mary's knee. "I'm on my way to see my daughter. Five years, she's been in London. Decent job, she's got, in the kitchen, but she's trying to work her way up. Says moving from Somerset was the best thing she ever did."

At least Mary was to become a housemaid, not a kitchen maid. And Thomas would be in London with her, so she wouldn't be entirely alone in a strange city. The train heaved and lurched. The fields gave way to houses, country lanes to wide streets, crowded with traffic. London was in sight.

With a whistle and a series of screeches, the train ground into a covered area and stopped. Carriage doors were thrown open, porters shouted and scurried, passengers spilled out. Mary climbed down gingerly, laid her bundle at her feet, took off her bonnet, and looked around. The station hall reminded her of the interior of the great church in Bath she loved to visit whenever she was in the city. The Abbey Church of St Peter and St. Paul it was called, but for local folk it was just "the Abbey." Here were the massive arches, the soaring ceiling, the echoing flagstones. But this was a church violated, as throngs of people rushed around her, and locomotives hissed and snorted. Above her, the glass ceiling was white with clouds of steam.

She put a hand to her face. The whipping wind had burned her cheeks where her bonnet failed to shade her. Her face felt flushed, but she was not sure if it was because of the wind or her nerves.

From her pocket she retrieved the paper on which Thomas had written instructions. She'd memorized the words but kept the paper in case something slipped her memory. *Go out from the station hall to the main street called Praed Street and you will see a row of omnibuses.*

Mary had seen omnibuses in Bath—large conveyances drawn by a team of at least two horses—but had never taken one; they seemed an unnecessary extravagance. Could she not walk? she had asked Thomas. The way was too complicated, he said, and she might get lost. *You'll like travelling by omnibus,* he wrote. *So long as you have some pennies for the fare, this mode of conveyance takes you quickly and easily to where you want to go.* She continued to scan the paper, reciting to herself, *Ask the driver for the omnibus that will take you to Oxford Street by Wardour Street. Get out at Wardour Street, and walk.* Then came a complicated list of twists and turns. But the destination address, and the name of the person she was to see, were clearly written at the bottom of the sheet, and these she could read. *Number 5, Bedford Court. Knock on the door and ask for Mrs. Scroggs.*

Mary looked around for the way out of the station. No one noticed her, no one stopped to ask if she needed help. Everyone was in a hurry and seemed to know exactly where they were going. She was not in Woolcot anymore, she reminded herself. Here, no one knew her. There was nothing and no one to remind her of who she was and what she had been. She was anonymous and invisible. It was a surprisingly comfortable feeling. This, surely, was why she'd come to London.

She put her bonnet back on, picked up her bundle, and set out towards the far end of the station hall, which was where she thought the way out must be. As she exited onto the street, she felt herself jostled this way and that by a sheer mass of people, more even that at the station hall. People of every class, every age, every situation, the rich and the poor, crushed together in the throng. Carts pushed their

51

way through, people scattered, gentlemen on horseback waved their crops and cried "Make way, make way." Ragged boys with brooms swept a path for elegant ladies to cross, ragged girls with winsome cries carried bunches flowers for sale, men pushed barrows piled high with fruit and vegetables, others carried sides of meat on their shoulders.

The noise and smells and activity were overwhelming, and Mary stood back for a few moments to gather her wits before picking a path through the throng to the line of omnibuses she'd spotted. "Sorry, excuse me," she said as she skirted around people, but no one paid her any mind. She found and mounted the correct omnibus, relieved the driver appeared to understand her and was helpful. She noticed stairs leading to the open top deck and began to climb up, hoping for some fresh air to breathe. But the conductor hustled her to the stuffy, crowded inside. "Gentlemen only on top," he said.

The conductor called out when it was her stop. "Here you are, my duck, Oxford Street at Wardour." At least, that was what she thought he said. She climbed down from the omnibus, and looked around. "Over there, duck, that's where you want to be," said the conductor, and pointed in the direction of a small street turning from the main thoroughfare. She thanked him, and recited to herself the directions to Bedford Court that Thomas had sent. She focused on following the twists and turns of the streets and memorizing landmarks along the way, lest she miss a turn and find herself hopelessly lost, but then found herself bumping into people or tripping on a kerb.

After several minutes, she came to a turning into a broad courtyard lined with solid brick houses and several shops. After the hustle and bustle of the surrounding streets, the courtyard was pleasingly quiet, homely almost, with just a few children at play on the cobblestones and mothers gossiping from their doorways. According to her memory, this ought to be Bedford Court, but there was no street sign. She noticed a young woman carrying a bundle emerging from one of the houses. She had a patched skirt and a shawl over her head, but good shoes on her feet. Mary called out to her.

"Pardon me, this is Bedford Court isn't it? I'm looking for Number 5."

The woman stopped and stared at Mary with a quizzical frown, then jerked her head towards the house behind her in an aggressive manner. "Number 5 is it you're looking for? Well, there it is then. 'Tis a lovely place you're going to. Oh yes, you'll like it there all right," she said and gave a short laugh. She spoke with a strong Irish brogue. From under her shawl, curls of copper-coloured hair framed her soft white face like a halo. What a lovely woman, thought Mary.

As the woman turned and walked briskly away, she called, "Good luck." Mary wasn't sure she meant it. The encounter made her apprehensive again as she stepped up to the door and knocked. It was a brown door, with a large white 5 painted on it. A maid answered her knock.

"Good afternoon, is this No. 5 Bedford Court?" asked Mary.

The maid pointed to the number on the door. "I should say it is. Who's asking?" she said, in a not very friendly voice.

Mary announced herself, and the maid's expression changed. With a broad grin she said, "Oh yes, Mary Piper. We've been expecting you," and ushered Mary in.

The hall of the house was long and dark, lit only by a small window above the front door. Bright floral wallpaper added a little cheer to the otherwise dingy hallway. To the right, a staircase, carpeted in a rich red and gold pattern, led straight up to a landing.

"I'm Polly, by the way," the maid said, "and you'll be in my room. There's a spare bed there now the other girl's gone. She didn't last long. P'raps you'll work out better than she did." Polly gave Mary a sly look, then grinned again, "Hope you don't snore."

Her words startled Mary. She didn't know whether she snored—her mother had never said anything and neither had Thomas. The lodger had snored, but perhaps she did too. After all, one did not normally know such things unless someone else told you. But no one had. It bothered Mary that she might snore and disturb Polly in the night—it would not a good footing to start her new life. Then she heard Polly snigger in a good-natured sort of way, and thought perhaps the girl had only been joking.

"Come with me. I'll show you the ropes."

Down the hall on the left were two doors. Polly pointed to the one nearest the front of the house.

"That's the front parlour. Mrs. Scroggs's quarters. She's the proprietor. You don't go in there unless you're called," she said. She pointed to the next door. "And that there's the back room, and you don't never go in there, not never. That's Miss Everett's room." She said it in such a way as to brook no questions. Mary was curious but kept silent. She followed Polly to a large dining dining room at the end of the hall, beside which another staircase, this one bare and wooden, led down to the kitchen in the basement. They would go there later, Polly said.

Polly led her back along the hall, past the mysterious back room door and the front parlour door, and up the main staircase to a large landing with several cream-painted doors. "That's where the boarders sleep," said Polly, "but us lot is up in the attic." She opened a smaller, bare wooden door, behind which was another narrow, wooden staircase leading to a small landing and four more doors. Polly entered one and Mary followed with her bundle. She found herself in a compact room nestled under the eaves of the house. A chest of drawers with a washstand, a wardrobe, and two narrow beds furnished the room. Mary put her bundle on the nearest bed, under the eaves, and Polly snapped, "That's my bed; you get the drafty one by the window." She sniggered again. "All the new girls sleep in that bed, but I've been here for two years, and I'm in Mrs. Scroggs's good books at the moment, so you'd better watch out."

Nonplussed by the maid's sudden sharpness, Mary moved her things to the other bed. She was not sure what to do or say next, but Polly went on with a stream of instructions, mostly, from what Mary heard, to do with time: what time they were to rise, what time breakfast was served, what time boarders had to leave for the day so that the servants could clean the rooms …

Mary felt slightly panicked. She had heard that here in the city people used clocks to keep time, but she had always relied on church chimes or the sun. She glanced out of the window. She could see no nearby church, and no sign of sun. The sky was a solid brown. Beneath it, smoke from neighbouring chimneys billowed, and rooftops stretched on and on, unbroken by hills or valleys. Time by the clock was one of many things she would have to learn.

Polly continued to talk, counting on her fingers the names of the current boarders, "Mr. Grey, he's a watchmaker, quite a gentleman, been here for over a month, then there's Mr. Wilkins. Commercial traveller. You have to watch him, he's a bit of a card. And then there's Miss Everett in the downstairs back room. Let me give you a word of advice. Miss Everett is Mrs. Scroggs's special friend, so you don't go near her room unless Mrs. Scroggs says you can. Not never. Remember what I told you. *I'm* allowed to take her tea in, but you won't be, so don't start thinking you can get favours from Mrs. S. by taking her friend's tea in … "

Mary wondered how she would ever remember all this as Polly rattled on, " … if you get on the wrong side of Mrs. S., you'll be out of here before you can say Jack Robinson. I've seen it myself, I've seen it all. Girls come here, they stay for a week, they upset Mrs. S, and out they go. Like the one what just left. You'll sleep in her bed now. You wouldn't believe why she was sacked. I might tell you one day. But you'd better watch out, Mary Piper."

Mary placed her hands to her temples and squeezed her eyes shut. Polly paused as if for breath and then spoke in a gentler tone.

"Ah now, don't you be furrowing your brow, young Mary. I don't mean no harm, just trying to help you get settled. Here, come down with me now and meet Mrs. Scroggs. She's not a bad old stick, as long as you do as you're told."

Mary looked up, and saw that Polly's eyes were kind. She was really a very pretty girl, thought Mary, with her pale blue eyes, small pointed nose, and freckly face. She herself, she knew, could not be considered pretty. Her skin was too sallow, her hair too mousy, her chin too square, her nose a little too prominent. But she thought she would enjoy living with someone as pretty as Polly. She was sure she hadn't meant to be sharp. She smiled.

"Thank you, Polly. You're very kind."

Polly smiled back, with a mouth full of crooked teeth that in an odd way made her even more attractive.

"Come on," she said. "Better wash your face and hands and smarten your collar. Mrs. S. likes a clean maid. First week's wages'll buy you your uniform, and you have to wash and iron it yourself, and keep it clean."

Polly led the spruced-up Mary down the stairs to the hall, knocked gently on the front room door, and opened it a crack to peek in.

"Come in, come in girl," Mary heard a voice. The two girls entered.

"Mary Piper, the new girl," said Polly.

"Come on then, let me look at you," said the voice.

Mary could see only a big armchair, with two feet in worn leather slippers sticking out, resting on a footstool. Then the occupant of the chair leaned forward, removing her feet from the stool, and Mary saw for the first time the woman who was to become her employer. A large head and broad face filled Mary's line of sight. The face had a ruddy complexion and small brown eyes that bored into her.

She curtsied and mumbled, "How do you do, Mrs. Scroggs," and the woman in the chair nodded, and then silently scrutinized Mary, starting with her face, and moving her eyes down to her dress, and finally her shoes. Mary became acutely aware that her dress was worn and had a patch on the sleeve, and her shoes were old and scuffed. She shifted around uncomfortably, and tried to cover the patch with her shawl.

At last, Mrs. Scroggs spoke, with a firm voice that allowed no argument. "Country," she said. "I don't usually take country girls. They're all as slow and lumbering as the cows they milk, and it takes too long to teach them. But you're Mr. Thomas Piper's sister, I gather. Your brother gave you a very good character reference, Mary Piper. He says you're a quick learner, honest and hardworking. But then he would say that of his own sister, wouldn't he? Still, he's a fine young man, I must say, a good Christian. I hope you'll be the same, and you won't let your brother down. My problem is I'm too soft-hearted. That's been my downfall in the past. Taken girls on out of pity, or because I like their brothers or their fathers, and then they let me down and I have to sack them. I hope you won't let me down, Mary Piper."

Mary didn't know what she was supposed to say, so she said nothing. Polly, who was standing behind her, gave her a little shove. Again Mrs. Scroggs, looking straight at Mary, said, "I hope you won't be like some of the country girls I've had."

Mary curtsied again and said, "No, Madam," and hoped that was the correct response. It was, for Mrs. Scroggs nodded again. "Very well. Polly will show you what you need to do. And now, for your first job, you can see to my feet."

Mary looked at her questioningly. Polly whispered, "She's a martyr to her feet," and sniggered, then more loudly said, "Here, I'll show you what you have to do."

"Good girl, Polly, that's the way," said Mrs. Scroggs, and put her feet back up on the footstool.

Polly took Mary down to the basement kitchen and introduced her briefly to the kitchen staff, who seemed to Mary to consist of a great number of women scurrying to and fro. Polly said their names in turn, but Mary could barely remember any of them.

Polly barked at one of the kitchen maids, "Mrs. Scroggs's bowl, Jane. And the kettle."

Jane took a large kettle that hung from a hook by the fireplace and carried it with a bowl to where Polly and Mary waited. Polly carefully poured hot water from the kettle into the bowl, and covered it with a clean cloth.

"Now you take this up to Mrs. Scroggs; careful now, don't spill it. Help her take off her slippers and stockings. Test the water with your elbow—you'll be in trouble if it's too hot, and more trouble if it's not hot enough. I take it you do know how to test water with your elbow?"

This was something Mary did know. She had learned from washing newborn babies how to gauge the temperature of water.

"Then you help her put her feet to soak in the hot water." Polly looked up at the clock on the kitchen wall. "It's nearly six o'clock now. Go back in at quarter past to take the water away."

Mary felt panicky again. She didn't know what quarter past six looked like on a clock. She glanced outside, but it was difficult on such a dull day to know what time it was. Perhaps by the time the light had fully faded it would be quarter past six. Or perhaps she'd hear a church bell strike the quarter hour. She carried the bowl upstairs and helped Mrs. Scroggs soak her feet. Then she curtsied again and made to leave the room.

"Don't go, Mary Piper," said Mrs. Scroggs. "Come and let me look at you proper-like. You can sit down."

Mary was surprised, but did as she was told. Mrs. Scroggs beckoned her and scrutinized her face. "Come closer, girl," she said.

Mary shuffled her chair and leaned forward. Mrs. Scroggs leaned forward too, took Mary's chin in her hand, and turned her face this way and that. This level of intimacy made Mary decidedly uncomfortable. Then Mrs. Scroggs let go of her face, sat back and smacked her lips together.

"I like the look of you," she said. "You lost your mother recently, didn't you?"

Mary nodded, and looked down. Thomas must have told her this, perhaps to elicit her sympathy for his employment negotiations on her behalf. She hoped he hadn't mentioned the other business.

"I'm a charitable woman, Mary Piper, anyone will tell you that. I'm highly respected in this neighbourhood. All the local people like to have their daughters work for me, because they know this is a respectable house. I train them up, so they can then go and work in some of the great houses. I've had girls go up to Kensington and Belgravia, working for judges and lords. Even had one go to Italy to work for a countess. I'm a good judge of character, you see. I was only saying that to Miss Everett the other day. 'Aren't I a good judge of character, Miss Everett?' I said, and she agreed, and she should know, 'cause she's a woman of refinement, is Miss Everett. You'll find out if you stay here. If you work hard and do as you're told I might even let you take Miss Everett's tea in."

Mary was intrigued to know more about this Miss Everett, who seemed to hold some special status in the house, but she recognized that it was Mrs. Scroggs, and not she, who had leave to ask questions. She simply curtsied again and said, "Thank you, Madam."

"You've got a strong jaw, and a firm nose, Mary Piper. I like that in a girl. Those little girls with their snub noses don't last long, let me tell you. I don't take a girl with a snub nose.

"I've made a few mistakes over the years, I won't deny it. Too soft-hearted I am, sometimes, and that's my downfall. But usually I know a good character when I see one, and I see a good character in you, Mary Piper. You're polite and, well, I don't mean to be unkind, but you're plain, and in my book that's a compliment. It means you won't be running after all the young men in the neighbourhood."

Mary, with her height and large bones, was not accustomed to feeling small in the presence of others. But Mrs. Scroggs had a dominance that quite overwhelmed her. The woman seemed to fill the room with her body and her voice, and her huge head. Mary tried to stand up straight before her, but found no matter how she tried, her shoulders insisted on bowing and her head on looking down at the floor. Working for Mrs. Scroggs, she feared, would be a challenge she might not be up to.

She spied the water in the bowl. Was it getting cold? Was it quarter past six yet? The light outside seemed a little dimmer, and the water in the bowl must be almost cold. Would Mrs. Scroggs reprimand her for this? Then she had an idea.

"Madam, how is the water? Would you like me to refresh it?"

Mrs. Scroggs looked astonished. "Well, now, aren't you a thoughtful girl? She took her feet out of the bowl and placed them on the towel Mary had laid down. "You can take the bowl away now. Goodnight."

With that, Mrs. Scroggs turned away. Mary, not knowing what else to do, picked up the bowl of water and started for the door.

"My feet," Mrs. Scroggs called after her. "Dry them first, then take the towel."

"I'm sorry, Madam."

"Just remember next time."

Mary gently dried the old woman's feet, upon which the woman appeared to fall fast asleep in her chair. Mary carefully carried the bowl out of the room and pushed the door closed with her foot. Her first encounter with her employer had been stranger than she could have imagined, but she'd survived. In the hall she almost bumped into Polly, who grabbed her arm, sloshing the water.

"There you are. I've been looking everywhere for you. What've you been doing? Supper's ready and Cook'll be angry if you're late."

With the mention of supper, Mary realized she was extremely hungry. She had not eaten since her early morning breakfast in Bath. She followed Polly downstairs to the kitchen, where a convivial group of women sat at a long table with plates and bowls in front of them. "We do the boarders' supper first, clear it away, and then have ours," said Polly.

The food was served by one of the kitchen staff, and it was good. Bread and soup with pieces of meat and potato. Mary ate hungrily, while trying at the same time to watch her manners and not slurp the soup too loudly.

It was a lively meal, with a lot of banter and chatter among the women. Next to Mary sat one of the kitchen maids, a plump girl with badly pock-marked skin. Mary thought her scars must be from smallpox, a disease she had heard was common in London. Martha, her name was, and she seemed a cheerful person, though Mary wondered how much she must have suffered to have been so scarred.

At the station and on the omnibus, Mary had noticed many red, raw, and scarred faces or waxen, yellow, unhealthy-looking skin. It must be, she thought, something about the London air, a miasma that descended and brought with it smallpox and other skin problems.

At one point during the meal, Martha nudged Mary and whispered to her, "Don't let that Polly push you around. It's always the same with her. Every time a new girl comes, Miss Nibbs gets on her high horse and thinks she's in charge. Well, she ain't. You make sure she don't make you do more than your share."

Mary thanked Martha for the advice, but was not about to enter into household gossip. "Polly's been very kind to me," she said.

Martha sniffed and nodded knowingly. "I'm just saying … "

After supper, Polly and Mary went back upstairs to the little attic room. Before they retired, Polly went through the list of chores that Mary would be expected to perform, starting early the next morning. They were beginning to sound familiar and Mary felt more at ease. Clean the dining room grate, bring in the coal, light the fires, fetch the tea and bread up to the dining room, ring the breakfast bell, strip, air, and make up the beds … Monday was laundry day, Polly said, and Mary would be responsible for washing the gentlemen's shirts, and their sheets, and changing the beds. Polly held out her hands, which were red and swollen.

"I don't do laundry no more. Mrs. S. brought in a daily woman when my hands got raw, but now you're here you'll have to do it."

That was fine by Mary; laundry was a chore she'd grown well used to these last months.

Tuesday was ironing, provided the sheets were dry; otherwise it would be Wednesday. But Wednesday was also mending day—sheets and tablecloths and blankets—so that would have to be fitted in too. And she had to be on call for the gentlemen when they rang the bell. Mary hoped she would remember everything.

"Polly," she said, "I don't want to make any mistakes. Will you be able to show me what I have to do?"

Polly's demeanour seemed to soften. "All right," she said, "I'll try to help you."

"I don't want to take you away from your own work."

Polly gave Mary a strange look, almost as if she were guilty about something, and turned her back, busying herself at the washstand. Mary was relieved that Polly agreed to help. She looked at the bed. Her very own bed. Even though she'd slept alone after her mother died, she had never really felt alone, for her mother's memory still occupied the bed. Even the indentation of her body remained more than two years after her death. That indentation had comforted her during these last months. She used to lay her hand on the shallow hollow and whisper goodnight to her mother. Often, she fancied she heard her mother's response, *Goodnight my Little Sparrow."*

It had been a long day and Mary was tired. Though unfamiliar images and confusing information had filled the first day of her new life, it had not been as frightening as she had feared. She undressed and quickly slipped into the cold sheets. Now she would really be alone, but it was, she thought a little guiltily, nice to have a whole bed to herself. Before she had finished the thought, she was asleep.

The lights in the neighbouring houses in Bedford Court went out one by one. Candles were snuffed. Gas was extinguished. The courtyard was peaceful now. Children slept. Women and men settled in their beds. A million fires burned down to embers, and the smoke and soot from their chimneys drifted in the yellow light of the streetlamps. All that could be heard was the distant clatter of traffic on Oxford Street and the other grand boulevards and avenues of London—coaches carrying the mail, farmers in carts headed home from markets, omnibuses taking workers back to their homes, policemen patrolling the streets with their truncheons and whistles. Later, the city would be quiet, but only for a short while, and the clatter would start up again even before the sparrows woke.

EIGHT

At the garrison, the days were long and tedious. Edward's body, though thin and wiry, had toughened from marches, knee-deep in mud, through bogs and over hills. Nights under canvas in Ireland brought the sleep of exhaustion. Here at the Woolwich barracks, the exhaustion was mental. Edward longed for that peaceful quality of sleep that had him wake refreshed and ready for a new day, but it would not come; his mind would give him no rest.

What little sleep he managed was fitful and full of dreams of a woman standing on a wharf, her red hair a halo against the morning sun, her shoulders pale and soft against her drab clothing. He turned from her, but looked again. She was drowning in the mud of the river, her arms like wings outstretched, begging him for rescue. Ribbons of riverweed streamed from the hem of her skirt. He saw words written on the ribbons as they were pulled along by the current. They were the words of the stories his sister Sarah had lulled him to sleep with when he was a boy. The enchantress who bewitched her captured knight, the sirens who lured sailors to their deaths on rocks. Sarah had warned him over and over. "People call us the weaker sex," she said. "They say we are fragile flowers. Do not be fooled, Edward. Women can mendacious, manipulative, and inconstant. Do not allow a woman to beguile you with beauty. Remember, a rose's bloom fades by October."

This woman, this Catherine Joyce who filled his dreams, was the very danger Sarah had warned him of. He vowed he would not see her again. He would not go to her. She cared nothing for him, had barely looked at him when he left. All she could think about was her Jack.

Oh, but ... if only he could get her loveliness out of his mind! Catherine was not the woman for him. He was a serious man, steady and of sober tastes. The kind of woman he needed should have a still and patient soul, a neat appearance, a quiet, obedient manner. This Catherine was a wild bird with unclipped wings. He was not the man to contain her or tame her, so why even think about visiting her?

Perhaps one day he might pay her a brotherly visit. Just to find out how she was settling down. If he left straight after Sunday service, he could be at Mrs. Scroggs's boarding house by noon. If it was Catherine's day off, he could take her for a stroll in Hyde Park, or to one of London's many tea gardens.

But why would he go? She was nothing to him, just a common Irish peasant girl who lived in a confused dream world and had lost her way for a while. All he had done was to be a gentleman and put her on the right path.

On the other hand, it would do no harm to pay a quick visit, just to say hello. For more than two days she had been his charge, under his guardianship. She owed him gratitude if nothing else. Yes, he would go and see her, just to make sure she was well and happy.

On the night of September 23, a full, golden harvest moon hung low in the sky. A soft, autumn rain had cleansed the streets of soot and grime and made the rooftops glisten. Edward rose early, well before roll call, even before the church bells chimed for the harvest festival, and spent extra time on his ablutions. He shaved his cheeks as closely as he dared, clipped his beard, combed and waxed his moustache, and applied aromatic pomade to his hair. Its camphor scent made him breathe deeply and square his shoulders. His uniform was clean and pressed.

He set out immediately after morning service and arrived on Mrs. Scroggs's doorstep just after noon. He rang the bell. Mrs. Scroggs opened the door wide and stood, broad-beamed, feet planted like trees, hands on her hips. A flurry of skirts behind her revealed Polly, the housemaid, peering from the stair banister.

"Well," said Mrs. Scroggs, "if it isn't *Mister* Harris, come looking for his wench, no doubt. One little thing you neglected to tell me, wasn't there?" A slow sneer formed on her mouth. Polly moved closer.

Edward looked puzzled. "What?"

"Just a little matter of the girl being, shall we say, a touch *unwell*."

Unwell? Catherine? His face screwed up with consternation.

"Oh, I see you looking all innocent, pretending you don't know anything about it. Well you can't fool me, *Mister* Harris. Thanks to my Polly here, I found out before it was too late. She's a bright girl, is Polly. They shared a room, and it didn't take long for Polly to see what was going on."

Polly leaned on the banister and smirked in the background.

A crowd began to form in the courtyard—curious women and children, hearing the altercation, lingered to watch and listen. What was Mrs. Scroggs on about this time? Edward was still puzzled.

Mrs. Scroggs took a step toward him and hissed, "In the pudding club, no less! And you brought her to this house!" Edward recoiled as the woman's spit sprayed his face.

It took a few moments for the meaning of her words to register. Catherine was with child! He had not known, nor suspected. Then it came to him what this must have meant for her. Of course. No wonder she had been so desperate to find Jack. No wonder she had pleaded and begged him to help her. Now he understood why she was adamant about not returning to Kildean. There could be no happy outcome for a girl like her in a closed Irish village. Yet in her innocence she had put herself in an even worse situation, for in London there was only the street or the workhouse.

He caught Mrs. Scroggs's steely glare and felt his colour rise as he understood her implication. He raised his hands and backed away.

"Oh no, no. Mrs. Scroggs, you can't think … I swear I knew nothing about this. If I had known, I would never have brought her to you. Good Lord … "

"You may well call on the good Lord, as may she, as only the Lord can save her now. Fancy you of all people bringing a woman like that to my door. You, your father's son, and your angel of a sister, what would she have thought?"

Edward thought fast, and decided his only defence was to invoke a similar level of righteous indignation. He drew himself up to a grave and soldierly stance as he faced the older woman's accusatory glare.

"Mrs. Scroggs. As I told you, I only met this girl on the day I brought her to you. I knew nothing about her, just that she seemed in a bad state. Like you, I'm a good Christian and felt duty-bound to help her. I knew you to be a charitable woman. But I knew nothing of this … this … had I known, I should never have brought her here."

Edward held Mrs. Scroggs's gaze. She frowned, her eyes narrowed, and then her face softened. "Hmm," she said, and folded her arms over her ample bosom. "Hmm," again, then, "well, I suppose I might believe that. Coming from you, Sarah's little brother. So, it looks like the little Irish minx fooled us both. There was you thinking she was a poor beaten thing, and me wanting to be charitable and help her out with a job and bed, and what do I get for my kindness?" She began to raise her voice. The watching women nudged each other, grinned, and moved a little closer. Their children, bored by grown-up talk, went back to their hoops and tops. "Of course, when I found out, I told her she had to go. I confronted her. She didn't deny it. Well, she couldn't, could she? You can only hide such a thing for so long.

"I gave her what for, I did, the lying little trollop. She looked me straight in the eye and as good as told me, so what? Said she didn't want to stay here anyway. I've never been spoken to like that in my life, not by the likes of a sinful girl like her. Out on her ear, I sent her. Packing, I sent her, with her bundle of clothes in her apron."

Edward barely heard Mrs. Scroggs's rambling indignation. Another thought had risen within him, that Catherine's running away from Kildean didn't have to be all about Jack. No doubt she thought she loved the man, but it was all about her predicament. In her heart of hearts, she must have known it was folly to believe she would ever find Jack, or if she did, that he would marry her. But in her situation, she was desperate, and clung to the only hope she thought she had. Now that hope had gone, but Edward was here.

Then, like two rivers that flow together into a broad, still delta, all his confused and conflicted ramblings of the last few days dissolved into one clear thought. He would marry her. In his head, the declaration felt like a victory shout, and he would have thrust his fist in the air and given a whoop of joy, but restrained himself. Catherine had left, and he had no idea where she was. He would have to find her before he could marry her. He straightened his back, brushed his sleeves, tugged at the edge of his jacket, and looked Mrs. Scroggs in the eye.

"You sent her away, Mrs. Scroggs. Quite right. But which way did she go?"

"Which way? Off to St. Giles, I'd wager, back to the Irish slums. Back where she belongs."

Polly, in the shadows, still snickering, pointed the way.

"When did she go? How long ago?"

"Took off yesterday. After I had it out with her. I wouldn't have her in this house for another Sunday."

Just yesterday. She had no knowledge of London's neighbourhoods, and its twisting, turning streets. She probably wandered for hours through unfamiliar courtyards and passages where unknown dangers lurked. Where did she sleep? Perhaps she stumbled into a doorway, a garden, a bridge; any place to shelter, while he had been tossing and turning in his bed. Was she afraid? Not once had she shown a modicum of fear or anxiety about anything—not at the wharf, nor on the ship, the train, and not even in the unfamiliar streets of London. She had shown only a ferocious and naïve determination to pursue what she believed was her destiny. Naïveté breeds self-assurance, he thought, and Catherine had both in spades, but she had little understanding of the what could happen to a beautiful young woman alone in a city like London.

With his face impassive, despite his leaping insides, he nodded and bowed to Mrs. Scroggs. "I understand, Mrs. Scroggs, and thank you." He turned to leave.

Mrs. Scroggs continued to grouse and grumble about the taint the girl had brought to her house. "Well, Edward, I can see you get my point, don't you? She's not the sort we want around here, is she? We don't need her kind, not when there's decent girls to be had. Just got a new one yesterday, a fine young lady, decent Somerset girl, comes with a very good character reference. Not like that Irish good-for-nothing. Good riddance to her, I say, and I'm glad you see it the same way. Out of my sight. I wouldn't have her in my house another minute … "

Edward hurried away. He headed east along Rupert Street up to Soho Square, passing St. Anne's Church, where he had been christened, taking shortcuts through passages and courtyards. The crowded streets and alleys, as usual, were a Babel of languages—Russian, French, and Italian mixed with English—as couples and families took their Sunday promenades.

He knew these streets; they had been mapped in his mind for years. But he had never had cause to cross over into St. Giles Parish past the eastern edge of Soho; he would rely on his internal mapping instincts to lead him. He knew the parish only by reputation as a neighbourhood thick with thieves and pickpockets, soaked in cheap gin, and rife with disease. At least, according to the stalwart gentlemen from St. James's Parish. They liked to write prolifically to the Letters page of the daily broadsheets that the hovels of St. Giles's rookery spilled over with Irish vagrants and prostitutes and numerous members of the criminal class. It was, they said, a veritable cesspool of criminality and depravity.

But Edward was not afraid. The things he read and heard about the Irish—a degenerate race, bestial in their habits, uncontrolled in their temper, dirty, criminal, and given to the demon drink—frequently left him shaking his head. Unlike many of his compatriots, Edward viewed the Irish as redeemable if only given a chance to improve their lot, and for most of them that was why they came to London, only to be further vilified and rejected. He did not doubt there was a large criminal element among the Irish of St. Giles, but he believed that for every Irish degenerate grovelling in the gutter, there were at least three or four decent hardworking men who sent money to wives and saved for their passage to a better life. The honest poor lived in the squalid St. Giles because they were barred from "respectable" neighbourhoods. Mrs. Scroggs, he knew, was by no means atypical in her categorical refusal to "take Irish."

Four years of marching through Ireland, measuring its terrain, and billeting in its towns and villages, had given Edward a healthy respect for what God and the English had served the Irish in their own land. He had seen for himself the hovels that he was sure surpassed even the meanest houses in St. Giles and contrasted so starkly with the fine manses their English landlords owned and hardly ever visited, while extracting ruinous rents for their meagre smallholdings. Despite their poverty, he had found the Irish a robust, resilient race with a rich history, and he recalled with gratitude the many kindnesses bestowed on him by cottagers, and evenings of laughter, music, and dancing. He was a rare breed: an Englishman, and a soldier at that, comfortable in the company of the Irish, sympathetic to their plight, hopeful for their future. And hoping to seal his own future, too, with an Irish woman. The memory of his sister flashed into his mind, as it did so often where Catherine was concerned, and he caught his breath for a moment. But Sarah would never know Catherine, and never know how deliriously happy the thought of marrying her made him.

He followed Old Compton Street to the notorious alleys of the Seven Dials. As he went deeper into the parish, he noticed the houses getting shabbier, the shops meaner, the street traders more raucous. The densely packed streets swarmed with men going in and out of the entranceways to the teetering houses that lined the streets, or sitting on doorsteps in desultory fashion, their clothing grime-coated, their hats battered, some without shoes. Others lurched from the taverns, their voices ringing out with songs he remembered from Ireland.

There were a few women, too, among the crowds of men. Here and there he saw the swish of a skirt or the high arch of a bonnet within the throng. The irony of searching for Catherine in this human hive, as she searched for Jack, was not lost on him. He glanced around him as he made his way through the crowds, peering particularly at the women, but none had Catherine's fresh young beauty. Not the fat old fishwives shouting in shop doorways, or the sad young girls leaning in the shadows, hands pawing at passing men. He passed a tavern where a pock-marked young woman sat on the pavement nursing a skinny child, her breast carelessly bared, her eyes glassy with gin, a grubby hand held out in vain hope of a coin or two. Edward shuddered and hurried on. God willing, he would find Catherine before this fate was hers.

From the Seven Dials circle, he turned onto Castle Street, and left onto Drury Lane, which led him to St. Giles High Street. Then he knew where he would find her, the obvious place where she would have spent the night. The ancient church of St. Giles-in-the-Fields. Sanctuary. She had known only the vague direction in which Polly had pointed. As the sun went down and the streets darkened, she would have walked towards the sound of the great old church clock sounding the hours and the half and quarter hours. The churchyard would have been a place for her to spend the night.

As he hurried along the High Street, he saw the spire of the church ahead of him. Morning services were over; congregants had dispersed. Would not someone among the congregation have seen her, a woman alone, seeking shelter in a church? Once seen, Catherine was not forgotten.

He entered the churchyard and moved stealthily along the short path that led through mildewed gravestones. The place was quiet and empty, a peaceful retreat from the clamour of the street behind him. Massive yew trees put the church walls in deep shadow and Edward squinted as he searched the west side of the church. Not a soul lingered. He turned the corner and looked toward the front steps. A stand of birch trees lining the front and east sides were turning russet and sparkled in the early afternoon sunshine. The church's front door was closed, the steps empty. A slight wind rustled the trees and carried with it a woman's laugh. Deep and full-throated, it was not Catherine's mellifluous tone. But someone was there, in the churchyard, on the other side perhaps. He slipped behind the birch trees and moved silently toward the east side entrance. Through the swaying branches he saw three figures on the steps. A man and a woman. And Catherine. He let out a sigh. Her shawl was around her shoulders, her hair loose, and her head slightly bowed. He moved forward, and sidled behind a tree to get a better look.

The woman crouched before Catherine, holding her hands, as if in persuasion. On her felt hat she wore flowers, and her skirt was made of some shiny green material. Her shawl was of fine, lacy wool, which nevertheless could not hide loose threads and large holes. Her face was pale, freckled, sharp-featured. The bearded man sat beside Catherine, a red cravat around his neck, a tight jacket, a size too small, torn at the side, and no hat. No hat, on a Sunday! His body was small and wiry, his beard was raggedly trimmed to a point on his chin, and his dark hair curled around his ears. His forehead revealed a bronze complexion, which gave him the look of a gypsy.

Edward felt his shoulders tense. Could this be Jack? Was it possible? Surely, she could not have found him so quickly. But if not Jack, this man and woman, accosting a young woman alone, were assuredly up to no good. The man had the temerity to place his arm around Catherine's shoulder with a smile. More like a leer, thought Edward. He felt an urge to strike him there and then. He had no weapon, but he had on his soldier's uniform. As a corporal and a military man, he knew how to adopt an authoritative demeanour. This scrawny youth should be no match for a trained soldier.

He stepped boldly up to the group and announced, "Ah, there you are my dear. Time to come home now." He turned to the man, looked him in the eye, and said, "Thank you, sir, for taking care of my wife. Sometimes she gets a little confused, but I'm here now, so you may leave."

Catherine started visibly and stared at him with wide eyes. As she recognized him, she frowned. "What?"

He beckoned, "Come on, let's go home, dear."

"Home?" she said. "What are you talking about?"

"Yes, indeed," said the man, still leering, "who by the saints are you, anyway? 'Tis best you take care of your own business, soldier, and leave this little lady alone."

His accent revealed him to be an Irishman, hardly a surprise to Edward, but it might be hard to pry Catherine from a compatriot. The woman with him shuffled closer to Catherine and grasped her forearm. Catherine glared at Edward and shifted her body toward the woman. The man moved to shield Catherine with his body.

The woman spoke with a sneer. "She's coming with us. We're her people. Best you go, soldier, and stop bothering her."

Catherine snuggled up to the woman, who stroked her face, for all the world as if they were sisters. The man stood, feet apart, in a threatening stance, his face an insolent mask. A slick red scar on the side of his face glistened in the noonday sun. Edward's forehead was damp with sweat. How was he to get Catherine away from these people? He had no sword or rifle, no physical weapon with which to threaten them. They had, apparently, not hurt her so he had no cause to call on the law. Then it came to him. He had the best weapon of all. Even so, the tension in the air made him tread carefully. Resolute, he stepped forward.

"Catherine, I know. Mrs. Scroggs told me."

"Mrs. Scroggs!" she said. "I'll not go back to that awful woman. You can't make me. Besides, she's already got a new girl. So even if I begged her, which I won't, she wouldn't take me back. I hated her.

I'm staying with my own folk. Miss Delaney here knows the circus trade, and she's going to help me." The woman nodded, her smile smug.

"Catherine, you don't understand ... "

Catherine pursed her lips, tossed her head, and moved closer to the woman. "Thank you, Edward. You've been good to me. But I'm all right now."

Edward felt the situation slipping away. He would have to employ a more direct approach. He dropped his voice to a whisper, but ensured it was loud enough for the man and woman to hear. "I know about it, Catherine. What Polly found out and told Mrs. Scroggs. You know ... this ... " he extended his hand towards Catherine's abdomen and glanced surreptitiously at the pair. He caught the woman's frown, "I'll take care of you, and the ... " The woman visibly flinched.

Catherine looked from Edward to the woman, still holding her arm. Her mouth moved as if she were struggling to speak, her brow furrowed.

"Catherine, please ... come now."

He saw the look of surprise on Catherine's face as the woman shouldered her away. The woman nudged the man, who had continued to glare at Edward, but who now turned away and punched his thigh with his fist as if in disgust.

"What ... ? Miss Delaney?" said Catherine. She looked from Miss Delaney back towards Edward.

"Hah." The woman pushed Catherine down the steps, where she sprawled on the ground. Edward crouched down to help her to a sitting position. The woman turned to her companion.

"Come on Jim. She's no virgin. It's with child she is. No use to us in that condition. The soldier can have her."

The man turned away from Edward and followed his companion. He spat at Catherine on the ground and gave her a little kick. "Filthy whore!" he said with an angry laugh. "Best of British luck to ya, with yer stinkin' soldier," and sauntered away.

Catherine looked after them with a stunned look on her face. Edward helped her up. She tripped and fell against him. Then the tears came, though he could see she was trying hard to hold them back. Edward took her back to the church steps and sat down beside her, cradled her in his arms.

"They were going to give me a place to stay and honest work among my people."

"Catherine, Catherine. Believe me, the work they wished to offer you was not work you should do."

Catherine pulled away from him, angry, defiant, "No, no, it was you. You scared them away with your soldier's uniform and acting all high-handed. You've ruined everything. I'm going after them." She made to stand up and lifted her bundle.

Edward tried to pull her back down, but she snatched her hand away and turned her back on him. But she didn't leave. He tried again.

"Catherine, listen to me! You're going to have a child. That means, well ... this Miss Delaney and her friend ... they thought you were someone different. They thought ... never mind. They were mistaken, that's all."

His years in the military had educated Edward on the proclivities of certain men. There was a high premium to be paid for a virgin. A one-time fee, of course, but that once would have been enough to keep that young man and woman living the high life for some time to come. There would be an ongoing fee, of course, after the initial prize, though with diminishing returns. But the cost-benefit of a pregnant woman, even a young and pretty one, made her virtually worthless.

"I think you're the one mistaken," Catherine retorted. She flashed her eyes at him. "Go away, leave me." But she was crying. She looked down, lacing her hands against her abdomen. "So, what did they think, since you know so much?" Her voice was angry and combative again.

"They ... they thought you might have been able to do something for them, but ... they changed their minds."

Catherine said nothing, but continued to scowl at Edward. He suspected she knew what he meant, but refused to admit it. He sighed. "Dear girl. This is London. There are men here ... men with certain tastes. Men you don't want to have anything to do with. You're young, you're beautiful, and you're alone. That puts you in grave danger in a city like this."

Catherine squinted. The momentary flicker of her eyes told Edward she had just lost a modicum of her innocence. She sank back down onto the steps, and pressed the heel of her hand to her forehead.

"Jack loved me. I know he did. He knew about the baby and he promised to take care of me."

"And so did Jim Delaney, just now."

She drew her knees to her chest and rocked back and forth. "You did warn me not to come to England, didn't you? But now you know why I couldn't stay in Kildean."

"Oh, yes. I do see that."

Above her, a flock of sparrows flitted and chirped among the branches of the trees, and she lifted her gaze upwards. "I have a dream sometimes, that I'm a bird. It starts off with me flying, feeling so free, and then suddenly I start to fall from the sky, down into the soft mud of a river. I suffocate in the mud, and I wake up gasping. Perhaps it's ... what is it called?"

"A premonition? No, Catherine, there's no such thing. It's just a meaningless dream. You didn't suffocate, and you won't."

She pulled at a clump of daisies on the lawn, picked off the petals and scattered them to the wind. "I hate Jack," she said. "I could kill him. How could he abandon me like that? I gave up everything for him."

He could have wept at the look of sadness that crumpled her face. "Some men don't want the responsibility ... "

Catherine tied the ends of her shawl around her shoulders and sat upright. "You're right. He's a rat. Let him go to Hell. I don't want to find him anyway, because I hate him." She looked up at Edward through teary lashes, and shifted a little closer to him. "What's to become of me now?"

Edward squeezed her hands in his, closed his eyes, breathed deeply. *Now. Now*, he told himself. *Say it now. There won't be a better moment.* He opened his mouth. When he said it, it came out in a rush, and his face reddened and sweat beaded on his brow.

"You could marry me," he said.

The silence was palpable. *Please, let her not mention Jack again. Let her understand that I am her only hope.*

He opened his eyes to see Catherine searching his face. In light of her new worldliness, was she calculating her odds? He didn't care. She must have known, even before he said it, that he wanted her, and had from the moment he first saw her. But did she believe he'd marry her, make an honest woman of her? This, she must see, was the best offer she would ever get in her condition. *Please,* he thought, *she doesn't have to love me. Only stay with me and let me love her.* He willed her to speak, to answer him, but he could not utter another word. She looked down, but kept her hands entwined in his. Her voice was soft and lilting, almost teasing.

"You would do that for me, Corporal Harris?"

The spring snapped, and a lightness filled the air. "Oh yes," he said, "and not just for you, but for me. Catherine, I want you to be my wife, I want to take care of you."

"What about ... ? It's not yours."

She didn't mention Jack's name, and he thanked her silently for that.

"I don't care. I'll make it mine. I'll take care of it, just as I'll take care of you."

Her face was blank, her eyes gazed past him. Was he losing her? Was she reconsidering? He found himself babbling. "Think, Catherine, of what I'm offering you. I have a good position in the Royal Engineers. I recently got promoted, and there'll be more promotions. I am respected. I can give you a decent life, and your child too. A respectable life. You'll always have a bed to rest your head on, always enough food on the table. You'll have money to buy clothes, and shoes, and beautiful bonnets. Perhaps we'll travel. You want to travel, don't you? Maybe I'll be posted abroad. I can offer you a stable home. And if you want, we can send for your sisters, and give them a good home, too ... "

At the mention of her sisters, she blinked and shifted her gaze, then went back to staring at a point somewhere above his shoulder. He wasn't sure if she was listening.

"Catherine. Look at me. I know I'm not the father of your child, whom you loved so much. I may not be the handsomest man in the world. But am I so ugly, am I so hideous, so deformed that you cannot conceive of being my wife ... ?"

The corners of her mouth curled up and she turned playful eyes on him. "Stop, stop! You're a fine man, Corporal Edward Harris. And handsome enough." Was she genuine, or putting on an act, mocking him? Was he ridiculous in her eyes? He could not have borne that. He swallowed hard.

"So, will you marry me? You know you have to. You know in your heart you have no choice. I'll be good to you. In time, you'll learn to love me. I'll give you everything you want … "

He was babbling again. He took her hand, held it to his chest, and waited. Her eyes flickered. He heard her rapid breathing, felt his own heart beating. What seemed like minutes passed. Then, in a firm voice she said, "All right, Edward. I'll marry you."

He closed his eyes and pulled her towards him. She did not resist. How sweet she smelt, a mixture of musk and grass. How soft the white shoulders he'd dreamt of, which now he could caress and make his own. He wanted to hold her forever, there in the churchyard, but the bells for the afternoon service began to ring, breaking the spell, and Catherine pulled away from him. Her face was grave but her eyes were soft as he took her hand and walked with her out of the churchyard.

NINE

By October they were married. Catherine had little say in the arrangements. Including the wedding dress. Edward bought that. A blue concoction, which he said matched her eyes. But it made her feel ridiculous. Ruffles at the sleeves and a high frilled neck that just about strangled her. The wedding ceremony, the reception at a tavern, Edward's colleagues from the garrison, his Uncle George and Aunt Fanny from Birmingham—it was all a fog. Except for one moment at the reception.

Edward had pulled her onto the dance floor in an ebullient, whirling dance that went on and on. She felt hot and tight and miserably damp with perspiration until someone opened the tavern door and a blast of cold air entered that took her breath away. That was when she saw that snarky Aunt Fanny staring at her, so she stared back as she waltzed around the room, then stopped, arched her back, and stuck her belly out at her. The look on Aunt Fanny's face was worth preserving in bronze, had she had the means!

Catherine had expected Edward to be furious—he was usually such a prude. What a surprise when he pulled her to him and kissed her on the lips, right there in front of everyone. Perhaps it was just the drink, but he whispered in her ear that he wished he hadn't bought her that prissy dress, that she should be in red silk and black feathers! They both laughed. A mad moment. It hadn't been repeated. Perhaps it never would be.

At night, on the little narrow bed, in the cramped married quarters of the barracks, she tried not to flinch when she touched the thin, translucent skin of Edward's arms. She would cast her eyes from his dun-coloured hair, his pale eyes fringed with lashes as yellow as sawdust, and tell herself: *Be fair. He is kind to you, he will care for you*

and your baby. He is not an ugly man or a bad man. Why can't you love him?
But when she squeezed her eyes shut, it was Jack's caress she felt,
Jack's scent she breathed. How was it that the man held such power
over her, with all his fine promises come to naught? Yet if she could
only see him, just once more, feel the touch of his hands on her
body, have him love her again as he did under the trees in Kildean.
Then she would give him up and throw in her lot with this soldier.

Edward constantly apologized for the primitive living conditions
at the barracks, and assured her that they would shortly move to their
own billet once he had permission and had found lodgings. One day,
exasperated by his earnestness, Catherine responded more sharply
than she'd intended. "Are you forgetting, Edward, where I came
from? Are we Irish not used to sleeping on earthen floors with the
pigs and chickens?" She'd meant it as a joke, but there was a harsh
undertone to her words and she felt guilty when she saw the
surprised look on his face. She had no call to be sarcastic with him,
but he was beginning to irritate her.

She felt an odd sensation in her belly.

"Oh!" she said in surprise.

Edward led her to the single chair in their quarters. "Is it the
baby?"

"I felt something. Maybe it moved."

Edward knelt beside her, laid his head in her lap, put his arms
around her waist. She went to push him away, but then the sensation
came again. Not a pain, but a flutter, as if a bird had lodged in her
womb and was trying to escape. Now she knew; she really was going
to have a baby. This, then, is why she married Edward, this plain
Englishman.

"I felt it too!" Edward exclaimed. He lifted his head and laid his
hand on her belly. "I can feel it moving!"

"Yes, yes. But I need to rest now, Edward."

Edward pulled back. "Of course. I'm sorry. You rest now."

Catherine watched Edward leave their little compartment. Such a
thin man, she thought, when he was out of his uniform. So puny.
The hair at the back of his head lay flat against his skull. His trousers
were too long for his legs. She turned her face to the wall.

* * *

In November, they moved out of the barracks to a billet in Southwark, an attic room in a tall brick building, a little dilapidated. The front door opened directly onto the street, which in turn bordered the river and was steps from Southwark Bridge. Their room was at the top of four steep flights of stairs, for which Edward, as was his wont, apologized profusely, showing particular concern for her "delicate" condition.

Again, she could not resist a sharp retort. "'Tis a well-known fact, is it not, that we Irish peasants are used to fetching and hauling and carrying even when we're heavy with child? You think four flights of stairs would defeat me?" She'd thought the crudity of her remark would annoy him, but he laughed, and squeezed her shoulder. Sometimes he surprised her. She recalled his reaction to her impudent gesture towards Aunt Fanny at the wedding; he had seemed proud and almost excited that she would show such disregard for proper decorum. Perhaps he was not as dull and prudish as she'd thought. Perhaps there was a more adventurous side to him. She should give him a chance.

The stairs were a trial, despite her rejoinder to Edward, and by the time they got to the top landing she was out of breath and felt the weight of her belly. She thought she might just stay on that landing and never leave, never have to go up and down those stairs again. Edward unlocked the door to their room, then picked her up and, with a shy smile, carried her over the threshold.

She had to admit to a certain pleasure on first sight of the attic room. It spanned the full width and half the depth of the house, with smooth, papered walls, a wooden plank floor, and a feeling of solidity.

A double-doored wardrobe stood against one wall, and a washstand with candlesticks and a china jug and bowl nestled against the opposite wall under the eaves where the ceiling sloped. Beside it was a wooden dresser with three drawers. Against the opposite wall was a rolltop desk and chair. In the chimney nook hung kettles, and a shelf beside the chimney housed a tea caddy, a bread bin, a butter box, and a sugar tin. A large easy chair and a wooden table and two chairs, one with its broken back tied up with string, took the space in front of the fireplace. In the hearth a bright fire crackled, lit earlier by

Edward to take the chill off the room. Maroon curtains made from some shiny fabric fluttered at a good-sized window to the left of the fireplace.

Dominating the middle of the room was a big, high, four-poster bed, enclosed in dark red velvet curtains, a little patched and worn in places. She ran to the bed, swept aside the curtains, jumped onto it, and laughed aloud as she sank into the soft feather mattress. She surprised herself with the laugh—it had been weeks since she'd felt such a spring of pleasure.

She lay for a moment to savour the luxury of the bed and felt an unexpected tenderness towards Edward. He was a decent man. Though often grave in his manner, overly concerned with status and respectability, she had also seen in him a light-heartedness, even a mischievousness, and a wry sense of humour that matched hers. She should try to be a good wife. Besides, what other option had she had? *Take one day at a time.* She propped herself up on one elbow, smiled at Edward, and met his eyes for the first time since that delicious moment of impudence with Aunt Fanny at the wedding. He ran to the bed to join her, and she didn't resist him.

As always, he was gentle in his ministrations, mindful of her condition. He treated her like lady, and not a rough Irish peasant who had grown up sleeping on a straw pallet on the earthen floor of a stone cabin in the poorest part of Kildean. After he'd made love to her, she lay against the pillow, running her thumb and forefinger over the fuzzy cloth of the velvet bed curtains, and looked around. Fingerprints, scuffs, and smudges on the walls, and nicks in the floorboards gave the room a comforting, lived-in look; this had been home to other people before, probably many other people over dozens of years. Had they been happy? Would she, could she be happy in this room? With Edward? Sounds drifted up from the street below—the clatter of carts, the clop of horses' hooves, the cries of street traders. Not pigs and chickens. This was a city room. In England, the place she'd dreamed of visiting as she watched the travellers come and go through Kildean, listening to their stories of the great land across the sea. The place Da had promised to take her to. Would Da still be proud of her now? The fire flared in the hearth. She shivered, despite the warmth in the room.

Edward, dozing beside her, put his hand on her belly. Instinctively, she pushed it away. She rose from the bed and rummaged in the bundle of her belongings. She found the fan her father had given her and laid it on the dresser, then took out the blue wedding dress and put it in the bottom of the drawer, laying her spare clothes on top. The last item in her bundle was the bone comb Jack had given her. This she tucked under the blue wedding dress in the bottom of the drawer. She had never shown Edward the comb. Then she sat down to warm herself by the fire.

Through the autumn and winter months, as her girth expanded and her feet swelled, she pushed away fatigue and regret to make a home for Edward and the coming child. She played her part so well that she could almost believe she was truly a happy, fulfilled wife and expectant mother. She rose early, built the fire to make her husband's tea, prepared water and soap for his toilet, sewed buttons on his shirts. At the market she bought rabbit for stew and fresh fish for his supper. She passed pleasantries with the neighbours, and gratefully accepted a borrowed crib and high chair. In the evenings, she knitted caps and coatees. Kind neighbours and soldiers' wives dropped off clothes and blankets for the baby.

In late February, Edward's Aunt Fanny arrived from Birmingham to supervise Catherine's confinement, and Edward moved to a mattress in the corner of the room. Catherine was relieved, despite having to share the bed with Aunt Fanny.

Edward told Catherine he wanted her confinement to be that of a lady, and Fanny, having worked as a lady's maid in her youth, said she knew exactly what that meant. Now that Catherine was within days of the birth, Aunt Fanny forbade her to perform any but the lightest of chores, or go to the market. She was either to be prostrate on the bed, or propped up with cushions in the chair by the fire. Aunt Fanny sealed the windows with rags and wax, drew the velvet bed curtains tight, and banked up the fire until Catherine felt ready to choke. By day, a pale wintry light seeped through the gaps in the window curtains. By night, a single yellow candle flickered. Catherine wondered if she would ever see daylight again.

When Fanny was out of earshot, Catherine protested to Edward, "Why do I have to be confined in this stuffy room?" Edward insisted that regardless of what might go on in Ireland, here in London, a respectably married woman in her condition must avoid breathing the city air, and must be kept warm and quiet indoors. Catherine scoffed but was too tired and too heavy to protest. Only a few more days and it would be over.

Catherine's labour began early on the Wednesday before Palm Sunday. Out of bed and in her nightgown, she held on to the bedpost as a wave of pain came over her. Aunt Fanny grabbed her clothes and tried to help her to dress.

Catherine flapped a hand at her. "Leave me alone. I can take care of myself."

Fanny tut-tutted. "Please yourself, young lady, but this baby's coming and we have to get to the hospital before you drop it right here and now."

Edward stood by the bed, wringing his hands. "What can I do, what can I do?"

"Nothing," said Aunt Fanny. "This is women's business. You get out of here right now. Off you go. We'll let you know. Come, child."

Catherine, who had pulled on some day clothes between contractions, allowed Aunt Fanny to drag her through the door, down the stairs, and into the street.

The Southwark Lying-In Hospital for the Wives of Soldiers and Respectable Working Men, where Edward had registered her, was a short walk away, but it seemed to Catherine to take hours to get there, as she had to stop every few steps to cling to Aunt Fanny or to a lamp post until the waves of pain subsided.

Aunt Fanny was in a panic. "It's coming too quickly," she said. "It shouldn't be like this. Something's wrong. Labour should take hours, not minutes. Hurry now!"

"Damn you, Fanny," said Catherine, under her breath, but she struggled the several more yards to the hospital and up to the registration desk.

A woman with a sour face looked Catherine up and down and sniffed. "You'll have to wait your turn. There's others ahead of you."

Aunt Fanny banged her fist on the desk. "She can't wait," she said. "Look at her. She's going to give birth here on the floor if you don't do something."

The woman drew herself up to her full height, shut her registration ledger with a bang, and manhandled Catherine into a ward full of moaning women. She pushed her onto a bed, pulled her legs up into stirrups, and, ignoring Catherine's protests, marched away, leaving an anxious Aunt Fanny to wring her hands and yell for a doctor. Catherine writhed on the bed and then let out a final wrenching cry, as she felt a heavy weight pushing out between her legs. *I'm giving birth to a monster,* she thought. *It's going to split me in two and I'll die here.* She tried to hold it back, but her body took charge and the thing inside her kept pushing its way out.

Less than twenty minutes later, and just two hours after labour began, the doctor handed a squalling baby to Catherine. "A quick and easy labour," he said, "and a healthy baby girl." The doctor performed a perfunctory examination on her. On realizing Catherine was from Ireland, he gave a knowing nod. Women of her race, he stated, being of inferior, less-civilized stock, often gave birth with a speed and ease redolent of the animal kingdom. He swept his hand around the ward, which echoed with the moans of labouring women. "Most of these English women will work much harder for their babies." Catherine, now recovered from the raw emotion of the labour and birth, threw him a look black enough to wither roses in the queen's garden, but he had already moved on to the woman in the next bed.

Aunt Fanny, calmer now, looked at the baby, wrapped in a receiving blanket borrowed from one of the garrison wives, and recited the old adage under her breath, checking off the days on her fingers, *Monday's child is fair of face, Tuesday's child is full of grace, Wednesday's child—is full of woe.* She shook her head. Catherine ignored her. She gazed at the tiny mite, but could see no feature that reminded her of Jack. She could be anyone's baby. She named the child Louisa Jane, which was Edward's choice.

Aunt Fanny reminded Catherine of how fortunate she was to have found a man like Edward to save her, because lying-in hospitals were for respectable married women only. "And don't you roll your eyes at me, young lady," she added, "maybe where you come from women push out their babies behind a tree and go right back to digging potatoes. But here in civilization we have hospitals and doctors, men of science, not fumbling country midwives, to attend to births, and you have to be married to receive their services. We're not living in the Dark Ages anymore." Catherine wanted to thumb her nose at Aunt Fanny, but instead stared at the wall beside her bed.

The doctor pronounced Catherine fit enough to continue her confinement at home, and discharged her. Aunt Fanny announced that Catherine was to remain prostrate and still for a full two weeks after the birth. "A month would be better," she added, "but I can't stay away from home that long. Who knows what nonsense George is getting up to."

For the next fortnight, the curtains remained closed, the windows sealed, the fire ablaze until the air in the room was as dense and hot as soup. Each morning, Fanny unwrapped Catherine's bindings to check her progress, noting her rapidly shrinking belly with what Catherine, even in the stupor the stuffy room had induced, detected was a slight disapproval. Fanny pulled the bindings tighter. "I must admit, you Irish women are robust," she said, "I suppose it must be all that hard labour in the fields. But for now, you'll lie still. It's not safe for you to get up yet."

Catherine, weakened by childbirth, bed rest, and a diet of invalid food was barely aware of Aunt Fanny coming and going, feeling her brow and feeding her soup and medicinal potions. The potions left her torpid and groggy, unable to generate the energy to lift her head.

Occasionally, as if at a great distance, she heard a baby cry, felt a pinch at her breast, heard Edward's low voice murmuring, and Fanny's grumbling whine cutting into sleep. Fanny grumbled about everything. She grumbled about the baby, and about Edward's constant fussing over her, picking her up, cradling her in his arms, burping her, kissing and cuddling her. Waking from one fitful sleep, she listened with irritation to their conversation.

"It's not fitting for a man to be so obsessed with his child," Fanny said, and, "The baby isn't crying enough. It should be exercising its lungs more. It's not thriving." And then, to Edward in a fierce whisper when she thought Catherine was asleep, "Edward, that wife of yours is a cold and distant mother. Why doesn't she ever ask for the baby? She only takes it when I give it to her."

If only I had the energy, wouldn't I get up and slap your fat face?

Edward was just as bad, but in a different way. His irrepressible optimism annoyed Catherine as much as Fanny's pessimism. "What could possibly be wrong, Aunt Fanny? Look at this baby—have you ever seen such a pink and chubby little mite? And of course Catherine wants the baby. Look at her now, nursing the child. You worry needlessly. Just let her rest. I'm sure the birth has been hard on her." Catherine heard Fanny give a hrrumph and muttered, "If that was a difficult birth, I'd like to know what an easy one is."

No point arguing with either of them. Instead, Catherine gave in to her drowsiness and drifted in and out of dreams. She thought she was back in Kildean. She smelt the must of the earth, the wet grass. She saw her sister Bridget carry chicken feed to the coop in her apron, Norah whip the pig out of the house. She woke, and the memories caught at her chest, but then the image faded, to be replaced by Ma's frowning face, eyes blazing, mouth spitting her name. *Katie, Katie, Katie,* Father Quinn standing behind her, smug and self-righteous. She heard the whispers, *Catherine Joyce had a bastard child by an Englishman.* She cried out and opened her eyes. Aunt Fanny put a cup to her lips. The anger faded and she dozed again.

She tried to recapture the joy of her summer with Jack, but the edge had gone, dulled by sleep and warmth and Aunt Fanny's potions. One time, she was almost there, she could smell him, feel the weight of his body against her, his skin on hers. He embraced her with arms that became feathered wings, and he lifted her up, and they flew together, wheeling and gliding as one bird. They soared over Kildean to the Galway Bay cliffs and out across the ocean towards America, then back to Ireland, eastward to the sea, where they looked down on ships tossing on the waves. They gained the English coastline, and swooped over green fields and downs and on to the foggy black of London. Then the feeling changed, became heavy. They fell from the sky into a watery place—a marsh, moist and deep and dark with mud. On her chest she felt a great weight press down on her. It was not Jack. Jack had gone, flown away. This was a dead weight. She could no longer fly. Trapped in the mud, she could no longer breathe. She struggled to be free, only to sink deeper. She opened her eyes to the darkened room. The weight was the baby that Fanny had placed on her chest. It smothered her, entangled her. Her limbs felt broken and twisted, her muscles atrophied. She struggled for air, then drifted down again.

She awoke some time later to a grating noise and the sense of light shining behind her closed eyelids. She opened her eyes and tried to sit up. Aunt Fanny was drawing back the curtains. Light flooded through the window, cast dancing shapes on the walls, smarting Catherine's eyes and making her squint. She heard noises in her head and realized they were church bells.

Aunt Fanny bustled over and laid a hand on her forehead. "Well, now, young lady. I think you're ready for a little light. It's Sunday morning and decent folks are already up and about."

Edward was by the window, removing the rags that had stopped the drafts. Aunt Fanny helped him push the armchair closer to the window, and then helped Catherine, on wobbly legs, grope her way to the chair. "There you are. The roses will soon come back to your cheeks. A few more days and you'll be strong enough to leave your room."

From the chair, Catherine could see out of the window. The view showed a clear day. How rare was that! The customary pall of yellow smoke that overlaid the sky like a piece of dirty netting had given way to bright sunshine and a deep blue sky. Catherine leaned forward. Through the soot and smudges on the glass, she saw the city laid out before her like a painting. How strange she had not noticed it before! The road in front of the house sloped down to the river, where steps led up to the bridge. On the other side was London proper, the East End, the West End, the North End. The river was alive with ships and boats. The bridge was alive with pedestrians, carts, cabs, omnibuses. Outside these four stifling walls, a living world existed, thrumming, buzzing, waiting. And out there was Jack!

Fanny handed her the baby and began packing her things. She would catch the evening train back to Birmingham. *Leave, yes go. Let me alone, for I have things to do, plans to make.*

Over the next few days, Catherine's head cleared by degrees, like a dulled knife repeatedly scraped on a honing stone. In the lightening evenings, she sat with Edward by the window, fed the baby, watched the setting sun dapple the river with blood, and asked Edward to tell her about the city. She kept her tone nonchalant. *What's that spire over there? What neighbourhood is that, who lives there? Which church is it? And that big dome? And the bridge, far off in the east? Who lives near that bridge? What is that massive brick building on the other side? What kind of people live near there?* Edward, with his passion for mapmaking and surveying, told her, with palpable enthusiasm, everything he knew about the layout of the city.

By the middle of April, when she was up and about, she had the great metropolis mapped in her mind. Thanks to Edward's detailed directions, she could picture the grand boulevards and squares of the West End that she'd passed through with Edward on her first day in London, and how they linked to the courtyards and alleys where the ordinary people lived, which cut through towards Lincoln's Inn Fields and St. Paul's Cathedral and on to the narrow streets of Shoreditch and the East End. She knew where the tailors lived, the tanners, the brickmakers, the goldsmiths, and the silversmiths. She could even see, when Edward pointed it out above the tops of the houses, the Monument to the Great Fire of London, from nearly 200 years ago, when half of London burnt to the ground. She could trace in her mind the route across Southwark Bridge to the new Billingsgate fish market, and the Covent Garden fruit and vegetable market, to Cheapside with its second-hand clothing stores, to grimy St. Giles, and to Spitalfields, the centre of the weaving trade.

She'd looked up sharply when Edward mentioned the weaving trade.

"Weavers? Would there be any there from Waterford?"

The idiot boy and his father at the wharf in Waterford, who gave up their places on the ship for her, were weavers. The boy claimed he'd seen Catherine with Jack, and he was the one who told her the circus had sailed. Perhaps he'd talked to the circus folk. Perhaps he'd talked to Jack. It was a link, a place to start. If she could find that boy and his father, they might know where she could find Billy Mather's Amazing Circus.

But Edward looked wary. Catherine lowered her eyes and fussed with the baby, realizing she should not show her cards so soon.

"Maybe. Maybe not. There are Irish all over London. I told you that before. And you know what nearly happened to you just after you arrived when you met up with London Irish folk."

"I do, I do, Edward. I won't forget, and I certainly won't make that mistake again."

"St. Giles, Spitalfields. All the same. Places a respectable married woman like you should never venture."

Catherine knew she should remain nonchalant but could not resist a dare. "But Edward, I thought you said you liked the Irish, that we're good, hardworking people. And after all, you married an Irish woman!"

Edward gave a short laugh and laid his hand on the back of her neck. "Very good, Catherine. Now, no more talking tonight. You should rest. Tomorrow evening we'll go walking. You'll like that, won't you? We can show off this lovely baby to the neighbours."

It was best not to challenge him further. Catherine had already risked raising his suspicions. She smiled at him as he kissed her cheek, and took the baby from her. While Edward settled Louisa in her crib, Catherine lay back in her chair and closed her eyes, pretending to doze for Edward's benefit, but her mind remained active.

There was a woman who lived in the basement who had befriended Catherine in the days since she'd risen from her confinement. Her name was Ellen Booth, and she seemed to want to be friends, keen to catch a few words with Catherine on the tenement steps where she often sat. One day, as Catherine left to buy provisions, the woman had asked to see the baby. Catherine drew back the blankets that covered Louisa in her basket. Ellen gazed at the sleeping baby and Catherine saw her eyes fill with tears. She confided to Catherine that she'd lost her own baby a couple of weeks earlier, and was still bothered by pains and tightness in her breasts.

"It's the milk," she said sadly. "It wants a baby, but the baby's gone." Ellen looked at Catherine with pleading eyes, as if she wanted to ask her something but could not bring herself to say it. Her husband was a brute of a man who blamed her for the death of his infant son and heir; she still bore the bruises on her arms, fading to yellow, from a beating he'd given her.

"Would you like to hold the baby?" asked Catherine.

"Oh, may I?" Ellen lifted Louisa from her basket and cradled her in her arms.

Catherine noticed the milk stain spread slowly through the woman's blouse. "It's all right," she said. "You can feed her if you like."

Ellen looked at her with gratitude. "This will heal me, and it might help bring on another babe."

* * *

The next day, St. George's Day, dawned bright and clear. Catherine had left her confinement nearly four weeks prior and she was ready. Once Edward left for work, she took out the new clothes Edward had bought her to replace the threadbare togs she'd arrived in. The pale-yellow cotton lawn gown was a perfect fit, and fell in a flattering way from just below her bosom to hide the remaining swell of her belly. Aunt Fanny had bought her stays. Catherine had never worn them, to Fanny's disgust, but could not have imagined how well they made her figure look, and they were not uncomfortable. They kept her back straight and accentuated the soft tumescence of her breasts, often full now with milk. She put on her shiny new leather shoes, and the new bonnet, sprigged with spring flowers. She admired herself in the mirror above the washstand. Since her confinement had ended, her porcelain complexion glowed with health, and her hair was shiny. *When Jack sees me again, won't he be impressed! "You look like a proper lady"* *he'll say in his funny English way.*

Of course, when she found him, she wouldn't take him back. Not after what he'd done to her. She would confront him, demand an explanation, make him realize how he'd almost brought her to ruin. He'd see how well she'd done for herself with her soldier husband, and he'd be sorry he'd left, because he could have been her husband, but he threw away his chance. Then he would redden with anger and jealousy and shame, and beg her forgiveness, but she'd turn away and pout. He'd plead some more, and she'd make him go down on his knees and grovel and weep. And maybe, just maybe, after all that, she'd let him love her again. Just once. Then she'd turn her back, and walk away. She would, she would.

She picked up the baby and carried her downstairs. Ellen Booth was on the steps as usual. Catherine held out the baby to Ellen.

"Mrs. Booth, I have to go out. Would you take the baby for me for a couple of hours?"

Ellen showed her delight by taking Louisa in her arms and putting her straight to her breast. Catherine nodded, turned, and set out along the path that crossed Southwark Bridge.

Though she held fast to the map in her head, she found the way was more complicated than she had thought it would be. So many winding streets, some with dead ends, others with sharp turns that led to other streets that did not connect the way she expected. She stopped a young woman with a child to ask the way to Spitalfields, but the woman shrugged and hurried away. Another older woman merely stared at her, and indicated a general direction with her hand. By afternoon, her head was spinning, her feet in her new shoes were aching and blistered, and her breasts were tingling. And she had not found Spitalfields. She returned downhearted. Ellen was still on the steps, cradling the baby.

"As good as gold, she was," said Ellen. Catherine sat beside her, took off her shoes, and massaged her sore feet. "Ever so quiet, she was," said Ellen, "never cried, not even a whimper. She likes my milk, Mrs. Harris, she really does."

Catherine put her shoes back on, and picked Louisa up. "You can take her again tomorrow if you want. I have to go out again."

"Oh yes, Mrs. Harris. I'll take her any time you want."

TEN

The days at Mrs. Scroggs's boarding house were full, leaving no time for Mary to brood, for which she was thankful. Besides, she had never been afraid of hard work.

Polly and Martha proved companionable girls, and Mary was touched by how openly they accepted her into their servants' circle. She'd always felt awkward with her contemporaries, never knowing what to say, and preferred the easy company of children and older women. She found she enjoyed the new experience of having companions of her own age who shared secrets with her.

But some of the stories Polly and Martha told about the boarders, past and present, were shocking. Such as the married man who, clearly forgetting his status, pushed Polly against a closed door and tried to lift her skirt. Or the two young brothers who took Polly and Martha down to the tavern on their night off, plied them with gin until they could hardly walk, and then … They stopped the story at that point and gave each other knowing looks.

They also exchanged knowing looks about Mr. Foulkes, who still had the room at the back on the first floor, and of whom Mary was strongly advised to steer well clear. She had seen him once or twice, marching downstairs and through the hall, twirling his walking stick. He looked like an upright sort of person, but when he smiled at Mary as she polished the hall coat stand, the glint in his eye unnerved her.

Polly and Martha and the other servants had much to say about Miss Everett, the lady tenant who occupied the back room on the ground floor. Apparently, she had some sort of special connection to Mrs. Scroggs.

"Though I can't imagine what they have to talk about," Polly had said. "I mean, you've never met a loopier person than Miss

Everett, stuck all day in that dark room, never leaves it, she don't. What can she possibly have in common with Mrs. S? When she talks it's all airy-fairy stuff. Don't make no sense."

Mary had ventured to ask, "But isn't she an invalid, and that's why she doesn't leave?"

Polly had rolled her eyes. "That's what she *wants* everyone to believe. If you ask me, she's just off her rocker."

Martha had said she reckoned Miss Everett had "one over" on Mrs. Scroggs and that's why she let her stay in that room.

Mrs. Parsons, the cook, who had been at the boarding house longer than anyone, agreed. "You've got that right. The old bag says she's her special friend, lah de dah and all that. Special friend my foot! Where d'you think Mrs. S. got the money to start up this house? Business arrangement, that's what it is. Miss Everett put up the money. Mrs. S. knows she's got to be nice to the crazy old bat. Or else ..." Mrs. Parsons made a chopping motion with her hand. Martha and Polly laughed.

Martha had said, "But what about the husband? I thought it was him what left her the money for the boarding house."

"Ah, but how do we even know there was a Mr. Scroggs? No one's ever seen him," Mrs. Parsons said with a sly grin.

One particular tale that Polly told stuck with Mary, about a young Irish girl who'd been deposited on the boarding house doorstep by a soldier, an acquaintance of Mrs. Scroggs. "Turned out she was ... " Polly had dropped her voice to a whisper, "... in a delicate condition when she arrived. You know, in the pudding club." Mary had frowned. Polly could be quite crude at times. Polly continued, "She was given short shrift by Mrs. Scroggs, I can tell you. Apparently, the soldier knew nothing about it. At least, that's what he *said,*" and she'd winked. "She slept in the very bed you're in now, Mary. But don't worry, we washed the sheets!"

Mary looked away. Polly's story left a bad taste. She recalled the young woman with a bundle coming out of No. 5 Bedford Court the day she'd arrived. Was that her? No wonder she'd seemed upset. How afraid she must have been, for herself and her unborn child. Where was she going that day? To meet the soldier? Was he her lover? She'd certainly been a beauty, but what could become of her in that condition? Perhaps the soldier might have been persuaded to make things right for her. Or perhaps not. She might have ended up in the workhouse, and her baby, too. How terrible that would have been. But when she expressed her concerns about the girl, Polly and Martha didn't seem to care. "Oh, she'll be all right, up with her folks in St. Giles," Polly had said. Mary hoped so.

Sundays were the servants' day off, and these were the days Mary especially looked forward to, for her brother, Thomas, would call to take her to church. On the way, he would pepper her with hopeful questions about her new position. He was a slight boy, not yet fully grown, and she towered above him, yet he'd smile up at her indulgently as if he were her older brother. She didn't mind; she appreciated his protectiveness and his pride that he had been the instrument of her finding a new life in London. She would chat happily about Polly and Martha and the others, but refrain from sharing the more salacious stories the women had told. He was still of a tender age and didn't need to know about such things. But she did ask him if, when he'd stayed at the Scroggs house on his initial arrival in London, he'd come across Miss Everett, the mysterious woman in the back room. He had not, having only stayed at the house for several nights.

The conversation would then turn to Thomas's job, and he would enthusiastically report that his employer had shown him much regard such that he was hopeful of promotion. They didn't talk about Somerset, or the event that had made her leave. That life and that event were in the past and did not need to be mentioned.

One morning, as they were making their beds, Polly, who seemed to relish regaling Mary with her scandalous exploits, told a particularly bawdy tale concerning a gentleman, who purported to be a Lord, and two young women he brought to his room, in complete violation of Mrs. Scroggs's rules. He then bribed Polly to help him sneak the women out early the next morning, and Polly willingly connived in return for monetary consideration. Polly acknowledged Mary's disgusted expression, stopped her giggling, and composed her face.

"You won't tell Mrs. Scroggs, will you?"

"Of course not, Polly. I would not betray you. But what you did was wrong, as wrong as what the man did."

Polly stared at Mary for a moment, apparently uncomprehending. Then, as if considering her words, she said, "Yes, you're right. Mary. You have a pure heart, and I think you're too good for this rotten old world. One day you'll make some bloke very happy."

Mary had never thought much about marriage. She considered she had neither the looks nor the personality to attract a suitor. Her features were coarse, her chin prominent, her nose large and slightly bulbous. Her waist was hardly smaller than her hips, and her fingers were as plump as sausages. As for her personality, beside the sparkling Polly or the jovial Martha, she felt dull and devoid of charm or poise. In Somerset these things hadn't bothered her, for she'd been comfortable with the role of "spinster midwife," which she'd assumed would always be hers. But now that role was no longer hers, and it seemed there was only one fate open to her.

She tucked the sheets of her bed in tight and murmured, "I expect I shall be an old maid."

Polly looked at her with an exasperated expression.

"Oh Mary, don't be so down on yourself. I think you're a fine person. Better'n me, that's for sure. You got good morals."

Mary laughed, touched her hand to her forehead in a self-conscious gesture, and looked towards the washstand. "The water in that jug needs replenishing," she said.

Polly stared at her. "Mary, I can see you one day as a mother, holding a baby in your arms. Wouldn't you like to get married and have children? You'd make a wonderful mother."

Mary pursed her lips and busied herself tidying the washstand. This was not to be discussed. Mary had never told Polly or anyone in London of her former life. They didn't know, and she would never tell them that she might never again hold a baby, never again hold one of God's new and perfect creations. But Polly had not finished.

"Listen," said Polly, "there's going to be a Christmas dance at the church on Saturday. Everyone in the neighbourhood will be going. I'm sure Mrs. Scroggs would give us both the evening off."

"I don't know," said Mary, turning. She'd once attended a dance in Somerset, and recalled the embarrassment of sitting with the old matrons for most of the evening while the pretty, fresh-faced girls danced away with the young men, and only the father of a neighbour finally took her hand, probably out of pity.

She shook her head, but Polly continued in enthusiastic tones.

"Why don't me and you go together. It'll be decent folks, don't worry, and we can have a rare old time. And you never know who you might meet." Polly had a mischievous glint in her eye as she said this. "Go on Mary. It'll take you out of yourself a bit. The only place you ever go is church on Sundays, and then to your boring old brother's house."

"Polly! My brother is not boring. He's a fine young man."

"I'm sorry. But he is a bit like a middle-aged bloke, you must admit."

"He's two years younger than me."

Polly rolled her eyes. Mary felt defensive and slightly peeved, but decided not to pursue the subject with Polly. She picked up the water jug to take to the kitchen, and smoothed her apron. She would go with Polly to the dance, but she doubted she would enjoy it.

Polly got Mary done up in her Sunday frock, pushed her down onto the bed, and grabbed a comb to dress her hair. She teased tendrils around the nape of her neck and pinned ribboned braids over her ears in the latest fashion. Polly held the looking glass before her. Mary was not sure she liked the result, but Polly declared her new image "handsome."

The church hall was brightly lit with gas lamps and a blazing fire, the air thick with smoke and noisy chatter. A long table at one end held bowls of oranges and raisins, all kinds of sweetmeats and a large punchbowl. Boughs of red-berried holly and yew hung from the walls. But pride of place was given to a large Christmas tree in the corner, which sparkled with tinsel and candles. It was the first Christmas tree Mary had ever seen, and she found it quite dazzling.

The hall was full of people, mostly, by their appearance, young servants and shop assistants, although the vicar and his wife also circulated, carrying greetings and blessings to the guests. Polly was soon at the centre of a circle of happy young men and women, laughing and chatting. Mary stood for a while on the edge of the circle, not knowing where to put her hands or what to do with her face—should she smile, try to look interested, try to join in the conversation? Since no one spoke to her or seemed to notice her, she moved away and pretended to examine the baubles on the Christmas tree. Someone handed her a glass of punch, but her smile of thanks felt foolish and false. When the musicians started up and the dancing began, she slunk over to a dark corner of the room and stayed in the shadows until the merrymaking stopped and the crowd began to thin out.

Polly, who suddenly remembered her existence, found her, and took her arm as they made their way back to the boarding house. Mary was embarrassed by the evening, but Polly seemed oblivious to her discomfort and wanted only to talk of the young man she had met at the dance. He was a footman recently hired by a grand house in Bloomsbury; she was sure he would want to call on her, and she would have to be careful not to let Mrs. Scroggs know about it.

Though the evening, as she'd expected, had been a humiliation for Mary, she found Polly's cheerfulness infectious. As she listened to her friend's happy chatter, she realized that Polly actually enjoyed sneaking around, doing little underhanded things that were against the rules. She had asked her once if she weren't afraid of getting caught, but Polly had merely shrugged.

Over the next few weeks, it became apparent that the liaison between Polly and Mr. James Sylvester, her new young man, had blossomed into a full-scale romance. Polly could talk of nothing else. Martha and the cook rolled their eyes and nudged Mary at mealtimes.

"Don't she go on?" they said. "Them stars in her eyes are going to set fire to this place if we're not careful."

Polly's romance required her to spend a considerable amount of time away from the house, without Mrs. Scroggs's knowledge. Since their employer spent most of her time either with her feet up in the parlour, or surveying the street from the front doorway, it was not difficult for Polly to slip away through the kitchen door into the back courtyard, through a small archway and out into the next street without Mrs. Scroggs knowing. Preparing for the clandestine meetings, however, took time and assistance from the reluctant Mary, who disapproved of the deceit but did not want to let her friend down. And she had to admit to a vicarious thrill at the thought of Polly in the embrace of Mr. Sylvester. For each encounter, Polly's face and hands had to be scrubbed and inspected, her hair pinned and re-pinned, her stays laced; "Tighter, tighter," she would command until she could scarcely breathe, and Mary worried she would faint right away.

One evening, three months after the Christmas dance, she did just that. Mary heard her creep home late. The stairs creaked as she climbed up to the little attic room, pushed open the door and fell onto her bed with a groan, "Oh, oh." Later she called out to Mary, "Get a bowl, quick, a bowl."

Mary grabbed a bowl from the washstand just in time for Polly to vomit up the contents of her stomach. Then she lay back, fully clothed, in a dead faint. Mary fetched a wet cloth to revive her and sat beside her most of the night, soothing her brow, as Polly, delirious and incoherent, alternated between shivers and sweats, tossing off her covers one moment, pulling them back the next.

By morning, still feverish and moaning, Polly broke out in a rash on her cheeks and forehead. With horror, Mary understood. She dressed quickly and ran downstairs to tell Mrs. Scroggs to call a doctor. The guests were calling for their breakfast, so she quickly resumed her chores, but found it hard to concentrate.

Later that morning, as she dusted in the hallway, she heard the doctor conferring with Mrs. Scroggs in the parlour, and stood aside as he left with his black bag. Mrs. Scroggs appeared at the door and called Mary in. In a grave voice, she advised Mary that Polly would be confined to bed for the rest of the day and possibly longer, and then she would decide what to do about her.

"You and Martha will take over Polly's chores for the foreseeable future."

She hardly dared ask the question, but she had to know.

"Is it the smallpox, Mrs. Scroggs? Is that what the doctor says?"

Mrs. Scroggs made a strange sound at the back of her throat, part snort, part laugh.

"Not the pox," she said, "something that might even be worse."

It was hard to imagine anything worse than smallpox, but the frown on Mrs. Scroggs' face told Mary to ask no more questions. Whatever it was, it was curable, for she was apparently expected to recover, which greatly eased Mary's mind.

Mrs. Scroggs beckoned Mary to her.

"Now with Polly … with Polly the way she is right now, I want you to be the one to take Miss Everett her meals."

Miss Everett. The invalid in the back room. Mary was surprised. No one except Mrs. Scroggs and Polly ever went into Miss Everett's room. It was surely an honour for Mary, the newest member of staff, and not Martha, to be granted the job of looking after Mrs. Scroggs's invalid tenant. Yet she remembered the gossip about Miss Everett and wondered what she was in for. Was she to be confronted with a lunatic? Would she shout at Mary, call her names, be angry that a new maid was bringing her breakfast?

With trepidation, she carried the tray up from the kitchen and knocked tentatively at Miss Everett's door. There was no answer. She waited. Nothing. She knocked again, opened the door a crack, and then, since there was still no reply, she dared to look in.

The room was surprisingly large, at least twice the size of the front parlour that Mrs. Scroggs occupied. Dark green velvet curtains at the windows kept the room in deep shadow, lit only by narrow shafts of misty light where the curtains didn't quite meet. The room appeared to be empty.

Mary stood nervously holding the breakfast tray in the doorway. Then a wispy, wraith-like movement caught her eye. More the sense of a presence than a solid object. It made Mary jump. Had she seen a ghost? Had some unspeakable thing entered Miss Everett's room? Though apprehensive, her eyes were pulled towards the wraith, which was now floating towards her like a wave. As it drew closer, Mary's eyes became accustomed to the dark, and with relief she saw a woman dressed in long, silky robes, the same colour as the velvet curtains, but made of something diaphanous that seemed to flow like water. Mary's hands shook as she laid the tray down on a small table. The woman held out her hand palm up to Mary and spoke.

"You must be Mary." Her voice was soft, slightly frail, yet there was an underlying firmness and conviction in its clear enunciation. "You'll be taking over from Polly, I daresay."

"How do you do, Madam," said Mary. "But it's only for a while, until Polly is recovered."

The woman smiled in a way that made Mary think she knew something about what had happened to Polly. She noticed the woman's eyes seemed to shine, even in the darkness, as though they had their own source of light. She prepared to curtsy and leave, but found herself transfixed to the spot, pinned down by those luminous eyes. A vague thought occurred that she should be frightened, but she was not. On the contrary, the woman's presence filled her with a serenity she had not felt for many months. A memory flitted through her, a ramble through wet fields in Somerset with her father when she was a child, picking spring primroses and listening to a skylark's song.

Miss Everett, now at the table, picked up her teacup and took a sip, and the image of Mary's father faded. A shaft of morning light shone through the window where the curtain had been partly drawn back, and at last Mary was able to see Miss Everett's face more clearly, so that she was no longer a misty presence and disembodied voice. What she saw was a pale, thin visage that might once have been beautiful but was now criss-crossed with lines. Yet her cheeks were still firm and not sunken, so she must still have her teeth. She seemed to Mary both old and young at the same time. She was supposed to be an invalid, but did not seem sick or weak, and was perfectly able to walk and sit without assistance. She looked fitter and younger than Mrs. Scroggs, with her bad feet and sagging girth.

The sense of calm that emanated from her filled the room. The only word Mary could think of to describe it was "contentment." Miss Everett, alone all day in her darkened room, was completely content. Would that Mary might someday feel such a pleasant emotion.

Miss Everett replaced her teacup on the saucer and looked at Mary.

"I see you are intrigued by me," she said.

Mary touched her hand to her hair in her usual gesture of embarrassment. As if she had been caught out wondering how it was this woman knew her thoughts.

"Some people think I am strange, or mad." She gave a tinkling laugh. "Some say I am a witch!" Mary coloured. Some people had said she was a witch, but some people had once said much the same about Mary after Harriet Pickard's death. Miss Everett held up a reassuring hand. "I am none of those things, I assure you."

Mary, still speechless, found herself gazing at Miss Everett's face.

"Now, Mary, I know you are worried about Polly, but there is no need. In a few days, she will be quite well again."

Though relieved to hear this, Mary wondered how Miss Everett, shut away in her room with no visitors, would know so much about the goings-on in the house.

Miss Everett inclined her head to Mary, and with a wave of her thin and delicate hand, and a soft, "Thank you, Mary," she dismissed her. Mary curtsied, took the tray, and left, closing the door quietly behind her.

Mary felt shaken by the encounter, but something within her wanted to return, to learn more about this woman. As she went about her chores, she felt Miss Everett's presence surround her like an aura. It was afternoon when she ran into Martha on the stairs and remembered Mrs. Scroggs's instructions about sharing Polly's chores with Martha.

"Martha, we'll have to manage without Polly for a while. We have to share her chores between us."

Martha laughed. "Oh, is that so? Well, that's going to be an easy one, 'cause Polly only has one chore, and that's to take that mad woman in the back room her meals."

Mary looked at Martha with a quizzical expression.

Martha gave Mary a friendly shove onto the top basement stair, and sat beside her. "Didn't I tell you on your first day? Don't let Polly bully you into doing all the work. But you didn't listen, did you? Oh, she runs the odd errand for Mrs. S., and takes her time at it too. She can take all day to go down to the market for a bit of soap or a spool of thread. Who knows where she goes, dawdling away while the rest of us is hard at work, so's we hardly even notice. She always gets back in time for Miss E."

Mary didn't know what to think. She recognized that Polly was often devious and could be lazy, but now she learned Polly had taken advantage of her over these last months, letting Mary believe she was as industrious as Mary was. She frowned, but Martha giggled, and patted Mary on the head.

"She took you for a sucker, didn't she? Piled it all on. Don't worry. You're not the only one. She does it every time a new girl comes. Always takes a while for them to catch on. Not me. I work in the kitchen, so she can't do nothing to me."

Mary gritted her teeth. Mrs. Scroggs had given her instructions and she would follow them, and Polly for all her faults was in trouble and needed their help. "Be that as it may," she said to Martha, "now she's ill, we should care for her. She was delirious in the night."

Martha laughed again.

"Delirious? Delirium tremens, you mean!"

"Delirium tremens? Martha, you're wrong. She had a high fever and a rash. You didn't see her. I even thought she had the smallpox, but Mrs. Scroggs seems to think she'll recover."

"Oh yes, she'll recover all right, and be out on her ear! Listen, Mary, what Polly was last night was drunk. Smashed. Three sheets to the wind. Partook a bit too much of the old mother's ruin with her fancy man. It doesn't agree with her. Makes her all hot and cold and gives her a rash. She should stay off the stuff. It's not the first time it's happened, but it's the last time. Mrs. S. warned her before, so this time she'll be gone. You mark my words."

Drunk! How could Mary not have realized! Martha must think her an ignorant country bumpkin. She wrapped her arms around her shoulders and rocked back and forth on the stair, feeling foolish and embarrassed. A tap on her shoulder made her look up.

"Oi, you, perk up then." It was Martha, still beside her on the stair, apparently oblivious to her turmoil. "Nearly time for the old lady's tea."

"What? Who?"

"Miss Everett. Her tea. Your job now and it's time."

Mary felt the tension drain from her shoulders. For some reason she could not fathom, the anticipation of seeing Miss Everett again brought a sense of calm. She hurried down to the kitchen to prepare her tray.

After several days, Mrs. Scroggs forgave Polly and kept her on. It was, she said, the Christian thing to do, and she hoped God would forgive her, in accordance with the words of the Lord's Prayer. Mary was pleased, but had a feeling that Miss Everett's hands were involved in Mrs. Scroggs's decision.

There were changes though. As punishment, Mrs. Scroggs took Polly off her former light duties. Mary would now be in charge of errand running, and taking care of Miss Everett's needs, while Polly was to take over the harder work that Mary had been doing. The slight guilt Mary felt for taking Polly's light work load, and the fear of Polly's likely resentment towards her for this, were overshadowed by her joy at the prospect of twice daily visits to Miss Everett.

Polly, to Mary's relief, showed no resentment towards Mary. She was defiant in her attitude towards Mrs. Scroggs and nonchalant about her new workload. Mary thought she ought to have exhibited at least a little shame. Her attitude made more sense when, a few days later as they prepared for bed, she announced, "Mary, I'll be leaving soon. I'm going to marry Mr. Sylvester and move to Wolverhampton."

Mary's immediate delight at her friend's news was quickly tempered by concern. Mr. Sylvester was the man who had made her so very ill. "Polly, are you sure he is the right sort of person for you? I mean after the other night … "

"We was celebrating, Mary! That was when he popped the question. Went down on one knee and everything. I just took a bit too much of the oh-be-joyful, that's all. It doesn't agree with me. I ought not to partake, but I'm right as rain now, and he's a good man. It's all official; we've set the date, and I've given my notice. So what do you think of that, Mary? I'm going to be a married woman!" Polly grabbed Mary's hands and whirled her around until they were both dizzy and fell on the bed laughing.

"I'm happy for you, Polly. But goodness, I shall miss you."

"Oh, you'll be all right. Mrs. S.'ll find a new girl—maids are two a penny 'round here, and you make sure you boss the tenderfoot around. You'll be cock of the walk when I'm gone." Polly took Mary's hands in hers again, and dropped her voice. "Now then, Mary, what I hope for you is that you find your own young man to marry, and then you can be as happy as I am."

Mary drew her hands away, and turned her face from Polly. She went to the washstand, and slowly washed her face and hands and unpinned her hair. She knew Polly meant well, but she was resigned to spinsterhood. Perhaps Thomas would marry one day, and have children. Perhaps she would hold a baby again, a little niece or nephew whom she could indulge; she would like that. She turned, wanting to reassure Polly that she had not intended to push away her questions, but Polly was already tucked under the covers asleep.

ELEVEN

Whenever she could, after Edward had left for work in the mornings, Catherine would bundle the baby up in her basket, take her down to the grateful Ellen, and set off across the bridge. Ellen never asked where she was going, and Catherine was confident she would not tell Edward of her forays; it was as if there were a silent pact between the two women, each with a secret she kept from her husband.

With each turn she made a mental note of landmarks and fitted them to the map in her head to help her remember her way—the curio shop on this corner, the grubby crossing-boy on that corner, the row of hansom cabs on the main street, the arcade of jewellery shops that teemed with finely dressed women.

She spoke to no one, and no one seemed to notice her. Everyone was busy, rushing hither and thither with their own business. The only ones not in a hurry were the occasional gentlemen who tipped their hats as she passed. That made her smile; she no longer looked like the poor Irish girl with a bundle in shabby skirts who had arrived not eight months previously. She rather liked being treated with respect. It made her want to thumb her nose at Ma and all the old Kildean gossips. They wouldn't believe it if they saw her now.

She always returned in time to prepare Edward's supper and greeted him with a glowing fire and a meal on the table. After supper, she cleared the dishes, sat demurely with her sewing, and fed the baby at the hearth.

Her shoes were loosening up with wear, and with each foray she travelled farther north and east than ever. But she was growing despondent, for she had still not found Spitalfields.

Then, one day, as she wound her way through yet more alleys and courtyards, she fancied she heard a rumbling, and above it, the faint sound of singing. She quickened her pace and hurried toward the sound. She turned a corner, which led into a large cobbled courtyard. From the open doorways of the side-by-side brick houses came the sound of what she recognized as shuttles moving back and forth, and the creak of looms being lifted and lowered to alternate warp and weft. Merchants hurried by with great skeins of silk and woollen thread on their shoulders. Shuffling women carried bolts of newly woven fabric to market stalls set up at the far end of the courtyard. This must be Spitalfields, and these, she was sure, were her people.

A smile touched the corner of her lips as she strained to hear the sound of singing above the rumble of the looms and the babble of chatter. The song was familiar. She headed for the tavern sign that hung creaking in the wind. Outside, men leant against the tavern walls, tankards in hands, talking and laughing. The cadence and list of their voices were familiar. They bowed slightly, lifted their caps as she approached. She saw surprise but no insolence in their expressions. No doubt they had taken in her fine clothes and may have noticed the ring on her finger. Nevertheless, she kept herself stiff, arms close to her sides, as she spoke.

"Pardon me, is this Spitalfields?"

The men looked startled to hear her voice. She chuckled inwardly. *Yes*, she thought, *I am Irish too, but I no longer look it, do I? They think I'm a lady, and they were expecting a different accent!*

"'Tis indeed," said one of the men. "Is there something we can do for you?" Before she could respond, an older woman ambled towards them. "Who's this then?" she said.

"See for yourself, Janet," said the man who had first spoken. "A lady, I'd say."

"Then there's to be none of your nonsense, Michael," the woman said. She turned to Catherine, looked her up and down, taking in her fresh clothes and sprigged bonnet, her shoes, and said, "Is it something we can help you with, dear?"

Catherine was cautious after her experience with Miss Delaney, and kept her tone nonchalant. "I was just out walking, getting to know my way around. I heard the looms and the singing and I was curious."

The woman gave her puzzled look. "Where are from dear? You're country. I can tell by the way you talk. Waterford county, I'd say. What's your village?"

Catherine was not ready to reveal her origins. For all she knew, these folk had heard of Catherine Joyce running away from Kildean. No doubt the news had spread from village to village and given the locals a juicy story to embellish. She evaded the woman's question and simply introduced herself as Katie Harris.

"Katie Harris. Well, now, let me think, I knew a Harris family in Cork. They ran a general store there, had three girls, I seem to remember, no boys. One of them married a fellow up in Dublin … oh," she glanced at Catherine's hands, "I see you're married. Harris is your husband's name, then." The woman gave a broad smile as if everything was now clear. "But where is your husband? Does he know you're out and about on your own?"

"Oh, he's away on business."

"A businessman?" The woman nodded knowingly. "And you're a bit lonely, bless you. Miss your people?"

Catherine nodded. The woman seemed kind. She was older than Miss Delaney, with a smooth round face and full-lipped smile, motherly in her manner. To hear her speak was like returning to a comfortable, well-trodden path. She reminded Catherine of the matronly teacher she'd had at the Hedge School in Kildean.

"Well, if you are from Waterford, you'll find lots of folk here from that neck of the woods. Waterford and Cork. Dublin too. Come and sit you down inside," the woman gestured Catherine into the tavern. "It's lunch break. You'll feel right at home here."

She did, as soon as she entered the tavern. It was like Friday and Saturday nights in Kildean, with a couple of men on the fiddle, a couple of women singing, and everyone holding their tankards aloft as they joined in the chorus. When the tavern emptied and the men returned to their looms, Catherine emerged on the arm of the older women, flushed and bright-eyed.

"You'll come again, Katie," said the woman, whose name was Janet O'Hara. "Come of a Saturday night."

Catherine wished she could, but evening visits were out of the question. But come again in daytime, that she would.

A few days later, Catherine again finished her chores early, handed Louisa to the grateful Ellen Booth, and left. In Spitalfields, Janet greeted her with a torrent of chatter and local gossip. Janet's friendliness seemed genuine, but Catherine remained cautious, having learned from her encounter with Miss Delaney how unwise it was to blurt out her intentions to a stranger. But on her third visit, she decided to trust Janet and dared to ask if she knew of any circuses in London. Janet had laughed. London was full of circuses of all kinds, big, small, whatever you wanted to see. Did Catherine ever see a circus, Janet asked.

"I did," she said, ready with her cover story, "about a year ago. I took my younger sisters. They were so excited. And the performers let them help groom the horses. The troupe left for London not long after. Now I'm here in London, I'd love to see them again and thank them."

Janet looked skeptical.

Catherine continued, keeping her tone casual. "But I can hardly recall the name. Billy Mater, Mather? I think it was Billy Mather's Amazing Circus."

"Well now, I've never heard of that one. Hasn't been round here as far as I know, and there's been quite a few."

Catherine tried not to let her face drop. She had counted on the weavers knowing something of Billy Mather's Amazing Circus, some clue as to where it might have gone. She tried again.

"I thought perhaps someone here in Spitalfields must have heard of it. It was only a year ago it was in Waterford, and they toured around Ireland. There must be people here who saw them then."

"A year ago? Let me think, now. Well, most of us have been here more than a year. Three Christmastides already I've been here. Haven't gone back. Well, why would I? Everyone says Ireland's done for. Now Michael McCann, you remember him when you first came here? He's been here longer than any of us. Still got a wife in Cork, and went back a few times, but not lately. His boys all followed him here some years ago, oh, but not the youngest one, he went to America, did well for himself too ... "

As Janet's musings meandered away from circuses, Catherine tried a new tack. The weaver man and his simpleton son, who gave up their places on the boat, had been bound for England. Did Janet know of such a boy, she asked. "Thin, about as tall as me, with fair hair and bad skin. Do you know of a simple boy like that, with a father who's a weaver?"

Her query provoked another stream of chatter from Janet, who began to recount the life histories of all the Irish she knew who might have arrived in the last few months, or not, several of whom might have met Catherine's description, or not. "There's a few simpletons, for sure, poor souls, but none from Waterford that I know of. Perhaps they went to Liverpool, or stayed in Bristol," she concluded.

It was hopeless. Catherine would have to think again, find a new plan. She pulled on her gloves and prepared to leave.

"Always lovely to see you, Katie dear. You're a sight for sore eyes around here." Janet laid a friendly hand on Catherine's shoulder.

Catherine made her excuses and left feeling downhearted. Janet, still chatting mindlessly, called after her.

"Come and see me again, Katie, and we'll have a drink together … And isn't it circuses you want? A lot of them come in the summer. I'll ask around, must be someone's heard of Billy Mather."

Catherine stopped and turned. Janet hadn't forgotten. She smiled and waved, her spirits lifted. Next time she visited Janet O'Hara, perhaps she would have news for her. She picked her way over the cobbles and through the winding alleys to the bridge. Ellen Booth was waiting on the steps with Louisa in her basket.

The following day, she left Louisa with Ellen again and made her way back to Spitalfields. Janet greeted her with her usual enthusiastic prattle, and then said, "Are you still looking for that circus, Katie? I heard there's one just arrived up in St. Martin-in-the-Fields, and another coming soon to Shoreditch."

Catherine didn't linger. She reviewed the map in her mind. She knew how to get to those places. They were a start, and even if they were not Billy Mather's Amazing Circus, people at those circuses might know where else she should look. If necessary, she would scour London and visit every circus ground she could find.

* * *

All through the wet summer of '45, the tavern in Spitalfields, in Janet's company, became a resting place for Catherine to replenish her energy for longer, more distant forays. Leaving Louisa safely in the willing arms of Ellen Booth, she went from site to site, field to field, heedless of the rain that soaked her clothes and the wind that blew her hair into tangles. She got as far as the West End and east to Brick Lane, even as far north as Hampstead and Holloway. At every street and square, she examined the billboards and posters advertising plays and concerts for information on circuses. At every theatre she asked in the box office, and with her sweetest smile, begged to be allowed to go backstage to ask the performers. She questioned horseriders and dwarfs, ropewalkers and clowns. But no one she spoke to had ever heard of Billy Mather's Amazing Circus.

After each excursion, despondent, she headed back to Spitalfields and took a cup or two with Janet and the weavers at the tavern. Being there among her people cheered her. They were not like the pinched and narrow folk from Kildean. These were the ones who had got away from that oppressive world across the sea. She enjoyed listening to their stories, and joined in their familiar songs, drank beer and whiskey with them, and laughed with them. The men looked admiringly at her, yet retained a respectful distance. They must have wondered what she was doing there. When she opened her mouth, they recognized her as one of them, but not quite. "You're a lucky one," one of the men said to her. "You found that pot at the end of the rainbow."

That made her chuckle. A corporal's salary did not a rich man make, nor a gentleman. To them in their grubby working togs she must have seemed wealthy beyond their imaginings, yet they seemed to bear her no grudge.

Being with her new friends made her all the more determined to find Jack and leave the stultifying embrace of Edward and his stuffy world. When she thought of the years rolling ahead with this bland Englishman, watching his thin white frame grow bent and old, his straight hair wispy and sparse, she wondered how she could ever have imagined being happy with such a dull man.

Every time she left Spitalfields to return to the attic room, she felt a boulder growing in her belly. Her feet dragged behind her as she crossed Southwark Bridge, and, with her breasts tingling, picked up Louisa from Ellen. If Ellen smelt the whiskey on her breath, she said nothing, only too happy to have Louisa for herself.

Catherine's life was now divided between the tedium of living with Edward and the hope of leaving him once she found Jack. The search for Jack was a fire burning within her. As soon as she returned to the attic room, the fire went cold. Edward's footsteps on the stairs each evening as he returned made her stomach lurch. He brought her violets, candied fruit, and a kitten (which she gave away to a neighbour's child). He gazed at her, and played with her hair in a way that made her squirm inside. The more he showered her with tokens of his love, the more she felt stifled by his earnest attentiveness.

When her conscience pricked, which it did with bothersome frequency, she tried to place Edward side by side with Jack in her mind. Then it was easier to disdain Edward, so proper, so obsessed with his mapmaking and his measurements, as if the whole world could be contained within lines on a piece of paper. Jack's world was so much bigger, and broader and deeper. How could Edward believe that she could truly love him when she had been loved by a man like Jack?

Sometimes the guilt caused her to become sharp with him, but when her sarcasm and cutting remarks seemed to make him adore her all the more she wanted to lash out and break loose from his embrace. She had tried to love Edward and hate Jack, but she could not. She was sorry for cheating him, sorry for not being the wife he wanted, for being unable to be true to him, but she could not love him. It was Jack she loved, Jack she wanted and needed.

The double life became second nature to her. She learned to be careful with money, purchasing cheaper cuts of meat, smaller pies, and day-old bread so that she could sneak some coins for her journeys. Edward never noticed the difference, and, she was sure, never suspected how she spent her days. Why would he? His work at the garrison consumed him by day, and she was always there when he got home, with food on the table and a clean hearth.

By late August, though, Catherine was growing increasingly disconsolate. The summer was already old and she had found not a single trace of Billy Mather's Amazing Circus. Her search had covered most of London north of the river. Janet's ceaseless chatter was beginning to bore her. None of the weavers in Spitalfields had been on the ship that day from Waterford, and none of them had ever heard of Billy Mather's Amazing Circus.

One day, after a midday drink with Janet, she wandered so far west she became unsure of the way back. She stopped at a tavern somewhere south of Piccadilly for refreshment and to review the map in her head. She sat alone, a glass of whiskey before her. She knew how it looked, a woman drinking alone in a tavern, but she no longer cared.

The whiskey, bought with Edward's pie money, blurred the edges of the fear she now faced that she would never find Jack, that she might have to give up the search and settle for a half-life with Edward. Would it be so bad to stay with him? To have a name, a home, food in her belly? Respectability. Edward was always on about respectability. It was the practical, sensible solution. That's what Edward would argue.

She shook her head and banged her fist on the table, ignoring the glances of the other patrons. Yes, it *would* be so bad. She would wither and die in those puny arms. His earnest adoration of her smothered her, as had Aunt Fanny's potions and blankets during her confinement. She called for another whiskey. There were still places to discover. And if London came up with nothing, she would fan out to places beyond, and up and across the length and breadth of England.

She rose from her seat and wandered into the street. The whiskey had gone to her head and she tripped and swayed, disoriented, unsure and uncaring of where she was or where she was going. Ahead of her was a bridge, but not Southwark Bridge. She staggered towards it. It was a bridge she had not seen before; it had several more arches and a steeper grade. She figured if she crossed the bridge and turned left she'd eventually end up in Southwark, but why would she do that? Rather than go back to Edward, she might lie down on the bridge and fall asleep into oblivion. Then she would never have to return to Southwark, and never spend another night with Edward. She giggled tipsily at the thought.

On the other hand, perhaps a bridge was not the best place to sleep, especially now a light rain had begun to fall. If she could get across, she might find a warm, dry doorway to sleep in. Her wavering gait took her over the bridge and slap up against the sight of a massive structure on the other side. It was a grand red brick and sandstone building with arched windows and an ornate pillared entrance, topped by a coat of arms. Numerous well-dressed people milled around in front of the building—ladies in fine silks and gentlemen in top hats and tailcoats. Grand carriages waited at the kerb, the horses munching oats from their nosebags.

But what caught Catherine's eye, even in her inebriated state, were the posters plastered on the front wall of the building. She stepped closer. One poster in particular was advertising a circus. And among the pictures of horses and acrobats, she saw him. Jack! Jack, in his strongman stance, feet apart, arms raised, fists clenched. The artist had rendered him perfectly, the curve of his cheek, the firm swell of his body, his clear, penetrating eyes, even the dark curl of hair on his forehead.

The fog in her head cleared, and a bass drum beat in her chest. She scanned the poster to find the name of the circus. Not, apparently, Billy Mather's. This was Astley's Royal Circus. She looked up at the building. On the roof was a huge sign reading "Astley's Amphitheatre."

Jack must have left Billy Mather to join this new troupe, this Astley's Royal Circus. How grand it sounded! Tears of joy and relief flooded her eyes. After months of searching every corner of London, here at last was Jack, no more than a few miles from where she lived. Had he been here all along? She peered at the small print on the poster. No. This performance was part of a travelling troupe on loan to Astley's Amphitheatre for one week only. One week!

Catherine was now sober and sharp as a knife. She marched into the foyer of the theatre and up to the box office. Patrons milled around, spilling out onto the porch, enjoying drinks at the bar, while their well-dressed children ran around playing peekaboo. These were, apparently, affluent people who didn't have to work during the day. But were they waiting for the performance to start, or was it already over? Her breasts were stinging for Louisa, so it must be midafternoon. Too early for the evening performance. She asked the man in the box-office.

"You're a bit late, my duck. It's half over. This is the break."

"Half over? What have I missed?"

"Equestrian events are finished, and the acrobats. But it's only the afternoon performance so there's still a lot of seats. The tightrope walkers and strongman are coming on next."

She hadn't missed him! She clawed back her dishevelled hair, straightened her shawl, and counted her last remaining coins.

"Here," she said to the man in the box office, "do I have enough for a ringside seat?"

"Not likely. Them's the most expensive in the house." Then, seeing her downcast face, he relented. "Tell you what. Since you've missed the first half, I'll let you in for a reduced price."

She handed over her money, stepped boldly into the theatre, and stopped. The size and opulence of the place astounded her. Seats from high above her were tiered down to the sawdust ring on the ground. The circular walls were decorated in rich gold and green, with crimson velvet hangings in the boxes. Fluted pillars and columns in white and gold rose up to the domed ceiling, from which was suspended a massive crystal and gold chandelier. There must have been room for a thousand people inside this magnificent theatre. And this magnificent place was where Jack was performing!

The man had been right about the ringside seats. They gave a perfect view, steps from the barrier separating the ring from the audience. Higher up, the people in the top balcony were far away from the action, and peered through what looked like spectacles or magnifying glasses. The more affluent audience members sat closer to the ring, and Catherine took her seat among them. Some of them looked at her curiously, and shifted away. *Well*, she thought, *they have no cause to spurn me just because I'm wearing cotton and not feathers and silk.* She felt like telling them that some people saw her as a lady. But evidently she was not sufficiently lady-like for this toffee-nosed crowd. She'd paid, and had as much right as they to sit in the expensive seats. She ignored them and looked up at the intricately carved ceiling, trying to calm her somersaulting stomach.

Trumpets sounded, and Catherine turned her eyes to the sawdust ring. A large man in a top hat and tailcoat entered. The next few minutes were a blur to Catherine. She sat nervously twisting her hands, trying to keep her breath even. She barely noticed the tightrope walkers or heard the "oohs" and "aahs" of the audience.

Why don't they hurry, she muttered. *Please, be quick, finish now, you've had enough time.*

The ropewalkers made their bows and ran from the ring. The drumroll sounded, as it had in Kildean. The audience fell silent. Catherine looked anxiously towards the curtained area from where the performers entered. The curtain was pulled taut. Nothing moved; the only sound was the dying echo of the drum. The audience waited; people began to shift in their seats and murmur. Still nothing. Then the curtain fluttered, was pulled back. And Jack stalked into the ring. Behind him came his sequined assistant. His body was as smooth and taut as it had been in Kildean. But this was a grander, more important-looking Jack, for now his costume sparkled with silver thread and his boots were tied with golden laces. He seemed taller, broader, even more handsome.

He surveyed the audience, his eyes glancing up and down, left and right, and then straight at Catherine, and recognition lit his face. Her heart jolted. He continued with his act, but the one raised eyebrow and the slight smile when his eye caught hers could not be mistaken. She watched him, spellbound as she had been the first time, and saw, as he left the podium, the flick of his head towards her that said, "Meet me afterwards," just as in Kildean.

She left quietly before the show was over, found a curtain across a doorway at the back of the building, and slipped through it. She entered a large covered area milling with people, performers waiting to go on, others leaving the ring. The smell of horse overwhelmed her; the sawdust on the ground was damp with their urine. It was a comforting smell of country fields and barns, but it was three times the size of the field in Kildean.

She snaked through the crowd, moving towards the far end of the space, where the horses were tethered. In Kildean, she'd always found Jack by the horses. This time, no one tried to stop her. With so many people, they likely assumed she was part of the circus. And then, there he was, his back to her, a red satin cape around his shoulders. Before him was his assistant, the sequined woman. Catherine had barely noticed her during the performance, and could not remember if she was the same woman as in Kildean. She wore a similar red dress, with her black hair piled in a complicated bun. Jack appeared to be remonstrating with her, waving his hands, and she, red-faced, was shouting at him. Then she turned and stomped away. Her face was angry. If it were the same person, she seemed to have aged ten years since Kildean. Jack held out his hands and shrugged.

Catherine tiptoed towards him. Her heart was pounding but her head was clear. She called out to him. "Jack."

He turned, saw her. His shoulders relaxed; he looked her up and down and the lazy smile that began at the corners of his mouth became a broad grin.

"Ruby Red, my Catherine. How fine you look, all dressed up like a lady!" Catherine had waited so long for this moment, longed for him, raged at him, loved him, hated him, and vowed to make him pay before she'd forgive him. If, indeed, she would ever forgive him. But then he smiled at her and she found herself speechless before him.

"I knew you'd find me one of these days!"

At that, something boiled up inside her and her face burned. What was he saying, that this was some kind of cat-and-mouse game? That he had abandoned her as a joke, as a challenge for her to seek and find? Had it all been a game for him? Had he even given any thought to what she'd been through these last months? How she had almost been brought to ruination? How she'd been forced to marry a man who made her skin crawl to avoid an even worse fate? How she'd left her sisters and mother to follow him, and tramped for months through London looking for him? How dare he make light of her predicament. He must be made to understand what he had done to her. She glared at him.

"I had the baby," she said. "Your baby."

His face grew serious. He looked shocked. Perhaps he even blushed. He held out his arms towards her, took her hands in both his, gently, possessively, as he had before. Her skin tingled at his touch. She should snatch her hands away, turn her back, walk away from him, go back to the husband who adoted her, the comfortable home that waited for her, forget these wasted months of mooning after a man who cared nothing for her. What did she want with this feckless gypsy? He would bring her nothing but misery. She willed herself to pull her hands away, but her will failed, and only the throbbing and tingling in her body and her head remained.

"Catherine, forgive me. I've done wrong by you. I'm sorry."

She pulled herself up, and tried to yank her hands from his grasp. He held on tighter.

"Why didn't you wait for me? I followed you. I followed you all the way to England. I've been looking for you everywhere."

He looked away, as if searching for the right response. "You came all that way, for me? Catherine … "

"You told me to come at dawn. You said you'd take me to England and care for our baby."

"I did, I did. I meant to, I really did. But we had to leave. The ship was sailing."

Now, now, was the moment to leave, before it was too late, but still she could not bring herself to release her hands from his.

"But you left me to come alone. You could have sent word, but you didn't. You didn't even bother to find me."

"Poor Ruby Red." That smile again. "Forgive me. I tried, I did, honest, but there was no time. I'm sorry. Tell me what you've been up to. And the baby. What was it?"

Her resistance was failing. She looked up at him through her lashes.

"A girl. Louisa."

"Fancy that."

"I could bring her to you, you can see her if you want." Louisa was his child. He should want to see her. When he did, he might truly understand what he had done.

He released her hands, and the tingling stopped. He stood for a moment, his hand on his forehead, deep in thought, then glanced over his shoulder. Then, "Tell you what, Catherine. You come again and we'll talk about things. Whaddya' say? There's something … well … we'll talk about it, all right?"

Talk, he'd said. *Something to talk about.* Something important he wanted to tell her. Surely this could only mean one thing—that he still loved her, that he wanted to be with her. She felt weak, as her anger fell away like shards of bruised skin. The months she'd spent in her quest, the journey from Ireland, her miserable marriage to Edward—forgotten, discarded, of no consequence. Jack still wanted her, and only this mattered. She clasped her hands together.

"Can I come back tomorrow, bring the baby with me? Will you be here?"

"Yes, come back. I'll tell them to let you in. If anyone tries to stop you, just say Jack's expecting you."

She felt her chest expand. He was telling her she was special, giving her a free pass.

"But look, best not bring the baby. I'll get to know it another time. Just come alone."

Alone. That meant he would love her again. Still, a sliver of caution remained. Could this really be happening?

"You will be here, won't you? You won't leave me again?"

"I'll be here. Come about this time, after the matinee, before the evening performance. And we'll talk."

He drew her close. She couldn't hold back. He placed one hand on the nape of her neck, the other on the small of her back. She sighed at his touch, wanted to stay, but he pulled away.

"Off you go. I've got things to do. I'll see you tomorrow."

Her body still trembled with the touch of him, and her breasts had grown hard and full with milk, as she left the building and set off home through the darkening streets.

TWELVE

Less than a month after Polly's engagement, Martha surprised everyone with the announcement that she, too, was engaged and her fiancé was a lad from her home village, a blacksmith's apprentice. The marriage was planned for the autumn, when her betrothed was due to finish his apprenticeship.

Polly's engagement and marriage were not a surprise—she was a girl who would always land on her feet. But Martha? With her pockmarked, sandpaper face? Mary thought it must be her cheerful disposition and talent for knitting up the whole kitchen staff in stitches of laughter. Such a contrast to Mary's own stolid dullness.

Martha's news, following so closely on Polly's, put Mary in a melancholic mood as she prepared Miss Everett's tea tray. She knocked on Miss Everett's door and pushed it open. Miss Everett, as usual, seemed to glide towards her in her flowing gown as she greeted her and indicated for Mary to lay the tray on the table.

Miss Everett sat down at the table and looked at Mary in the same penetrating way she had on their first encounter.

"I see you are feeling sad today, Mary."

Astonished, Mary could do nothing but nod wordlessly.

Miss Everett poured tea into her cup from the teapot, and placed the pot back on the tray.

"Because Polly is leaving? And Martha too?"

Again, Mary nodded. She would miss her friends. Polly's happy-go-lucky attitude and Martha's down-to-earth approach to life had often given Mary pause to reflect on her own diffidence in her early days in London. In their easy company, she'd felt her comfort with her new life grow day by day.

"I'll miss them," she said. It sounded feeble.

"Of course, you will. But this melancholy is not just about Polly and Martha. There is more, is there not? Their leaving has brought something else to the surface."

How insightful Miss Everett was. Mary felt tears pricking. There was more, and she wanted to tell Miss Everett. About Somerset, the village she grew up in, the river, tramping with her father through lush fields, her skirts soaked to her knees, collecting hedgerow herbs with her mother. The babies she'd cradled, the mothers she'd comforted. The world she thought would always be hers. And how she'd lost it all one day in spring, when the sun was bright and the daffodils were in bud along the river, and she didn't know that an unspeakable thing would happen in the night, and how the next morning the water in the washtub ran red, and after that she burned her herbs and put away her tools and followed her brother to London. She wanted so much to tell Miss Everett, but the words would not come. Only tears. She no longer tried to hold them back.

Miss Everett did not move or speak while Mary sobbed, but remained composed in her chair, her hands clasped in her lap. Then Mary remembered her position and quickly recovered her composure. "Oh, Miss Everett, I'm so sorry. Please forgive me, I have behaved unconscionably."

"Nothing to be sorry about, Mary dear. Tears are Heaven's healing fluid. You lost something in Somerset. It was something important to you. And now you feel fragile, like a bird with a broken wing."

Again, Miss Everett seemed to know Mary's unspoken thoughts. Mary gave a wan smile. "My family always called me Little Sparrow."

Miss Everett smiled. "They named you well, Mary, because the sparrow is one of the strongest birds in the air. It may look fragile, but it is not to be underestimated. And broken wings heal." She pushed the breakfast tray towards Mary and sat back in her chair. "Now, with Polly leaving, you will be busy, but when you have time, you and I will talk again."

Mary straightened her collar, composed herself, and took Miss Everett's tray. The glow she felt as she left Miss Everett's room stayed with her for the rest of the day.

* * *

By Easter, Polly was married and had moved to Wolverhampton. She wrote advising everyone that they must now address her as Mrs. James Sylvester. Mary could almost see the cocky snoot to her nose and the wink of her eye as she wrote that.

Through spring and summer, a succession of new girls arrived and left, none living up to Mrs. Scroggs's exacting standards. Mary was rushed off her feet directing each new girl, teaching her how to launder the sheets, clean the hearths, dust the drapery, see to Mrs. Scroggs's feet. But with each brief lull in activity, Mary took the chance to linger in Miss Everett's room. To Mary's relief, there was no repeat, and no mention, of her earlier outburst.

Mary had often wondered why Miss Everett was considered an invalid. She didn't seem like an invalid—she ate well, and was able to walk without assistance. Her voice was firm and clear. Only the pallor and permanently drawn curtains suggested a sick room.

As she became closer to Miss Everett, she felt more confident to ask her, "Miss Everett, what is your illness? People say you're invalid, but you seem quite well to me."

"Ah, I wondered when you were going to ask me. The question is not what is my illness, but what is my wellness?"

Mary was confused, as she often was by Miss Everett's enigmatic responses, and her propensity to answer one question with another.

"Hmm. What is your wellness?"

"Wellness of mind, wellness of heart. Do you see me as unwell in my mind and my heart?"

"I don't think so. But I do wonder why you don't leave your room."

Miss Everett rose and went to the window, pulling the curtain aside. The light from the window revealed her face. Again, Mary was struck by her faded beauty. Once, she would have been stunning.

"Mary, if you think hard about it, the answer will come to you."

Mary didn't know how to respond. Miss Everett, as if she recognized Mary's puzzlement, rested a gentle hand on Mary's wrist.

"I have no family, as you may know. I was an only child of an only child—that is a special status given to very few people. It helped to make my father a wealthy man. But I think you and I both understand the hollowness of the material world."

Mary nodded.

"Some people see these four walls that I never leave as my prison. They do not understand. You see, Mary, here alone in my room, I am … unencumbered. I am emancipated."

Emancipated. The word was strange to Mary's ears. She could not remember ever having heard it before. But so many of the things Miss Everett spoke of were strange, and this was simply one more.

Miss Everett stood with her back to the window, and the light peeking through the edges of the curtains put her in silhouette. She held up a hand to Mary and said, "Go now, Mary. You have a pure heart, and an inner strength you are not yet aware of. Remember that. I'll see you in the morning."

Mary left the room, feeling at peace as usual when leaving Miss Everett, but still a little puzzled by her words. It seemed Miss Everett had actually chosen the role of invalid, and seemed supremely comfortable in her choice. But why? Had she once been like other beautiful young women, preoccupied with dreams of love and marriage? Had she been unlucky in love? Badly let down by a man? Mary thought not. In the place Miss Everett occupied, Mary was sure, no space was given to such concerns. By claiming to be an invalid, Mary realized, her friend was able to avoid the demands and pressures of the material world, and in so doing had found true serenity and peace of mind.

As Mary lay in bed that night, pondering these things, she wondered if she too would ever find the serenity and peace of mind she so envied in her friend. She thought about what Miss Everett had said about sparrows being the strongest of birds, and how broken wings can heal and fly again. As she drifted into sleep, she felt her mother's warm presence beside her in the bed, stroking her wing, breathing strength into its sinews, and fancied she saw Miss Everett's shadow hover like a candle glow by the window.

THIRTEEN

The sun was already low by the time Catherine got home. There was no sign of Ellen or the baby. Edward must already be home—he was early. She didn't care. Edward no longer mattered. Jack had talked about their future together.

When she stepped through the door, Edward confronted her. He held Louisa in his arms. And his face was like thunder.

"Explain!" he said.

She stood before him, defiant.

"Explain what?" She laughed, baiting him. It was cruel, but she couldn't help herself.

"How dare you cheek me. You are my wife. You are a mother. You have duties and responsibilities. Now I hear stories about you from the neighbours that make me ashamed—how you neglect your duties, how you leave your baby to be raised by a common wetnurse, and walk out alone in the morning and don't come back till afternoon."

Catherine shrugged. Ellen must have talked. No doubt Edward had threatened to speak to her husband.

Edward went on. "Do you not know how it looks? Do you not realize how you have dishonoured me?" He moved towards her and she thought he might strike her, but he held back and paused for a moment. "You've been drinking, there's whiskey on your breath! Catherine, this is unacceptable. You have disgraced me, you have disgraced my family. I am a respectable man, I have a position to uphold, and you as my wife are supposed to be my helpmeet. Instead I find you've been behaving like a loose woman. I will not tolerate it … I cannot … "

Catherine, triumphant, glared at him. "Then don't tolerate it. You won't have to anymore, because I'm leaving."

Edward's face turned red. "Leaving? Hah! You know you can't leave. I've shown you what happens to a woman alone in London, with thieves and scoundrels and people up to no good. Don't you remember how it was when you left Mrs. Scroggs? It will happen again if you leave. And now you have a baby. I am your husband and I will not allow you to leave."

Not allow her to leave? Marriage certificate or not, she would not be held. Not now that she had the chance to be with Jack. "You will not allow me, hmm? Well, what if I say I'm leaving anyway? Because I've found Jack, and I'm going away with him."

Edward's face changed from red to white, and he stared at her, speechless. She couldn't help feeling a little sorry for him and guilty about what she planned to do. But she would not let sympathy turn her heart faint.

"I see you're surprised. You thought I'd forgotten about him, didn't you. You thought you could replace him. But you didn't know, did you, that I always meant to find Jack? I never stopped wanting him. I told you before he'd be waiting for me somewhere, and he was."

Edward looked stunned. She relented a little; no need to be cruel to the poor man.

"Look, Edward, I am grateful for all you've done for me. But you must know I don't love you, and I never will. And now that Jack is back in my life, I will not stay with you."

"You are my *wife*," Edward responded through gritted teeth. The baby began to cry. Catherine moved towards Edward to take her, but he pushed her away, and carried the baby to her crib. He then came back and grabbed her by the wrists. He shoved his face close to hers; his spit sprayed onto her face.

"As my wife, you *will* obey me, by God and by the vows you made in church."

"Hah, those vows mean nothing to me!"

His nails dug into her skin.

"You're hurting me," she said. "Let go."

But he held on all the tighter until the pain of his grasp brought her close to tears. She kicked his shins, spat at him, but he would not let go. His eyes bore into her. She tried to wrench her wrists away, but he held fast. With an almighty effort, she thrust her knee into his groin. He dropped his hands from her wrists and staggered back, doubled in pain. He recovered, but still bent and clutching his groin he came towards her again. She stood her ground, glared at him, holding her knee at the ready, her hands up defensively, her wrists still aching. He glared back. The fury in his eyes terrified her; although her well-aimed knee may have stalled him temporarily, he was stronger than her and there was no telling where his anger would lead him.

She held her defiant position as he advanced, and then, instead of grabbing her again, he stopped dead. His mouth was a contorted grimace. He said nothing, but grabbed his coat, turned, and left, slamming the door behind him.

Catherine sat on the bed and rubbed her sore wrists. If she had felt any guilt or discomfort in leaving Edward, that had gone. He had hurt her, and she had every reason to leave him. She feared him now, having seen the rage in his eyes, afraid of what he might do to her when he returned, whether he might return with his soldier friends or with Ellen's brutish husband, and force her to stay.

She must leave now, this evening, and go to Jack. She glanced out of the window—it was not yet dark, so the evening performance would still be on. If she hurried, she would be able to catch Jack before he left the theatre. She didn't know where he was living—was it a caravan, or a room somewhere? What if she could not stay with him? But she would not, could not think of that. He would take her in, especially when he saw their baby.

For the second time in a year, Catherine bundled a few possessions together and prepared to leave for a new life. Unlike last time, she now had several fine cotton frocks to pack, and a small valise to put them in. In the bottom drawer of the dresser, tucked under the folds of her wedding dress, was the comb Jack had given her. She slipped it in among the clothes in her valise, but left the blue wedding dress in the drawer.

She tucked Louisa up in her basket, covered her with her shawl, put the basket over one arm, grabbed the valise with her other hand, and left the attic room. She left Edward, and Aunt Fanny, and Uncle George, Edward's friends and colleagues at the base, and the neighbours who, it now turned out, had told tales about her, just as people had in Kildean. She crept down the stairs, hoping no one would see or hear her, but as she went through the front door, she could not avoid running into Ellen Booth, on the front steps as usual, shelling peas into a bowl. Ellen looked shamefaced when she saw Catherine.

"Oh, Mrs. Harris, I'm so sorry. You were late, and your husband arrived, and I didn't know what to say to him. He kept asking me questions, and on my life, I couldn't tell a fib. It was as if he knew, even though I swear I never breathed a word before, but he got it out of me, with all his questions. I'm sorry if you got into trouble."

"It's all right, Ellen, it doesn't matter now. I'm leaving."

"Leaving? Oh, but Mrs. Harris, you can't leave on your own. What will become of you?"

Catherine gave a sly smile. "Don't worry about me. I'm going to be fine."

"Isn't he a good man, then, your Edward? He seems a decent man, but I s'pose you never can tell. Look at me, and my Jimmy. Everyone said he was a good man, too, and see what he done to me last night." Ellen bared her shoulder to show Catherine a fresh bruise.

"I'm sorry for you, Mrs. Booth. But it's not like that with me. There's another reason I have to leave."

Ellen looked longingly at the bundle of Louisa in the basket on Catherine's arm.

"I'll miss her, that I will."

"You can see her again if you want." It was rash to tell Ellen her plans, but Catherine was bursting with the news, and had to tell someone. And if it weren't for Ellen taking care of the baby and keeping her secret for so long, she would never have found Jack.

"You must promise me not to tell anyone. Especially not my husband."

"Ooh, I promise, I do."

"Well, walk along the river west, count three bridges as you go, and you'll come to a big square building. It's a sort of theatre. That's where I'll be."

"You going on the stage, Mrs. Harris? That's not a proper profession for a married lady like you."

Catherine chuckled. "I'm not such a lady, Ellen. You don't know me. But just come, before the end of the week when you get a chance to slip out. Then you'll understand. And you can see Louisa again. But remember, tell no one." She winked at Ellen and set off.

The basket with Louisa in it and the small valise of belongings were heavy, but Catherine didn't mind. She felt young and strong and ready for the world.

When she got to the theatre, people were already filing out. The evening performance was over. She pushed her way through the thickening crowd, and as before pulled aside the curtain and entered the space behind the ring, confident this time that she would be allowed to pass. There were people sweeping and scattering fresh sawdust. A man and a woman, still in costume, were leading a line of horses out to the stables at the back. No one stopped her.

But there was no sign of Jack. She headed through the crowd towards the horse corral at the back, and almost ran into a woman coming towards her. The woman looked familiar; was it the bearded lady from Kildean? It was! Except that she did not have a beard at all. How odd. Had she shaved, or had the beard been false? Catherine didn't know or care.

"Excuse me," she said. "I'm looking for Jack, the strongman. He's expecting me."

The woman peered at her. "I remember you, love. Well, he knows how to pick 'em, does Jack," she said in a cheery way. "There he is now," and she pointed to a caravan at the far end of the area. Jack was sauntering towards her. He must have come from the dressing area for he wore trousers and a shirt, with a cap on his head. His shirt was open at the neck, the sleeves rolled up. Her heart pounded. She put the valise on the ground by her feet. He came up to her, took her by the shoulders, and kissed her cheek. The bearded lady grinned in the background.

"Couldn't stay away, could you? Didn't I say tomorrow?"

She laughed, unsure if he was teasing her.

"I've brought your child," she said, and laid the basket down. Louisa was sleeping. Jack peered into the basket.

"Pretty little thing, isn't she? Is she a good baby? Does she cry much?"

Catherine was not sure how to respond. She realized she had spent little time with Louisa over the past weeks. When she was around, Louisa was usually sleeping or feeding. It was Ellen who had cared for her during the day. Ellen knew the baby better than she did. But what else could she have done? Louisa was in good hands with Ellen. And besides, she had done Ellen a favour by letting her care for and feed Louisa. That was a good thing to do. Now that she was back with Jack, she would take care of the baby herself.

"Yes, she's a good baby. As good as gold." That was what Ellen had said. Then, "Jack, I need to tell you something."

"Uh oh!" he said, raising his hands in mock horror. "Last time you had something to tell me … " He glanced down at Louisa and grinned.

Catherine clicked her tongue. "This is serious, Jack."

"Come on then, girl, out with it."

"Jack, I'm married."

"Oh. I see." He raised one eyebrow.

"But I've left my husband and I'm not going back."

She kept her eyes cast down, realizing for the first time that Jack may not understand that she had come to stay, not just for a visit. She felt she should give him some more explanation.

"He helped me when I was in trouble, after you left me, when I was all alone in London." She looked at him through narrowed eyes. He looked away, and she hoped he still felt ashamed. "But now I have no reason to stay. The child is not his, the child is yours, you know that."

He took off his cap, ran his fingers through his hair, paced back and forth a few times. He crouched down, and gingerly poked his index finger at the bundle of Louisa in the basket, then moved his finger to her face and stroked her cheek. He stood up, paced a little more, and then he spoke.

"This … this husband," he said. "What sort of a man is he?"

"Just a man. A soldier, English. He knew I was with child. I had no choice but to marry him, the way things were, but I don't love him, and I'll never go back to him."

"A soldier? Is he going to come after me with his musket?" Jack asked with a smile. As if Jack could be afraid of a man like Edward! But Catherine could not tell if he truly meant it as a joke.

"Of course not, Jack. He's a small man. You're much stronger than him. And he doesn't know where I've gone, and he has no claim on me. The child is not his."

"But he's your husband, legal and all?"

"Well, it wasn't a Catholic church, so it's not really legal is it?"

"Ah," said Jack. He was silent again, pacing again, crouching to look at the baby, then looking Catherine up and down, deep in thought, then smiling. Catherine wanted to scream, to cry, to throw her arms about him, but she stood silent, waiting, and then at last he took her hands in his and smiled.

"Good lord, but you're a beauty, Ruby Red. Why did I ever leave you? I must have been mad. But now you're back, with your hair and your eyes, and well, after you came by earlier I got to thinking ... Of course, you being married and all, and the child, well, it complicates things a bit ... "

"But I told you, the marriage means nothing ... " *Please don't send me away.*

"See, I need a new assistant. Someone young and pretty, who'll look good in a sequined gown. The crowds, they like me, but they like to see me with a pretty lady too. She completes the act, you know. Like a partnership. So, what do you think, Catherine? D'you think you could do that, yourself? Could you be my new assistant?"

Would she? Why would he even ask? This was more than she had dreamed about back in Kildean when she used to meet him under the trees. She'd begged him then to take her into the circus. He hadn't said "Yes" but he hadn't said "No." Now he was saying "Yes." And more! To be the sequined woman in the red dress! There in the ring with him, before hundreds of cheering people!

"Oh, Jack," was all she could say.

"Only thing is ... the baby," he said. "How would we ... ?"

"Oh, but ... " She had not thought this through. She no longer had Ellen, who would, she was sure, have helped her work something out. But she dared not go back to the house for fear of meeting Edward.

"See, we'll be leaving here in a couple of days. Off to Liverpool first, then we sail to America."

Catherine's eyes grew wide.

Jack stroked his chin. "Well, look, I'll ask around. She's a good little thing, don't cry too much, right? There's a woman I know who looks after circus babies. I'm sure she'd do it for a small consideration. Leave it with me. We'll get the little tyke fixed up tomorrow. Now, follow me."

He took the baby's basket and her valise and led her to a caravan parked in the field behind the theatre. She climbed the steps and looked in. What a mess! A typical man's mess—clothes strewn on the floor, the bed unmade, dirty dishes in a bowl.

"Oh, let me get at this," she laughed. "You men! I'll have to give this place a woman's touch."

"Not yet," he said, and grabbed her from behind, laughing, and pulled her down onto the bed.

In the morning they awoke to a ruckus outside the door. Jack was already pulling on his shirt and trousers, and going to investigate. Catherine leapt from the bed, pulled on her shift, and wrapped her shawl around her. She heard shouting. She knew even before she went to the door, peeking around Jack, that it was Edward, striding towards the caravan in his soldier's uniform. An old man pulled at his arm, others shouted, telling him he was trespassing, calling out to Jack in warning. Jack quickly closed the caravan door, pushed Catherine onto the bed. "I thought you said he wouldn't come after us."

They heard Edward clamber onto the running board, and more shouts from the gathered crowd. The caravan rocked as he hammered on the door. "I didn't think he would," said Catherine. "I don't know how he found me, but he has. And he's going to break the door down, Jack. Let me go to him. I'll talk to him."

"All right, but I'm right behind you. I'll take care of you."

She shot him a grateful look, went to the door, and opened it a crack. As soon as he saw her, Edward stopped shouting and lashing out. The shouts from the performers now crowded around the caravan quietened down. Edward stood back from the door. His face was grim, and exuded a steely truculence as if to defy any man who dared to oppose him.

"Catherine, I've come to take you home, you and Louisa. Please get your things together and come at once."

A few jeers rose up from the watching crowd.

Catherine opened the door wide. Jack stood behind her, his hands on her shoulders, towering above her. The crowd's jeers turned to cheers. She indicated him to Edward.

"Edward, this is Jack. I told you I'd found him. I always knew I would. I'm sorry, but I cannot come back to you."

Edward looked Jack up and down, taking in every inch of him, and his combative demeanour seemed to evaporate before her eyes. For he only had to look at Jack, Catherine thought, to know why she had to be with him. Edward, for all his militaristic posing, was a pitiable sight beside him. Even in his fine soldier's uniform, with the high cap that made him look taller than he was, he looked small and weak. His mouth twitched and turned down at the corners. He looked away from Jack and from her and she thought he might begin to cry. If he did, she would turn away too and close the door in his face, for she couldn't stand the embarrassment of a man weeping, especially in front of Jack.

Then he seemed to recover his composure and stretched his hands towards her. "Catherine, please, why are you doing this?" His voice was no more than a whisper. "Haven't I made you happy? I've bought you fine clothes, I've given you a warm and comfortable home, money to spend. A ring on your finger, a name for your child … I've accepted her as my own. And you want to leave it all behind for … this?" He swept his hand contemptuously around the caravan, and, indicating Jack, his voice rose, strident, "and as for you … you, sir, are a despicable blackguard and you should be ashamed."

He regained his soldierly stance—shoulders back, head up— looked Jack straight in the eye, clenched his fists, and took a step towards him. Another cheer rose from the crowd; perhaps they hoped for a fight. Jack retreated behind Catherine, but said, "Now, who might you be insulting, here, Mister Soldier. You'd do well to listen to the lady. She told you—she's with me now." Jack tightened his grip on her shoulders. Catherine reached up and placed her hand on his knuckles in a gesture of solidarity.

Edward ignored him and the increasingly rowdy crowd, now alternately hissing, booing, and cheering. He addressed Catherine again. "Catherine, you're not thinking straight. This man abandoned you when you were in a most vulnerable situation. That means nothing to you?"

Catherine pursed her lips. "He's explained what happened."

Edward stared at her in disbelief. "Oh, he's 'explained' has he? He's explained why he walked out on you when you were expecting a child? Why he never bothered to get a message to you? Why he never tried to find you? And you've forgiven him for this?"

Catherine pushed the palm of her hand towards Edward's face. "Yes," she said, defiant, "and *you* wouldn't understand."

"I wouldn't understand, eh? I wouldn't understand that you're giving up everything for a gypsy. What kind of life do you think you'll have with this … man? Living with circus folk. No home, no fixed address, no future. Don't you know what a miserable life you'll have, in this caravan, going from place to place, never settling?"

More jeers from the crowd.

"Just maybe, Edward, this is exactly the kind of life I do want. I don't suppose you've thought of that," said Catherine. "It's called freedom, Edward. You wouldn't know what that means, would you? You and your respectability, trying to turn me into a lady. Well, I'm not a lady and I never will be, and never wanted to be. You can keep your miserable respectability. It's a prison and I don't want it."

Applause and laughter from the crowd.

She attempted to close the caravan door, but Edward put his foot out to hold it open, grasped her by the bodice of her shift, twisting the fabric in his hand. Jack kept his hand on her shoulder from behind. More hisses and boos from the crowd.

"And you really think he'll stay with you? That he won't abandon you again when he tires of you? When you become inconvenient to him?" Edward let go of her shift and shook his head in exasperation. "Well, Catherine, *wife*, you may throw your life away for a circus man. But what about your daughter—what kind of a life for her? I accepted your child as my own. I love her as my own. If nothing else, I will not let you take her away from all that I can give her."

Catherine took a step forward. "Hah, you have no claim on Louisa. She's mine and Jack's."

Edward's voice dropped to a fierce whisper again and he wagged his finger at Catherine. "I have every claim on her, Catherine. I am your legal husband, and as such, Louisa is mine as much as yours. I think you will find the law is on my side." He raised his voice against the hoots and hollers of the crowd. "Do what you will with your ... *Jack*. Ruin your own life, but do not ruin Louisa's. I take the child. Do you understand?"

Catherine put her hands to her ears, shaking her head. The crowd began closing in on Edward. Jack, who had been looking at his feet, stepped forward, shielded Catherine, and drew himself up to his full height before Edward.

"Time for you to leave, Mister Soldier. But the child stays. If you don't leave now, I'll have you thrown out for trespassing." Catherine nodded her assent and clutched Jack's sleeve. A cacophony of cheers from the crowd drowned out any response Edward might have made. He glared at Jack for what seemed like minutes. His fists were clenched, his face was red, his eyes bulged, the vein in his forehead throbbed, and his mouth was twisted as if he were trying to speak but the words would not come. Catherine thought he might have an apoplectic fit. Edward jabbed a finger at Catherine.

"Go then, be damned into ruination. I should have known better than to trust you, but the child will be mine." He turned his pointing finger at Jack and spat, "And you, sir, have not seen the end of me. I'll be back, and next time I'll bring the constables with me." Jack raised his fist, but stepped back, pulling Catherine in front of him. Edward turned, climbed down from the caravan and walked away fast, pushing his way through the cheering crowd that now fell back to let him pass. The show was over.

Catherine collapsed on the bed, shaking. Jack comforted her. "Don't worry, Catherine, we'll find a way to hide the baby. He won't get her. And we'll be gone from here in a few days." He cupped her face in his hands, wiped the welling tears away with his thumb, and brushed his lips to her throat. She moved her body close to his. Louisa woke and began to cry. He pulled away from her.

"Best see to the baby, then. I'll be off to fix things up for her so's he'll never find her, or us. You just wait."

She picked up the baby and fed her, still shaking, but her heart was full and grateful.

FOURTEEN

Edward paced back and forth from one end of the attic room to the other and slapped the wall, covered his face with his hands, hit his head with his fist, slapped the wall again. His head pounded with the memory of Catherine in the door of the caravan, hidden behind that varmint, her hand in front of her face, as if to push Edward away.

It was unbearable, unthinkable. He had saved her, protected her, given her a home and future. And loved her. What did that Jack, with his muscles and his arrogant stance and his looming height, know about love? The man was handsome all right, but she was *Edward's wife*. How dare she dishonour him in this way? Even if she wanted him back, which she didn't, it would be beneath the dignity of his station to accept her. She was capricious, impetuous, faithless. She disgusted him.

But how could he not want her back? Nights without the divine warmth of her body beside him? Days without the anticipation of her waiting for him at home? The home he had made for her. And worst of all, to lose Louisa, the child he had loved as his own from the moment she was born—it was unendurable.

He should not have trusted her. Why had he not been more vigilant? How was it he could read and measure every minor bump and fissure on a flat landscape, yet he failed to detect the signs of her perfidy? Whatever misgivings had arisen in his mind, he'd chosen to dismiss, preferring to convince himself that he could make her love him. When she'd questioned him about the Irish in Spitalfields, or when she'd gazed into space but never at him, never caught his eye in flirtatious play—he ought to have realized she wouldn't stay. She'd given away the kitten he'd bought her, allowed his gifts of flowers to wither. There was the sharp tone, the sporadic sarcasm; instead of reprimanding her for her insolence, he'd preferred, in his complacency, to believe they added spice to their marriage.

And yet she had given him no concrete cause to doubt her. Supper was on the table each day when he got home, the floor was swept, the bed made, water and coal replenished. Louisa appeared to be thriving. How could he have known?

All day he raged. Self-pity fought with self-righteousness, sorrow with anger, longing with contempt. At suppertime, he threw away his bread and cheese, went down to the tavern, bought a bottle of cheap gin. Back in the attic room, he downed two shots in quick succession. He was not used to hard liquor, and the drink cramped his stomach into a tight knot. Like a twisting knife. A knife in the heart would kill the execrable Jack. He could run the man through with it, or shoot him with his musket, and take back his wife and child. He put his head in his hands. He was not a killer—that was fantasy.

His head spun from nausea and more cramps tore his stomach. Bent double, he sat on a chair, his head between his knees. He could not hold her if she willed otherwise. And he could not compete with a man like Jack. The heart of a woman like Catherine was too big, too deep, too passionate for a commonplace man like him to contain. She'd talked of freedom. He remembered what she told him, the day he found her in St. Giles. Her dream, of being a bird flying high, then she'd fall, become mired in mud and wake up gasping; she could not be trapped, not her. She could not be tamed. He took another shot of gin and lay, fully clothed, exhausted, on the bed.

That night Catherine and Jack appeared to him in a dream as red demons, oozing mucus; their long, white teeth burrowing into his abdomen. They consumed his insides and left a hole, where Louisa lay fast asleep, cradled by blood and sinew. They grabbed the baby, pulled her out, and laughing, plunged their fists into his hollow abdomen. He cried out, and his cry woke him.

Church bells tolled in the distance. Sunday morning. He would miss services today. But as he lay groggy and drained, he realized the dream had done something to him—expunged his self-pity and helpless rage, and cleared away the mess and detritus of the last two days. In place he felt a new energy and sense of purpose rise. This was a challenge that required military discipline to tackle. As an experienced military engineer, who had crossed raging rivers, scaled sheer cliffs, and waded knee-deep through bogs, this should be an easy assignment. He got up, straightened his clothes and washed his face.

From the drawer of his desk, he took a sheet of paper and a quill, dipped the quill in the inkwell, and began to write. He laid out his plan with the precision of the mapmaker he was. Clear lines connected one action to another. Potential barriers were identified, options considered, clear paths drawn up with a network of linkages.

His first course would be to find a sympathetic lawyer to plead his case. He would ask everyone he knew at the barracks and write to Uncle George. The case would be built on putting a child in moral jeopardy, in an unstable, peripatetic environment by a mother who had clearly exhibited wanton behaviour and child neglect. He wrote down the name of the theatre and the name of Jack's circus and made a note to find out their itinerary. The lawyer would likely advise a full investigation of Jack's background; he might need to hire a special investigator. Money for legal and investigative services would be required; he had the nest egg his father's tailor shop provided, and might need to dip into that. He placed several £ signs at key points on the paper and underlined them.

He would need witnesses. Neighbours? Aunt Fanny? (He remembered that scene at the wedding.) Though reluctant to call on Ellen Booth, the wetnurse could testify to Catherine's neglect of her child. He would need time to pursue his case, and would claim family illness to beg compassionate leave from his commanding officer.

By early afternoon he had filled two sheets of paper with his neat handwriting. He rose to prepare an early supper of bread and cheese and a glass of porter, and sat down to review his plan and consider any gaps. He made some further notations as he ate and drank, and then heard a light tap on the door. He ignored it—just the wind—and continued to read and amend his plan. The knock came again, louder. He turned the paper over, laid the pen down. Who might be coming to the door at this time on a Sunday afternoon? He got up, smoothed his hand over his hair, wandered to the door, and opened it. Jack stood on the threshold of the room. In his arms he held Louisa, her basket at his feet.

Edward stared at him, stupefied. "You … what … ?"

Jack gave a sheepish grin. "Well, you see, Corporal, she changed her mind, did Catherine. She thought about what you said, about the circus not being the right sort of place to bring up a child and all, and, well, she agreed with you. So, here I am—delivering the baby to you."

Jack held the baby at arm's length. Louisa held out her fat little hands to Edward, and Edward scooped her up, rubbed his face against hers.

"Aah," said Jack, still grinning foolishly, "see, she likes you. Well, so there you are then."

A dozen or more questions formed in Edward's mind. Why? How? What had made Catherine change her mind? Why had she sent Jack and not come herself? Was Jack telling the truth or another of his lies? And most of all, what kind of a man was this Jack to hand over his own child and stand there grinning like an idiot? But he would not question the varmint, for whatever he might tell him would likely be a lie. He felt almost nauseous with disgust but held Louisa close to his chest and breathed in the sweet warmth of her; he would never let her near this demon again.

"Well, then," said Jack again. He shifted from one foot to another, and held his hat to his chest, apparently reluctant to leave. Edward was not going to ask him in. He would not sit down with him and talk man to man. But the fellow was waiting for something.

"So, I'll be on my way." Jack said. "Just I thought, you know, a little consideration might not go astray ... " He rubbed his thumb and forefinger together. "If you know what I mean, just to help me and Catherine out a bit."

The penny dropped with a thud. Now the words formed on Edward's lips, and he spat them out. "You, sir, are a good-for-nothing scoundrel. You will leave my house right now and you will not dare to show your face again, or I shall have the law on you."

Jack backed away. "Righto," he said. "I'll be off then."

Jack clattered down the stairs. Halfway down, he stopped and turned towards Edward. Edward held on tight to Louisa.

"I do love her, you know," Jack said. "Catherine. I'll treat her right, honest I will. I won't let her down again. It's just that ... "

Edward closed the door. He cupped his hand over the downy

softness of Louisa's head. She snuggled her face into his shoulder. The front door downstairs opened with a creak and then clicked shut.

FIFTEEN

The summer of '45 was cold and wet. Rivulets of rain ran down the gutters without cease. It was impossible to get the laundry dry, for no sooner did the sun come out than the rain returned. Much of Mary's time was spent heating irons to take the worst of the damp from the sheets. Windows rattled in the wind, condensation ran down the inside of the walls, mould grew in the corners and crevices of the house, and the hall was slippery and wet from the boarders' dripping boots. The constant wind and rain got on Mrs. Scroggs's nerves.

"This weather is doing me in," she said. "I'm not one to complain, everyone knows that, but I can't stand this weather. It makes me short-tempered, and I'm not one to be short-tempered. Patience of Job, I have, that's what people tell me. 'How do you do it, Mrs. Scroggs,' they say, 'with all you have to put up with, all them girls coming and going and the gentlemen in and out with their dripping boots and soaking clothes?' Well, I've a peaceful and pious soul and it gives me patience, but this weather is doing me in."

As July and August rained on, Mary and the other staff saw little of Mrs. Scroggs's self-proclaimed patience. She was grumpy and crabby, and increasingly unleashed her displeasure on Mary, snapping at her, blaming her for the other servants' ineptitude. Her changed attitude puzzled Mary, for until the wet weather began, Mrs. Scroggs had treated her as one of her favourites. Now she wondered if she was about to be let go. She confided her concerns to Martha.

"I know the weather is miserable, but I can't help feeling there's something I've done to upset Mrs. Scroggs."

Martha shrugged. "Wouldn't worry about it, Mary. It's happened before. We've all seen it. She has her favourites, then she goes off them. Who knows why? Could be the weather, but I doubt it. If you want my opinion, it's all about that Miss Everett."

"What? Why?"

"Well, think about it, Mary. You and Miss Everett, you've become a bit too close for the old bag's liking, haven't you? You've cut old Ma Scroggs out of it. She's just jealous, that's all. The old green-eyed monster. She wants to be the only one in Miss Everett's pocket."

Mary was astounded.

"But why? Oh, Martha, no! In any case, why would she not just have one of the other servants take care of Miss Everett?"

"Oh, she won't do that. She'd never admit she's jealous. Besides, if Miss Everett says she wants you to go on bringing her meals, then that's the way it'll be, 'cause she won't want to upset Miss Everett. That old witch has got a few things over Mrs. S., you mark my words." Martha inclined her head towards Mary and dropped her voice. "You know what Cook says, about how it was Miss Everett, not Mr. Scroggs, what put up the money for this house. The thing is, what I say is they need each other. This big house ain't much good to Miss E. seeing as she's an invalid. So she hires Mrs. S. to run it for her, and she gets to stay in her own room mixing up her witch's brew. But she owns the house, got the upper hand she has, and can send Mrs. S. packing any time she wants."

"Oh, Martha, you don't know Miss Everett. She's no witch. And she's as gentle as a lamb."

Martha sniffed. "Well, you asked me my opinion. I'm just saying ... "

Martha was entitled to her opinion. And it might be true that Miss Everett owned the house. She was, after all, an educated woman of some breeding, and it made sense for the house to have been an inheritance. Certainly, having Mrs. Scroggs run the place as a boarding house was a benefit to both women, for it provided income for Mrs. Scroggs and a home for Miss Everett. Mary saw nothing about the arrangement to make her respect Miss Everett any less than she did, or Mrs. Scroggs for that matter.

Martha's theory that Mrs. Scroggs was jealous did give her pause, though 'jealous' was perhaps too strong a term. That Mrs. Scroggs was wary of Mary's growing closeness to Miss Everett, or felt possessive of her friend, might be closer to the truth.

Mary didn't want to cause trouble between the two women, and wanted to reassure Mrs. Scroggs that her relationship with Miss Everett was no threat to her. As the summer grew old, the work in the boarding house became less onerous. With fewer gentlemen and less work cleaning and lighting fires, Mary put yet more effort into pleasing Mrs. Scroggs, while continuing to find time to linger in Miss Everett's room on her thrice-daily visits.

One morning Miss Everett greeted Mary with a broad smile. Laid out on her table was a collection of leather-bound books that looked brand new.

"Mary, do you remember when Polly and Martha announced their engagements, and you told me your pet name?"

Mary nodded. It was the day she'd wept like a child in Miss Everett's room. The memory still embarrassed her. "Little Sparrow," Mary said.

"Little Sparrow," Miss Everett said, "with her broken wing."

Mary felt her throat constrict. That tender spot was still there, under the surface, and it still ached. She'd hidden it from everyone else, but of course, Miss Everett knew. She had always known. Mary bit her lip and turned her head away. She didn't want to cry again in front of Miss Everett.

Miss Everett invited Mary to sit down, and indicated the books on the table. "Mary, see these books. They expound a wonderful new discovery to which I am party."

"A discovery?"

"A healing life force or energy. Mysterious to most mortals but I am one of the few on whom the gift of this power had been bestowed."

"A life force? What is that?"

"It is called animal magnetism and it was discovered by a very great doctor in Austria. His name was Franz Anton Mesmer. Hence, many people call this power 'mesmerism' after Dr. Mesmer, who first learned how to harness this force to heal the broken spirit."

Mary shifted her chair a little closer to Miss Everett. "Heal the spirit," she said. "It sounds like something Jesus might do."

"You are right. In fact, according to many believers, myself included, animal magnetism was the source of our Lord Jesus's miracles. He was the greatest of all magnetizers. Remember how He cast out evil spirits, and brought Lazarus back to life?"

Mary frowned. She knew her Bible stories, and she found what Miss Everett was saying slightly discomforting.

"So ... to practice this ... this thing ... isn't it ... a ...?"

"A blasphemy?" Once again, Miss Everett had read her mind. "Not at all, my dear. Have no fear of any trespass on your faith." Miss Everett smiled and leaned forward to pat Mary's shoulder.

"And ... Satan?"

"Satan dare not be pulled in by these magnetic forces. He runs screaming from them. Mesmerism heals; it does not destroy. The angels protect it."

This was intriguing. "Tell me more, Miss Everett. How does it work?"

"I can show you if you like. I can help to heal that tender spot on your wing." She told Mary to sit directly facing her and relax her arms by her sides.

"Close your eyes and breathe deeply," said Miss Everett, "in, out, in, out. Feel the rise and fall of your chest. Concentrate on your breath. Now, open your eyes, slowly, and look into mine."

Mary did as she was told. Miss Everett stretched out her hands towards Mary and gently fluttered her fingers up and down. Mary followed the movement, nodding her head up and down to the rhythm of Miss Everett's hands, until, after several minutes, she became drowsy and her eyes closed again.

"Now let your mind drift into the void of space; allow it to seek the healing fluid that connects all life to the stars and moon."

With her eyes now closed, Mary sensed Miss Everett moving to stand behind her; she smelt her lavender perfume and her honeyed breath, and felt her fingers touch her head. As softly as leaves falling from an autumn tree, Miss Everett's fingers began to massage Mary's forehead and temples, reaching deep, touching her mind, unravelling twisted sinews and painful knots, then moving to the back of her neck and her shoulders, leaving her with a profound sense of well-being. Too soon, Miss Everett moved her hands away and whispered to her to open her eyes. She had returned to her chair in front of Mary.

"You are feeling relaxed, contented, almost sleepy, are you not?" she said.

"Yes, I am. What ... what did you do, Miss Everett? What happened?"

"I mesmerized you. I used the powers of animal magnetism to relax your spirit, rebuild your strength, and help you heal."

"Does this mean I'm fully healed?"

"Nearly. Perhaps not completely. But I think you are now strong enough to fly."

"Fly? Where would I fly to?"

"Where would you like to fly to?"

Mary considered Miss Everett's words. Since coming to London, she had lived day by day, learning London ways, keeping her mind on her work, and pushing away memories of Somerset and her former life.

She had not seriously considered the possibility of going anywhere else. Besides, where would she go? To another boarding house, another housemaid's position? What other choice was there? Going back to Somerset was not an option. She would never return to midwifery. And for all Mrs. Scroggs's recent bad humour, she had been given a level responsibility over the new servants, and she did feel settled and comfortable here. She enjoyed the companionship of the other servants, the special friendship with Miss Everett, and the pleasant Sunday outings with her brother, Thomas. But now Miss Everett had made her question if she wanted to stay in Mrs. Scroggs's house indefinitely.

Miss Everett patted Mary's hand, and glanced at the tray containing her breakfast cup and plate. This signalled it was time for Mary to clear her meal things and leave. Still pondering Miss Everett's words, she rose reluctantly, took the tray, and closed the door behind her.

As she started down the stairs to the kitchen, she became vaguely aware of a male voice coming from the hall. She peeked around the bannister. Mrs. Scroggs was in conversation with a young man in a soldier's uniform. He removed his cap and bowed stiffly to her. She seemed to be acquainted with him and greeted him with enthusiasm. Another new boarder? There were several vacant rooms and if he were to stay tonight she would have to get one of them ready. Time to stop daydreaming. There was work to be done.

SIXTEEN

"My wife is dead." The words spilled from Edward as he stood in Mrs. Scroggs's parlour, holding his cap to his chest and bowing stiffly. He hadn't intended to say them. Not like that. He hadn't known quite what he would say, but as he left the attic room, crossed the bridge, and headed to Soho, the story emerged and ran through his head.

He had married a fine woman, he'd say, not long after he had last seen Mrs. Scroggs, when he had inquired after the Irish girl. He had met his wife through the church before his stint in Ireland, he'd tell her, and she had waited for him. He married her as soon as he returned. She was everything a wife should be: clean, attentive, clever with her hands, still with her voice.

He'd pondered whether to suggest a comparison with his sister, Sarah, whom Mrs. Scroggs had so admired, but decided it would be going too far to implicate that good woman in his concoction. Though perhaps it was his sister's swift death that sparked the idea of claiming his own dear wife had died tragically just last week, from a fever that swept through his tenement, and now he was left alone to raise their infant child, and was turning to the good Mrs. Scroggs for her assistance in finding a nursemaid.

Louisa he had left in the care of Ellen Booth, much against his better judgement. Mrs. Booth was a rough woman and had, moreover, been complicit in Catherine's betrayal. But the baby needed milk, of which Ellen had copious quantities, and she had after all been instrumental in helping him locate Catherine, even though on pain of him informing her husband she had been wetnursing a baby with no monetary compensation.

Edward hoped any deleterious effect of the milk from a woman like Mrs. Booth on the baby's character would be reversed by the love and care he would give the child. As a wetnurse, she could continue to feed Louisa until she was weaned—he would come to an arrangement to compensate her—but he would need a nursemaid of excellent character to care for the child's moral upbringing.

Leaving Louisa with Mrs. Booth was also a prudent move. Better for Mrs. Scroggs not to see Louisa, now five months old, lest she wonder about her size. He hoped Mrs. Scroggs would not ask too many questions about dates. If she did, he would have to compound his story with further untruths about when the baby was born, for the truth would reveal the child was conceived months before Edward returned to England and purportedly married his paragon of virtue.

Edward brushed aside his feelings of guilt at the thought of the blatant lie he was to tell Mrs. Scroggs. Louisa had unleashed in him such protectiveness, and Catherine and Jack such rage, that he would do anything to keep the child—lie, cheat, even steal. Now that he had her back, he would not let her go.

There was one more precaution he had taken. Instead of going directly to Mrs. Scroggs's house, he took a detour to Astley's Amphitheatre. He pulled his collar up and his cap down, and peeked through the main door into the foyer. All was quiet. He'd counted on performances not taking place until afternoon. He relaxed and walked into the foyer with an authoritative manner. The box office was open; a man sat behind a desk, and leaning against the wall behind him was a coarse-looking woman with rouged lips and cheeks.

"Can I help you, sir?" asked the man in the box office.

"Tell me, my good man. Has the circus left already?"

Before the man could answer, the woman behind him leant forward and thumped her fist on his desk.

"Bleedin' right it's gone, ain't it?" she said. "Left for Liverpool this morning, it did."

Good news. But he needed to know more.

"What about the performers? All left too? The strongman, for example?"

"That bastard," said the woman, "took off with his new fancy woman, didn't he? Left me in the lurch. I was his assistant, wasn't I? Not no more. Not once he got his new bit of fluff. The bugger."

The tension lifted from Edward's shoulders, but the pain in his chest remained. Catherine had gone. She was with Jack now. But at least Louisa was safe. He left the foyer and continued on his way to Soho.

Mrs. Scroggs beamed when she saw him, and invited him in to share a pot of tea. In her parlour, he stood to attention before her, yet felt his resolve begin waver in the face of her commanding presence. A slight panic took hold of him. He had lied to her before, about Catherine being a poor girl thrown out by a wicked employer, and Mrs. Scroggs had taken her in, with less than satisfactory results. Now he was about to deliver an even greater lie. She indicated a chair, but he declined; standing made him feel more in control. While Mrs. Scroggs called for tea, he ran through his story in his mind. The tea arrived. Mrs. Scroggs poured, insisting he sit down. And Edward's words spilled out unbidden.

"My wife is dead."

Mrs. Scroggs looked taken aback. "What?"

He ought to have said, "A terrible family tragedy has befallen me," or "My dear wife has passed on," or even, "My dearest angel of the home has gone to a better place." Those were the proper sorts of words to use on the occasion of a bereavement, but what came out was that bald, stark announcement.

Mrs. Scroggs sat for a few moments to digest Edward's words, murmuring, "Dead, you say? So young. And I didn't even know you were married."

Mrs. Scroggs's bewildered response gave Edward a gambit, and he started to recount his story with a renewed confidence. Oh, he assumed she had known of his marriage, he said. He was sorry she had not been informed. No, he had not been keeping it a secret, merely that his bride came from south of the river, where her family lived, and they rarely had an opportunity to travel north. And now, this terrible turn of events, so sudden, to lose such a wife, and what was he to do with their child, this poor, motherless baby girl, so young, so helpless? By the time he had finished, he was almost enjoying the pained look on Mrs. Scroggs's face.

"You poor boy," she said. "And when was the baby born?"

Edward steeled himself to answer the question he'd hoped she would not ask.

"Was she a Monday's child, or a Tuesday's child? Perhaps she was born on a Sunday and will be healthy, wealthy, bonny, and gay."

Edward smiled with relief. Hoping to divert her from further questions, he said that she was still a very young baby, not yet weaned, but that he had been able to engage a wetnurse for her.

"Oh!" said Mrs. Scroggs, sitting upright in her chair. "You want to be careful Edward; some of those women are not to be trusted. Make sure she doesn't add a dose of gin to the mother's milk. You keep an eagle eye on her. I hope you haven't farmed her off to the country for nursing."

"No, she's a good woman, lives in my tenement building. I know her husband." Edward winced inwardly at his own words. "But I will need a nursemaid, which is why I have called on you to help. I can't pay much—I have a little money saved from my father's tailor shop, but my soldier's wage is meagre. There's a family in my building willing to provide room and board for a nursemaid for a reasonable rent, but I shall have to pay the wetnurse too."

Mrs. Scroggs scratched her chin. "Hmm."

"I trust you, Mrs. Scroggs. I know you to be a God-fearing Christian woman, and you know all the families in this neighbourhood. I do hope you can think of someone who can help me with this poor baby."

Edward almost relished his own obsequiousness; if it would help Louisa, he didn't mind crawling to the likes of Mrs. Scroggs. Whatever else she was, or claimed to be, Edward was confident of her judgement in the matter of domestic affairs.

"Hmm," said Mrs. Scroggs again.

Edward inclined his head towards her, encouragingly.

"Well. I think I might be able to help you. I've got a girl who's about ready to move on. I've trained her up as best I can for housemaid work, but I've had it in mind to let her go. She's been here since last September, and she's taking up space now that I could give to a local girl. She's a pious young woman, I'll say that for her. You won't catch her in any hanky-panky, not like some of the girls who come here. And I've heard it said she once worked as a country midwife. Not much call for that sort of thing here in the city, but it does mean she probably knows something about babies. I think she might just suit you fine. Come back about noontime and we'll get it all settled."

Edward went to a nearby coffee shop. He had told the lie, convinced Mrs. Scroggs, and now he felt drained. He brooded over his coffee, and relived the past forty-eight hours. Too much emotion, too much anguish, too much sorrow. He could not go on like this. He must put Catherine and Jack and his abortive marriage behind him. His one concern now was Louisa. It was time for him to chart a new course, and build a decent and normal future path for Louisa. He looked at the clock on the wall. It was almost noon. He paid for his coffee, picked up his cap and made his way back to Mrs. Scroggs's house.

SEVENTEEN

"A baby?" Mary said. "I'm to look after a baby?"

This was not what she expected when Mrs. Scroggs called her in. She had prepared herself to be reprimanded for something she had done or neglected to do in her work, and had wracked her brains to know what it might be. Had one of the gentlemen complained? Was breakfast too long coming, or too hot, or too cold? Were the bedsheets not properly laundered?

For weeks, Mary had received only scowls from her employer. But when she entered the room, Mrs. Scroggs was all smiles. She explained that a position of nursemaid had opened up in a very respectable household and she had recommended Mary for the position. The mother of the child had died tragically from a fever, she said, and the child was not yet weaned. A wetnurse had been hired, but Mary would be in charge of the child's moral upbringing. The father was a fine young man, she said. "I've known him since he was a little nipper. And now, the poor boy, what a terrible thing to be so young and left to raise his child alone. His whole family, I tell you, are tragic. His sister, well, you couldn't have met a more pious woman. Like a saint she was ..."

Mrs. Scroggs chattered on, but Mary scarcely listened. All she heard was that she was to be in charge of a baby. The turn of events was not something she could ever have imagined. She thought her heart might explode, so hard and fast was its beat. When she left Somerset, she believed she would never hold another baby in her arms, but now she was to have a child here in London to love and to nurture. Not her own baby, but a baby nonetheless, and a poor, orphaned mite; what a wonderful opportunity God had given her! She beamed at Mrs. Scroggs and clasped her hands to her chest.

There was a knock at the door. "Come in, come in Corporal," said Mrs. Scroggs. The door opened and a young man in a soldier's uniform, erect and unsmiling, entered the room. Mary recognized him as the man she'd seen earlier at the front door with Mrs. Scroggs.

"This," said Mrs. Scroggs, "is Corporal Harris, the father of the child, and your new employer, Mary. Edward, this is the girl I told you about. I do believe you will find her very satisfactory."

The soldier nodded towards Mary, and she gave him an awkward curtsy. She hardly knew where to look or what to do with her hands, which were now damp with perspiration, and she could feel her face had become hot.

The man glanced towards her and spoke. "I assume Mrs. Scroggs has explained my situation to you. She assures me you will be a reliable and competent nursemaid. But to be clear, I shall demand nothing less than your absolute devotion to my daughter's upbringing. Do you understand?"

Absolute devotion! Mary closed her eyes briefly, then looked the soldier in the eye and said, "Oh yes, sir, I understand very well. Thank you, sir."

Corporal Harris nodded at Mary again, thanked Mrs. Scroggs, and left.

Mrs. Scroggs closed the parlour door behind him, and turned to smile at Mary. "You're a lucky girl, Mary. I knew you'd be right for this job."

"Oh, but are you sure I am acceptable to Corporal Harris?"

Mrs. Scroggs lifted her eyes to the heavens. "Who am I, Mary?" she said. "Mrs. Scroggs, right? People know me around here, and they trust me. Corporal Harris trusts me. I told you, didn't I, that I've known him all his life. Lived just around the corner from here, on Rupert Street. He cuts a fine figure in his uniform, doesn't he? I knew his sister well—what a fine woman she was. Died young, you know. Oh, she had a lovely funeral. His Uncle George pulled out all the stops, black feathers on the horses and all, and the neighbours lining the streets to pay respects. And that poor boy, now a widower and so young. Such a shame. Seems tragedy follows some people around like a shadow. First his mother, then his father. A good man, his father. A tailor, you know, and respected hereabouts. His shop's still there in Rupert Street, run now by a Mr. Charles. But it was his sister who brought him up. Well, he couldn't have asked for a finer person to raise him. Such high morals, she had, and so does he. I was the one, you know, who laid out her body, called for the undertaker. People in this neighbourhood trust me, you see. And, now, who does Mr. Harris—I should say, Corporal Harris—come to when he's in trouble? Mrs. Scroggs, of course. So don't you worry, he'll like you just fine. You won't let me down, mind?"

"Oh no, Mrs. Scroggs, I won't. I don't know how to thank you. You've been so good to me." The words gushed and Mary could not stop them, even though Mrs. Scroggs was no longer smiling, and had jerked her head towards the door.

"Go and get your things packed up. You'll start straightaway. You'll be boarding with a family in Southwark, in the same building as the father and the baby."

So soon. Mary thanked Mrs. Scroggs again and left. Martha was outside the door when she emerged. She must have been half-listening, and she grinned at Mary as Mary outlined what Mrs. Scroggs had proposed.

"Good for you," said Martha, cheerful as ever. She took Mary's arm affectionately as they went down to the kitchen together. "Polly's gone, I'm leaving. Now you. Mrs. Scroggs is cleaning house. Wonder who she'll get in here to take your place. She's always got someone up her sleeve. No one ever stays here for long. Well, I'm happy for you, Mary. You don't want to stick around here forever, waiting on that queer old stick in the back room."

Miss Everett! Mary couldn't wait to tell her the news. She ran back upstairs, tapped gently on Miss Everett's door, and opened it a crack. Miss Everett beckoned her in, and indicated a chair.

"So you're leaving us, Mary," she said. Miss Everett's words came back to her. She had said she was ready to fly. How was it that Miss Everett always seemed to know about things before they happened?

"I suppose Mrs. Scroggs told you. Isn't it wonderful? But, oh, Miss Everett, I shall so miss our chats."

Miss Everett smiled. "No need for parting to be sorrowful," she said. "The French have a term they use at times like this. They say *au revoir.*"

"O revar?" Mary tried to imitate Miss Everett.

"It means 'until we meet again.' Nothing is forever, Mary. You and I shall meet again."

"I would like that very much."

"I cannot say when. But I will be here for you when you need to return. And you will need to return. Now you'd better get ready before Mrs. Scroggs comes after you." The glow Mary always felt in Miss Everett's company was now magnified by the joyful anticipation of her new job.

Mary got Martha to help her write a note to Thomas. She knew he would be delighted with her news, and he was, sending his enthusiastic response by return post. "I hope, dear Little Sparrow, that your new employer will condescend to allow you to attend church with me on Sundays," he added. Martha giggled and rolled her eyes as she read the pompous words, but Mary was too full of happy anticipation to notice.

By late afternoon she was packed and ready to leave. Corporal Harris sent a boy to take Mary and her belongings to her new position. The walk to Southwark was not arduous. The boy took her across the bridge and entered a tall tenement. At the top of four flights of stairs, he stopped and knocked on the door of an attic room.

A male voice said, "Come in."

Corporal Harris sat at a desk, a pen in his hand, a sheet of paper before him. She hoped he was not writing instructions for her, for she did not want to confess to her lack of facility at reading. He looked up as she entered, his pen poised in his hand. Now that she was calmer, she was able to observe him properly. Sandy hair, blue eyes, regular features, not very tall, a serious face. Of course, for he must be in deep mourning, hence his passive expression. Her heart went out to him. She curtsied, and looked down.

Corporal Harris got up, gave the boy a coin, and walked to the far end of the room, where there was a cradle. Mary felt her heart flutter. The corporal picked the baby up and held her so gently and lovingly that Mary immediately warmed to this poor man, widowed so young, who obviously loved his child deeply.

When he spoke at last, his voice was without expression. "This is Louisa, your charge. I have arranged for you to board with a family on the third floor. The Dawsons. A potter and his wife and daughter, both dressmakers, quite respectable. Two grown sons. You will share a bed with the daughter. That is the best I can do for you until the child is weaned, as I have to hire a wetnurse."

Mary had got used to having her own bed. She had only ever shared with her mother, and never with a stranger. But she would make the best of it for the baby's sake. The corporal continued.

"You will have sole charge of the child during the daytime as I must take the train each day to my garrison in Woolwich, and do not get home until tea time. You will then bring the baby to me, and she will sleep here, and you will return to the Dawsons for your supper. You will have Sundays off to spend however you please.

"I have one more very important rule. The wetnurse—her name is Ellen Booth. She lives in the basement. You are not to have any conversation with her, you are not to discuss my business with her, or speak about Louisa to her, and you are never to mention Louisa's mother, my dear departed wife. You will hand her Louisa only as and when Louisa needs feeding, and then you will take her back. Once the child is weaned, you will have no further communication with Mrs. Booth. Do you understand me?"

"Yes, sir." Mary knew the reputation of wetnurses, and understood this loving father's concern for the moral and physical well-being of his child. Some of these women gave their charges gin or laudanum to quieten them, or left them for hours while they went to the tavern and came back reeking of liquor. Very few of them were to be trusted and a prudent mother kept careful watch on her child when obliged to hire a wetnurse.

Mary was only too pleased to comply with the father's rules, but she was finding it hard to stand still and keep her hands by her side, for she longed to take the baby from him. The baby began to cry, and as if acting from instinct alone, Mary rushed over and held out her arms. "Oh please, sir, may I?" she said.

For the first time, she saw the glimmer of a smile on the corporal's face as he handed her Louisa. As soon as Mary took her, Louisa stopped crying, reached out a hand, and curled it around Mary's finger. Mary gazed at her, taking in every inch of her round face framed with tiny golden curls, her soft, white skin, her eyes as blue as cornflowers. She touched her finger to the baby's cheek, gave the chubby little feet a gentle squeeze. How sweet she was, how perfectly formed. She smiled at the baby, and the baby smiled back, a melting smile that lit her face and set Mary's heart pounding. Mary pulled the baby close and breathed the warm milky scent of her face and neck. "Sweet child," she murmured, "my sweet Little Sparrow."

EIGHTEEN

Edward had always considered himself an honourable man, so he was surprised at the way he was able to pile one untruth upon another. It was as though Catherine's betrayal had transported him to a place where lies and deceit could be justified, so long as they matched the lies and deceit served on him by Catherine and her vagabond lover.

After he had announced Catherine's death to Mrs. Scroggs, it was easy to repeat the lie to all and sundry. When his colleagues showed sympathy, he expressed pious thanks for their concern. He did not flinch when neighbours enquired as to why they had not seen Catherine about. When he told them in short measure of her sudden passing, they said nothing, too shocked to respond, too shy to probe about funeral arrangements. He wrote to Uncle George with the news, and received a long sympathetic epistle in response. Fanny wanted to come and take care of him and the baby, but Edward quickly wrote back to say he had made arrangements and all was well.

His final touch was particularly ingenious, he thought; a gesture to the fashion for creating jewellery from the hair of departed loved ones. In a small box in his desk drawer was the lock of hair he had stolen from Catherine while she slept on the ship from Ireland. He hired a local woman to weave this into a watch chain, which he wore ostentatiously on his waistcoat. Since he had no watch, he attached the end to a button, which he hid in his waistcoat pocket.

The lies, he told himself, were all for Louisa. He could neither allow her to be raised by vagabonds, nor grow up to learn her mother had abandoned her. Further, by putting it about that Catherine was dead, he could avoid the shame and humiliation of people knowing his wife had run away with a circus performer. Instead, he could mourn her as dead, and pour all the passion he once had for

Catherine into loving and caring for her daughter. Before long, he almost believed the fiction to be fact.

Dealing with Ellen Booth, the wetnurse, had required some forethought. She was the only person who knew Catherine had run away, and she was unlikely to believe the story of her sudden death from fever. Threatening her might work, especially if he invoked her husband. That ploy had worked the day Catherine left and he got Ellen to spill the beans.

But despite his contempt for Ellen's type, it was not in Edward's nature to issue threats. A more effective approach, he decided, was to buy her silence with money, a small weekly emolument for her continuing services; that would keep her quiet, satisfy her brutish husband, and provide sustenance for Louisa. Now that everyone believed Catherine was dead, even if Ellen did talk, they were not likely to set much store by the gossip of a woman like her. Edward was well-respected in the neighbourhood and at the barracks, and he suspected people would sooner believe him than the vulgar woman who inhabited the dank cellar of Edward's tenement.

Louisa appeared to thrive, growing into a chubby, rosy, happy infant, and his concerns that the quality of Ellen Booth's milk might pose moral danger appeared unfounded. Any future deleterious effects would, he hoped, be counteracted by the solicitous care provided by Mary Piper, the nursemaid, who was proving most satisfactory. She had a strong body, large firm hands, and was plain enough that she was unlikely to become distracted by the attentions of any young men who might cross her path. She was efficient, punctual, and she and Louisa seemed to have made an immediate connection. Edward had steered his life back to an orderly course. His status, his reputation, and his self-respect were intact. And he had Louisa.

Only then did he realize how on edge he'd been during his marriage to Catherine, uncertain of her loyalty, and full of niggling self-doubt about whether she could ever truly love him. Those doubts confirmed, he set his mind to relegating Catherine, and the brief, heady months when she had held him in thrall, to that place in memory where dreams evaporate into the light of a waking dawn.

By Michaelmas, a comfortable routine had been established. Each evening, Mary brought Louisa to him, and sat demurely while he dandled the baby on his knee. Then she washed the baby, swaddled her, and readied her for her cradle before leaving for the Dawsons. Louisa slept well, and Edward watched over her until he too fell asleep. Each morning, Mary arrived early to take Louisa for her feed, and Edward left for the barracks. On Sundays, Mary's brother, an inoffensive fellow called Thomas, often came to take Mary and Louisa to church, and occasionally Edward joined them, which seemed a pleasant arrangement for everyone.

It was Edward's habit to read the newspaper in the evenings over a nightcap of porter, while Mary attended to Louisa. One day in late October 1845, near to All Hallows Eve, he noticed a particular item in the newspaper. It was towards the bottom of the front page, and he might have missed it had it not mentioned Ireland. It warned of coming trouble in that land. A blight had been observed in Ireland's fields that turned the potatoes to black mush.

Crop failures, he knew, were no stranger to Ireland. There had been terrible times in the past when people in the poorest parts of Ireland actually died from hunger and the fever that came in famine's wake. Potatoes were the staple, often the only food the impoverished Irish were able to grow on their small, sub-divided plots, so news of a blight was alarming.

Edward laid his newspaper down and took a draught from his tankard. If there were to be another crop failure in Ireland, so be it. It meant nothing to him. Besides, the report said it was expected this failure would be followed by a bumper harvest in '46. That was the usual pattern—good years followed the bad. The weather had been exceptionally cold and damp this summer, so obviously, some of the potato stores had rotted. But enough would be saved until the next year's crop, so there was nothing to be concerned about. That's what the experts were saying.

Edward got up and walked to the fireplace, warming his hands against the flames. He had built a stone wall around his memories of Ireland, for they brushed too closely to Catherine. But now random images pushed through his defences. One image in particular: Catherine on the wharf at Waterford, her hands stretched out in pleading, her face glowing white against the halo of her hair. He poked the fire with such force that cinders flew onto the hearth. He stamped them out, and threw more coal on the fire.

Mary had finished swaddling Louisa and brought her to Edward. He walked her up and down in his arms, kissed her, played piggy toes with her until she gurgled and giggled with joy, and then handed her back to Mary. In Ireland, the newspaper report had said, a shipment of Indian corn was shortly to arrive, sent as relief by Mr. Peel, the prime minister. Indian corn, it said, was a nourishing alternative to potatoes. The situation in Ireland was under control.

By the spring of 1846, it was clear the situation in Ireland was far from "under control." More than half the winter stocks of stored potatoes were rotten with blight. Mr. Peel's corn had all been used, and no further relief was forthcoming as the government wrangled over repealing the *Corn Laws* and refused to release to the people the stores of grain stockpiled in Irish ports for export to England and beyond; to do so, it was claimed, would go against the established laissez-faire policy of allowing the market to prevail, which would resolve the situation without government interference. There was food in Ireland, said the newspapers, great quantities, but the stores were not for distribution to the Irish; there was hunger amid plenty. Edward threw the newspapers down, and told Mary to use them for kindling.

The next day, Mary advised Edward that Louisa was fully weaned and would no longer need Ellen Booth's services. Ellen, she said, was expecting her own child and was moving away with her husband. Edward nodded in satisfaction at the news. He need no longer worry about Ellen Booth and what she might know or do or say. That same day, Louisa took her first steps. Edward watched the delight on her face as she wobbled across the floor and fell into Mary's arms. The scene evoked in Edward a sadness he could not explain.

That night he dreamt of Catherine for the first time in months and fancied he felt the warmth of her body beside him in the bed. He woke with sweat on his brow, though cool morning air had drifted through the open window.

As he got ready for work that morning, he took the newspaper Mary had placed at the fireplace and tore it into shreds. He would allow no more newspapers in his house. He informed Mary of this, and told her to use dry leaves instead to light the fire.

But although he no longer purchased newspapers, and averted his eyes from the headlines scrawled on the billboards, he could not escape overheard conversations on the streets, on the train to and from the garrison, in the churches and taverns all through the summer and autumn of '46. The blight had returned to Ireland. The leaves of the young potato plants were turning black even before the tubers were set. The people had no food. At least three-quarters of the harvest had been lost. Workhouses in Ireland were overflowing. Peasants were being evicted for want of rent money, their homes burned to the ground.

Edward could also not escape what he saw around him on London's streets as the autumn gave way to winter. A trickle at first that one could perhaps ignore; just a few more Irish voices than usual. A few more Irish beggars. But by December, it was clear that Ireland's people were leaving their land in droves, emptying the blighted countryside like oats from a pannier, and filling London's streets. Many arrived hungry, penniless, lousy, and in rags.

Angry debates in the churches, the taverns, and the corridors of power alike pitted one side against another. Some preached compassion and demanded more action from the government. Charities were set up but were soon overwhelmed by the depth and breadth of the migrants' misery. Others blamed the Irish for their self-inflicted dependence on the lazy potato, which required little labour to produce. Many people expressed revulsion at the parlous condition of the migrants, and feared they came to take jobs from the honest working English, spread disease, commit crimes, or overburden parish relief. Edward's company, though not a fighting force, was ordered to be on standby should military action in Ireland be required to quell growing unrest. More often than not, Edward went home grim-faced and angry.

One day, just before Christmas, an agitated crowd stood around a newspaper billboard near the station. More bad news. Edward tried not to look, but before he knew it, he was among the crowd, reading the words splashed in large black letters on the billboard. "IRELAND. MASS DEATHS FROM STARVATION REPORTED." Edward hurried away to catch his train. When he got home he went straight to Louisa, telling Mary he would see to her and put her to bed.

The next day was Sunday. Mary, up early and in her Sunday best, asked Edward if he would accompany her and her brother to church for Christmas services. He glared at her, his face thunderous, and raised his hand. She shrank back in fear. But the hand was not for her, it was for himself. He covered his eyes, and swiped his hand down his face.

"Church!" he said. "Go! Just go!"

Mary lingered, stepped towards him, stepped back, then, as he shook his head and gestured to the door, she picked up Louisa and left.

Edward sat with his head in his hands. Then he rose, put on his jacket, stepped out into the street, and headed west along the river in the direction of Astley's Amphitheatre.

He didn't really think she would be there, but the only place he could think of to go to was the last place he had seen her. Since it was Sunday, only one employee stood guard in the box office. He could not tell him when or if the circus would be back, or where it was now.

"Come back tomorrow," he said. "We're always getting something new. Maybe the boss can tell you."

Edward headed home by way of a tavern. When the patrons got merry and the music started up, a woman in a red dress sidled up to take his hand into a dance. He pushed her away and left. It was for her family, he told himself, not her. He cared nothing for her. It was her sisters. They were innocent children, and she must be worried about them. Even her mother, whom she must have loved even as she reviled her. If he could find Catherine, he could help bring her sisters and mother to safety. Or perhaps she had already brought them over. In which case, there would be nothing for him to do. But he must find her to know. Then he could be satisfied.

The following evening, he returned to the theatre, but no one there could give him news of Astley's Royal Circus. It was travelling, they said. Could be anywhere—America, Yorkshire, Scotland.

"Ireland?" he asked.

"Not likely," they said. "Not with all the trouble over there."

The tavern drew Edward back that night. The woman in the red dress was not there. He sat in a corner and drank steadily until the clock struck midnight.

When he got home, Mary was asleep on the rug before the fire, Louisa in her arms. Ashamed, he lifted the child, woke Mary, and sent her downstairs to the Dawsons. This must stop, he told himself. Neither Catherine nor her family were his concern anymore. He would not allow her to bewitch him again. Louisa stirred in his arms and rested her head against his neck. He laid her in her cradle and doused the lamp. Embers from the fire still burned. He sat by the fireplace, closed his eyes, and listened to Louisa's rhythmic breathing, calm in his certainty he would not go back to Astley's Amphitheatre.

NINETEEN

From the first day of her new employment, it was clear to Mary that Corporal Harris was so deep in mourning he seemed barely aware of anything outside his own grief. He was like a man in a dungeon with no light and no hope of release. Except for Louisa, for whom he seemed to hold a fierce love, which she noted in the softening of his eyes and his mouth when she handed her to him. How great must his love for his wife have been for him to grieve so deeply, she thought. What had she been like? How had she died? He never spoke of her to Mary, but then he rarely spoke to Mary of anything, nor looked her way.

She wondered if the Dawsons, with whom she boarded, might know something of what happened. She'd found the Dawsons to be generally decent folk. Alice Dawson, with whom she shared a bed, was a friendly, inquisitive girl, if a little impertinent. She loved books and read a few chapters every night before she blew out the candle.

When Mary asked her what in the books could so hold her attention, she began reading aloud to Mary, and before long was gladly helping Mary to improve her own reading and writing. This meant Mary she could maintain a correspondence with Polly and Martha and Miss Everett. At first, she found it hard to form the words neatly and avoid ink blots, but soon became more fluent, happily writing about Louisa and her progress, and about her own delight in being her nursemaid. About Edward, she wrote only that her employer was decent and fair-minded.

Their return letters were full of news—Polly's pregnancy, Martha's wedding plans, still on but delayed again. And Miss Everett's short and cryptic notes, usually with lines of poetry that Mary found soothing but enigmatic as usual. But she found the books Alice read, with their tales of honour, gallantry, love, and sacrifice a little ridiculous.

Alice's twin brothers, boisterous and outgoing, came in and out, stopping for supper and then dashing off out again until bedtime, so Mary hardly had a chance to get to know them. Mr. Dawson was a distant, insubstantial man who, even in his chair in the corner, seemed barely present. But he was not unpleasant.

Mrs. Dawson was the hub of the family. She was a round, no-nonsense woman, her hands always busy with a needle or a cooking pot. She'd taken a shine to Louisa. "Here comes the little cherub," she'd say when Mary passed her on the stairs on her way back from the market, and Louisa would reward her with a smile and a gurgle. Louisa had begun to charm everyone who saw her. Her golden curls, her huge blue eyes, and her sunny disposition made people want to pick her up and rock her and kiss her rosebud mouth and plump cheeks.

One day, Mary dared to ask Mrs. Dawson if she had known the corporal's late wife, and, if so, did she think Louisa took after her? Mrs. Dawson had not, for she and her family were new arrivals in the building and had barely met any of the neighbours, barring the old man from next door who apparently knew everyone. It was he, presumably, who recommended the Dawsons to Corporal Harris as a suitable family for Mary to board with.

"All I know," said Mrs. Dawson, "is from what Mr. Whatsisname next door said, it was a dreadful tragedy. A beautiful woman, she was, glowing with health, he said. And suddenly, pfft! It happened awful quick, poor man."

Mrs. Dawson, it seemed, knew no more about the matter than that.

As the months passed, and Louisa grew from babe-in-arms to babbling toddler, Mary expected Corporal Harris's melancholy to lift. But that had not happened. If anything, it seemed to have deepened. She could not forget his strange response on the Sunday before Christmas when she invited him to attend church with Louisa and Thomas. And his being out when she returned; he'd never before gone out alone on Sundays. Sunday was his day to spend with Louisa. Twice in the last week, he had left in the evening and returned after midnight, his gait unsteady and alcohol on his breath. This was out of character; she'd never known him to drink anything but his evening tankard of porter. Had he been a woman rather than a man, and had he not been her employer, she might have reached out to him in friendship. Instead, helpless, she watched him grieve from afar.

One evening, as she shared a nightcap with Alice and her mother, she found herself so lost in thought that she broke her own rule of diplomacy and said, "How can I help him? He seems so lost."

Mrs. Dawson looked at her with raised eyebrows.

"Corporal Harris, she means," said Alice, catching on, "the grieving widower upstairs."

Mrs. Dawson frowned. "Help him? Good heavens, Mary, he's your employer! It's not for you to be helping him."

Mary coloured. Alice cast her a sidelong glance.

"Besides," said Mrs. Dawson, "he'll get over it. Men always do. And they don't let the grass grow for long under their feet either. He's probably out there now courting a new woman. That would explain the late nights. You just mind your own business, Mary, and don't be worrying about things that don't concern you."

That night, before they went to sleep, Alice read aloud for a while as usual and then laid her book down.

"I think," she said, "that Miss Mary Piper too often these days has a certain person on her mind."

"What on earth do you mean, Alice?"

"I think you know what I mean. And why not? He's a good man. And he's available."

"Alice, how can you speak like this? He is a widower, still in mourning for his wife. I only meant that I wish someone could help him in his grief."

"But you didn't say 'someone.' You said 'you.' You asked how *you* could help him."

Much as Mary had grown fond of Alice, she could be uncomfortably direct at times. Mary rolled over. "Time to go to sleep, Alice. Goodnight."

TWENTY

All through 1847 and into 1848, the news from Ireland became more dire by the day. Mass deaths, evictions, and burnings continued. People who could still walk rioted in the streets; those who could not withered and died in their hovels. Migrants continued to flood the streets of London, Liverpool, and all the major cities in England.

Edward no longer even tried to avoid the news. And soon could no longer suppress his longing to know what had happened to Catherine and to see her again. His good intentions withered with every mention of Ireland. He stopped even pretending it was for the sake of her sisters and mother that he had to find her. It wasn't. It was for her and her alone.

Whenever he could get away from the garrison, he returned to the theatre, but there was never any word of when the circus would be back, only that it would return at some point. Each time he stopped at a tavern on the way home and brooded in the corner over a tankard of beer. If only he could find her, talk to her, make her see sense, that Jack was a rogue who would never love her the way he, Edward did. Surely by now she must know what a terrible mistake she had made. Running away with Jack was nothing more than a youthful indiscretion that Edward would forgive. If he could make her understand how foolish she'd been, she would come back to him. They could send for her sisters and mother, and with Louisa they could be a proper family.

He didn't know if she was even still with Jack in the circus. He might well have abandoned her again. In which case, she might be living somewhere up in St. Giles, perhaps alone, in desperate need of help. He gave up on the theatre, and wandered up to St. Giles, where he kept his eyes peeled, looking, watching, glimpsing a figure here, another there—was that her, over there, hurrying along the thoroughfare, mounting an omnibus, entering a shop? Several times he was almost sure he saw her and he followed, slipping through the crowds, weaving in and out, only to realize it was not her at all, but some stranger.

In St. Giles he mingled with the ragged new arrivals from Ireland in the cellars and doorways. Thin and hungry, at least they could afford passage, but left behind others who had no option but to die of starvation or famine fever. He wanted to feel their misery in the hope it would assuage his own, but the dull ache refused to shift. There was no sign of Catherine among these blighted people.

One afternoon, he drifted east to Spitalfields, where the weavers on the ship that brought her to England might have headed. He remembered how her face had lit up when he told her it was the centre of the weaving trade. Perhaps she had gone there looking for people from Waterford. Perhaps she'd brought her sisters over to live among the weavers.

He wandered around for a while, and was accosted by a woman leaning in the doorway of a tavern, watching children playing in the street.

"Ho, soldier," she said, "look at you in your fine uniform. What are you doing here among us poor wretches?" Her speech was slurred and Edward could smell alcohol on her breath.

"Just walking. Taking the air."

"I knew a woman once, married to a soldier. Used to come here all the time. Looking for a circus. Set herself up real nice with her man, dressed up all fine like a lady. That was before ... before all this ...." The woman swept her arms out, taking in the ragged beggars in the doorways.

The sweat in Edward's armpits felt cold. His voice was urgent.

"When was this? How long ago? Was it summer or winter that you saw her? Was she alone, or was she with ... someone?"

The woman swayed and steadied herself against the wall. "Long time ago. Two years, maybe. Never comes anymore. Well, why would she? Nothing for her here, nothing but poor starving souls."

The woman stumbled off. Edward thought to stop her and interrogate her some more, but there seemed little point. It was more than two years ago that Catherine had started leaving Louisa with

Ellen and taking off each day to look for Jack. It seemed Catherine had been here, but not recently. He let the woman go, but then she turned, her hand held out.

"Spare a penny, sir? Times is hard, and they keep on coming, these folk. Every day there's more and there's not enough jobs for us all. Spare a penny. The tikes are hungry."

Edward gave her some coins. She seemed hardly able to stand. He could not judge her, any more than he could judge himself. He walked back to the river, tracking west to Westminster towards the bridge. He stopped by a tavern, drank steadily until the sky turned pink, and headed after all to the amphitheatre. One more try, then he'd leave it alone. He would.

When he arrived, he found a new poster plastered on the wall. Astley's Royal Circus was back! For one week only. There it was, after all this time. His fists curled, his nails dug into his palms. There was no picture of the strongman's act, but if he was still performing, by God he would meet him after the show, and this time he might even kill him, consequences be damned. Strike him through his miserable belly with his bayonet, watch him bleed to death. And then take Catherine back. If she was still with him. If not, he would force the man to tell him where she was before he put an end to his sorry existence.

He fumbled in his pocket—he had just enough change left for a ticket. He entered the theatre and took a seat near the front. He sat through the equestrian events, the tightrope walkers, the acrobats. An hour passed, and one act followed another.

Finally, a drumroll announced the final act. And there was the fellow, sauntering into the ring, muscles bulging, mouth an insolent curl, hair slicked back and shiny. Edward's fingers bristled to place themselves around the man's throat. He clenched his fists again and remained seated, waiting.

Then, there she was. She sidled in behind Jack, holding a skein of silver chains aloft, and strutted around him, turning this way and that to smile archly at the audience. He noted with disgust that her cheeks and lips were rouged. Her red sequined gown hugged her body in an obscene way that revealed her curves, the plumpness of her breasts as she bowed low, and the white glow of her bare shoulders. At the end of the act, she curtsied, then lifted her hem to reveal a silk-stockinged ankle. She threw the audience a coquettish grin, parted her lips, tossed her head back., winked, and ran from the ring.

Men in the audience whistled and hooted, stamped their feet, and called "Encore, encore," while women averted their eyes and opened their fans. Catherine tripped back into the ring for an encore, hand in hand with Jack. She lifted her hem again to expose her legs almost to the knee, and did a little swivelling jig.

The audience erupted again, and Catherine, as if egged on by the pandemonium, let go of Jack's hand and stalked around the perimeter of the ring, stopping here and there to flirt with the men in the ringside seats. She patted one man on the cheek, pulled another by his jacket towards her, sidled up to another and shook her shoulders at him. The men reached out their hands to her, but she ducked away skillfully before anyone could touch her. Then, in the continued uproar, she ran back to Jack, took his hand, and they bowed again to the audience and left the ring. All the while, the seductive smile had never left her face.

Edward pushed his seat back and marched out of the theatre. Despite the drink he had imbibed earlier, his head was clear, and his rage was stone cold. He took the long way home, crossing and re-crossing bridges. His brisk footsteps echoed in the rain-slicked streets. Every few minutes, he was interrupted by a wave of nausea as the image of Catherine's shameless performance swam before his eyes. Dizzy and sick to his stomach, he'd stop, clutch his abdomen, squeeze his eyes shut, and recite, "No more, no more," until the nausea faded and he was able to continue walking.

He had walked for more than an hour when a new rain began to fall, light at first, then in driving sheets. Within seconds, the road was filled with deep puddles and water gushed along the gutters. Edward stopped, removed his cap, and lifted his face to the sky. The water ran down his cheeks, poured in rivulets from his hair, soaked through his clothes. He let out a cry, part laugh, part sob, and held out his hands to the rain. People all around him hurried for shelter and stared from shop doorways at the madman standing alone in the pouring rain, his arms wide, his face upturned. He closed his eyes tight. The blindness was comforting, it bore no images, only blackness. No sounds, but the drumbeat of the rain. No feeling but the cool wetness on his cheeks.

The downpour abated and Edward, heedless of his drenched clothes, opened his eyes, turned eastward and south, and began his clipping pace again, straight towards Southwark Bridge two miles away. As he walked, he left behind him Astley's Amphitheatre, and the circus, and the disgraceful sight of Catherine, of what she had become, of what this Jack had made her become.

At Southwark Bridge he slowed, then stopped. He stood by the railing. Below him, the black river water lapped and the lightermen's boats twinkled. He ran his hands along the bridge railing. The steel was smooth and hard, the angles true and clean. A sturdy structure, engineered to last. People had returned to the streets after the downpour, and the bridge was full of pedestrians, horses and carts, omnibuses. The hour was late, but London never slept. Edward looked around him. All that he saw and heard was real. Solid. True. Real lives being lived by real people. And a future grounded in reality, not fantasy.

How had he veered so badly off course? He must regain control of his life's map, for Louisa's sake, and his own. In a few months he expected to be promoted to sergeant. Then he would be able to afford a bigger home for Louisa and nicer clothes. He would enroll her in school and would ensure she learned to read and write and study geography and history, and perhaps even Latin and French.

In a dozen or so years he'd be discharged from the military. He fancied he would sell his share of the tailor's shop to Mr. Charles, his father's old colleague who was managing the business, and use the proceeds to open a map shop in Soho—his own shop, like the one he used to visit, and which first got him interested in becoming a surveyor with the Royal Engineers. Back when his sister, Sarah, was still alive. It was an ambition he'd had for years, even as a boy, but had almost forgotten. For the first time in many months, he thought fondly of Sarah.

He shook the railing of the bridge, and observed with satisfaction that it did not budge; it was as firm as rock, iron-strong. When he had his shop, he would teach Louisa how to use the instruments and take her out to the countryside to show her the bumps and dips that translated into wavy lines on paper. She would become adept at reading and evaluating maps and would help Edward in his shop, just as Sarah used to help his father and Mr. Charles in the tailor's shop. A good life. A real life.

Louisa. Louisa. He gripped the railing again. Now that clarity had returned, he knew what he must do for Louisa, this very night. How had it taken him so long to see what was before his eyes? He turned from the bridge railings and headed home to the tenement building.

He climbed the stairs, turned the key in the lock and entered the room as he had done without thinking so many times before. Mary was waiting for him by the hearth as usual. He hung up his wet coat and cap and went to Louisa, asleep on the bed, and stroked her cheek. Then he asked Mary to sit at the table and join him for a drink. She declined the drink but came to the table. She looked at him, her eyes wide, slightly alarmed.

"What can I do for you, sir?' she asked.

Edward poured himself a tankard of beer, but did not drink it. He set it on the table and rested his chin on his hands.

"Sir?" said Mary, "are you feeling all right? Can I help you?"

Edward looked up at her. "Yes, Mary, you can. You can marry me. Will you?"

Mary gave Edward her answer the next evening. He held out one hand to Mary and the other to Louisa, cradled happily on Mary's hip, and held them tight.

"I have today received some news that may make you change your mind."

Earlier that day he'd learned he had been posted to an island in the north of Scotland to undertake a geodesic survey.

"The journey will be long and uncomfortable, and the place we're going is cold, bleak, and isolated. You may be lonely."

Mary's eyes shone. She assured Edward that such a prospect held no anxiety for her, that she was comfortable with solitude, and as his wife she would follow him wherever his career took him.

Edward gazed at Mary as if he were seeing her for the first time. He pulled back to look at her where she stood in her dull grey dress; tall, large-framed, square-jawed, muddy-complexioned, brown hair pulled back in a tight bun. No one would describe her as pretty. A plain young woman, but she surely loved Louisa as much as he did, and now as he looked at her with the child in her arms, he saw that her face took on such a glow that she could almost be described as beautiful.

"You are pure gold, Mary Piper."

The pending move to Scotland was fortuitous. He would leave London behind, through more than six-hundred miles of winding road and tossing sea, and the Scottish island would make things right. He told Mary they would post the banns as soon as they arrived. Mary did not ask why they would not marry here in London, but accepted, as she seemed to accept everything he told her. He realized she did not have a shrewish bone in her body. She was loyal, grateful, and she loved Louisa.

PART II

Stornaway, Scotland
London, England

1848-1857

TWENTY-ONE

The view from the ferry towards the Isle of Lewis was of a land of brooding indigo skies that cast shifting shadows over low, mossy, green and gold hillsides. A lonely place where cold winds rippled down to the sea, with few trees to break their course. A few modest thatched houses sparsely dotted the landscape above Stornaway, a charming town enclosed by the island's harbour, which seemed to have emerged naturally from the rocky shore and green hills that surrounded it. Mary was immediately captivated.

On arrival, Mary and Edward, with Louisa in tow, unloaded their trunk and travelled by horse and cart to their new home, a little stone cottage in the centre of town. It was smaller than the attic room in Southwark, but was cosy, and had a kitchen garden with parsley and mint and a few marigolds for Louisa to pick. Mary loved it. So, too, did Louisa. She was now nearly three years old. Daintily built and curly haired, she was a happy, outgoing child who seemed as captivated with this crisp, cold world as Mary was.

Edward was part of a larger company of surveyors and engineers, many of whom had wives with them, and in the weeks that followed, they drew Mary to their clique. They were friendly enough, but it made her sad to see how closed their minds were, roped to their own tight circle of gossip and constant complaints about the weather and the isolation and the coldness of the local people. She found herself mostly on the outside of their gatherings with little to contribute to the conversation.

Not long after their arrival, Edward was promoted to the rank of sergeant and his responsibilities increased. He spent much of his time supervising survey work on the moors and bogland with his men, tramping in the wet turf and sleeping under canvas. Trips to neighbouring islands and the mainland often kept him away for days and weeks and Mary was left alone with Louisa. To pass the time, she began to explore the town and the surrounding countryside. This land, she found, did not trumpet its majesty the way London did, with its great monuments and royal palaces. It was, rather, a place that opened to her little by little.

First, she explored the harbour in Stornaway, where she took Louisa to watch the boats rocking on the water, and the fishermen unloading their nets.

"Look at the silver fish, Louisa, see them jumping in the nets?"

Louisa would laugh and clap her hands, and the fishermen would smile and nod. Their wives stood in the doorways of the little houses that lined the harbour, hands on hips or arms folded, and exchanged shouts with the men. They spoke a strange dialect, and at first Mary had difficulty understanding them, but soon picked up on their cadence and learnt a few words from their language. They would discuss the size of the morning's catch, what kinds of fish had been caught, what price they expected to get at the market.

As Mary became a familiar sight, the fishermen's wives began to pass the time of day with her. "Cold today, mother, make sure you wrap the bairn up well," or "Nice to see a bit of sunshine, mother, but a storm's brewing for later."

Mary would ask politely if she could purchase some fish for her husband's supper.

"Of course, mother," they'd say, followed by more shouts to the men. "Find a good plump fish for the lassie here." Then they would smile at Louisa and say something to her in their language, and she would smile back and repeat their words. And they would laugh and say, "Would you listen to the little sassanach? She'll be one of us before long."

In the afternoons, she often dressed Louisa in a warm knitted smock and took her up to the moors to wander among the crofts, where the country women crouched over their gardens in their thick tweed skirts. As she became a familiar figure there as well, they would wave a greeting to her. As a country girl by birth, Mary felt comfortable walking among these women. She loved the way her feet sank into the turfy grass, and her skirt brushed against clover and gorse, leaving a mist of purple and gold on the fabric. When rain stippled her face, she held Louisa close and dry inside her cape; when the rare sun came out, Louisa toddled happily behind her, collecting stones and grasses to take back to the cottage.

In their wanderings, they discovered the ruins of castles and ancient mysterious stone circles that revealed the long history of human habitation in this seemingly lonely land. On rocky outcrops, gold and rust with lichen, she would hold Louisa fast against her, brace herself against the wind, and with the cry of the seagulls in her ears, would think that nowhere could be more heavenly than this place.

In the solitude of the moors, Mary often went over in her mind the events that had led to her happy situation. Edward's proposal of marriage had been a surprise, and she'd asked him if she could have a day to think it over. That evening she'd confided in Alice Dawson as they prepared for bed.

"It came out of the blue, Alice," she said.

"Out of the blue? Really?" Alice had said with a knowing look.

"What do you think, Alice? Should I accept?"

Alice had rolled her eyes. "You mean you haven't said yes yet? Oh really, Mary. Sometimes you are such a dolt. After all, you love him, don't you?"

Her comment made Mary blush to her roots. Alice could be very impertinent at times.

"I don't know. Do I?"

"Of course, you do. It's as clear as the nose on your face. Has been for weeks."

Mary had wondered if Alice had been too influenced by the romantic books she read. Whatever she felt for Corporal Harris was not the sort of love one found in Alice's novels. She loved Louisa, there was no doubt about that. But love Edward? She had not lost her appetite, she did not moon around all day thinking of him, there were no fireworks, the world had not grown rosy. But she did care about him, she worried about him, about how he was mired in a grief that seemed to have no remiss, and wished she could find a way to lift him out and bring him some peace. Perhaps that was love of a different grain. A quiet love that would grow deeper with time. And a love that she now realized had been growing within her, if not in Edward, for some time.

"Yes," she said, "I think perhaps I do love him, Alice. But does he love me? He didn't tell me he loved me, only that he wanted us to be married."

"What does it matter so long as he wants to marry you? You've said yourself that he's a good man and treats you with respect. You know, these books I read—they're all fantasy. Have you ever known a couple who behave like the people in those books? Look at father and mother—they barely talk to one another."

Mary listened intently and Alice continued.

"What Corporal Harris is offering you is real: security, respectability, a decent standard of living. He may not be a rich prince, but he has a regular income. Do you want to remain a servant for the rest of your life? And end up a miserable old maid? And what's more, with Edward you'll have a ready-made family! You'll never be alone in your old age. Of course you should say yes. It's a wonderful opportunity for you Mary, and I envy you. I would love to meet and marry a man like Corporal Harris."

Now, as she walked with Louisa up among the Scottish crofts, or sat knitting by the fire of their little Scottish home while Louisa played with her doll, Mary knew she had been right to accept Edward's proposal. Mary appreciated Alice's sensible attitude. She did after all know the difference between the infatuation of her storybook lovers and the true love between a husband and wife that needed deep roots to flourish. With Louisa as the enduring link between her and Edward, those roots would surely grow.

She recalled the rush as they prepared for the weeks-long journey to Lewis by coach and ferry. Thomas, beaming with pleasure at his sister's good fortune, came to help them load their bags on the coach. Edward shook his hand and patted him on the back. Mary did wonder why they could not have married before leaving London, which would have made the sleeping arrangements along the way more convenient, but Edward was adamant they would marry in Scotland. And why not? Naturally he wanted to start his new life with her away from London with its memories. She knew all about starting a new life and leaving memories behind.

A few doors down from their house on the main street was a draper's shop, run by Angus and Sally McPhee. Sally was the first island person to befriend Mary, the first to even speak to her on any topic other than the weather. She took a particular shine to Louisa, whom she presented with a wooden bobbin on a string. Louisa said, "Oh, thank you kindly, Mrs. McPhee," and gave her a smile so bright that Sally's eyebrows shot up.

"My goodness, the child looks like the fairies had a hand in her creation," Sally said. She patted Louisa on the head. "And would you look at her curls. Like coils of gold turning to copper. And her skin is so white you'd think she might glow in the dark."

Mary was acutely aware of Sally looking at her in a puzzled way, as if she could not quite believe that plain Mary could have given birth to such a lovely child. Mary touched her own dark hair self-consciously, and laughed. No reason to be coy.

"She is my stepdaughter," she said, "by my husband's first wife, now deceased."

"Ah," said Sally, as if that explained everything. Then, "You're not like the others. How come?"

"The others?"

"The other engineers' wives. You're set apart from them for sure."

Mary smiled. "I think they find it a little isolated here."

"And you do not?"

"I like solitude. I was lucky to find a few good friends in London, people I worked with. But I'm not always ... I'm afraid I'm not always very good with people."

"What people? You're well-enough liked by folks around here."

Mary was embarrassed that she had been noticed.

"I'm sorry," said Sally, seeing her discomfort. "I only meant, well, you're a woman who knows when to speak and when to hold her tongue. That's something to be admired in this town. But you always walk alone, and I wonder if you're happy here."

"Oh yes, Mrs. McPhee. I'm very happy. I couldn't wish to be anywhere in the world but here, on this island, with my husband and child."

Sally's grin lit her face. "Would you like to come in the back and have a cup of tea with me? I have some scones still warm from the oven."

Mary's smile matched Sally's.

Afternoon tea with Sally became a regular event, at least whenever Sally's husband, Angus, was home to look after the shop. He was a large, black-bearded, bear-like man of few words but with an amiable manner. The shop was the converted front parlour of an old stone house on the corner of the main street. A heavy curtain divided the shop from the small back parlour, which was Sally and Angus's living space. This had a cheerful, welcoming warmth, with several comfortable armchairs strewn with knitted patchwork throws and soft cushions. A colourful rag rug warmed the stone floor. The walls were whitewashed. Thick felt curtains at the windows kept the wind out. A dresser against one wall held dainty cups on hooks and a large china teapot, with a drawer containing silver cutlery—items, Sally said, from her trousseau many years ago. A steaming kettle was always on the hob by the peat fire in the grate, which sputtered and sparked and then glowed when Angus added more fuel, while the appetizing aroma of pies or oatmeal biscuits seemed to emanate permanently from the oven set above the fireplace.

From the parlour were three doors: one to the outside, one to Sally and Angus's bedroom, and a third that Sally always kept closed. Mary wondered about the third room, but did not ask. These were not the kind of people one could question about such personal matters, which Mary appreciated for she too did not like to be questioned. If Sally had secrets, so too did Mary.

Once when Mary arrived unexpectedly early for tea, after shopping in town, she met Sally coming out of the room, which she closed behind her in a furtive, hurried movement. Mary did not want to discomfort her friend, so she turned away and busied herself rearranging the purchases in her shopping basket. Sally recovered her composure and the incident was never mentioned, or repeated.

Conversation with Sally was quiet, sporadic, never gossipy, and the silences between the two women, as they sipped tea, ate buttered scones, or knitted together by the fire, were always companionable. Strong but gentle, the McPhees, like the other local people, minded their own business, and left her to hers. They reminded Mary of the cold-climate flowers on the moorland that kept themselves closed and contained, hiding their beauty against the wind and rain, waiting for rare moments of sunshine to open their petals.

If Scotland suited Mary well, it also did wonders for Edward's demeanour. She had never seen him so relaxed and content, like a new man. When he arrived home after his days out in the countryside, or his nights away, he would hold out his arms for Louisa, and hug her and kiss her as if could not bear to ever let her go. Then he would stroke Mary affectionately on the back of her neck and kiss her cheek. He ate with enthusiasm, praised her cooking, laughed and joked, and was always loving and gentle in bed. Intimacy was difficult for Mary at first. She was shy, embarrassed for him to see her body, touch her in her private places, but with his help she learnt to relax and enjoy his discovery of her body, as she too discovered his.

One evening, close to Michaelmas in their second year in Scotland, when the nights were drawing in and the hillsides were purple with heather, Sally McPhee confirmed what Mary had suspected for some time. She could tell, Sally said, just by looking at her.

"You'll be needing some new swaddling clothes soon, then, Mrs. Harris," she'd said. Mary turned pink with embarrassment. "I'll save some skeins of that soft wool for you, for the knitting."

She felt shy as she told Edward, uncertain of how he might react. He was playing on the floor with Louisa, but when she announced her news, he stood up, took Mary in his arms and held her so tight she could hardly breathe. In the months that followed, it seemed a smile never left his lips. He sang in the mornings as he shaved, and sang in the evenings as he prepared for bed. At night, he held Mary close, stroked her tenderly, told how happy he was, how grateful to her he was that she had agreed to marry him. "He's on top of the world," Mary told Sally when she asked how Edward was taking the news of her pregnancy.

As her confinement drew near, Mary tried to dismiss the qualms that arose, the memories that resurfaced of another time, another place, another world. Memories of a woman who laboured all day and all night, and bled all day and all night, and whose womb, in the early dawn hours, gave forth a creature that ought never to have been conceived. As Mary entered her own labour, attended by one of the fishermen's wives, she felt her body freeze.

"You must relax, Mrs. Harris," the midwife told her. "Everything is normal."

But still, with every wave of pain, she tensed, clenched her fists and her jaw, and curled up her knees. When at last she felt the release, and saw the smile on the midwife's face, she breathed a sigh of relief and said a silent prayer of thanks. William Oliver was placed in her arms, perfectly formed, with a pair of lusty lungs and a shock of black hair. Mary felt healed and strong as she cradled her own perfect child.

Edward wrote to Uncle George and Aunt Fanny in Birmingham with the good news. Aunt Fanny wrote back to say she longed to see the new baby but that at their age the journey to the north of Scotland by bumpy coach and rough sea would be too arduous for her.

"When are you coming back south?" she wrote. "And when are we going to meet this new wife of yours, about whom you have been so mysterious?"

It was true, and Mary had noticed. Edward had been circumspect about their marriage, having sent a brief note to Uncle George informing him of his move to Scotland and remarriage there. But to dwell on questions about Edward's first wife might lead her to doubt the solidity of her own happy situation. Besides, it seemed reasonable to her that he would want to leave sad memories in the past.

Mary wrote to Thomas, Polly, Martha, and Alice with her good news, and received enthusiastic letters in return. Polly herself now had a little boy. Martha's wedding plans had been delayed as they waited for her young blacksmith to find a good position, but she said they would be married before the year was out. Thomas had news of his own.

My dear Little Sparrow, he wrote, *I trust you will delight at my news as I delight at yours. It gives me great pleasure to advise you that Miss Tabitha Turcotte has consented to be my wife. Miss Turcotte is a dressmaker of fine character, the daughter of a cheesemonger of this parish, and I do believe she will be an admirable addition to our little family.*

Mary welcomed the news of her brother's betrothal, but frowned at Edward's wry amusement when she read Thomas's letter to him. He'd always regarded Thomas with a touch of disdain.

"I'm sorry," he said with a chuckle. "Maybe this Miss Tabitha Turcotte will be the making of him."

Miss Everett was the last person to whom Mary wrote. She composed the letter with great care, writing slowly to avoid ink blots and smudges. It was Miss Everett's response she most looked forward to, and her opinion—on babies, on marriage, on life in northern Scotland, on anything—that she most valued. She often thought of what Miss Everett had said the day she was hired as Louisa's nursemaid, about Mary being ready to fly. Did even Miss Everett imagine just how far Mary had flown?

When Miss Everett's response arrived, it contained only two lines of text. At the top, Miss Everett had written that the lines were a short poem called *Love, What it is,* by a famous poet called Robert Herrick, who had lived nearly 200 years earlier. The poem read as follows:

Love is a circle, that doth restless move
In the same sweet eternity of Love.

Mary read the poem four times and still could not understand its meaning. Dear Miss Everett. It was so like her to write in mysterious terms. So often in the past Mary had found Miss Everett's words puzzling, until she learned to listen instead to the rhythm of her voice and feel the sense of peace it conveyed. She read the poem again, and tried to imagine the words unfolding in Miss Everett's voice, bringing her the sense of calm she had known so often in Miss Everett's presence. She folded the letter up and put it with her other correspondence. No doubt the poem was Miss Everett's message of love toward her and her baby.

William Oliver thrived in the brisk Scottish air, growing into a hearty boy with sturdy legs and rosy cheeks. In 1851 and 1854, two more babies followed, both healthy girls, whom they named Rebecca and Amelia. Mary now had a quartet of children to care for, and though they kept her busy, it was a happy busyness.

Then, in the spring of 1855, the call came for them to return to London. They had been nearly seven years in Scotland. Louisa was already in school, William Oliver was a jumping jack full of beans,

Rebecca was a demanding toddler, and Amelia a happy, compliant infant.

Mary would have stayed in Scotland forever if she could, but Edward's new posting made her proud. He was to work on a grand new project, surveying a site in Kensington for a massive museum to showcase the best of British art and design, the brainchild of none other than the Prince Consort, Queen Victoria's husband. It was an honour to be chosen for the project.

Though sad to leave Scotland, she looked forward to seeing her brother, Thomas, and meeting his betrothed, as well as renewing old friendships, especially with Miss Everett. They planned to stop in Birmingham on their way back, so she would at last meet Uncle George and Aunt Fanny as well.

She wondered at Edward's apparent lack of enthusiasm about the pending move. From the day he told her, his mood seemed to pall, and he was often twitchy and irritable. She tried to dismiss the pinprick of anxiety his frowning face at the dinner table provoked in her. Surely, after all these years, far from London, the pain of his bereavement must have dulled. In nearly eight years of marriage and three children, hadn't Edward shown his commitment to her?

She raised the issue in the most loving way she knew. "Edward, I'm so proud of you for having been awarded this project. No doubt you're a little anxious about it? And about returning to London?"

His eyes flickered. He blinked, glanced down at the children playing on the floor, and then, to Mary's relief, his face softened. "Well, we've had a good life here, haven't we Mary? So yes, I'm sad to leave. I'm sure you are, too."

"We'll make the best of it. It'll be a new adventure for the children," said Mary.

Edward nodded and drew William Oliver to his knee and, to the boy's delighted chuckles, launched into a rendition of *London Bridge is Falling Down* with full hand gestures. Louisa, with Rebecca in tow, ran over to join in, Louisa helping her with the correct hand movements. Baby Amelia on Mary's lap laughed at the fun, and Mary laughed with her.

TWENTY-TWO

Aunt Fanny and Uncle George's house was grander than any Mary had lived in, apart from Mrs. Scroggs's large boarding house. It had a proper parlour at the front, with an array of chairs and small tables, a large and comfortable kitchen, and a scullery at the back with Aunt Fanny's pride and joy, newly installed piped water.

"Such a luxury, my dear," she told Mary as she showed her how the tap turned on and off. "Saves me such a lot of work, all that fetching and carrying. Of course, we have a daily girl now who helps, and it's much easier to keep servants with piped water. She's a dull girl, but the best I could find. Servants! They're all the same."

Mary smiled. Perhaps Aunt Fanny didn't know that Mary had once been a servant. But then Fanny put her hand to her mouth and exclaimed, "Oh, I know you were once in service, my dear, but not for long, was it? I can see you are not the usual type." Her voice trailed away, and she busied herself with seating everyone at the kitchen table. Mary was kind enough not to mention that she knew Fanny herself had once been in service as a ladies' maid.

Aunt Fanny had prepared a sumptuous supper of cold ham, duck, rabbit, some kind of a large fish that Mary did not recognize, and various sweetmeats. The meal was convivial and satisfying. The children were quiet and minded their manners. George congratulated Edward on his promotion, and peppered him with questions about his work. Edward was in his element as he recounted in minute detail how he measured every bump and dip in their Scottish island's terrain.

Mary became aware that Aunt Fanny was watching her. Judging her, perhaps. Fanny had known Edward's first wife, and may have felt that she, Mary, had usurped her place. She touched her hand to her forehead in her usual self-conscious gesture, realizing Fanny's approval might need to be earned.

After the meal, Uncle George invited Edward into the parlour and left the ladies at the table with the children. Aunt Fanny closed the door quietly behind them and, smiling broadly, sat beside Mary and took her hand. Mary was surprised at this sudden intimacy.

"I can see you've been good for Edward," she said.

"I try to be a good wife to him, but he's very kind, so it's not hard."

Aunt Fanny continued to beam and patted Mary's hand. Mary felt she was about to say something else, but decided not to. Mary wanted to ask her what it was, but her throat constricted and the words died before they reached her mouth. It was about Edward's first wife, Louisa's mother, she was sure.

Aunt Fanny turned to the children, playing on the floor. She held out her arms to William Oliver.

"Oh, come to your auntie, you sweet little boy."

She petted the boy, and held him up to the sink to see how the tap turned on and off. Then Rebecca wanted to try, so they both played with the taps. Fanny then turned her attention to little Amelia, taking her in her arms and pinching her chubby cheeks. She ignored Louisa. Mary noticed that when Louisa caught Aunt Fanny's eye, and smiled at her in her usual engaging way, Aunt Fanny averted her eyes. Most people who met Louisa were enchanted by her winning personality and fetching looks. For a woman to ignore a child like Louisa was unusual. Was it because Louisa reminded her too painfully of Edward's first wife? Did she blame the child for the mother's death, coming so soon after her birth?

Here was a woman who had known Edward's wife intimately, who had been present at Louisa's birth, nursed her through her confinement. Who might even have been there at her death and might know the circumstances. Mary could come right out and ask. *Aunt Fanny, what was she like? Was she truly very beautiful? Were they very much in love? How did she die, was it a very painful death?* But she could not bring herself to do it. The silence around Edward's first wife had become a habit. She had always reasoned his silence was because he did not want to hurt Mary by raising the spectre of another woman.

Besides, he had shown in many loving ways his devotion and commitment to her and his children, so there was no need to rake up the past. Still, her inability to break the silence rankled her. She had nothing to fear, no cause to doubt Edward's fidelity.

While Aunt Fanny was occupied with the other children, Mary took Louisa aside. The child must have been crushed by her aunt's rejection.

"I'm proud of how nicely you smiled at Aunt Fanny."

"She doesn't like me. But I don't mind."

"Of course she likes you. Everyone does."

Louisa gave her an old-fashioned look. "Not her."

"No Louisa, I'm sure she likes you fine. In fact, I think you make her think of your mother."

Louisa put her arms around Mary's waist. "*You* are my mother."

Mary decided not to pursue the matter.

"Uncle George is nice, though," said Louisa. "He gave me a penny. Look." She reached in to the pocket of her smock and took out a coin. "May I go and join Papa and Uncle George now?"

"Go on then." Mary said. How strong Louisa was. Resilient and self-confident, the very qualities Mary still sometimes doubted in herself. Even after so many years, that sore spot still pained her at times; still would not fully heal.

In the parlour, Uncle George retrieved a dusty bottle and two glasses with a flourish from the sideboard cupboard.

"Something I've been saving for a special occasion such as this."

He poured a brandy and handed it to Edward with a broad smile. The two men stood with their backs to the fire, rocking gently on their feet, and sipped their drinks. George wanted to talk about the Irish troubles, as Edward feared he would.

"Government sent the army in, Edward. Quite right too. Can't have people rioting in the streets."

"Yes, well … "

"Quietened down now, but not for long I don't suppose. More trouble to come, they say. Rebellion. More riots. Army's still on alert. 'Course, they wouldn't send the engineers, only the fighting forces. Lucky for you, eh, Edward. You wouldn't have wanted to be back in that quagmire."

Edward nodded, wondering how he might steer George to a different topic. To his relief George finished his quaff and slapped Edward on the back.

"You've done well for yourself, my boy, with that Mary. Proud of you. Tell me, has she made you happy?"

Edward thought for a few moments, and then replied, "Yes. Yes, she has. I'm fortunate she came into my life, and the children are a joy."

"Hmm. Glad to see you found some sense at last. What I mean to say is, well, Mary's a decent sort of girl, ain't she, you can tell just by looking at her. Sorry of course, I was, to hear of … well, that other business with the Irish girl. Bad do, her dying so suddenly. Bit hard on you. But you've bucked up now, like a good lad, and this Mary's done you proud, from what I see. Reminds me of your dear sister. Demure, modest, loves the children. A good still tongue in her head. Quite the angel, I would say."

"Yes, she is an angel. She's loyal, and good, and sweet-tempered."

"Good lad. You look after her now."

They stood together in silence until the ladies joined them, bringing the children for goodnight kisses. Fanny set up a borrowed mattress and some blankets for them all in the kitchen. The next day their journey to London continued.

At King's Cross Station, Thomas and his wife, Tabitha, were waiting for them. Mary had been looking forward to meeting her new sister-in-law. Thomas had described her as a "fine young lady," and when Mary saw her at a distance as they walked from the train she had to agree she had not only a fine but a refined look. She was small, with a dainty figure and a fashionably slim waist. Her hair, peeking from her bonnet, was shiny and brown as a nut and framed a narrow, heart-shaped face with a pert, pointed nose. As they approached and Mary extended her hand, she noticed Tabitha's eyes. An unusual colour, light brown flecked with gold, but it was their shape that made them stand out—wide-set, narrow but long, with strong brows that gave her face a surprised look. She had an old look about her young face, and a slight frown between those extraordinary eyes.

Beside the delicate Tabitha, Mary felt big-boned and clumsy. She curtsied awkwardly as she touched her hand to Tabitha's, but Tabitha did not return the gesture, which made Mary feel even more awkward. Like a nurse bending to reach a child's level, but Tabitha was not a child; she was a grown woman.

Thomas fussed and flapped and dithered around them, looking as pleased as Punch to be finally meeting Edward on equal terms rather than as the brother of his daughter's nursemaid. He alternately bowed to Edward, then slapped him on the back, kissed Mary's hand, patted her on the head, and petted the children. He introduced Tabitha twice to Edward and Mary, and then scolded himself for his own stupidity.

On Edward's request, Thomas had arranged accommodation for them in Lambeth, close enough by steamer to the Woolwich barracks, but convenient for Edward's new worksite in Kensington.

"Come, come everyone," said Thomas, "let us make our way to your new lodgings, and then we can have some tea. Tabitha has arranged everything for you. Here, let me help." Thomas went to pick up their large trunk, and immediately dropped it. He called a passing porter, who ignored him, then looked around in agitation for another. Tabitha raised her hand and a porter came running over. Edward quickly negotiated a price for taking their luggage to the omnibus. Thomas beamed. "Very good, very good," he said. Tabitha led the way, followed by Mary, Edward, and the children, while Thomas trailed behind.

Now that Edward was a sergeant, he could afford two rooms with a proper kitchen. Their new accommodation in a large, squat brick house in the better part of Lambeth, upriver from the odiferous tanning factories, was bigger, though not as cosy as their home in Scotland. But Mary was pleased to have a large floor area for the girls to crawl around on. In the following weeks, she took pride in turning the rooms into a comfortable family home, with knick knacks, a warm rug, pictures for the walls, a rocking horse for the children, and a vase of fresh flowers always on the table.

Sunday afternoon tea with Thomas and Tabitha became a regular part of their routine, and at first, Mary enjoyed these times—she had missed her brother's comfortable presence more than she realized. But after a few months she found herself agreeing with

Edward that Thomas's apparent business success had rather gone to his head, and that Tabitha had doubtless had a hand in that.

If Thomas's pomposity evoked mild sarcasm in Edward, Tabitha's intrusive inquisitiveness drew a stronger reaction. Her tongue, he said, was as pointed as her chin, and her nose was long enough to look round corners. Mary tried, in a halfhearted way, to defend her.

"She's curious, that's all. She means no harm, Edward."

Edward scoffed and warned Mary to be wary around Tabitha. "I don't trust her, Mary, and neither should you. She's a sly one. Make sure you watch yourself around her."

Mary wanted to like Tabitha, who, for all her faults, was family. But she did find herself discomfited by Tabitha's "curiosity," which consisted of her pestering Mary with questions about Edward, their marriage, his background, what she thought he got up to when he wasn't at home—which she peppered with asides on the well-known reputation of soldiers.

"You're too trusting, Mary," Tabitha said. "I'd keep more of an eye on him if I were you. I know where my Thomas is at any time of the day or night."

Mary was not always quick enough to steer the conversation away from Edward and her marriage, and the questions bothered her more than she liked to admit. Now that they were back in London, Edward seemed to have lost the gentle, teasing demeanour he'd sported in Scotland. He was quieter, more serious, his manner often brusque and veering towards rudeness. His distracted moods reminded her of how he'd been in that first year when she had been nursemaid to Louisa. In fact, the only time she saw Edward smile these days, apart from when he was with the children, was when he was mocking Thomas and Tabitha, and that was always with a scornful smile. She put his stern moods down to the stress and responsibility of his new job, and tried to dismiss Tabitha's insinuations.

Not long after their return to London, during one of their Sunday meetings, Tabitha whispered to Mary that she was to have a child in the New Year. Mary told her she was delighted for her, and that the children would be thrilled to have a cousin to play with.

"Of course, I shall be having a proper doctor to attend me," said Tabitha with a smirk, "They know what they're doing, unlike certain country midwives who make a mess of things."

Mary was stunned. Was this a casual throwaway comment or was it deliberately aimed at Mary? If so, how could Tabitha know? What had Thomas told her, or rather, what had she interpreted from what Thomas told her, for surely Thomas would not have betrayed her on this of all matters? She had never spoken to a soul about what had happened that day, but if she were ever to discuss it, it would not be with Tabitha. Since this was not a jab she could challenge, she had no choice but to ignore it and hide her anger. She swallowed hard, clenched her jaw, and gave Tabitha a watery smile.

Although Tabitha had a way of making Mary feel foolish and naïve, she was kind to the children. Except Louisa, whom she mostly ignored, after warning Mary that Louisa had a cast in her eye that would spell trouble down the road. One time, they sat drinking tea in Mary and Edward's rooms. Louisa sat cross-legged on the floor, remonstrating with her doll and her stuffed bear about some imaginary misdemeanour.

"You're a naughty bear," said Louisa. "You mustn't bite Dolly. I shall have to whip you and send you to bed with no supper."

Tabitha frowned at Louisa. "That child has bossy nature, Mary. You should teach her humility."

Mary reared in defence of Louisa. This was a slight she did not have to ignore. "On the contrary, Tabitha," she said, looking directly at Tabitha and trying to keep her voice steady. "Louisa is not bossy. She's strong, loyal, and fair-minded. I'll give you an example. Last week, I watched Louisa stand up to a bully who was tormenting younger children in the school playground. Even when the bully pushed her, Louisa came back at him, stood her ground, and wagged a finger at him until he walked away." She stirred her tea. "I consider those to be fine qualities in a child, Tabitha."

"Oh, tish," said Tabitha, reaching for the teapot. She officiously poured for Mary and herself. Louisa took no note of the women, though she did get up and move a distance away where her bear and doll could carry on their dialogue.

Mary had stood up to Tabitha, Tabitha had backed down. A small victory, but it gave Mary little comfort. She inclined her head to Tabitha.

"May I offer you another slice of cake, Tabitha?" she said.

There were two pieces left, one of which Mary had been saving for Edward. But Tabitha grabbed both pieces, dunking them in her tea, and gave a sly grin. "Eating for two," she said. Mary sighed. Edward would have to go without his cake.

TWENTY-THREE

In the years they'd been away, London had grown even bigger and busier, with throngs of people, coaches and carts, omnibuses, hawkers, and beggars, all pushing and pulling, all in a hurry to go somewhere or return from somewhere. A city that moved urgently, onwards, upwards, and outwards to fill the world with its magnificence. Though Mary missed the solitude of hills and braes, the bobbing boats in the harbour, the nods of the crofters, and the kindness of the draper's wife, she could not help feeling moved by the vibrancy of this monumental city.

Buildings seemed to shoot up overnight. grand stone and brick edifices glorifying the British Empire, the apotheosis of which was the enormous Crystal Palace that had housed the 1851 Great Exhibition. Even in the north of Scotland, Mary and Edward had heard of the wonders of this monument to industry, science, and art. Though the exhibition was over by the time they arrived back in London, the grand crystal edifice that had housed it remained, and they took the children to see it. It was, Edward pronounced, a triumph of modern engineering, and pointed out to the children, wide-eyed before the structure, the angles and joints and struts that held it together.

The sight of it reminded Mary of the day she arrived in London, confused and nervous, and thought how the soaring railway station ceiling resembled Bath abbey. How much had changed for her since that day! She stared in awe at this new edifice, more massive than any abbey or cathedral she had seen, a monument to Man's glory, not God's. She felt a momentary discomfort in this new world that seemed to place mammon alongside God.

The children had grown restless with Edward's technical explanations. He hoisted William Oliver onto his shoulders so he could see higher up. Louisa was now more interested in drawing circles in the dust on the pavement, while Rebecca hung on to Edward's leg, begging to be lifted too. Edward set William Oliver down, took Rebecca on his shoulders instead, and jogged around with her until she shrieked and begged to be put down. Laughing, he set her down and ruffled her hair.

As Mary, holding Amelia in her arms, watched Edward's antics with the children, her apprehension about this new world evaporated. She was strong now, and she was back in London where her healing had begun all those years ago; a different London, but as the city had changed, so too had she. She was no longer the fragile bird who had arrived, reluctant and nervous, at King's Cross Station. She was a strong woman now, and she would meet the future with a confident and stout heart.

She had, however, forgotten how foul London's air was, how the dust that settled on every surface was black with soot, and how, no matter how hard she scrubbed, the rings on Edward's collars and the grime on the hems of the children's skirts would never come out. The mists that came down from the hills in Scotland were white as snow, and she had walked through them as if walking on a path up to Heaven, but London's fog was thick and yellow and choking. On some days, she was afraid to take the children out, for fear of diseases lurking in the foggy miasma.

But here in London was Miss Everett, alive and well and a bare hour's walk away, less if she took an omnibus. She had written to the lady of her impending return and Miss Everett replied that she was to come and see her soon as she was settled. Edward gave his permission, clearly pleased she had a friend to keep her company, and gave her leave to take the children with her. They chattered and babbled on the omnibus, kneeling at the window to watch the passing scenes, clapping their hands in delight every time the bell rang and the omnibus pulled up to a stop.

Much of London may have been changing, but when Mary stepped off the omnibus and walked with the children to the little courtyard off Rupert Street in Soho, she may as well have walked back in time. True, Martha and Polly had moved on, and the boarding house was a little more dilapidated—the window sills could have done with a lick of paint—but the cobbled street, the standpipe at one end, the corner grocery store and dress shop, the dusty children and aproned women in the doorways were all there. The familiar feel of the place was comforting to Mary, a place of fond memories and fast friendships; especially the friendship with Miss Everett.

She stepped up to Mrs. Scroggs's doorstep, gathered the children into her skirts, took a deep breath, and rang the bell. Mrs. Scroggs opened the door herself, pulled back in surprise, and then, as she recognized Mary, greeted her with great fanfare as if she were a long-lost relative.

"Come in, come in, my dear girl. Tell me all about what you've been doing. Oh, you've been busy I see. I heard about you marrying Mr. Harris. Well, I did you proud, didn't I? You see, I always look after my girls. That's why the neighbours send their daughters to me, because they know I'll train them up properly, and send them on their way. My, what lovely children. Come in, come in." She ushered them into the parlour and drew up a chair.

Mary sat down and the children, shy and quiet in the presence of this imposing woman, sat at her feet. Mrs. Scroggs beamed at the children, reaching out to ruffle their hair. "Well now, those three little dark-haired ones, anyone can see at a glance they're yours. Image of you, they are, Mary. But this one," she said, indicating Louisa, "she's the pretty one, isn't she? From the first wife, I suppose." Mary bristled. Louisa glanced up at Mary, and put a protective arm around her siblings.

A servant entered with a bowl of water covered with a towel.

"Oh, yes, this was your job, wasn't it, Mary?" said Mrs. Scroggs. "Now, Susan, this is Mary Piper. Oh, Mrs. Harris now, and she can teach you a thing or two about that bowl of water." Susan laid the bowl on the floor for Mrs. Scroggs's feet, curtsied quickly and fled. "What a time I've had, Mary, you just can't get the same caliber of girls anymore. It's not as if I haven't tried. They should thank me for taking them on and paying them a decent wage, and they get their room and board, but some of them, well, young girls nowadays just don't seem to know the meaning of work. Not like you."

Mary inclined her head towards Mrs. Scroggs and smiled.

"Now, let me think. You remember Martha, don't you? Well, she's gone. Oh, but I do miss her, she was a lovely girl, wasn't she? Married, you know. Found herself a good man, a blacksmith. And that Polly too. I was fond of her for all her mischief. Got half a dozen little ones now, I hear, and a fine living up in Wolverhampton with her footman.

"Well, many of my girls fix themselves up with decent men, I make sure of that. Like you, my dear. Mrs. Scroggs did all right for you, didn't she? And look at you now! A passel of babies, all good and healthy. Course, I knew you'd do well with Mr. Harris. I've known him all my life. Knew his sister, Sarah, too. Such a fine woman, and so tragic. Died young you know … "

As she listened to Mrs. Scroggs, Mary couldn't help wondering why Edward's sister was so frequently mentioned—by Mrs. Scroggs, by Uncle George and Aunt Fanny—and always in glowing terms, while Edward's first wife was not. Edward, too, talked openly about Sarah, how she had raised him after their parents died, and joked that everything he knew about women and marriage he had learned from Sarah. "It wasn't much," he'd said with a chuckle. "I think a man learns more about such things from his wife than his sister." She wondered if he had learnt anything from her, Mary, he hadn't already known from his first wife.

Mrs. Scroggs paused for breath, and Mary turned her attention back to her.

"Yes," she said, hoping to bring Mrs. Scroggs's monologue to an end, "you've been so good to me, Mrs. Scroggs. I don't know how to thank you."

"Don't thank me, my dear, thank your Lord. He's the one who gives and He's the one who takes away. I knew you'd do well from the first time I saw you. I'm a good judge of character, you see. I've made some mistakes, mind, but not many. Now, will you stay for some tea?" She winked at the children. "I might be able to find a biscuit or two."

Mary did not want tea. She hoped the children hadn't heard the word "biscuit." They were becoming restless. Amelia, who'd crawled onto her lap, whimpered and rooted for her breast. Rebecca picked at her skirt and began whining, "Mama." William Oliver was making "choo choo" sounds with the toy train he'd brought along. Louisa had a possessive arm around Mary's legs and kept pulling at her. Mary wanted to ask Mrs. Scroggs to please forgive her, for her time was limited, and she wanted to drop in to see Miss Everett before she left. But she felt awkward bringing up the subject of Miss Everett. After all, Mrs. Scroggs considered Miss Everett to be her own special friend, and had given Mary the cold shoulder when she became aware of her friendship with the invalid. Did Mrs. Scroggs know that Mary and Miss Everett had been in regular correspondence over the years? She suspected not. Mrs. Scroggs had rarely picked up the mail that arrived at the house; that job was given to one of the maids, who handed the letters out to the addressees.

Now that she was face to face with Mrs. Scroggs, she felt guilty that while she had written to Miss Everett and Martha and Polly, she had never thought to write to Mrs. Scroggs. She didn't want to hurt Mrs. Scroggs's feelings by revealing her continuing friendship with all these women. She fiddled with her bonnet, adjusted her collar, hushed the children, and wondered how she was to deal with the situation. In the end, it was Mrs. Scroggs herself who saved the day.

"Well now, you remember Miss Everett, the poor invalid woman in the back room, don't you? I think it would be a courtesy if you were to pop in and say a quick hello to her. I seem to remember you were in charge of taking her meals in for a time while you were here."

Relieved, Mary rose and gathered the children. Not only had she never told Mrs. Scroggs about her correspondence with Miss Everett, neither, apparently, had Miss Everett.

"Thank you for the offer of tea," she said, "but we really must be going." She said her goodbyes to Mrs. Scroggs, and left her to her armchair, footstool, and soaking feet. Rebecca pulled at her skirt. "I want a biscuit, Mama." Mary hushed her. "Later, Rebecca, I promise."

With Amelia in her arms and the other children trailing behind, she walked down the hall to the door on the left at the end of the hall. Miss Everett's room. She hesitated, and then knocked quietly. There was no reply. She knocked again, and heard Miss Everett's frail voice. "Come in Mary, my dear." She smiled. How did Miss Everett know it was her? When she entered the room with the children, she found it to be dark as usual, with shafts of autumn light that shone through the cracks in the curtains and gave the space a filmy look.

Miss Everett emerged like a wraith from in front of the draped windows.

"Mary, my dear," she said, "How pleased I am to see you, and how well the little sparrow's wing has healed."

Mary responded with a broad smile. The older children hid in her skirts, their restlessness giving way to silent awe. But when Miss Everett bent down and extended her hands to them, and Mary gave them a little push, they shyly approached her and turned their faces up to her, as if they knew she was a friend.

Miss Everett laid her hand on William's head.

"This is the boy," she said, then she snatched her hand away as if she had touched something hot.

"What is it?" Mary asked, feeling a little alarmed.

Miss Everett shook her head.

"He is of the angels," she replied in her usual mysterious way, "a special child."

"William is a special child. Of course, all my children are special, but for a man to have his own son ..."

"And there will be another one soon."

She nodded towards Mary's abdomen. Of course, Miss Everett knew. No one had told her, but like Sally McPhee, the draper's wife, she could tell just by looking at Mary. She hadn't even told Edward yet. Mary gave a chuckle.

"How could you tell, Miss Everett? Are you a mind-reader?" she asked, teasingly. "But you're correct. And perhaps it will be another son. Edward would like that, but I shall be happy with a daughter. So long as the child is healthy." She patted her abdomen.

"Yes," said Miss Everett. Her voice was dreamy. She placed her hand on the head of each of the girls, one by one, but when she came to Louisa, she let her hand linger. "Ah," she said, "the magical child."

"She is magical to me. You could say it's because of her I now have a husband and three more children. I feel so fortunate."

"Indeed," said Miss Everett, "but there is more." She ran her fingers through Louisa's curls, then cupped her hand to the child's chin. "This child has twin birds within her, and they will form a heavenly union when they emerge."

Mary gave a wry smile. Dear Miss Everett; she hadn't changed a bit, and was still prone to talk in riddles. Mary used to assume the riddles had hidden meanings, but, if she were truthful, the years had made her a little skeptical of some of Miss Everett's strange ideas. She also used to think she wanted to be like Miss Everett, living alone in contented solitude on a plane that hovered somewhere above the day-to-day world. That was before she found her own kind of happiness, and understood that love of solitude did not have to mean being alone.

But it had been Miss Everett who, with her kindness and perceptiveness in the early days in London, when Mary was confused and unhappy, helped to put her on her path to healing and fulfillment. For that, she would always be grateful and always feel a special bond with her friend.

Mary sat down, and the children, becoming sleepy, settled down around her. Baby Amelia yawned and Mary laid her on the floor beside her sisters.

"How have you been, Miss Everett? I've missed you, and it's good to see you still looking so well."

"I have been away, Mary," she said.

"Away? Where? Where did you go?" Mary was surprised. She had never known Miss Everett to leave the house, or even her room.

"Ah, I see I have confused you. One does not have to leave a room to go away. Not anymore. Something wonderful has happened to this world, Mary. God has given us a new gift. It came first to two little sisters in America, called Kate and Margaret Fox, and it spread like a gospel across the sea. Now it is here in London, given to a few chosen people. I am one of those privileged people."

Mary, as usual, barely understood the words, let alone their meaning, but she listened politely.

"You see, it had to happen. It is a matter of evolution. You may have heard of Mr. Darwin's theories about evolution of the physical form. But there is also evolution of the mind and the soul. First, we learned the healing powers of mesmerism and animal magnetism. You remember we talked of that, many years ago."

Mary nodded and smiled. This she did understand. The day Miss Everett had mesmerized her with what she called a healing force was the day that changed her life for the better. For on that same day, she was hired by Edward to be Louisa's nursemaid.

Miss Everett continued. "We now know that was but the first stage of our contact with the soul. Now some of us have evolved to the second stage."

Miss Everett's eyes shone as they always did, and as so many times in the past, Mary felt an energy radiate from the silky folds of her robes. While the children drifted to sleep in the dim room, Mary felt alert and eager to hear more.

"Communion with the spirit world, Mary. We are now able to contact the souls of those who have passed over. We always knew they were there. Sometimes we feared them. Other times we longed to see them, to speak with them, but they lived beyond our reach. Now we know how to converse with them."

"Are you speaking of ghosts, Miss Everett?" Mary felt a slight shiver go through her.

"You may call them ghosts, or spirits, or simply the souls of the dead."

"You can speak with them? How?"

"I have learnt the new way. That is what I mean when I say I have been away."

"Away? Where have you been?"

"Where I have been, dear Mary, is the Other Side."

Mary was still puzzled, but curious. "The other side? Of what?"

"The Other Side is what we call the spirit realm, where our dear departed souls wander. For thousands of years they have been trying to contact us. I have heard their cries, their pleas, and felt their longings to speak to their loved ones, to deliver their messages of hope.

"At first, when I was a new recruit to this art, the voices were so loud they hurt my ears, such a cacophony, each voice drowning out the next. I had to be firm and tell them, 'one at a time please.' You see, their relief was so great, to discover at last that someone on this side was hearing them. With great practice, I learned to control their voices and to command them to come only when called."

Mary's head spun. Spirits of the dead? Ought they not to be left in peace? She touched Louisa's head, smoothed her copper curls. Miss Everett had always assured her she had the church's assent to everything she believed in—mesmerism, animal magnetism, spiritual healing—because it was all for good works. But the idea of communicating with the dead made Mary profoundly uneasy.

"Miss Everett, what does the church say about this? Are you sure you're not ... what ... usurping God's power?"

"You are not the first to wonder that, my dear. Isn't it strange, that whenever a new idea or a new invention comes along—steam engines, spinning machines—there are some people who worry that it goes against God's will? What they forget is that God is the Great Giver, and He gives us these things to make our lives happier and healthier."

"But how do you know it's not the Devil who's deceiving you? Even Jesus was tempted by Satan."

Miss Everett sat in silence for several moments. Then she took Mary's hand in hers.

"Mary, I would like you to come here next week, on Saturday evening. Bring your husband. I have invited a few people, some friends of mine, for what we call a séance."

The word sounded strange, but what astonished Mary was the thought of other people being in Miss Everett's room. She realized she had no idea what sort of social contacts Miss Everett had, and had assumed she was rather alone in the world, barring the occasional social visit by Mrs. Scroggs. She gave Miss Everett a querying look.

"A séance is a gathering of people who wish to receive messages from their loved ones on the Other Side. They are all good, God-fearing people. I even have the wife of the vicar of St. Anne's in my séance. Her husband is quite approving, and says he might come himself one of these days. Many important people have already discovered this new movement. You may have heard of the renowned poets, Mr. Robert Browning and Miss Christina Rosetti. They are faithful adherents. And it is said even the Queen and Prince Albert regularly attend séances at the palace. But I would like you to come and see for yourself. When you have experienced it, you will realize this is God's work, not the Devil's."

Mary was intrigued, but was uncertain of how Edward would receive the news. He showed so little interest in matters of the spirit or the church, and she doubted he would assent to their involvement in anything as strange as this.

"I see you hesitate, dear Mary. I understand. This is truly a new world that has opened its doors to us mortals. I can only assure you that if you come to my séance you will be astounded. But if you prefer to wait, I will not mind. Mull it over with your husband. If you decide not to come next Saturday, then you will come another time. There will be a need for you to do so."

There was a knock at the door. Miss Everett rose. "I believe my tea has arrived. Come in Susan." The maid entered with a tray. It was time for Mary to leave. She picked up Amelia and woke the other children. "Time to go," she whispered.

"Wait a moment," said Miss Everett. From a plate on her tray, she took three biscuits and handed them out one by one. "One for William Oliver, one for Louisa, one for Amelia." The three children took their prizes and beamed their thanks. But there was none for Rebecca. Her face fell and she looked about to crumple into tears.

Louisa put her arm around her sister and chuckled. "She's teasing you, Rebecca. Look, there's still one left on the plate."

"Oh," said Miss Everett, "Louisa is correct. I have one more biscuit. Who might that be for?"

Mary smiled, as Miss Everett handed the fourth biscuit to Rebecca.

Louisa took Rebecca's hand and marched her up to Miss Everett. "Go on Rebecca, be nice now." Rebecca flung her arms around Miss Everett's legs. "Thank you for the biscuit," she said.

"And thank you kindly for having us, Miss Everett," said Louisa. "I hope we weren't too badly behaved."

"You were angels," said Miss Everett. "Goodbye, Louisa, take care of your mama." Louisa flashed her a smile as they left.

On the way home in the omnibus, Mary felt cold, despite the warm weather and stuffy interior, and wondered if this was because she had rejected her friend's invitation. Had she upset Miss Everett, and had her dear friend withdrawn from her? Surely not. Miss Everett would never do that, and their goodbyes had been warm and friendly. It was her imagination. And Miss Everett had said she could attend another time, when she felt a need to do so.

She shivered again and felt a pain like a sharp dagger, low down, and a rush of liquid. Nausea rose in her throat, and her head swam. She clutched at her belly and gasped for air. The pain increased.

When they arrived at their omnibus stop she was doubled over in pain. Louisa, looking concerned, helped her the few yards to their rooms and up the stairs where she collapsed on the bed.

"Bring me some rags, Louisa, you'll find some in the cupboard in the kitchen."

"Mama, what's the matter? Are you dying?" cried Louisa.

She shushed Louisa and begged her to bring the rags, and then take the others out to play. Then she curled up in bed and silently wept. Later, she'd explain to Louisa.

For too long she'd sought to protect the girl. But what had she been protecting her from? The innocent curiosity of a girl child, or from her own trauma? There were things Louisa needed to know about as she grew from childhood to womanhood. It was time to tell her. Once this was over and she was feeling better. She'd explain to Louisa everything she needed to know about being a woman.

But there were other things she never wanted Louisa to know. That she would never tell her. Such as the memory that flooded through her now with the waves of pain, about the bright spring day, so full of promise, when she walked along the river to Harriet Pickard's cottage, of what emerged from Harriet's body as she slipped moon-white into the night, and how, the next morning, when she scrubbed and rinsed her clothes in the washtub the water still ran red. She turned her head as if to banish the thought and hugged herself.

By the time Edward arrived home, Louisa had settled the other children in a game, and was making soup for Mary. Mary struggled to get up to greet Edward, but he consigned her back to bed. While he fed her soup, Louisa prepared supper.

"It's all right, Mary. There will be other babies, you'll see."

Mary nodded, grateful for Edward's kindness and Louisa's help, but something in her heart told her there would be no more babies. She did not know why she felt that way, but she had been told that a woman should always trust her intuition, and this was Mary's intuition. She had four beautiful, healthy children, counting her precious Louisa as one of her own, so she should not be selfish. With God's grace, she would get over this grief.

TWENTY-FOUR

If the knock were to come, it would be in the night. Constables liked to come when you were least expecting it. Heavy footfalls on the stairs to startle you awake. The rat-a-tat-tat on the door from a truncheon, loud enough to make the house shake and even the innocent to tremble with fear. But Edward need not worry. The knock wouldn't come. Not after all these years.

In Scotland, with time and space between him and London, Edward had felt safe. Even with their impending return to London, he felt only a fleeting anxiety. The sojourn with Uncle George and Aunt Fanny on the way back to London had solidified his new life in their eyes, even if they'd had any suspicion. And why should they suspect anything? Uncle George's approval of Mary and what he called Edward's steady footing helped to square things with Edward's conscience.

When they arrived back in London, Mary's brother, Thomas, did them proud with the new accommodation in a neighbourhood where no one knew him. Thomas and Tabitha welcomed him with enthusiasm as their brother-in-law. Funny chap, Thomas, and his wife a bit hard to take, but they were family now and that ought to give him a warm feeling.

Mary was a good woman, and he could not have found better. Her character was impeccable, her behaviour beyond reproach. Never had he had cause to raise his voice to her, never had ire risen in his chest from anything she had said or done. No act of disobedience, no sour look, no defiant stance. She raised no questions, begged no explanations, and accepted him in his present entirety, as if her life began and ended with him. He could find no fault with her and, yes, he loved her. He truly loved her.

Sometimes he wondered if she would be less devoted to him if she knew the truth, but he dismissed the thought as soon as it entered his head.

The children were the light of his life. Louisa—loyal, inquisitive, insightful, and mature beyond her years—was already at school, learning to read and cook and sew. Rebecca and Amelia, like their mother, dark-eyed and innocent. And his son, William Oliver, his pride and joy.

His work on the Kensington museum was absorbing and tested his supervisory skill now that he was a sergeant. All was well.

Even so, as soon as they were back in London, he felt a creeping anxiety. He started imagining things: a shadowy presence that followed him as he walked home from work. What if someone had talked? Ellen Booth, perhaps, or someone from the garrison, or the neighbours in Southwark. The Dawsons, with whom Mary had lodged when she was nursemaid to Louisa. Mary was still in touch with Alice Dawson. Suspicions raised. Rumours flying. People whispering to the vicar. The police informed, investigating ...

It was nonsense of course. All in his head. Fear and guilt did strange things to a man's mind. Ellen Booth must be long gone to another cellar with or without her brutish husband. The chaps at the garrison had all moved to new postings across the empire. Alice Dawson had moved with her family to the south coast.

Besides, for he all knew, Catherine really was dead. The thought made him shudder. He went to the box in the bedroom and took out the watch chain made from Catherine's hair, from the lock he had stolen as she'd slept on the deck of the boat from Ireland. One did not make hair watch chains from a person still living. If confronted, he would produce the watch chain as evidence.

But what if Catherine herself, abandoned again by Jack, came looking for him? What if she wanted Louisa back? Louisa was her flesh and blood, not Edward's. Louisa, who derived no inheritance from Edward, not her coppery curls, nor her eyes as blue as her mother's. If the matter came to court, the watch chain would not help him.

Perhaps he could throw himself on the mercy of the judge. Catherine had abandoned him for a vagabond, left him with a child; he hadn't meant to deceive, and he regretted his actions; six years of unimpeachable living had surely erased his guilt; what would it benefit his innocent children and the woman who knew nothing of his deceit to send him to prison?

These thoughts and fears, irrational though they were, occupied him daily, and Catherine began to enter his mind more often than he wanted. More than once he fancied he saw her advancing towards him among the crowds in the street, and he turned up his collar, pulled down the brim of his cap and hurried away. Or he might be pouring himself a cup of tea, and see her slim white fingers on the teapot handle beside his. Her breath at his neck, the turfy, Irish smell of her. Her face might appear in the flames of the fire, her lips parted then closing, eyes slanted then wide, then gone in the smoke.

Once, as the morning sun streaked the window pane, he saw her face reflected in the dust, and he reached towards her, though he knew it was only his imagination. Another time, he thought he heard her voice transposed onto Mary's as she sang to the children, so that momentarily he fancied she had returned and was there beside Mary, singing to Louisa. Each time it happened, he squeezed his eyes shut, and clapped his hands against his ears until reason returned. Yet still he dreaded the knock on the door.

When the knock came, it was almost a relief. It was a January evening in '56. Snow, wet and heavy, had been falling for days, and Edward had stoked the fire to draw the damp from the air. Mary was tucking in the children.

It was not a loud knock, not the expected ra-ta-tat-tat of a constable's truncheon. More of a tap-tap-tap, such as an overhanging tree branch might make at a window, or the tentative knock of a stranger looking for a particular address. But a knock nevertheless.

It was not normal for visitors to call so late in the evening, especially in such filthy weather. Through the open bedroom door, Edward saw Mary bent over the bed, heard the children's giggles, Mary's laugh. The knock came again. He could simply ignore it, pretend he was out. But they would return. They would bring reinforcements, take him away by force. Better to go quietly than resist. Get it over with. He closed the bedroom door with a gentle click, went to the front door, and listened. The tapping came again, more insistent. He opened the door a crack.

It was not the constable, not the law, not the church. He hadn't truly thought it would be. It was her. Catherine. She stood dripping melted snow on the step, her hair dishevelled, her eyes wild. Against her left shoulder, she carried a baby wrapped in a ragged shawl. On her bare right arm, a purple bruise.

"Edward," she said.

"No," he said and pushed the door. But she stopped it with her foot and had hold of his sleeve with her spare hand. "No," he said again.

"Please," she said. Her eyes were softer now. Her touch on his arm was warm. As he looked at her, she seemed to transform before his eyes, and a memory caught at the ragged edges of his heart. The usual memory. Catherine's upturned face, hands out, pleading on the wharf, her face silhouetted against the sun, her hair a golden halo, and that white shoulder. He caught his breath. *She is bewitching me again.*

"How did you find me? What do you want of me?"

"Edward, I know you owe me nothing. And I haven't come to cause trouble. But it's my baby. She's sick, and she needs medicine. I'm afraid without it she might die. I've nowhere else to turn. I was hoping you might help." She held her head on one side, her lips parted, her eyes pleading.

As if from afar, he heard Mary's voice wishing the children sweet dreams, Louisa's singing, Amelia's babble. He turned briefly towards the bedroom, then back to the apparition on his doorstep—just a beggar woman in rags, clutching now at his shoulder. He extricated her hand from his shoulder and pushed her foot out onto the landing.

"No, he said. "Leave me be."

"Edward, here." She thrust a damp piece of paper into his hand. "This is where you'll find me. You helped me before. You were so good to me. Please help me now." Her eyes shone bright in the shadow of the doorway.

"Go!" he said, "I don't want your paper. Just go!"

"Please, give me a few moments."

She tried to lean in to the door, but he was too fast for her. He shut the door in her face, bolted it, and stood for a moment, looking at the hand that had touched her, that held the piece of paper she'd given him. It trembled. Mary came into the room, and he hid his shaking hand in his pocket, pushing the paper deep inside.

"Was that someone at the door, Edward? I'm sure I heard a knock."

"It was nobody."

"So there was a knock. Who would be calling at this time of night in this weather?"

"Nobody, I told you. A beggar. An Irish beggar woman, that's all."

Why had he felt compelled to tell her this? "Nobody" was all Mary needed to hear. Why mention a woman, and an Irish woman at that? As though part of him wanted her to know?

"An Irish beggar? Oh, Edward, you didn't turn her away? These poor creatures have suffered so much. Surely, we could spare some charity. Please, call her back and I'll prepare a bowl of soup for her. It's a cold night."

"It was nobody, I tell you." Edward did not mean his voice to sound so harsh. Mary recoiled, looking puzzled. He softened. "She was looking for someone. An address." In his pocket, he fingered the piece of paper Catherine had given him. "She came to the wrong house. I told her where to go."

This satisfied Mary. He put a hand on her shoulder.

"Make some tea, Mary, and sit with me by the hearth."

TWENTY-FIVE

The January snow was followed by a thick yellow fog that brought with it one of London's feared miasmas. Folks on the street pushed posies of sweet-smelling dried flowers into their faces or waved handkerchiefs dipped in rosewater as they walked. Edward came home from work each day with new reports of sickness and death. Everyone was afraid. Mary kept the children inside as much as possible.

In February, William Oliver turned pale and weak. It started with a cough, dry at first, then retching, followed by a fever that would not break. While Louisa kept the other girls quiet, Mary kept vigil by her son's bed, kneeling to pray for his recovery or, if God willed it, his easy release. Edward, his face drawn and equally pale, joined her each night, holding his son's hand and whispering his name, over and over, "William, William, William."

Then, early one morning in March came the blood spots that spattered the sheets like red starbursts. Edward took the rainy-day money Mary had saved in a jam jar and spent it on a doctor, who arrived creaking up the stairs with his black bag, a sad-looking man who had seen too much misery and sighed as if he could not bear to see another sickly child.

"It's the London air," he declared. "You must take him to the coast as soon as possible. A full week of cold sea air. I cannot guarantee a cure; he may be too far gone, but it is the only advice I can give you."

Edward paced the floor, muttering. "London, London air. Filth and soot and dirt and fog. In Scotland he was the healthiest of all our children."

It was true. Mary recalled her robust little boy in Scotland, who ran, and jumped, and laughed in the salty air, flying his kite in the wind, leaping from rock to rock on the moors.

"He left his spirit in Scotland," she said.

"London be damned, curses on it," said Edward.

Mary flinched to hear him use such language, but she took his hand.

"We'll take him to Brighton, Edward. We'll raise the money. Thomas will help, I'm sure. I'll go and see him tomorrow."

"We'll need more. My father's shop, old Mr. Charles—there's still some funds left there. That will help."

"What about your Uncle George? He'll give us a loan, surely."

"Uncle George. Yes. I'll write to him." Edward went to his desk, scrawled a note, addressed it to Uncle George, sealed it, and stamped it. "Louisa, come here ... Louisa, come here at once when I call you!"

Louisa, unaccustomed to having her father shout at her, ran to Mary's side.

"It's all right, Louisa," said Mary. "Papa is worried about William. Please do as he says. Take the letter."

Edward told her to run down to the post office and send it by express mail.

"We'll get the money. We'll go to Brighton. I'll tell the barracks it's an emergency. Yes, yes ... " Edward had fallen into mumbling, "When he breathes the sea air ... yes, he will recover."

Mary put her arms around his neck, and stroked the back of his head until he grew calm.

The journey to Brighton in the second-class carriage was hard on William Oliver. Mary held him close, wrapped in a blanket, and tried to soothe him as he moaned with every bump and lurch of the train. The air in the carriage was no better than the air in London's streets, with men smoking pipes and the soot and smoke from the engine that seeped through the windows.

Edward sat across from Mary, his back rigid, his hands clasped tight. He ignored the younger children, and pushed them away when they fidgeted and squabbled and begged to be held by him. Louisa tried to occupy them with games: I Spy, and counting cows and sheep.

They booked into a boarding house close to the seafront. It was pleasant enough and provided both breakfast and supper, but all guests were required to be off the premises from 10 o'clock in the morning until teatime. Mary kept William well hidden in the blanket lest the landlady protest at having sickness in her house. In the mornings, she bundled him up and carried him to the rented deck chairs on the paved promenade above the beach. She struggled to keep Edward occupied, hoping to calm his anxiety.

"Edward, the girls are fractious and bored. Could you take them to see the pier? And then, if it's not too cold, they could go down and play on the beach for a while."

"Yes, yes … of course," Edward said, as though he had only just noticed his daughters.

The girls, excited to see the sea and the boats moored off the pier, ran off happily. Edward trudged behind, leaving Mary with William Oliver.

It was early in the season. In a few weeks, the spring visitors would arrive, but most of the people on the wide, paved promenade at this time were other invalids taking the air, hoping for a cure: rows of old women, men in bath chairs, and mothers, like Mary, nursing sickly children, all staring out at the tossing white horses, watching the tide come in and go out. A few early-season promenaders walked by and peered at the pale boy wrapped in a blanket as they passed. They furrowed their brows in sympathy, but moved silently away.

Mary was happy to be alone with William Oliver, so she could pray for him in solitude. The regimental band played on the pier, the notes wafting to the promenade. For early March, the weather was mild and dry, and the breeze salt-clean and rich with ozone.

On the fourth day, William Oliver stirred and struggled to sit up. Mary helped him, but it was only to cough, a long, deep, wrenching cough that left him exhausted.

Yet still he was able, as he fell back, to smile and murmur, "Mama, the air feels so fresh. Are we back in Scotland?"

This was the first time he had spoken since their arrival. Mary put her hand to his forehead. His skin was cool to her touch. The fever had broken. Her husband had been right. Edward was on the beach helping the girls pile pebbles into uniform heaps. She called down to him, "Edward, come quickly, see our boy."

Edward ran up onto the promenade, the girls close behind him.

"See, Edward, he's awake and his fever's gone. He thinks he's in Scotland! That's how good the air is for him."

Edward bent down and gently kissed the boy's forehead.

"That's my lad," he said, "that's my son. You're on the mend."

They stayed for another five days, and William continued to perk up.

"If only we could stay a little longer," said Mary. "He's much better, but he needs more time to regain his strength."

But the money had run out.

For want of a nail the shoe was lost, for want of a shoe, the horse was lost, for want of a horse the rider was lost ... Mary had often recited this rhyme to her children, and they loved to imitate the actions of nailing a shoe and falling off a horse. It made them laugh, but taught them a good lesson too.

Each time she thought of this rhyme in the days that followed, she wept. If only they'd had the money to stay longer in Brighton. For want of a shilling ... But, she told herself, at least God was merciful, for William Oliver died quickly, less than a week after their return from Brighton.

In the weeks that followed, Louisa was silent and sad, her eyes often blurry with tears. Rebecca whined and fussed even more than usual. Thankfully, Amelia, in the innocence of infancy, remained her usual bubbly self. Mary, often joined by a solemn Louisa, took her comforts in the churchyard, kneeling at her son's grave, praying for his soul. Her faith, and Louisa's steadfast support, sustained her and helped her return to the tasks of the day. She knew the saying, "Time heals all things," and it was true that she had recovered from the loss of her unborn baby, and though the scar would remain, she would recover from this loss, too, as would Louisa and her sisters.

But for Edward, there seemed to be no comfort. On the day of William Oliver's death, Mary had held her husband as he sobbed. She had never seen a man cry, and for a man of Edward's military bearing and self-discipline, it was profoundly shocking. As time went on, he grew silent and remote.

Through the spring and summer of that terrible year, she scoured the market for sweetmeats and exotic delicacies to tempt him—a basket of quail's eggs, a perfect orange from Palestine, bananas from Jamaica, candied chestnuts from France. She helped Louisa make a clown rag doll for Rebecca with scraps of fabric, hoping it would make him smile to see his daughter's delight, but it didn't. She starched and ironed his shirts with special care, and read uplifting passages from the Bible to him each night. She stretched the housekeeping money to buy extra butter, flour, and sugar to bake a cake for Louisa to present to him. "This is special for you, Papa, to cheer you up," Louisa said, but it didn't, and Louisa's face dropped.

Summer turned to autumn, then winter, and nothing she or the children did took the grey pall from his face. He pushed Amelia away when she tried to crawl onto his lap. When Rebecca whined and fussed, he ordered Louisa to take her outside. He no longer embraced Mary, but stared into space for hours, silent and brooding. His grief at William Oliver's death seemed to go beyond what might be considered normal for a man. He had closed in on himself and she feared for his sanity.

She remembered what Miss Everett had told her last year, about the Other Side and how she was able to talk to the spirits of the departed, and how this congress helped to assuage the grief of bereavement. Perhaps Edward would be willing to attend one of Miss Everett's séances. She broached the topic with care. For the first time since William Oliver became ill, he laughed; but there was no joy in it, only bitterness and disdain.

"Spirits of the departed. What nonsense," he said and turned away from her to stare at the fire.

"If you would just come with me, dearest. It can do no harm, and perhaps it might bring us both comfort."

Edward poked the fire. The flames lit his face, accentuating his wrinkled brow and the worry lines around his mouth. *How he has aged,* she thought. He was not yet forty but was as sad and stooped as a man twice his age. Finally, he spoke.

"You wish to go, Mary? Then go."

"But I would like you to come with me. Please, Edward. Maybe it will help us both."

Edward sighed and stood up. "Whatever you wish," he said, his voice dull as it commonly was these days. "I'll come with you."

She wrote to Miss Everett the very next day, and received an immediate response. The next séance was to be Tuesday night. Mary arranged for Tabitha to come and watch the children. It would be a treat for the girls to visit with Tabitha and their new cousin.

To Mary's relief, when she and Edward arrived at the boarding house, Mrs. Scroggs was nowhere in sight. A sullen girl answered the door and showed them in to Miss Everett's room. There were already several people sitting at a large oak table in the centre—two elderly women and three men, one of whom Mary was glad to see wore a clerical collar. The sullen young woman who had answered the door sidled into one of the chairs at the table. Her slovenly appearance suggested she was of the servant class, and it surprised Mary that such a woman would be part of Miss Everett's world.

Miss Everett, dressed in a long silky gown of dark green, greeted them warmly, settled them in chairs at the table and introduced each of the participants. To Mary's right was the Reverend Potter, the long-necked vicar of St. Anne's Church, and his similarly long-necked wife. To their right sat Mr. Poulson, a pale, sad-looking man with long, slender fingers, a silversmith by trade they were told. Beside him were portly Mr. Strembinsky, a Polish watchmaker, and his ample-bosomed wife. Finally, the sullen young woman, who was introduced only as Lottie.

"We are so pleased that you have all gathered here. I can feel already the spirits in this room are active, leaning in, peering through the spirit membrane, longing to bring you messages of love and hope," said Miss Everett. "Lottie, the gas please."

Lottie went to the gaslight sconces on the wall and turned each one down so the room fell into even deeper shadow than usual. She went back to her seat beside Miss Everett.

Miss Everett extended her hands to the table.

"Let us make the circle of the séance," she said, and bade each person take the hand of the person beside them. "Now we are connected, we are an eternal chain, we are one, united in our love, united in our longing for healing."

Mary glanced at Edward. His face was impassive, but he joined in the circle.

Miss Everett continued to speak in her usual soft, murmuring tone. Some of her words sounded familiar to Mary from her previous encounters, with many biblical references and excerpts from the ancient tomes that lined her walls and from which she had often read to Mary. But as usual, the words mattered less than the rhythm and cadence of her voice, which gave Mary the profound sense of peace that she had become accustomed to in Miss Everett's presence.

Miss Everett stopped speaking for a few moments. Then she addressed the company in a clear, firm voice.

"Please close your eyes, breathe deeply, and listen. Open your hearts and your minds to hear the souls of the departed speak through me, their medium. I shall now call upon my spirit guide."

Mary closed her eyes, checking first to ensure Edward had closed his, and waited. The only sound in the room was the soft breathing of the guests and the hum of the gaslamps. Then, from the vicinity of Miss Everett's chair, came a moaning sound. Not sad, Mary thought; more a purr of anticipation. *It's happening*, she thought, *it's truly happening. That must be one of the spirits trying to get through. Oh, please let it be William Oliver!*

Then from Miss Everett, "Are you there? Are you there? We are waiting. Please let us hear you."

The purr rose to a crescendo, and a deep, male voice coming from somewhere above the table spoke.

"Yes, friends, I am here."

There was a collective exhalation of breath in the room. The gas sputtered.

"Welcome, dear Spirit Guide," said Miss Everett. "Who will you bring to us today?"

The male voice replied, "I have a message for a lady who is sitting at your table right now."

Mary held her breath. The voice changed, became that of an elderly woman.

"Dear Lilian," said the croaking voice, "you were a good daughter to me and I want you to know that I am now truly in a better place. You do not need to grieve anymore."

Mary couldn't stop herself from peeking. She looked around the table and saw that Mrs. Potter, the vicar's wife, was silently weeping. She must be the daughter to whom the spirit spoke.

The croaking voice faded as the purring sound returned, to be replaced by another voice, and then another. One by one each of the people around the table received a message of hope and love from a departed one—a parent, a sibling, a son, or a daughter. By now, people had begun to open their eyes and look around. A murmur of contentment circled the table. Only Mary and Edward were left.

Perhaps, Mary thought, it will not happen this time. Perhaps she had been too eager. Miss Everett called for quiet.

"There is one more spirit who wishes to speak," she said. "Please close your eyes and maintain silence."

The room went quiet, and after a few moments the purring returned, followed by the spirit guide's voice again.

"I have here with me someone recently arrived who wishes my help in making contact with his loved ones. He is but a child."

Mary felt a jolt, and then a tug at her chest as though she were being pulled by gentle hands to the edge of a cliff. Her breath came in heavy spurts and she tried to control it. *It is him, it is him.* William was standing at the precipice, waiting for her to embrace him. *William, I am here, Papa is here. Speak to us.*

Then Edward, who had been sitting quietly beside Mary throughout the proceedings, made a strange noise. It was not a laugh, nor a sob, but something in between. Mary froze and squeezed his hand, hoping to calm him, to bring him back to the moment, to her moment, to their moment. *Edward, not now, please.* But again he made that sound, now more like an explosive sob, and pulled his hand away from the circle, causing Mary to open her eyes and jerk her head towards him. His eyes were open too, glaring, their pale blue turned to midnight. She felt a thump within her, her shoulders slumped. She had been so close only to be pulled back at the last moment.

Edward stood up, and all eyes popped open and turned towards him. The vicar's wife, whose other hand he had been holding, exclaimed, "Oh!" The vicar shook his head and muttered, "What, what?" Mrs. Strembinsky pulled her hands away from the circle, too, and touched them to her heart. Mr. Poulson jerked his head back, his mouth a startled "O." Lottie, sitting opposite, scowled at Edward, but said nothing.

Mary, defeated, was now mortified by Edward's behaviour. She tugged at his sleeve, urging him to sit down. He resisted. Miss Everett, pulled back from her spirit wanderings, opened her eyes, turned her face toward Edward, and addressed him in a soft, sweet voice.

"Dear Sergeant Harris, to lose a child is a terrible, bitter pill and your pain is unendurable. Your wife hoped I might help you find that solace you so dearly crave. But we all grieve in our own way. For each person grief is a journey, and I see you still have many miles to travel, many rivers to ford, many mountains to survey. You are not yet ready to meet with your little boy across this table, for you have … unfinished business to attend to. As you map out your hard road, I wish you to ponder these words: 'Love is a circle that doth restless move, in the same sweet eternity of love.'"

Mary caught her breath. She knew those words. They were the poem Miss Everett sent her when William Oliver was born. But they seemed as mysterious now as they did then. She looked up at Edward, trying to discern if he understood, but his face was expressionless.

Miss Everett continued. "Love is a circle, Sergeant Harris, and three is the number that makes a circle complete. Only when you understand the meaning and power of three, will you find the means to heal." Still Edward's face remained blank, and as usual Mary was puzzled by Miss Everett's words.

"Though you may wish to leave," Miss Everett went on, "I beg you to let your dear wife stay to hear her child's message of love and hope."

Mary's eyes filled with water. She tried again to control her ragged breathing. She could not meet Miss Everett's eyes, nor those of the guests, all now sitting back in silent shock. Edward stood stock still at the table. The room was hushed. Mary finally found it in her to peek at Miss Everett and saw that she remained serene and smiling. Edward's face was red, his lips pursed closed as if he were trying not to speak, lest he lose control completely. Finally, in a hoarse whisper he said, "Come, Mary. We are leaving." Mary let go of his sleeve. She felt sick to her stomach.

Edward turned to Miss Everett and gave a stiff bow. "Miss Everett, I apologize for disrupting your … evening with friends. I thank you for the support you have provided to my wife. But I'm afraid we must both take our leave of you now."

Miss Everett nodded politely to Edward as he took Mary, red-faced, by the wrist and led her from the room. Mary trailed behind him, wishing she could pull back and rejoin the séance, but knowing she could not defy her husband. She was saddened, disappointed, embarrassed for herself and for the company, concerned for Miss Everett, whom she felt she had let down, but most of all horrified that she had angered Edward and, instead of helping him through his grief, had only brought the grief closer still.

When they got out to the street, Edward stopped, and took several deep breaths.

"Charlatan!" he said. "Mary, for goodness sake, I know you're fond of this woman, but she is a charlatan. A fraud. All this poppycock about talking with spirits. It's all fake. I don't believe any of it, and neither should you. Come, we'll go home and we'll have no more of this nonsense. You are not to visit this woman again."

Mary was desolate in the weeks that followed. Though she longed to return to her friend and complete the séance, she dared not disobey her husband. She feared that she had forced his hand before he was ready, and the experience had done irreparable harm to him. One evening after supper, he put on his coat and hat and left without a word. Mary would have liked to have taken the children and gone with him, but his stiff demeanour made it clear to her he wished to be alone. It happened again the following night, and the night after, and on and on, week after week. She worried he might have turned to the demon drink, but he did not seem inebriated on his return, only as sad and silent as ever.

Her earlier intuition, that she would have no more babies, proved right, for he lay rigid beside her at night, and they no longer touched. At her wit's end to know how to help him, she sought the counsel of the Church, drawing the vicar aside after service one Sunday. He said only that it was abnormal for a man to grieve so long and deeply for a child.

"Women grieve, men carry on," he said. "Your family has reversed the proper order of things. You must look into your heart to see what error you have committed to make him behave in this way."

Mary's anger burst from her, then, like an explosion. Usually, when Mary felt anger rising for any reason, she suppressed it. It was not good to allow the blood to become heated. This time, she gave in to raw rage and marched home with the children running behind to keep up. When she got home, she told them to go and play in the yard, went inside, and slammed the door closed.

Edward, as usual, was nowhere in sight. She felt abandoned by him, abandoned by the Church, even by God, who had placed man above woman, husbands above wives, and in so doing, ordained her impotence. She paced the floor of the room until the heat in her blood dissolved into a morass of misery. Too exhausted to weep, she lay down on the bed and felt her body sink into its depths.

When she awoke, the fire was out, the room was cold, and Louisa was curled up beside her, stroking her face. The younger girls were asleep at her feet. She was startled by a knock at the door and a cheery greeting. It was Thomas, with Tabitha. She had forgotten they had said they would visit on this day. She had told Edward, and intended to prepare tea and sweetmeats. After her encounter with the vicar, their visit had slipped her mind.

Thomas called out again, and knocked more firmly on the door. Mary sat up quickly, smoothed her hair and dress, composed her face, and went to answer. As she ushered them in, Tabitha, as usual, pushed past Thomas. Mary took Tabitha's little boy in her arms. The baby smelt of milk and his warm body against hers soothed her.

"Oh, how you've grown," she said, and called Louisa. Louisa, who was already an accomplished little mother, was always delighted to spend time with her little boy cousin, and happily took him off with the girls to play.

Mary pulled up chairs, but Tabitha remained standing, her narrowed eyes scanning the room.

"Edward not home again?" she said. "Sunday afternoon. I didn't see him in church this morning either. I suppose now he's a sergeant he has to work on Sundays."

Mary felt her fists clench, as her rage rose within her again, but she kept her face impassive, her tongue silent, and went to prepare the tea.

TWENTY-SIX

The medium knew. Edward did not know how, but she knew. He'd assumed it was all stuff and nonsense. The darkened room, with the shades drawn, all that chanting and intoning, the lilting, lulling voice, quotes from the scriptures, the eyes that glinted through the blackness, calling on the spirits of the dead. Pure chicanery! Preying on people's grief and fears. And the voices! A confidence trick. And that meandering speech! A witch's brew of balderdash with bits from the Bible thrown in to give it the illusion of legitimacy. She was a good actress, he'd give her that. Easy to see how vulnerable people could be fooled by such a performance. Clever too, how she got the gaslight to sputter on cue. But a charlatan nonetheless. At least, he'd thought so, but …

He'd only gone along with it because of Mary. She thought the world of the woman, said she had the power to heal broken spirits, and claimed she had the Church behind her. Mary wouldn't have gone in for anything satanic, so he had no worries there, and if it would help Mary with her grief, he had been prepared to sit gamely through the whole charade.

But when the so-called spirit guide had called upon the child, he felt something. A probing, like fingers worming deep within him. He'd opened his eyes, seen the woman staring straight at him, and felt a scratching and scrabbling inside him as if a tight knot of some substance was being pulled, tugged, and drawn to the surface.

Panic had washed over him at that moment. The medium continued to stare at him. The gaslight on the wall sconce behind him flared. The rest of the participants remained in shadow, their eyes closed, oblivious of him, and he was caught in the light, exposed like a lone actor on a stage. That was when her eyes told him she knew.

He'd never believed in occult powers, but this was something he could not explain. Was she speaking through God or the devil? Whichever. It didn't matter. She knew what he had done. She saw his guilt.

In the days that followed he scoured his brain to explain what exactly had happened at the séance, and why the experience had so unnerved him. He sought escape in the streets. Walking helped him to think. The medium had said he had "unfinished business," and something else too. It gnawed at him but he could not quite remember. The woman had talked in riddles, about circles and love, but he felt there was a grain of something important, like a message, buried in her words.

One Sunday, he walked out early, before church. He could not face services these days, and usually made excuses to Mary. He walked for an hour along the river, further than his usual route, out of the neighbourhood. Perhaps the unfamiliar streets would help him remember what the medium had said about unfinished business.

At the corner was a tavern. The sign hanging above it struck a chord. "THE THREE BELLS." It came to him. *Three makes the circle complete.* That was what the medium had said. And more. She had said that once he understood the meaning of the circle of three, he would find the means to heal.

He sat on a bench outside the tavern and repeated the medium's words to himself. Slowly, the thoughts that had been scurrying like a nest of mice in his head began to settle and organize themselves into a logical pattern, like a map. Maps were familiar things. He could make sense of maps. All he had to do was to lay out, like an ordnance survey, the bumps and hollows and rills and streams of his life since his marriage to Catherine, and then find the connection to the number three. It was clear from the way the medium had stared at him, probed him, and unnerved him that she saw unresolved guilt in the flush of his skin. Guilt ran like a river through the map in his head. In the broad and peaceful expanse of Scotland, he'd thought to escape it, but one step into London's troughs had brought it worming its way back.

Passersby gave Edward a wide berth as he sat on the bench, muttering to himself, drawing imaginary circles and lines in the air. The nest of mice in his head began to scurry again. He took several deep breaths. *Think! Think! List your transgressions. Count them up.* He'd lied about Catherine's death. That was number one. Then he'd lied to Mary, to the Church, to the law, to the world, and to God, when he entered a bigamous marriage. That was the second transgression. And for each transgression, there'd been a punishment. Mary's miscarriage was the first. A lost embryo and a barren womb, which caused unending pain for Mary. And the second punishment: the death of his beloved son, William Oliver, a loss almost too great to bear. *How can I live knowing my actions made my wife barren and caused the death of my only son?*

Two transgressions, two punishments. But there must be a third. *Three makes the circle complete.* A nearby church bell chimed three times. Mary would be home with Louisa and the other children by now.

Louisa. Was she the link? In the map in his head, he drew a line from Louisa to all the main points along the way—when she was born, when Catherine left, when Jack brought Louisa back, when he told the world Catherine was dead, when he married Mary …

A sudden wind disturbed the still air and blew rubbish along the gutters—old newspapers, a tin can, whirlwinds of dust. The air grew cold. A pauper woman hurried past Edward, her head down against the wind. The hem of her skirt was muddy and ragged, and blew around her ankles. Her shawl was laced with holes. She had no shoes and her feet were black with grime. Edward watched the woman disappear around a corner, and Mary's words came back to him. "Edward, surely you didn't turn her away?" But he had. As Catherine had abandoned him, so he had abandoned Catherine. On a cold January night, she had begged him to save her child, the child who was Louisa's sister, and he had refused. How humiliating it must have been for her to come begging to him of all people. How desperate she must have been.

Edward gave his head a shake. This was madness. He owed nothing to Catherine or her miserable child. It was she who had wronged him. Her precarious condition was not his concern. Turning her away was nothing compared to what she had done to him.

But what if the medium were right about the number three? There was a curious symmetry to the idea that Edward's mapmaker mind could not dismiss; turning Catherine away was the third transgression that made the circle complete. And with each transgression, there had to be a punishment. An eye for an eye, as the Bible said. One lost embryo. One dead son. One more life?

Edward's hands grew ice cold. Louisa's visage swam before him: her golden almost turned to copper now, her white skin, the many moods of her eyes, soft and loving, fiercely loyal and steadfast. He heard her bubbling laugh.

He thrust his hands into his pockets. His right hand touched something—a piece of paper. When he pulled it out, he saw it was the paper Catherine had given him the night she came to his rooms. He hadn't disposed of it. Perhaps he knew he might need it one day, but he hadn't looked at it since the night he turned Catherine away. The scrawled writing, a little faded now, was of an address in St. Giles. Catherine had come to his doorstep in January. It was now May, more than a year later. What were the chances she was still in the same place? For all he knew, Jack had returned and taken her away. Or she'd found some other fool to help her. What of her child? Was it still alive? He had to find out, if only to prove the mad medium wrong and preserve his own sanity.

He turned towards the bridge, crossed it, and headed north and west in the direction of St. Giles. He entered a crowded warren of dilapidated buildings that leaned against one another like drunken men outside a tavern, and systematically searched one courtyard after another. In the thick and sultry afternoon air, gritty dust floated through the weak light and drifted down into piles on the cobbles. The oppressive heat of one of London's May heatwaves had drawn people out of their poorly ventilated dwellings and they wandered aimlessly, their noses covered against the stench rising from the drains. Others leaned in the shadow of overhanging buildings, or sat, hunch-shouldered, in doorways. Occasionally a woman in a doorway lifted her skirts and beckoned languidly as he passed. The odd tattered man held out a hand and said, "Please, Mister." Edward was glad he'd worn his soldier's uniform. It gave him a gravitas that allowed him to pass freely, though most of the people he passed seemed too defeated to make the effort to accost him. The famine in Ireland might be over, but its aftermath was etched on the faces of these people.

He squinted again at the address on the paper and asked a man standing on a corner for directions. The man pointed in a lethargic way towards a narrow passage that led deep into the innards of the rookery. An arch at the end of the passage opened to a particularly mean courtyard, too narrow to ever see the sun. He waited for his eyes to adjust to the dim light, and looked around. A few men lounged against the walls of a tavern at the far end. Children played in the dust and stared at him with blank faces, their mothers squatting in doorways, in desultory fashion, as if too weary to sew another patched skirt, or boil another pot of bone soup. Lines of grey washing strung across the courtyard hung in the still air as if stiff with the dirt and dust of the streets.

He saw her at the far end of the courtyard. She sat on the step of a tumbledown house, the infant in her arms, her head drooped forward, her skirt carelessly draped to reveal bare legs and red, swollen feet. The child must be nearly two by now, yet looked hardly bigger than it had when Catherine came to his doorstep. Its mouth was open to Catherine's bared breast, but it was not suckling, as if the effort were too much for the listless child to make.

From the shadow of a boarded-up doorway he watched her, his heart on a relay race from disgust to pity, hate to remorse, anger to guilt, and back to disgust. This filthy courtyard, this threadbare skirt, these shoeless feet, this starving child—these were her just desserts. Be this misery on her head. He should leave now. Why linger? But the medium's words tumbled back into his head. He could not leave.

He took a few ginger steps towards her. She raised her head and turned. She had seen him. Her shoulders lifted, her eyes brightened, and she smiled. Edward noted with a shock that several of her teeth were missing. Her smile had once been rare and special, for her teeth had been astonishingly straight and white.

"Edward," she said, "you've come."

As if in sudden realization of how she must look, she smoothed back her hair, and with a quick flick of her free hand, pulled her skirt down, and covered her naked breast with her shawl.

Edward pointed to the infant, and tried to keep his voice steady. "The child?"

"I call her Violet. Pretty name, isn't it? But she's small for her age and is often sick."

"That day. When you came. She was sick then."

"She got a little better, but she's still thin and weak." Her voice dropped to a forlorn whisper. "I'm afraid she'll die, like the others."

"The others? Catherine, you've had other children?" He would not mention Louisa, but he wished he could dispel his creeping sympathy for what she might have gone through.

She shook her head, and looked tearful. "I want Violet to live. Three babies gone would be too many." That number three again.

Did she even remember Louisa? Was she including her among the lost children? Rising anger fought with sympathy.

She looked up, and her eyes glinted in a way that made Edward catch his breath momentarily.

"That was why I came looking for you that day, Edward. I was desperate. It was so cold, I was weak with hunger, and Violet needed food and medicine."

"How did you find me that day?"

"Ah," she said, and tilted her head to one side, "how do you think I found you?"

Her look was almost flirtatious. She was putting on a show for him, like the performer she was. Had she no shame, no sense of propriety, sitting on the steps of a filthy slum in such a parlous state, her child lying limp in her arms? *Don't let her pull you into her game.*

"I don't know. You tell me."

The show was brief, as if the effort were too great. Her eyes grew dull again. She shifted the baby to her other arm and put her to the breast. Edward waited.

"You remember that house you took me to when we arrived in London? I went back there."

Edward swallowed hard. Mrs. Scroggs. To whom he'd first lied that Catherine was dead. Had he finally been caught out? Did Catherine tell Mrs. Scroggs that she was Edward's wife?

"I thought someone there might know where you were. That old battle-axe, Mrs. Scroggs, wasn't home, but I talked to the other woman."

"The other woman?" At least, it seemed, he was safe from Mrs. Scroggs.

"She remembered me, and she knew all about you. She told me where you lived."

"Who was she?" But Edward knew before she said it.

"The mad old invalid in the back room."

Miss Everett! It was all down to her! He clamped his hand on the back of his neck and looked skyward. That old witch had played him for a fool, and he'd almost been taken in by her nonsense about ghosts and spirits and the number three. He could almost laugh at the gall of the woman. She'd tried to make him believe she could see into his soul, but the only thing she knew was what Catherine had told her.

The infant whimpered. Catherine settled her over her shoulder and rubbed her back, giving Edward a few moments to think through the meaning of what Catherine had told him.

To what end had Miss Everett done this? Was she just a crazy old woman, or did she enjoy meddling in people's lives, playing with their minds? The best gloss he could put on her actions was that she truly believed her own nonsense. To learn that Edward had another wife still living, and that his marriage to Mary was bigamous, must have given her twisted mind the grist to invent a convoluted riddle about circles and numbers. Then it had been easy for her to entice Mary to take him to that ridiculous séance.

Following her logic, she had to get Edward to make amends with Catherine to assuage his guilt at William's death and somehow make his peace with Mary. His initial surmise about her was correct; she was a charlatan, and probably insane too. What Catherine had told him changed everything. He needed time to digest it.

"She said you had a wife and a family. I didn't want to cause you trouble, so I gave you my address on the piece of paper. I hoped you would come, but not for me. For Violet. She's so thin and frail."

"Whose child is she, Catherine?" Edward asked.

Catherine held his gaze. Then she shrugged and looked away.

"Does it matter?"

Edward said nothing, waiting. Catherine laid the now sleeping child on her lap.

"All right, yes, she's Jack's. And you can say what you like, I don't care. You don't know him. I do, and that's all."

Jack! It was still all about Jack! He looked down at the shrivelled infant, sunken-eyed with fleshless arms and legs. She already looked half-dead, too weak to cry from hunger. He didn't ask where Jack was now, when he left, or why he left. He didn't want to know anything about dead babies, or how she had been living these last months and with whom, or, for that matter, how she got the bruise on her arm that day in January. He was a free man.

The old witch, Miss Everett, had done him a favour after all. There were no messages from the Other Side. No occult powers worming into his soul. The circle of three was nothing but the wild imaginings of a crazy old woman. William Oliver had died from a random fever. Mary's unborn child died from a random miscarriage. There was no unfinished business. And Louisa, his Louisa, was safe.

He took a handful of change from his pocket and threw it down on the ground before Catherine.

"Feed your child," he said, and walked away. She called after him. "Edward, you'll come back, won't you? I promise I won't make trouble." He didn't look back. He didn't want to see her eyes, her hair framing her face like a halo, or hear any more of her duplicitous pleas.

He strode out of the rookeries and onto the broad boulevard where the air was fresher. Thunder rolled in the distance and sent the first fat drops of rain ahead. They patterned the pavement like a Paisley print, and the acrid smell of dampened dust rose from the ground. He quickened his pace to keep ahead of the storm. At the bridge he turned to look at the black sky over the North and East Ends of the city. The thunder was distant now. The rain had barely touched him. Ahead, to the south, the sky was bright and the storm was behind him. He crossed the bridge. He would not go back.

When he arrived at his rooms, he fished his key from his pocket, opened the door, walked in, and stopped. He would have liked to be alone for a few minutes to let the stale air of St. Giles leave his chest. But Thomas and Tabitha were there at the hearth with Mary, the kettle steaming on the hob, Louisa reading a book, the other children cross-legged on the floor playing fivestones. The adults all turned in their chairs as he entered, their teacups frozen in their hands. Tabitha grinned slyly. Thomas beamed.

Mary rose and came to him. "Edward," she said, "let me take your coat and cap, and come and sit with us. You must be tired from working all day. The tea is still hot. So glad you got back in time to visit with Thomas and Tabitha."

Edward closed his eyes briefly, then nodded at his visitors and sat down. Louisa brought him a cup of tea and a plate with a slice of cake. He leaned forward to embrace her, and felt his limbs lighten. "Thank you, Louisa," he said.

Mary's smooth, broad face shone in the firelight. Mary—his sweet, loyal Little Sparrow. Did she know what he had done to her? Did she suspect? She must have wondered where he went when he walked out alone. But she had remained silent, hoping perhaps that her steadfast loyalty would bring him back to her. He didn't deserve her, and now he was free he would change; from now on he would strive to be a good and faithful husband to her.

He took a deep breath. Then he turned his attention to his guests. He listened attentively to Thomas's chatter about his job and promotion, and smiled benignly at Tabitha, holding her gaze in the face of her smug suspicion. The rest of the afternoon was spent in small talk while the children played by the hearth.

TWENTY-SEVEN

There was no need to go back now. The medium's spell was broken and Catherine's bewitching of him had been all in his mind. The reality was prosaic. Catherine had not found him by some magical divination, but because the Everett woman told her where he lived. Only when she was destitute and alone did she discover she needed him, and hoped to exploit him. He wouldn't go back to be used by her again.

But what about the child? This Violet. A starving child needed daily sustenance. The few pennies he'd tossed at Catherine would only suffice for a single meal. He argued with himself. This was London, not Ireland; they would not starve to death. There must surely be honest ways for a woman like her to earn a living to care for her child. But that, he knew, was a ludicrous thought. She had no character reference, no work experience, and her former beauty was ravaged. No one but the lowest of men would look at her with her child. Which left only the parish workhouse. Allowing the parish to take her in would pile one wrong on top of the others.

And there was Louisa, too. She was Catherine's child, and sister to the infant Violet. Although another man had sired Louisa, Edward loved her as his own. Why should Louisa's sister not have the same love and care?

So for the child's sake, and only that, he went again. And again. Every Sunday, through the rest of May, through June, July and August. His resolve to be faithful to Mary faltered, but he couldn't tell her the truth. He had to go on lying to her, for the child's sake, for Violet. Well, lying to Mary had been his habit for years. Pennies disappearing from the rainy-day jar; if Mary noticed, she said nothing. If she should ask, he would come up with some story. Mary always believed him, trusted him. How twisted he had become! But it was all for the child. Only the child. He could not think beyond that, or he might begin to feel compassion for Catherine, and he could not allow himself to do that.

He never asked Catherine anything about her life since she'd left. Each time, he stayed for five, ten minutes to check on the child, then gave her money and left. By the middle of September, her belly was full, the child was rounding out, toddling on sturdy legs. The rent on the hovel was paid, and she wanted to talk.

"Stay just a little while longer," she said. "There are things I need to tell you." He resisted, held his hands up, made to leave. There was nothing she could tell him that he wanted to hear. But she implored him, and finally, one day, he stayed. Perhaps he wanted to hear of her suffering, and compare it to his own. Or perhaps he was simply tired of resisting.

A wind had got up and she suggested they shelter inside instead of on the steps of the house. The room was dark, the single window having broken a long time previously and been boarded up. There were no chairs or table, only a couple of wooden boxes. Catherine lit a candle. They sat on the boxes, while Catherine, with Violet on her lap, talked.

Jack had abandoned her not long after Violet's birth. But, she told Edward, it hadn't always been that way. The early years with Jack were magical. They travelled from town to town all through England, and then to the West Indies and America.

"Oh Edward, you should have seen America. It was just as I'd dreamed. People lined the streets and cheered when we came to town in our yellow-painted caravan."

She still hasn't asked me about Louisa.

"In the Indies, there were black people. They wore such colourful clothes. The women were funny-looking, but the children were sweet." A winsome look crossed her face. "On our first trip to America we stayed in the south because it was winter. In some ways it reminded me of Ireland, the way people talked and dressed. There were black people there too, and they lived in miserable dwellings, just like us in Ireland. Next spring, we went up north to Canada, and, well, you never knew such cold. We tried to warm ourselves by the campfire, but no matter how much we built it up, we couldn't stop shivering, even though it was already nearly April. I thought to myself, daffodils will be blooming in England, and here there's still snow on the ground."

Does she not wonder about Louisa? Is she ever going to ask about her?

"There were Red Indians in Canada. Jack said they might shoot us with their bows and arrows, and I was scared at first, but he was only teasing. The Indians were friendly. They wore fur boots and leather. Look," she pulled at a red-and-blue bead bracelet on her wrist, "one of their women gave me this; she didn't have money for the show but she had beads instead. The white people made the Indians sit in their own part of the tent. I didn't think that was fair. Jack said it was just the way it was, that Indians were an inferior race. Well, that's what they say about the Irish too, isn't it? I liked the Indians just fine ... "

She prattled on about Jack and their travels, the circus troupe, and the people they met on their way, Indians and black people, plantation owners in fine silks and satins, others who were called white trash, farmers and trappers, and fishing folk.

Then, as though all her energy were spent, she stopped talking. Her shoulders slumped, and she pulled Violet towards her breast.

Edward had heard enough and rose to leave.

"Stay," she said. "I have more to tell you. Something to explain."

What is to explain? He made for the door. She called after him.

"Edward," she said. "I know I betrayed you and hurt you. I wish I could make you believe I'm sorry. I did care for you, truly, but Jack ... Jack and I ... "

He didn't want to hear any more about Jack, but she begged him again to stay.

"It was something in here," she put her hand to her chest, "something I couldn't resist. I still can't. Can you understand that?"

Edward stared at her face, now clean and rounded out. She had combed the rattails from her hair. Her complexion had lost its muddy look and was pink and white and plump. It shimmered in the candlelight of the dim room. She had filled out her threadbare clothing and begun to resemble the girl he met on the road to Waterford, who stood pleading with him on the wharf. *Oh yes,* he thought. *I understand that.* He longed to stretch out his hand and touch hers, but instead he patted the infant Violet's hand, and nodded.

"You do understand, don't you? I had to be with him. I've told you about the life we had. It was all I wanted, to be with Jack and travel the world."

Edward noted the past tense. "And where is Jack now?" he said, bitterly.

She shrugged. "He said he was going back to America, but he couldn't take me with a child. But he'll come back one day, he always has. He does love me, you know."

But he left you here alone, with no money, no food. You had to come begging to me as your last resort. And still you won't give him up. Edward sighed and shook his head. She still had not asked about Louisa.

"You may not believe it, Edward, but in the early days, Jack was loving and kind. And all the travelling we did helped me to forget."

Forget what? Your life with me? "Forget?"

"Louisa. That was the first thing. Then my sisters."

Hah! Finally, she wanted to talk about Louisa. A surge of protectiveness enveloped him. Catherine gave up all moral rights to her daughter when she left. He would not discuss her with Catherine. He jumped in to steer her away from the subject of Louisa.

"Your sisters? What about them?"

She brushed a hand on her cheek. "We were in America when I heard about the famine in Ireland. It was awful, thousands of people starving and nobody helping them. I wrote to Father Quinn begging him to book passage for my sisters and mother, but ships weren't leaving for America at that time. I asked him to tell them to head for London, to St. Giles, and I'd find them when I got back. Jack sent the letter to Father Quinn and their passage money with a friend of his who was travelling to Ireland."

Jack again! Edward doubted the money had reached Kildean, if it had even existed.

"I found out when I got back to England, from people who'd managed to get out. The famine hit our village hard. There was no food. People I knew, our neighbours, all starving. Our family was one of the poorest. They got to the workhouse, but it was too late. They died of famine fever."

The news brought the horrors of the famine back to Edward. "I'm sorry," he said. Sorry for her family; not for her or Jack.

"Both my sisters, and my mother too. My whole family." She wiped her eyes with the ends of her shawl. "I felt so guilty, as if it were my fault for leaving them. It was a terrible blow, especially after Louisa."

What about Louisa? Edward clenched his fists, but steeled himself to hear her out. After that, the subject would be closed. He would not utter Louisa's name to Catherine, and would certainly never agree to her seeing Louisa. His face was stony as Catherine continued.

"I know you loved her, and I ought to have sent word to you, but we left so soon after it happened. Jack said it was best as it would be easier for me that way, that I'd be better able to forget her."

Edward was confused. What was she saying? What ought she to have told him?

"But he was wrong about that. You don't forget these things. It's still hard for me to talk about it." She paused, pressed her hand to her forehead.

"Go on," said Edward.

"It was a few days after you came to find me at the Amphitheatre. Do you remember?"

As if he could forget.

"We were to move on the very next day. To Liverpool, where we were to perform for a month. And then we were to sail for the West Indies, and on to America from there. Jack said it was best for Louisa to stay in London while we were performing and arrange for her to join us later for the journey to America. He knew a lady who would take care of her until we were ready to sail. It was only for a few weeks. Jack assured me she was the one who always looked after the circus babies. That was her job. Lots of the circus folk used her when their children were young. Jack said she was a good woman, very caring."

Edward was suspicious. "Did you actually meet this wonderful woman?"

"Oh yes. Jack took me to meet her. She had lots of babies she was looking after. Babies and toddlers and little children around her skirts. Very motherly. Jack said it was best to leave her there and then because ... well ... the truth is, I was afraid."

"Afraid?" Edward leaned forward in his chair.

"Well, we had to hide her because … because you were so angry, Edward. You were acting like a crazy man. Jack said you might come after us and abduct her. I'm sorry, but … So I kissed Louisa goodbye. We left for Liverpool the next day. I was happy. I was with Jack and Louisa was in good hands. But then … " Catherine's voice broke. She wiped her eyes again. "It was just before we were due to sail for America. A letter came. Jack showed it to me. Louisa … "

"What? What about Louisa?"

"I know you loved her and that was what made you so angry that day. And now these last weeks you've been coming to see me … Well, you haven't asked, but you must have wondered."

Wondered what? "Go on."

"Oh, Edward, I'm so sorry. I should have sent word to you but I was too upset. The letter said the diphtheria got her. She passed away, and I wasn't there to nurse her." Catherine was now weeping profusely.

Edward could scarcely believe his ears. He wanted to grab Catherine, shake her, box the stupidity out of her ears. How could she have left her child with a stranger? How could she love a man who concocted such monstrous lies? He belonged in prison. Perhaps he already was. Yet even as the terrible ire he felt for this man rose in his gorge, the meaning of it all also dawned. Catherine believed Louisa had died. How much, he wondered, did Jack bribe the woman to take part in his deception? No wonder Catherine had never asked about Louisa.

What a fool she was, how stupefying was her naïveté, even after years with this man, not to see him for what he was! It must have been a kind of madness that drove her to love a man like that. And it was a kind of madness that had driven him, Edward, to love a woman like her the way he had.

Catherine was still talking, telling her story. *Let her talk, let her finish.* It was now almost amusing to hear her and see her and to feel neither compassion nor contempt for her, neither love nor hate. Nothing at all.

"The next day, we sailed for America. Jack was kind to me, he comforted me when I wept. I had another baby in America, a little boy. And he died too, not long after he was born."

Edward pushed away the memory of William Oliver on his deathbed. *Babies die. All the time, nothing unusual, babies are always dying.*

"Two babies lost. And then Violet came. Another girl. But Jack said … "

Catherine stopped.

What did Jack say? Despite himself, Edward was curious.

"Jack was upset. It was getting harder to find bookings. And it would be even harder with a child. He wanted to go back to America, and wanted me to give Violet to the woman who had looked after Louisa. I said no. I couldn't. I knew it wasn't her fault that Louisa got the diphtheria, but it was the memory, you see. And the other little baby I lost. And the guilt. Oh, such guilt. Because I did wonder, if I had kept Louisa with me perhaps she wouldn't have died."

Guilt. Yes, Edward knew all about that.

"But Jack got angry. He didn't mean it. He'd never hit me before—he wasn't like that."

Edward remembered the purple bruise on Catherine's arm the day she came to see him. Catherine continued. "He was just worried about the show. He needed a good assistant. In the end, he said it was best for me to stay here in London and he would do the show without me—he'd find a new assistant. So he left. He said he'd send money. But that was so long ago." Catherine's eyes had become vacant.

Surely, she could not be so blind.

Edward spoke in a fierce whisper. 'Catherine, it's been, how long? Well over a year, nearly two. He has sent no money. You cannot truly still believe he will come back to you. You must see what sort of a man he is."

Catherine looked up at him through lowered lashes. "What sort of a man he is?" She fingered her shawl, pulled the baby closer to her breast, and gave a deep, shuddering sigh. "I know what sort of a man he is, Edward. I am not as blind to him as you may think. But what would you have me do? Admit my whole life has been one enormous mistake? Admit I should have stayed in Kildean and spent my days tilling fields and peeling potatoes? Admit that I was a fool to give up everything I had, everything you gave me, to be with a man who lies to me, cheats me, abandons me over and over and over again? No, Edward. I will not do that. Because I know that Jack has loved me, and I believe, in his way, he always will. And I will always love him. So, no, I will admit to no mistakes and no regrets. Not for loving Jack, and not for the life I lived with him. I did what I did because I had to."

Edward was done, spent, all emotion drained. He rose, threw Catherine his last few pennies, and gave a stiff bow.

"I'm sorry about … Louisa," he said. "I'm sorry about your sisters and mother. But I'm leaving now, and you will not see me again."

Edward got up and walked out of the dark house. He turned his face upwards to the sky. A sliver of sun had finally found its way to the courtyard, shining a patch on one of the rooftops. Edward felt his eyes smart as he looked up at the unaccustomed light. He crossed the courtyard at a clipping pace towards the arch that led to the passage and out into the street. Mary was at home with the children. She would be making supper. Perhaps she had found some good, fresh fish at the market. Louisa would be playing cat's cradle with Rebecca and Amelia. After supper, Edward would have his pint of porter, and then they would all take a walk by the river to enjoy the cool evening air. The children would be excited to watch the watermen's skiffs ferrying people across the river. He might promise them a pleasure-boat ride one day. That would make Rebecca and Amelia jump up and down. Louisa would put her small hand in his and smile up at him.

As he approached the arch, his footsteps on the cobblestones echoed. The patch of roof where the sun had shone was in shadow again. He reached the arch and began to enter it. Then he heard a noise, like a sudden whoosh, and a crackle. Then people shouting, feet running. He turned back. Smoke was pouring from the ramshackle house he had just left. People swarmed from the burning house like ants leaving a poisoned nest. Screams, shouts of "Fire! Fire!" A crowd gathered. Some people ran to the standpipe to fill buckets of water, but it was too late. Orange flames emerged from the thick smoke. The house was tinder dry and burnt like straw. The worst of the smoke billowed from the room where Catherine and Violet lived.

Edward did not have time to think. He ran back to the house, shouting, "Quick, there's a woman with a child in there."

"No chance, mate" said a man from the crowd, "it's a tinder box."

"Someone help her," shouted a woman. "She's got a child with her."

"Water, water, put the flames out," yelled another.

"God help us, it's going to burn to the ground," said another.

Edward took out his handkerchief. "Give me some water, quick," he said, and dipped his handkerchief into the proferred bucket, wrapped the cloth over his nose and mouth.

"You're not going in there, mate?"

"Wants to be a hero, him."

"But there's a woman with a child in there."

Edward bent down through the burning doorway, entered the wall of black smoke, and dropped to his knees, crawling on his elbows. He knew where she was—he had only just left her, sitting with the child on the wooden box. Almost blinded by the smoke, he saw through the dimness the outline of her body on the ground, beside her an overturned candle still burning—the culprit that started the fire. He pulled at the slumped body, felt the child beneath her, and dragged the two of them across the earthen floor. The dust and dirt from the floor flew up and smothered them both, but dampened the flames around them. Coughing and choking, he emerged with the woman and child, to the cheers and shouts of the gathered crowd.

The woman who had spoken earlier ran over with a wet cloth, with which she wiped Catherine's face, and put her arm around her. Edward sat up and coughed the smoke from his lungs until he felt dizzy with the effort. He looked at the burning house. There was no hope to save it and the men were now working with buckets of water to prevent it spreading to the neighbouring houses. An older man watched, hands on hips. "All these houses should burn to the ground. Not one of 'em is fit for human beings, but they expect us all to live like animals." He hawked deeply and spat on the ground. Edward, his head clearing, turned his attention to Catherine and Violet. Both appeared to be unconscious.

The old woman slapped Catherine's face, and she opened her eyes, came to and sat up coughing and choking.

"My baby," she said, and reached for Violet, who was also slowly reviving. She looked at Edward, and then at the house, which was now little more than a smouldering heap of ashes. "The candle," she murmured. "I knocked the candle over. It was so quick. I tried to get out, but the smoke was too thick, and then everything went black." Her eyes were streaming, leaving white rivulets on her smoke-smeared face.

"It's all right," said Edward, "you're safe now. I'll take care of you, I promise. I won't leave you."

The full import of the burnt house was coming home to the escaped residents. Women wept and wailed, men stamped the ground in anger. "Where are we to live? Where can we go? Everything's gone."

The same thought had come to Edward. Where would Catherine and her child go now? And what had he done? What had he just promised her? He could not have left her and the child to die in the burning house while others ran away or stood paralyzed amid the mayhem. But having played the hero, all obligations were discharged. He had thought to be free of her. He had walked away from her and her miserable life. Catherine's story, the abominable lie Jack had told her about Louisa, how she'd chosen to believe him, and chosen to stay with a man who doomed her to serial abandonment—this had evened the score, and cancelled his own guilt. And now he had heard himself promise to take care of her?

He looked at her soot-stained face and knew that he was still tied to her, and would be for all time. It was not Louisa that bound him to her. It was her. He still loved her. He had never stopped loving her. He did not want to stop loving her. He wanted her more than ever, rich or poor, with another man's child or not. He could not leave her now. He would take care of her. Somehow, he would find a way through this, because he was tired of dishonesty and guilt, tired of his double life. Mary would need to know. She would be hurt, that could not be avoided. He would be gentle, and somehow make things right with her. They would face what was to come together. But he would not leave Catherine.

He cleaned Catherine and the child as best he could with the wet cloth the old woman had handed him, and picked her up. The child was in better shape than Catherine and could walk, and she toddled behind the pair, holding on to Edward's coattails, as he carried the still barely conscious Catherine through the courtyard, acrid with the smell of charred smoking wood, pushing his way through the still-agitated crowd with its men in line handing buckets of water. When he reached the main road, he hailed a cab. The cabman looked askance to see the pair of them, their clothes and hands charcoal grey from smoke, both bedraggled and groggy.

"A fire," muttered Edward, "need to get to a doctor. Please help."

"Righto, sir," said the cabman, shaking his horse's reins. "What address?"

"Mr. Thomas Piper, 23 Red Lion Street, Westminster."

"That's a doctor is it, sir?" The cabman seemed doubtful.

"My brother-in-law. And his wife. They will see to things. Hurry, please."

TWENTY-EIGHT

The look on Tabitha's face when Mary answered her knock, as well as her unexpected arrival, told Mary something terrible had happened. Tabitha's cheeks were pink as if she had been hurrying, but the tip of her nose was white and shone like a candle's flame. Her mouth was set in a thin, straight line. Mary's first thought was Thomas: an accident, he was hurt, or worse.

Tabitha did not wait to be asked in, but pushed Mary aside and marched into the room. "Tell Louisa to take the younger children outside," she said. "What I have to tell you is not for their ears."

Mary did as she was told, then indicated a chair for Tabitha. Tabitha pushed the chair aside and paced back and forth.

"You understand, Mary, that Thomas and I can have nothing to do with this. There is Thomas's job, his profession; this could look very bad for him. I will not allow your husband's conduct to influence my family. I have nothing against you, of course, you are my dear sister. But we cannot have anything more do with you or your family. If anyone should find out. Thomas depends on his good character ... "

Tabitha was babbling, but when she mentioned Edward's conduct, Mary felt she almost knew what was coming. It would hardly be a surprise to learn that Edward had—strayed, though the thought of it still made her heart sink. She knew the word that began with an "m" but she could not say it even to herself. Yet if it were true, it would explain his absences, his distracted behaviour, his coldness in the bedroom, coins missing from the jam jar. Still, there had always been hope, wishful thinking, a fervent belief that she was mistaken, that there was some innocent explanation for his behaviour. Now, it seemed, Tabitha had come to confirm her worst fears.

As Tabitha continued her prattle, the story came out. Edward had arrived at their house with a dirty, ragged woman who seemed at death's door, trailed by an equally dirty and ragged child, and begged a mattress for them to lie down on. Edward claimed he'd saved the woman from a fire. At first, Tabitha said, she'd felt sorry for the woman and the child, and they'd provided them with a spare mattress. As Thomas went to fetch a doctor, Tabitha got some cool water for her to drink and went out to buy some soft cloth.

"I thought that would be it—we'd clean her and the child up and they'd be on their way. But when I got back, the doctor had been and gone, but I could see she wasn't going anywhere. Just lying there, with Edward hovering. It was his behaviour that made us both suspicious. Thomas asked him straight, 'Why have you brought this stranger to our house?' But we both noticed she didn't seem like a stranger to Edward, not the way he mopped her brow, propped her head when she coughed, put the cup to her lips. Very peculiar.

"A proper little Florence Nightingale, he was," said Tabitha, "a man behaving like a nurse. You never saw such a thing. I said to myself there's something fishy here. Something very fishy. Thomas saw it too. He's perceptive, is my Thomas.

"Well, I'm not one to poke my nose into men's business, but I drew Thomas aside. 'There's something fishy here,' I said to him. 'You've got to do something about it.' And d'you know, it made me proud the way he handled it. 'Who is this woman?' he said to Edward, straight out like that, 'and what is she to you?' He wouldn't reply straight away. Just gave him that withering look he always gives to my Thomas. He's never shown any respect to Thomas. I've kept my mouth shut about that for the sake of family harmony. But this, well ... "

Tabitha was becoming irritating and Mary's apprehension was growing. "Tabitha, please tell me in plain words. What is going on? What did Edward say it was all about?"

"I'll tell you what it's about."

When Mary heard Tabitha's words, spoken in flat, bald terms, she sank into her chair and covered her ears for the reality was worse than she could have imagined. Had it been only the word that began with "m," which Tabitha herself had no qualms quoting—"mistress, mistress" she had said with a vicious hiss—Mary might have been less shocked. But this, what Tabitha was saying, was something much worse.

Mary was not entirely naïve and knew even wives of the utmost devotion and obedience could not always hold their husbands faithful. There had always been the bothersome thought at the back of her mind that Edward had married her primarily to be a mother to Louisa. Though she knew she could never replace that first wife, whom he had loved so deeply and so privately that he could not even say her name to Mary, she believed her loyalty and faithfulness over the years had led him to love her. And until recently he had been a kind and attentive husband. Since she was no beauty, she knew she was fortunate even to have a husband at all, and children of her own, so if Edward had … strayed …

But this? "Yes, much worse, Mary," said Tabitha. "Not his *mistress*, but his *wife!* The wife he told us all was dead. But she lives."

Much later, after Tabitha had left with a flounce and a wagging finger, and Mary was alone with the terrible news, she realized the full ramifications of what her sister-in-law had told her. Edward had another wife. His first wife, whom she thought was dead, whom she thought he had mourned all those years ago, was still alive. It was she whom he had been visiting all these months, and whom he had saved from a fire. As if that were not enough, there was a child. Edward's? She could not bear the thought.

She ran to the secret drawer in the bureau where he kept important documents. There it was, the hair watch chain that Edward had worn when she first met him, every day until their wedding day. Only then did he remove it and put it away in a drawer. She always assumed the watch chain was made from a lock of his first wife's hair, and that when he stopped wearing it he was no longer in mourning, and was newly committed to Mary.

She puzzled over the hair watch chain. Such artifacts were customarily made from a deceased person's hair, not from a living person. Where did he obtain the hair? Was it truly from his wife or did he purchase it, perhaps from a morgue, to deceive and present himself to the world and to Mary as a grieving widower?

But this was not the Edward she knew, the man she married and with whom she bore three children, a decent man, affectionate, serious but with a healthy sense of humour. There must be another explanation. Perhaps he truly did not know his wife was still alive. Perhaps he truly believed she was dead. But no. Tabitha was very clear. Edward had confessed he had known all along that his wife was still living, had known it when he "married" Mary.

Now everything she had thought was true was a lie. Edward, of all people, had deceived her for years. He had hidden the truth from her, from Thomas and Tabitha, even from Louisa, from everyone. Living a double life. Visiting his wife while pretending to be married to Mary.

Married to Mary. But not married to Mary. What did it matter whether he knew or did not know that his wife was living? Such details were insignificant to the reality that now dawned on her. *My marriage is illegal. My children—Amelia, Rebecca, even William Oliver—all illegitimate.* Conceived in sin, raised in sin. They would carry the stain of bastardy through their whole lives and beyond. And Edward knew that. This was a monstrous betrayal.

He would be charged and go to prison. Tabitha had been very sure of that. The penalty for bigamy was harsh, she said. And Mary— she would be regarded as a fallen woman, shunned by society, shamed, and humiliated. Thomas would not help, not with Tabitha around. With no means of support, she would have to fall on the charity of the parish. They would take her children to be farmed out as cheap labour, where they would never escape their birthright. And for her, the workhouse. A wail arose in her throat that she could not control.

She ran to the door, not even bothering to put on her bonnet, and headed down the stairs. She almost ran into Edward climbing up the stairs. He stopped when he saw her, his face stricken. If Mary still held a spark of hope that Tabitha had been wrong, it was dispelled by Edward at that moment. Guilt was etched on his face.

"Mary," he said, "I'm so sorry."

She pushed past him, knocking him against the wall, where he slipped and fell on the stairs.

She was out in the street and running before he had a chance to follow her, running towards the bridge, where she stopped and looked around, unsure for the moment where she was, as if some external force had deposited her in a new world she did not recognize. The streets looked strange; she saw houses as she had never seen them before, taller, narrower, in brighter colours. The sky swirled above her, the pavement swayed and dipped beneath her feet, the bridge seemed to divide before her to reveal the serpentine river writhing below her. She shrank back, and the bridge closed up again, reforming into an undulating rhythm like a ship on rough sea.

Her mind flew from her body; her feet took charge and carried her along such that she hardly felt the pavement beneath her. They knew where to take her. Across the bridge, through the labyrinths of the East End, on to Westminster, Soho, the little courtyard close to Oxford Street. Her feet deposited her on the familiar doorstep.

The world stopped moving. She knew where she was, and who she needed to see. She rang the doorbell, breathless. The door was opened by a tall, thin girl in a maid's uniform; not someone she recognized, but Mrs. Scroggs employed many successions of girls; this one must be the latest.

"Yes?" said the girl.

"I'm here to see Miss Everett."

"Miss Who?" The girl's manner was insolent.

"Miss Everett. She lives in the room at the back." She fought the quaver in her voice to enunciate the name clearly.

The girl gave a mirthless laugh, and Mary saw that she was older than she had first appeared, more a woman than a girl, close to middle-aged.

"And who, may I ask, is wanting to see her?" said the woman, peering closely at Mary, taking in her dishevelled appearance, her hatless head.

Who? Who indeed? Who was Mary? Not Mrs. Harris, the name she had borne, now falsely she knew, for the past nine years. But not Miss Piper. The naïve young girl from Somerset hoping for a new life. She hesitated, then said, "Mary. My name is Mary."

The woman smiled lazily at her. She made no move to stand aside to let her enter, but stood squarely in the doorway. "Well, *Mary*," she said, with barely disguised sarcasm, "and what might *you* be having to do with Miss Everett?"

"She … she is a good friend of mine. Please let her know she has a visitor."

The woman laughed aloud now, and her mouth twisted into a sneer. "Well, *Mary*, Miss Everett ain't here no more."

"Not here?" Miss Everett never went out. "I think you must be mistaken. Miss Everett is an invalid and is confined to her room."

"Is that so? Well, I'm telling you she ain't here, and I'll tell you why. Fact is, your Miss Everett got took off to the loony bin not a fortnight since. Mad as a hatter she was."

"What?" The woman was talking nonsense. Mary gathered her wits. "Forgive me, I beg you, but I think you must be referring to someone else. Miss Everett is a special friend of the proprietor, Mrs. Scroggs. She has lived here for many years, and she is certainly not insane."

The woman scoffed. "Sez you! You shoulda seen her. Completely off her rocker she was. Crackers. Wandering up and down the stairs, mumbling about seeing dead people, talking to them, singing at all times of the day and night. When she started screaming about how a man was coming to get her, we called for the vicar but he couldn't do nothing for her. Said she'd dabbled in the dark arts and was riddled with evil spirits.

"We couldn't put up with it no more, what with the gentlemen boarders complaining and the servants giving notice—she quite put the wind up everyone. Had to get the doctor in and he ordered her off to the loony bin."

Mary felt nauseous. Miss Everett, in an insane asylum! This, on top of the news about Edward, sent the world spinning again. She had sat with Miss Everett so many times, listening to words that washed over her like balm and sent her away with a lightness in her step. Had any of it been real? Had she misread Miss Everett just as she had misread Edward? The other servants always thought Miss Everett was mad, but Mary hadn't believed it. She could hardly believe it now. But if Miss Everett were mad, perhaps she was too, for she had hung on everything Miss Everett said, whether or not she understood her words, because she trusted her completely. As she had trusted Edward.

The woman on the doorstep continued to scrutinize Mary, and said, as if she had read her mind. "A friend of hers, you say you are.

Well, if you're a friend of that mad woman, I figure you must be mad yourself. Looking at you, I'd say that's a fact if ever I saw one."

Mary was suddenly aware of her appearance. She was flushed and perspiring, her hair had fallen from its bun, and her clothes were dusty from her run. She must have looked a sight. Like a mad woman. Mad like Miss Everett. She backed away from the door.

"That's right, time you were on your way," said the woman. "Mrs. Scroggs wouldn't want your type hanging around."

Mrs. Scroggs! Perhaps she could help Mary. She tried again with the woman, forcing herself to inject some authority into her voice.

"Mrs. Scroggs knows me. I'm sure she would be pleased to see me. Can you tell her I'm here?"

"No, I can't, because she ain't here right now. She's gone off to Brighton, ain't she, with the silversmith, her gentlemen friend. Anyway, she'd tell you the same as me, 'cause it was her what called the doctor. So off you go, *Mary*, on your way." The woman waved Mary away and closed the door.

Mary was already halfway down the street, running as fast as she could, heedless of her unfastened hair, of the puddles and mud that dragged at the hem of her skirt, her arms flailing, her shawl streaming behind her. As she ran, she slipped and wove past hands that seemed to reach out from every doorway. Voices in her head accused, condemned, shamed; imaginary fingers pointed. Tabitha's face, her mouth in a twisted pout, telling her she was a fool to be so trusting; Thomas shaking his head at her, turning his back on her. Tabitha's voice rising to a shriek and merging with the sound of a single church bell ringing a single, somber, repeating toll.

The river was in sight. She stopped to catch her breath, and bent down as blood rushed to her head and saliva to her mouth. After several deep breaths, the thumping of her heart slowed, the tolling bell stopped, and her head began to clear. She limped onto the bridge, and went to the railing.

Tabitha was right. There had been clues from the start, which she had chosen to ignore. Why the insistence on marrying in Scotland? Why was there no grave? Why did he never mention her name or acknowledge her as Louisa's mother? Other clues. His insistence she not talk to Ellen, the wetnurse; Ellen must have known her. Puzzling looks from Aunt Fanny. The Irish woman who came to the door last January, whom Edward turned away. Was that her?

She had been too timid to ask awkward questions, too grateful that a man would want to marry her at all. Then, with the birth of the children, she gave in to a comfortable complacency. But this? Surely even Tabitha with her suspicious nature could not have imagined this?

A fog had risen and enveloped the river, turning it to a grey abyss and muffling all sound but the gentle lapping of the water below. The world disappeared. All that was left was her and the grey oblivion around her. It would be so easy to let it embrace her, carry her away, down the river, out of the grime and soot of London, westwards through fields of wheat and oats, back to her childhood home.

Her mother in the garden gathering herbs, greets her. *Come, my Little Sparrow, I need your help.* Later, she holds a slippery baby as it emerges, wraps it in a towel, while her mother watches and nods in approval. *You're ready, Mary.* Years pass and Mary has birthed a hundred babies. That's what she does and the village loves her. She's the spinster midwife. She has the love and respect of the people. Mothers ask her to teach their daughters to do what she does. She doesn't need a husband ...

Something tugged at her skirt. She brushed it away. *Leave me.*

In springtime, primroses paint the hedgerows yellow. Daffodils line the river banks. When she walks from her cottage into the village, people greet her. *There goes Mary Piper, a good and virtuous woman, our own village midwife.*

The tugging came again, more insistently. A small voice drifted through the fog.

"Mama, Mama."

Another tug. Mary turned. It was Louisa. Mary was jettisoned back to the bridge. Louisa looked up at her with a worried face. Mary sank to the ground, and pulled the girl to her. Louisa struggled to be free. At twelve years old she was a confident, insightful child who often acted older than her years, and she seemed to know this turn of events could not be dismissed with a simple hug.

"Mama, Papa is home. He sent me to find you. You must come."

Mary rose, turned away from Louisa, and gripped the railing of the bridge. Yes, it would be easy to jump, and be carried away to another world. But she was in this world and if she jumped, what then? Whether she lived or died, her children would suffer. Death was easy. It would put an end to her suffering in this world, but her suffering in the next world would be eternal, for suicide was a grave sin. Her children would be doubly tainted, as the bastard children of a mother who died by her own hand. Sin surrounded her, at every turn. It would be a sin to continue living, but a worse sin to die.

Louisa continued to tug at her skirt. "Mama, please come back."

She looked at Louisa's upturned face and clear eyes. Then she took her hand, and they walked home together. With Louisa's steadying hand in hers, she mounted the stairs and entered their rooms. Edward stood at the far end of the room; Amelia and Rebecca played on the floor beside him. Louisa, as if knowing what was to come, ran to her sisters and shepherded them out to the yard. Edward's face was a blank sheet. He moved towards her as she entered, extended his hand. She raised her palm as if to say, come no closer.

"Mary." His voice was a coarse whisper.

She swallowed hard and forced herself to look him in the eye.

"Who am I, Edward?"

"You are Mary. You are the mother of our children."

"But not your wife. Not Mrs. Harris."

He looked down, wringing his hands, and shook his head.

"Mary ... I cannot ... I wish ... I never meant ... Tabitha shouldn't have ..."

"Do you love her very much? Have you always loved her? Do you want to be with her?"

"She's dying, Mary. She has perhaps weeks, months at the most. The fire burnt her lungs. The doctor holds no hope for her."

"Then you must go to her, Edward. She is your wife, and you are her husband."

"Mary ... "

She remained silent.

"Mary ... what about you?"

"Me? I am nobody, Edward. I have no position in this family."

"Mary, please, I … that's not true … I didn't want you to find out like this …"

"Oh? And how did you expect me to find out?"

Edward looked down, shamefaced.

"It's clear that you didn't want me to find out at all. Did you? You expected to live this lie forever."

Edward said nothing. His silence steeled Mary's resolve. She drew herself up to her full height. Head up, hands stiff by her sides, her stance as erect as a soldier's.

"Edward, I will not stand in your way. I cannot in conscience take you from your legal wife. I have no hold on you. And I think you will find the law is not on my side in this. As I say, I have no status."

Finally, Edward looked up. His expression was pained. "Mary, what can I do? Please. Let us find a solution together."

"Solution? What solution? You have not denied you love her. You have not asked me to stay. And even if you did, I cannot. I will not live in sin with you, Edward. You must take your children, and you must go to her."

Edward's face, already pale, seemed to turn paler still. He sank into an armchair.

"Oh, perhaps you are afraid?" said Mary. "Shall you go to prison? Bigamy is a crime. Perhaps Tabitha can be prevailed upon to keep quiet. I have some influence with my brother. I'll talk to him, but that's all I can do for you, and I do it only for the children, for it is yet another error to evade the law, if only by silence. And then you shall go to her. You have no obligation to me, I shall … "

Mary was shocked by the vehemence of her own words; they welled up like a waterspout from some dark place inside her that had newly revealed its existence. With a supreme effort, she willed the words to stop their flow and cease in mid-sentence. At the silence, Edward looked up.

"You shall? What shall you do? Please, anything. Whatever you wish?"

Mary thought for a moment, and then she knew.

"I shall go back to Scotland. To Stornaway. Alone."

"Alone?"

"Yes."

"Mary, please. Can we not ... you can't go alone. I don't want you to leave. The children need you."

"You can send the children to Aunt Fanny in Birmingham. She'll be quite willing to have them. In fact, it will be best for them to be away from this unpleasant business. Please wire her at once, tell her I am indisposed, suffering from some illness. I am sure you can find a suitable *lie* to tell her." Rarely had the word "lie" ever been uttered from Mary's lips, but now she had said it, it seemed easy to say it again. "*Lie, lie.* Lie to Aunt Fanny. Lie to the vicar. Lie to our neighbours. Lie to the children. Most of all, to the children. You've proven yourself a past master at calumny.

"But Edward, let your lies be for the children's good, to protect them from the stain of bastardy. Louisa will be your challenge. At her next birthday, she will be thirteen and will need a position. Future employers will want to know of her background. Say whatever is needed to protect her. Spread whatever falsehood you wish. Deception has become your profession, and it has so tainted me that I cannot stay."

Mary turned from Edward and walked to the window, where she held onto the window frame with both hands. Edward, still in his chair, seemed flummoxed and quite unable to face Mary or respond to her tirade. How easy it had become to hate him, and easier yet to hate the woman who had led her to ruin. Yet how dreadful, were these feelings that raged like a fire lost to all control. Such unfamiliar emotions left her feeling ragged and exhausted. But she could not let Edward see even a moment of weakness. She laid her forehead against the window pane. It was cool on her skin. She longed for the cold, cleansing air of Scotland.

"How long ... how long will you ... ?" asked Edward.

"I don't know. Weeks, perhaps months. That's what you said, not I."

"And after that? You'll return? For the children, if not for me?"

Mary closed her eyes, and tightened her grip on the window frame. "I don't know, Edward. I don't know."

Edward stood up and ran his fingers through his hair. "Well then," he said, and paused, perhaps hoping to open a more reasoned discussion. Mary ignored him. "Scotland. Alone. How do you propose to travel? Where will you stay?"

Mary went to the dresser, took out clothes, folded them, and selected a few personal toilet items to pack in a bag. "I shall find my way. I'll wire Mrs. McPhee at the draper's shop. She was a good friend to me in Scotland, and she'll help me now."

Edward rose and watched her from the other end of the room. Still Mary ignored him and continued to pack.

"Well then," he said again. "Um. Let me at least arrange your safe passage. You could travel with a family as a companion. I could write a letter for you."

Mary considered this, and nodded. "That will be acceptable."

Edward went to his desk and took out paper and a pen.

"You will ... write?" Edward asked.

"I shall keep the children informed of my welfare."

That evening, she sat Louisa down and explained to her what was to happen. Edward loitered in the background, wordless, his face haunted, his eyes moist.

Louisa looked at Mary with wide, puzzled eyes.

"Mama, where are you going? Why?"

Mary felt her resolve cracking.

"It's not forever," she said gently. "Mama is a little unwell and needs some special air."

"I'll come with you. I'll look after you, Mama, get you well again. Mama, *please*."

"No Louisa. Please try to be brave. You will go with your sisters to your Aunt Fanny in Birmingham. I'll be back before you even miss me."

Wrong of her to make a promise to a child she was not sure she could keep. She didn't know if she would ever be back. Edward was lost to her and lost to her children too, and there was no possibility of her caring for them alone. No, the only chance for the children to avoid the stain of their birth was for Aunt Fanny to care for them. She was a good woman, and she would do her best to protect their reputation. Louisa would mourn for a while, but she was strong and resilient, and would get over it.. As for the younger girls—they would soon make new friends in Birmingham and forget all about London. Perhaps, in time, they would forget about her too.

PART III

Stornaway, Scotland
London, England

1857-1858

TWENTY-NINE

Since their first journey to Scotland nearly a decade earlier, a network of railways had reached from England into Scotland as far as Glasgow, and the journey was faster and pleasanter than before. Scotland had opened up to summer holidaymakers, and although it was already late September, it had been easy for Edward to find a well-to-do family taking the coach from Glasgow north to the ferry terminal for Stornaway.

The Galbraiths were a pleasant couple, making the journey to visit Mr. Galbraith's family, and happy to chaperone Mary in return for her companionship of their two young sons. Keeping the two boys entertained helped to take Mary's mind off all that had happened. There would be time for brooding once she arrived on the island.

In her wire to Sally McPhee, she cited "convalescence from illness" as the reason for her return to Stornaway—another lie, thought Mary as she dictated to the telegraph boy—and asked her to recommend her to a lodging house near the harbour. When she arrived, Sally and her husband, Angus, were waiting for her at the ferry port with Angus's old horse and cart.

"It's good to see you again, Mary," said Sally. "I'm sorry to learn you've been ill. Angus and I hope you'll come and stay with us, in our spare room. I've made it up for you."

Mary was surprised by this news. The only spare room she knew of in Sally's house was the mysterious one that no one but Sally entered. No matter; she was happy to have a place to stay with her old friend.

Angus hoisted her bag onto the cart, helped Mary and Sally up onto the seat, clicked at the horse, and they set off. While Angus, silent, drove the cart, Mary felt Sally's keen eyes on her. Her gaze made Mary self-conscious, for she knew that while her face was drawn and her forehead striated with worry lines, her body, as strong and stout as ever, betrayed no sign of frailty. Sally must guess, she thought, that what ailed her was not sickness of the body but of the heart. Mary's surmise was confirmed by Sally's next words.

"I ken you'll be with us for a while, Mary, for you've some healing to do. If you help me in the shop, I'll not charge you rent. If you work hard, I might stretch to some pocket money for you."

Mary felt moved almost to tears by the generosity of this gentle woman. Edward had paid for the train and ferry, the Galbraiths had not charged her for the coach, but the money she had taken from the rainy-day jar for her keep would last no more than a fortnight.

During the seven-day journey, she had thought about what she would do in Stornaway, how long she would stay and how she might live once her money ran out. She quickly rejected any thought of returning to her former calling as a midwife; that bridge had too long ago been burned. But she could be a nursemaid. That would suit her fine. Or there was always housemaid. Ironic, she thought, to fall back down to where she'd started in London, before Louisa, before Edward, before her marriage which, it turned out, was not a marriage at all. Yes, a housemaid might be best for it would be hard now to care for another woman's children. But these thoughts remained vague and swamped by the one imperative that had led her to leave in such haste—to get away from Edward, and to be alone, quite alone to think, to grieve, and once again, to heal.

When they arrived at the McPhees' cottage, Sally showed Mary into the room that had always remained closed. It was simple and clean, containing a bed with a patchwork quilt, a chair, a washstand, and a small chest. Nothing apparently unusual about it, but she'd always suspected that something sad had happened in that room.

Sally and Angus were not ones to gossip, or to poke into other people's affairs, and Mary was grateful that in the following days and weeks, Sally refrained from inquiring into the nature of Mary's indisposition or the reason for her travelling alone to Scotland. Mary bore her pain alone, especially at night, as she lay in the little narrow bed in Sally McPhee's house, the smell of smoldering peat and drying fish filling the air. And there was, she realized, something else in the air of that room—a memory of something which caused Sally to close it off. Why now had she decided to open it up for Mary? Perhaps, one day, Sally would tell her.

Edward wrote her a spare, regretful letter; a confessional in which he reprimanded himself for his perfidy and abased himself as a sinner before her. But he did not beg her to return to him, and he said nothing of his wife. His address had changed. He must have given up the family lodgings and moved with his wife to a new place in Clerkenwell. *His wife*. How alien that sounded to her ears. His letter made her angry. She did not respond to it.

Letters came from Aunt Fanny and Louisa. There had been some tears at first, Fanny wrote, and the usual tantrums from Rebecca, but they had now settled down happily. Louisa was quiet and obedient, and was a big help with the younger girls; Mary had raised her well, she said. Rebecca sent a drawing of her holding hands with Aunt Fanny, Louisa, and Amelia. Stick figures in crayon with big smiling faces. Louisa's letter was restrained and polite, as if she were holding back her own distress so as not to worry Mary. She enclosed a pressed flower and added three kisses.

The letters, though bittersweet to read, confirmed to Mary that her decision to leave was correct. As a woman alone with three children, two illegitimate and the other, Louisa, to whom she had no legal claim, there was no future for them with her. And the very idea of them going to Edward was unthinkable as long as he was living with his dying wife.

Better for the girls to be with their Aunt Fanny than to be with her in a life of ignominy and deceit, or, worse, with Edward. Yet how it hurt to read their letters. She didn't know when, if ever, she would see her children again, yet every day and every night she ached to hold them.

Life in Stornaway took on a rhythm. In the mornings, Mary stocked the shelves of the shop with bolts of tweed and tartan, spools of thread, and boxes of needles, and helped Angus load peat stacks onto his cart. In the afternoons, when she wasn't busy in the shop, Sally showed Mary how to prepare traditional Scottish foods. She learned how to make cock-a-leekie soup, scones and oatcakes, and proper porridge. Angus showed her how to smoke herrings to make salty, soft-fleshed kippers. She attended Sunday services, chatted with neighbours, and brushed up her rusty knowledge of Gaelic words and phrases.

Sometimes, when sadness took hold of her, she climbed up to the crofts and retraced the moorland paths she had walked before. The brisk air was invigorating. The wind and the cold filled her lungs, and her ears, and her head, and blocked out all thought and all memory. When this happened, for a few moments she felt liberated from loss and pain and regret and anger, and from everyone and everything in her former life. Was this what Miss Everett had meant by "emancipation"? It was a good feeling, a sense of being free from encumbrances. Unencumbered. That was another word Miss Everett had used.

She thought about Miss Everett locked away in an asylum, and fancied this might have been her own fate had this island and the McPhees not saved her. She felt she ought to try to find out where they had taken her. She could write to Mrs. Scroggs, or Polly and Martha might know. But she didn't write. She didn't write to any of them. When she left London, she left her old life behind, and that included Miss Everett.

THIRTY

Three days after Edward packed his daughters, along with a letter, on the train to Birmingham, Uncle George arrived on his doorstep. Edward bowed stiffly and ushered him in. George looked around at the half-filled packing boxes, took out his pipe, and began to fill it. Edward, erect and silent, waited for his uncle to speak. George drew on his pipe a few times, took it out of his mouth, and pointed the stem at Edward.

"Well, lad, it's a bad do, and no mistake."

Edward said nothing, and went back to putting things in the packing boxes.

"You've upset your aunt something terrible."

Edward felt the tension in his shoulders, but he kept his voice impassive. "I'm sorry. Please thank her for taking the girls. She's a fine woman."

"Hard on the girls. Been a lot of crying. Tantrums."

"They'll get over it." They would. Amelia's tears would dry, Rebecca's whining would cease. The angry look on Louisa's face as she'd shepherded her sisters onto the train and refused to wave goodbye to him would fade. Children were resilient.

"The fact is, my lad … "

Edward interrupted him. "Uncle George, you really didn't need to come all this way to see me. Everything you need to know is in the letter I sent you. And frankly, I don't need your advice."

George puffed his chest out. "I'm not here to give you advice, lad. I'm here to ask you what you intend to do about this business."

Edward continued to fill the boxes. He would not be intimidated by his uncle. "Exactly what I am doing," he said. "The right thing. It's about time. I've written to Mary, told her everything and expressed my deepest regrets for hurting her. I don't expect her forgiveness. I've come clean with you and Aunt Fanny. You know my position. I've done what I can to protect the girls and I know they'll be safe with Aunt Fanny. And now I'm going to take care of my wife. I've rented a room in Clerkenwell and will be joining her there, along with her young daughter. Now, if you wish to be of any assistance in this matter, you can help me carry these boxes downstairs."

George grew red in the face. "The right thing? This is what you think is the right thing? Come on now, lad. You're not thinking straight."

"She is my wife. I have responsibilities."

"Responsibilities? And what about your family? What about that sweet gal you sent off up to Scotland on her own?"

Edward flinched. "That was Mary's choice. She wanted to go. She's got friends up there who will take care of her. Good people. I'm sorry that Mary had to be hurt, but she'll be all right now." George looked skeptical. Edward pushed away the memory of Mary's face on the day she left—pale, lips pursed, eyes ice cold. He gave his head a shake. He would not think about Mary.

George went to the fireplace, knocked out his pipe, and blew on it to make sure it was out. Edward continued his packing.

"Hmm," George said. He stood with his back to the fireplace, holding the bowl of his pipe, and rocked on his heels.

"Seems she's got quite a hold on you, this Irish girl. What's it all about, lad? What do you think you're doing?"

Edward said nothing. George put the pipe back in his pocket. "Come on, now, my boy," he said, "this is not the way and you know it."

Edward looked up from the box he was packing, and held his uncle's gaze.

"Oh. And what is the way, Uncle George? What action do you propose I take? I could continue to live by lies and deceit. I could leave my wife for the parish to take. Let them bury her in a pauper's grave. Is that what you want? As I said, she is my wife. My legal wife. You saw us married. You heard the vows we made."

Silence hung between them. George shifted uncomfortably, hunching his shoulders, running his hand over his balding head.

"Yes, well," he said, then paused. "What am I tell your Aunt Fanny?"

Edward gave a short laugh and shook his head. He felt the tension leave his shoulders. "Aunt Fanny," he said. "Here's what you tell her. You tried. Tell her you tried. But you failed, because Edward wouldn't see sense. Just tell her that."

George coloured again. His forehead was shiny with sweat. He took a handkerchief from his pocket and mopped his brow. More moments of awkward silence passed as Edward tied up the boxes.

Then, "Yes, well, right-o, Edward. Nothing I can say, then, to change your mind? Nothing at all?" Edward kept his head down, concentrating on stacking the tied-up boxes by the door.

"It's what I need to do, Uncle. And it is the right thing, by God and the Church. You could call it my duty if you like."

"Ah yes. Duty. Well ... " George hesitated, then picked up a box and followed Edward downstairs. "I'll tell your Aunt Fanny that as well."

In the street, Edward called a carter over and arranged delivery; he would follow on foot. He turned to Uncle George and shook his hand. Uncle George responded with a firm double handshake, and patted Edward on the back. "Be on my way, then, Edward. Sorry and all. You're a good lad. Wish it could be different. We'll look after the girls. Sorry about poor Mary up in Scotland." Edward looked at his feet. George continued. "Of course, we'll be here for you as and when ... you know."

Edward closed his eyes briefly and gave his uncle a watery smile. "Thank you, Uncle George. If you hurry, you can catch the evening train. I must get over to Clerkenwell straightaway."

Weeks, perhaps months, was what the doctor said. Since that was all the time he could have with her, he took it and made each moment as if it were their last. For him, there was no past, and no future, only the present. It had been like that on the day he'd met her, when he took her on the boat with him. He would gladly have drowned on that boat journey if it had meant being with her forever. And still would. Even more now that she was dying and there was so little time left for them.

On her good days, while she was still able to leave her bed, they strolled arm in arm through London's parks, with Violet holding fast to his hand. Once they went to the Zoological Gardens where they laughed at the antics of the monkeys in the monkey house, and watched with awe the lions and tigers pacing, Violet on Edward's shoulders holding tight. They took a pleasure boat trip on the river, and Catherine trailed her fingers in the water while Edward and Violet threw bread crusts to the gulls.

When she could no longer leave her bed, he fed her soup and oranges and sweetmeats. On bad days, he cooled her feverish brow, and propped her pillows to help her breathe. They both delighted in Violet, who was learning to talk and kiss and cuddle. At night, they slept with her between them and Edward sang to her.

The weeks, perhaps months, were nearly up. Autumn passed into winter, and then to early spring. He didn't notice the tiny buds on the trees, or the green shoots pushing through the melting snow in the parks. The days were mostly bad now. She was rarely well enough to walk in the park. Her cheeks had grown hollow, her breathing was laboured. But when she opened her eyes, it was him she saw, him she smiled at, and his hand she clasped.

In Ireland, there had been a bird, a kestrel. It had belonged to the landlord's son, and the boy would let it out each day. Edward used to climb to a rocky outcrop and watch the bird wheel and dip above the hillside. Then, its freedom flight over, it would return, hover, and swoop down to alight on the boy's arm. No matter how far and how high the bird flew, it always came back. As, in the end, Catherine had come back to him. In the end, she loved him, of that he was sure. These last days they spent together were sweet and for this short while, his soul was at peace.

THIRTY-ONE

By November, the Hebridean nights were fast drawing in. In the evenings Mary sat around the fire with Sally and Angus, winding skeins of wool for Sally to knit the thick, oily jerseys the fishermen wore, and the McPhees chatted about local events and happenings. They told her some of the other Hebridean islands had suffered from the same potato blight that had destroyed the harvests in Ireland.

"It was not too bad for us, here," said Sally. "We had the fish, you see. And the barley and oats. But for the crofters on some of the other islands … " She shook her head.

Mary wanted to change the subject. Mention of the potato blight inevitably led her to thoughts of Ireland and the Irish, which in turn opened a crack in her defences that allowed Edward's wife to enter. She could not allow herself to imagine this woman. Edward had never talked about her, and she knew only that he had met her in Ireland. Louisa, she always assumed, with her startlingly blue eyes and golden curls turning to copper, must take after her.

December and January passed. There was no further word from Edward. Letters from Aunt Fanny and Louisa became more sporadic. Then in February, Uncle George wrote to say he had arranged for Louisa to take up a position at the Marylebone home of Colonel and Mrs. Graham. Colonel Graham was the illustrious son of one of Uncle George's former commanding officers. The Grahams kept a full complement of staff, and Louisa would be no less than assistant nursemaid to the Grahams' two young boys, Percival and Ralph. The news made Mary happy, but wistful. Her children were growing up and she was not there to see them blossom.

When she'd left Somerset all those years ago to start a new life in London, she'd found healing and strength and self-worth and love such as she'd never imagined could be hers. But now that new life had proved to be a fragile edifice, and she didn't know if it could ever be rebuilt. That night, as on so many nights, she dreamt of her children: Louisa's loving heart, Amelia's chubby face and sunny disposition, even Rebecca's whine and stamping foot. And William Oliver. In the little room with its mysterious memory, his thin, wracked body was always there with his sisters in her dream. It was as if he belonged in that room.

The following evening, as Mary sat with Sally by the fire and Angus worked out back, she told Sally about William Oliver's death. Sally had known him as a young infant, but in her discreet way had never asked about him.

Sally laid her knitting down and stretched out her hand to Mary's. She held it for a long time, until they heard Angus's heavy footsteps outside the door, and she let go. Angus came in with a pile of peat and banked up the fire.

"Off to the barn to bed the horse," he said. Sally rose, watched him go, then closed the door softly and came back to her chair.

"I had a child once," she said quietly.

Mary let out a long breath.

"I expect you must have wondered." Sally glanced at the door to the room where Mary now slept.

Mary inclined her head to Sally. She didn't want to appear probing, but she hoped Sally was now ready to tell her what had happened in that room.

"If you want to tell me ... "

Sally nodded. They sat for a few moments in silence, and then Sally spoke.

"A little girl. We called her Ailsa."

Mary smiled encouragingly.

"She was ... stillborn."

"Oh," Mary said. An involuntary shiver touched her shoulders, like a breeze from the past, a memory still clear, even after all these years. A memory of how the daffodils were in bud, the willow trees were leafing out, and the springtime sun was bright the day Mary took the riverside walk to Harriet Pickard's cottage, carrying her bag of tools and bundle of herbs.

"I was forty-two years old," Sally said. Her words brought Mary back to the present. "Angus and I had waited twenty years for that baby. We made the room up, the one you're in now. I had so many plans, Mary. All through the months of the pregnancy, my days were filled with thoughts of the joys that were to come, after so many years of waiting. And then ... "

"Oh, Sally, I'm so ... "

"It was a difficult birth. A long labour. All day and all night."

On that spring day, Harriet Pickard's labour had begun early in the morning, and stretched on into an unending night.

"They said I was too old." Sally wiped her eyes with the corner of her apron.

They'd said that about Harriet Pickard, too. Well over forty, they'd said. Too old to be having her tenth child. Mary didn't know. She was only eighteen at the time.

"But I wonder," Sally continued, "about the midwife who delivered her. She said I waited too long to call her. And then, all that pushing and pulling. The yanking. It just about tore me apart. I was sure I would die. She was just a young girl, inexperienced. I think she didn't really know what to do. She tried, but ... "

Mary closed her eyes. Had she also been too young and inexperienced that day? Had she pushed and pulled too hard? Had she miscalculated the timing, the position of the child, the condition of the cervix? If her mother had still been alive and with her that day, could she have stopped the bleeding? Saved poor Harriet Pickard, lying moon-white on the bed, before her life slipped away into the night? She'd been haunted by these questions, but the answers had never come.

Sally was still talking. "They let me hold her, just for a few minutes. The women in that room, and that young midwife. They handed her to me, wrapped in a blanket, and I held her."

Harriet Pickard had never held her baby. Mary told the other women in the room to take it away, while she tried to stop the bleeding. Harriet must not be allowed to see it, she said. You must never tell her, she said. She must never know. The women nodded, silent, shocked.

Sally was smiling, her eyes shining. "Mary, she was perfect. Perfect little hands and feet, a sweet face. To this day, I can still see that little face."

Mary had seen the face of Harriet Pickard's baby that day. A face with no eyes to see with, no ears to hear with, no mouth to cry with. She saw its whole body as it lay, like a mound of jelly between Harriet's legs, on the blood-soaked sheet. A body that had ... fins? Fins in place of arms to wave, and legs to kick. It squirmed, it flapped, and it expired. Mary picked it up, gave it to the women, and turned back to Harriet. She had to stop the bleeding.

Sally continued. "Then they took her away. They cleaned me up. My body healed. I was up and about within days. But here, inside ... " Sally tapped her chest.

Harriet Pickard had not healed quickly. She had not healed at all, because Mary couldn't stop the bleeding. It had soaked through the bedsheets, the mattress, flowed onto the floor, stained her apron, her blouse, her skirt. It had drained from Harriet's body like a river until she'd slipped away. Sally's baby had been perfect. But Harriet Pickard's baby could not have survived. And Harriet Pickard could not have survived such a birth. No woman could have. In her heart she knew it, but ...

Mary took a deep breath, and opened her eyes. These were memories she'd tried to bury, things she'd never wanted to think about, but they kept coming back, all through the years, coming back unbidden. Things she had never talked about to anyone, not even Edward, or Louisa. Especially not Louisa. Even her brother Thomas had only heard the story from others.

Sally gave a wan smile. "I kept that room as a place to come and pray and think about Ailsa, about what might have been. At least I gave away the cradle. But Mary," Sally's expression became intense, "I couldn't give Ailsa up. You see, she still lived inside of me. She still does. She lives and grows and runs on the brae. Can you understand that, Mary?"

Mary blinked and touched her palm to back of Sally's hand. *At least I have real memories of William Oliver. I had him for seven years and he lived and breathed and played on the brae. I do not need to invent a childhood.*

"Yes," said Mary, "I can understand that, Sally."

Sally stared into space. "The hardest part," she said, "was learning to forgive."

"Forgive?" said Mary, eyebrows raised.

"Set aside blame. Forgive that young midwife, forgive God for making this happen, forgive Angus for not finding a way to prevent it. Forgive my body for failing me, and above all, forgive myself for whatever faults of my own had caused this to happen."

"Sally, it wasn't your fault. Sometimes these things just happen. No one is to blame." A platitude. *No one was to blame for Harriet Pickard's death, or for the womb creature that could not live and could not allow its mother to live. But still, I blamed myself.*

"I know that now," said Sally. She gave a regretful smile. "But it took me nearly fifteen years."

"I never knew," said Mary. Her chest felt tight. Her thoughts crowded in: anger, regrets, sorrow, guilt, self-pity. They pounded within her, rising to a crescendo, then converged on one single word: forgiveness.

"Because I kept it all inside," Sally put her hand on her breast, "and inside that room. And then your telegram came, and I knew it was time." She smiled. "Ailsa would be fifteen now. A young woman. Out on her own, perhaps even courting. It was time to leave her childhood behind, put away my self-pity, open up that room, and open up myself to help another woman in distress. Angus was relieved, I think. He's been very patient."

Mary felt Sally's eyes on her. "Mary," she said. "Don't wait fifteen years."

The tension lifted from Mary's chest, and she breathed normally.

The two women sat in silence until they heard Angus returning from the barn. He came in through the back door, stopped, looked at Sally's red-rimmed eyes, then at Mary, and nodded. He gave Sally's shoulder a gentle squeeze, and patted Mary's arm.

The next morning, Mary wrote two letters, one to Louisa at her new employer's address in Marylebone, and one to Edward. She asked Louisa to book her a room at a lodging house, and to expect her arrival within a fortnight. Louisa wrote back by the next available post, telling her how thrilled she was with her news, and she knew of exactly the right sort of lodging in a mews house a few doors from her employer's home.

To Edward she wrote simply that she was returning to London and wished to meet with him.

When she told Sally of her decision to return, Sally took both her hands in hers and smiled. "It's the right thing to do Mary," she said. "You'll keep in touch?"

"I will."

Angus piled her belongings onto the horse and cart, and then from the cart to the ferry, and helped Mary across the gangplank. She waved as the ferry steamed away, and Stornaway and the Isle of Lewis faded into the mist.

PART IV

London, England

1870

THIRTY-TWO

It has rained in the night and Louisa's footsteps echo on the damp cobblestones as she hurries through Soho to her father's shop. The rain-washed spring air smells fresh this morning and white clouds scud in a pale blue sky. Louisa crosses Soho Square, takes a shortcut through St. Anne's churchyard, past the red brick hulk of the workhouse, and through the Berwick Street Market. The flowergirls at the market are already selling bunches of March daffodils in bud, and Louisa stops to buy some, as she does every year on this day. Later, she will go with her parents and sister to visit the grave of a woman she never knew but whose memory has embedded its threads into all their lives.

Louisa continues through Soho's narrow lanes and passages to a little courtyard off Rupert Street. Near the corner, squeezed between a pawnshop and a cheesemonger, is her father's shop. Well, not entirely *his* shop. She looks up at the sign and feels the usual frisson of pleasure at the name: "HARRIS AND DAUGHTER, FINE MAPS AND PRECISION SURVEY INSTRUMENTS."

She unlocks and enters. The pungent aroma of metal polish, the musty smell of old paper and ink always arouse in her a shiver of excitement. When her father retired from the military in 1860, he bought the shop from Mr. Makepeace, the former owner. At the time, Louisa was a nursemaid to two boys in the Graham household in Marylebone. When the Graham boys went away to school, Louisa came to work alongside her father in the shop and he added "daughter" to the sign. She stays in touch with the two Graham boys, up at Oxford now, and with Mrs. Graham. But it is here among the maps and brass instruments she has found her calling. *Like father, like daughter.*

Her father has made very few changes to the shop, and Louisa would like to modernize it. Piped water would be nice, and one of the new flush privies at the back. But she agrees with her father about the instruments. Some of them, like the intricate brass theodolite, the compass still in its leather case, and the polished wood and metal sextant in a glossy wooden box, are almost antiques, too precious to sell. They remain displayed in the window to draw in curious customers.

Louisa fills a vase with water from the large pot at the back of the shop, and arranges the daffodils. On this day twelve years ago, her mother led her through London to see a dying woman. She closes her eyes to recall, in a series of sharp, disassembled images, the woman's hollow cheeks, her ragged breath, her corkscrew curls, and the startling moment she opened her eyes and looked at Louisa.

The daffodils are a little limp, but the water will perk them up. Louisa places the vase in the window of the shop with the antique instruments, and turns the sign hanging on the door from "CLOSED" to "OPEN."

March 15, 1858 was three days after her thirteenth birthday and Mary, her mama, was back from Scotland after more than six months away. They had met by arrangement on a bench in a small park in Marylebone were the wind had blown last year's dry leaves into piles and daffodils were pushing up through the grass. Her mama had said she had something important to tell Louisa. But Louisa was too excited to listen and wanted only to talk about her job, and her two little charges, Percival and Ralph, the fun she had with them, the mischief they got up to, and how she missed her sisters, who were still in Birmingham, and she thought Aunt Fanny liked her now since she'd been such a help with the girls, and how Mama wouldn't believe how much Rebecca and Amelia had grown, and now Mama was back, wouldn't she send for them so they could be together as a family again?

As Louisa chattered on, Mary took her hand and led her through unfamiliar streets and boulevards to a tenement building, where they climbed to the second floor. Louisa grew uneasy. "Where is this, Mama? Why are we here?" Mary squeezed her hand but said nothing. With the other hand, she knocked on one of the landing doors. Her knock was firm. Not the polite way her mama usually knocked on a door. Rather, the sort of knock one might expect from Mrs. Graham.

A dishevelled-looking woman opened the door a crack and said in a sharp, unpleasant tone, "Yes?"

"I am here to see Mrs. Harris," Mary said.

Louisa was puzzled. Mary was Mrs. Harris. Who was this other Mrs. Harris?

"Just in time, too, I'd say, whoever you are," said the woman. She had a grubby face, untidy hair, and a downturned mouth, features Louisa found alarming. "And you can tell Mr. Harris, if she goes in the next hour or so, I'm still charging for the day."

"You may leave now," Mary said to the woman. Louisa had rarely heard her mama speak in so sharp a tone.

"Please yourself. I'll be downstairs if you need me." She pushed past to leave the room, and Louisa caught a whiff of her breath. She knew that smell; she'd smelt it on the breath of men and women who lounged outside taverns.

Louisa sensed there was something in the room she wouldn't want to see. She bit the inside of her cheek and pinched her lips together. Mary took her hand. They entered the room, and closed the door behind them.

The shop is cold. Louisa really must get her father to repair the cracks in the walls and windows that let in the wind and the damp. She screws up newspaper for the fire, lays kindling wood on top, and coal from the scuttle. Once the fire is ablaze, she goes to the cupboard at the back of the shop and takes out a bottle of metal polish and a chamois leather to polish the brass survey instruments, one of her favourite jobs. She'll use a bit of elbow grease to get them up to a high gloss.

On the countertop is a large map of Africa. A customer came by yesterday and perused it, and her father left it out in case he returns to buy it. Louisa will need to be in on the price negotiation, lest her father sell such a valuable map for significantly less than its worth. He cares little for money, but Louisa has to consider the viability of the business.

The fire has warmed the shop and the daffodil trumpets in the window have opened. Louisa's father will be here soon. She tidies the shelves, takes the metal polish and chamois back to the cupboard, and closes the cupboard door.

The tenement room was dark and stuffy. Its odour reminded Louisa of the smells that pervaded Smithfield Meat Market and Billingsgate Fish Market at the end of a warm day. At the far end of the room a prostrate figure lay on a bed under a blanket. On a small table beside the bed was a glass of water, a medicine bottle, and a cloth.

Mary pulled a chair towards the bed, beckoned Louisa over, and gently pushed her down between her knees. Louisa was apprehensive, but curious about the woman in the bed. She peered at her. The woman's cheeks were hollow, her eyes sunken. But her chest rose and fell. She was still alive.

Louisa turned to Mary with a questioning look.

Mary whispered, "Louisa, this is the person I told you about. This is your real mother. Whom you believed to be deceased. But it was a mistake. Your father ... made a mistake."

Her real mother? Louisa struggled to break away from Mary's grasp. This could not be true. Her real mother died when she was a baby. The shrivelled creature in the bed had nothing to do with her.

Mary pulled her back and stroked her hair. "Hush, Louisa," she says, "I know it's hard for you, but you are old enough to hear the truth, and I know you are strong and brave."

The words Mary had spoken earlier began to register with Louisa. They were to visit her real mother, who was dying. That was what she'd said. But Louisa had been too excited to listen. Little by little, the puzzling events of the past year started to make sense. Mama on the bridge that night, her sudden departure for Scotland over some mysterious illness, her father shipping her and her sisters off to Aunt Fanny. This woman, this half-dead creature, was the reason everything fell apart that day.

But ... but, if this were truly her real mother, was she also her father's first wife? Whom she believed to be dead, yet now lived? And if so ... that meant ... Louisa shook her head, to push the awful truth away. Her father would never do such a thing. Why had Mama brought her here to this stinking room with a living corpse of a woman who meant nothing to her, and these terrible thoughts that could not be true but which must be true, for her mama never told a lie?

Mary lifted her chin and said, "Louisa, listen to me. We are here to help this woman die in peace. There is no greater love we can give to a dying person. And one day, I promise, you will understand how this love will lift us all."

Understand what? That her father was a bigamist? She knew that word. She was old enough to know it meant her mama was not properly married to her father. It meant her father had committed a crime. And her sisters were ... what was the word they called children like that? Bastards? No, she could not, would not understand these horrible things. They couldn't be true. She felt a lump in her throat,

She shrugged away the hand Mary laid on her shoulder. She started as an eerie, jagged breath bubbled up from the woman's chest. The woman's eyes sprang open and she struggled to sit up. Her white face was framed by tangled red hair. Mary put her hand out and touched her chest.

"Catherine," said Mary. Mary reached down for the woman's hand, and entwined their fingers together, "I am Mary. Do you understand?"

The woman's eyes focused and her head gave a faint nod. Her lips moved but no words came.

"And this child is ... " Mary stopped, as if she couldn't say Louisa's name.

The woman's gaze shifted from Mary to Louisa. Her eyes were a startling blue. Louisa noticed the woman's curls formed tiny corkscrews just the way her own did. Perhaps once she was beautiful. She wanted to say something to the woman and wondered if she should introduce herself, but the lump in her throat stopped her from speaking.

Mary stroked the woman's face and smoothed her hair. "This child ... "

The woman's head nodded again. She lifted her hand to touch Mary's arm.. Mary put the glass of water to the woman's lips, dipped the cloth in the water and laid it on the woman's brow, all the while talking to her in a soft murmuring voice. Louisa watched, she didn't know for how long—it might have been minutes or hours. The air tingled, seemed to grow lighter. Louisa's skin prickled; she felt as if something rare were happening, something between these two women, a joining, an understanding, and a few moments of mutual tranquility.

From the shop window, Louisa sees her father striding towards the shop, head up, holding on to his hat against the wind. She smiles. He still walks like a soldier. And never misses a day in the shop. Even today, when they'll shut up early to get to the cemetery before twilight. She could run the shop single-handedly. She already does most of the ordering and keeps the accounts; knows, too, how the instruments work, and how to read the ordnance survey maps. How the far-apart lines indicate broad plains and plateaux, while the closer together the lines are, the greater the undulations of the terrain. At the tops of mountains or in the dips below sea level, the contour lines almost meet. Her father doesn't have to tell her, because she already understands, that he reads his life as a survey map. It's the way he deals with things.

He crosses the road, stops at the shop window, sees the daffodils, and nods. The bell on the shop door jangles as he enters.

The door to the tenement room opened with a click. Edward stood on the threshold. In his arms, he held a sleeping child. A feeling of unease, almost a panic, rose within Louisa. Who was this child?

"Louisa, Mary … " said her father.

Mary's eyes were dark and cold. Edward looked wary. These two people, whom Louisa called Mama and Papa, who used to be so affectionate to each other, were now cold and distant strangers.

"This is the child?" said Mary.

Edward nodded. "Violet is her name," he said. His voice was flat. "She is two years old. Nearly three."

"And the father?"

"Absent."

Which father, Louisa wondered? And who was the child's mother? The dying woman?

He blinked. "She'll be an orphan."

Mary, with Louisa holding fast to her skirts, strode toward Edward and took the child from his arms. "Then she will need a home," she said.

Louisa's head was in turmoil. She felt her breath coming fast. The child Violet, on Mary's hip, held out a chubby hand towards the woman in the bed. "Mama," she said, and began to whimper. Louisa bit her lip, blinked hard, looked away, then turned back and looked at Violet. She reached up to hold the child's little hand, and touched the fat folds on the back of her neck, twined her fingers in her curly hair, golden turning to copper.

Mary shifted Violet to her other hip and continued speaking in a matter-of-fact tone. "I've taken it upon myself to see to your wife's final hours, Edward. Clearly, you were not coping well. I've dismissed the nurse. She was most unsuitable. You'll find her in the tavern downstairs, and will need to pay her."

Louisa was only dimly aware of what Mary was saying, or of Edward's laconic responses. All she heard was the word "wife." His wife. Catherine. The word was a sharp stone in her stomach. The floor seemed to rise beneath her, listing like a ship, and the walls closed in. The room seemed to fill with water. Waves of it came at her, rising higher and higher, to her neck, to her face—she was drowning. With choke and a sob, she broke away from Mary and the child, and ran to Edward, beat him on the chest with her fists, kicked his shins with her feet. He tried to pull her towards him, to envelop her in his arms, but she struggled free, punched him again, and ran back to Mary, clinging to her skirts.

A cry came from the half-dead woman in the bed. In horror, Louisa watched her father's face pucker and a look of such intense pain flood his eyes that she felt her throat constrict. In one swift movement, he was across the room and kneeling beside the woman, and her hand was in his. Mary pulled Louisa to the corner of the room and sat her down with Violet, with her back to her father. She heard the sound of murmurs and gentle sobs from the bedside. Her father was weeping. Weeping, like a woman. She turned to look.

"Louisa," said Mary, and grasped her face, turning her head back to the wall, "look away. This is not for us to be part of."

Violet laid her head on Mary's chest. Louisa, trying to hold back tears, stroked the child's cheek with the back of her hand until the weeping by the woman's bed stopped and Louisa turned to see what was happening. Edward had walked to the other corner of the room, where he squatted, rocking on his heels, his head in his hands. *He is so sad*, Louisa thought. *We are all sad.* Mary went to the bed and draped the sheet over Catherine's body. Then she knelt to pray, and returned to the corner with Louisa and Violet. When Edward stood up, his head and shoulders were slumped, his knees bent. Louisa was afraid he might crumple to the ground. Her father, always so erect, so soldierly, was now defeated.

"Mary," he said, "What can I do?"

Mary's voice was clear. It didn't waver. "What you can do, Edward, is contact the undertaker and make arrangements for the funeral." Mary added, "Did she know about Louisa?"

"I never told her. Not even after the fire and all. I couldn't ... I couldn't bear to tell that it was all a lie what he told her, about Louisa."

Mary nodded, her lips pursed. "Perhaps for the best. I also did not tell her and neither did Louisa. But ... perhaps she knew."

Mary's tone was firm, but not in a bad way. In a way that made Louisa feel confident that Mary would make things better.

"Well, Edward," she went on, "Louisa is almost a woman, but Rebecca and Amelia are still in need of care. And this child of Catherine's, this Violet, will need a home and a family. I am willing, if you are, to return to your employ as a nursemaid and housekeeper. If that is what you wish, you will need to send to Aunt Fanny for Rebecca and Amelia, and arrange new rooms for your family. The girls cannot live here, not in this room, in these ... circumstances."

Edward seemed to pull himself together; he put his shoulders back, but his head remained bowed. "I'll see to things, Mary. Thank you ... for what you've done today. I can't imagine how ... "

Mary cut him off with a sharp turn and a swish of her skirt. She took Louisa by the hand, and with Violet on her hip, walked out of the door.

Louisa is writing up orders at the back of the shop, while her father serves customers at the front. The fellow who was interested in the Africa map has come back. Louisa hears their animated conversation and hopes her father stands firm on the price, but he probably won't, and she'll need to intervene at some point.

She puts her pen down and sits back in her chair. It still stings, the memory of that day twelve years ago. The shock of it. The anger. Her father a bigamist, her real mother alive and then dead, a sister she never knew she had. The betrayals—everyone betrayed, Louisa, Violet, her sisters, Catherine, Mary, and Edward too. All those lives, torn apart. But the aftermath of that day ...

The clock on the wall strikes two. Louisa hears raised voices and genial farewells from the front of the shop. The customer is about to leave. She pops her head in; apparently, he has decided not to purchase the map, for it is still on the counter. Another day perhaps. It is nearly time to shut up the shop.

The funeral was a small affair. Louisa sat between Mary and Edward. Rebecca and Amelia, back from Birmingham, stayed home to care for Violet. Louisa glanced around the church to see who was there: a few curious strangers off the street, the undertaker and his assistant, a couple of church employees.

As the service began, a dark-haired man sidled into the back pew. Louisa couldn't take her eyes off him. He'd been handsome once for sure. As a young man, he must have had girls falling all over him. But time had given him a weather-beaten look. Cheekbones once high were now sunken, betraying a loss of teeth. His hair was thick but greying. Edward must have noticed Louisa staring behind her, for he turned to look, stiffened, and clenched his fists.

When the service ended, Edward marched up the aisle, ahead of Louisa and the rest of the family. The dark-haired man had already snuck out of the church but Edward caught up with him and collared him. Louisa watched the confrontation from a slight distance. Her father was not tall, but he drew himself up until he seemed to tower over the man, and stared unflinching into his eyes, until the man glanced away.

"I should strike you here and now, but we are on hallowed ground," said Edward.

The man held out his hands in a gesture of defeat.

"I loved her, you know. Honest I did, like no other woman I've ever known."

"Love? You dare to speak to me of love?"

"I was all mixed up, see. I lost my job. Tried to get another, but they wanted a younger man. And it was all too hard for me, too complicated with the child and all. But I loved her, and I'm sorry for the things I did, sorry she's gone."

"You'd better leave before I kill you, church or no church," and Edward moved towards him in a threatening way.

Louisa remained stock still behind him, watching the scene play out. She had never seen her father so angry. Edward continued to glare at him. The man moved away, head still down, turned to leave, then looked back.

"I just want you to know, I'm sorry. I wish I'd been a better person. That's all."

At that moment, Mary appeared and pushed Edward away. She held out her hand to the man.

"It's Jack, isn't it? Thank you for coming, Jack," she said, "but you should leave now. I wish you well. I am sure that somewhere within you there is goodness. I hope you find it."

He looked up, and Louisa saw a lopsided smile twitch at the edge of his mouth. He said something to Mary, she couldn't hear what. It might have been, "Thank you. You're a good woman." Or perhaps that's what she hoped he said. His defeated demeanour changed. He gave his head a toss, put his shoulders back and left. Louisa watched him go. There was a strut about him, a sort of swagger, but as he went out of sight, his shoulders slumped. This once-handsome man was her real father. He was the man whom this woman in the grave loved so obsessively, she gave up everything to be with him. Edward had loved this woman in the grave just as obsessively, such that he transcended public standards of decency, legality, and loyalty to be with her.

She grasped Mary's hand. It was large and warm and comforting. Mary held fast to her hand, as together they scattered handfuls of earth into the grave.

Edward has his coat and hat on. It is time to go home. Mary will be waiting for them at their flat in Marylebone, with Violet, on half-term holiday from school. Amelia won't be there as she is on shift at the military hospital where she is a nurse, training in midwifery. But she won't forget—she never does. She says she'll try to drop by tomorrow. Rebecca, who married last year and moved to rooms in Holborn, is having a difficult pregnancy, but sends her greetings; she will come by later if she feels up to it. Louisa takes her cloak from the hook and links arms with Edward. Before they lock up and leave the shop, they turn the sign in the window around to read "CLOSED."

THIRTY-THREE

When they get home, Louisa changes into a ruffled, black bombazine dress, and pins on a simple black satin hat. Mary is already dressed in her black taffeta mourning dress. Not one to spend money frivolously on fashion items, she wears the same gown she wore last year and the year before, updated with fresh ribbons or an altered sleeve. Louisa helps Edward into his black jacket; Mary brushes him down and straightens his tie. Violet appears from the bedroom wearing a fashionable narrow black skirt, white blouse, and black armbands.

Edward, silent, leads the way to the cemetery, Louisa and Violet beside him, and Mary a respectful distance behind. The great church of St. Giles-in-the-Fields is not far from their pleasant Marylebone flat, just across Oxford Street at Tottenham Court Road, and on to St. Giles High Street. The birch trees shading the steps to the church are pale green with young leaves. Sparrows flit and twitter among the branches. They enter the main gate of the church and head to the back were the graves lie. The grass is wet from the morning's rain and soaks the hems of the women's gowns.

As soon as they round the corner of the church, Violet grabs hold of Louisa's arm. "Look, Louisa. They're still there."

"And every year there are more," says Louisa. "There must be a hundred of them now."

It was Violet's idea, five years ago when she was just ten, to plant daffodils around Catherine's grave. She'd been not yet three when Catherine died, and had only a single memory of her mother; a crystal image of being in a park, where Catherine picked a daffodil for her and put it in her hair. Now the daffodils have spread as far as the stone wall at the edge of churchyard. Within days, as they open, they will form a golden carpet.

"Papa, Mama, may I?" asks Violet. Edward nods. Louisa squats down with Violet to pick the daffodils. Violet lays one bloom on top of the gravestone, and hands one each to Edward, Mary, and Louisa, who each lay their flower on the grave. They stand silent for a few minutes. Violet kisses her palm and lays it on the stone. Edward removes a large handkerchief from his breast pocket and wipes his eyes, his head bowed.

Louisa watches her father. She wonders what memories swirl around him when he visits the grave. Shame and sorrow, guilt and anger? Love? Gratitude? A messy brew, no doubt, that boils up every year on this day. But his face is impassive. At Catherine's bedside on the day she died, he'd shown a passion for her she had never seen him show for Mary. But he loved Mary too. Through it all, he loved Mary too. Mary was the placid lake, the calm counter to the rushing river of his passion for Catherine.

Placidity was not something Louisa felt in the aftermath of that day in the tenement room, with its heavy smell of decay which still fills her nostrils whenever she remembers the scene. It took her a long time to understand what Mary had done and why she had done it. The supreme selflessness of her actions. But in time, she came to see that Mary was lifted up that day, as if to a higher plane, where love and forgiveness defeated anger and sorrow.

And because of what Mary did, Louisa found she, too, was lifted up, and she too could love and forgive. Love Violet, the unexpected sister. Forgive Edward, the man she called Papa. And Catherine, the mother she'd never known. And even Jack, with his twisted little heart. Yes, Jack, her real father, who had betrayed everyone, but who had given her and Violet life. That little surprise, that it was Jack and not Edward who was her real father, only came much later.

By then, it seemed almost irrelevant, because after a respectable few months, which Mary insisted upon, Mary and Edward were reconciled. Yes, Mary took him back. The wedding this time was proper and legal, and Mary moved back into their home as his wife rather than his employee. Mary made them a family again.

Edward lifts his bowed head. Louisa takes his arm and, with Mary and Violet behind, leads the way out of the graveyard. Above them, s kestrel hovers, then swoops down to alight on the fence behind Catherine's grave. Like a guardian, Louisa thinks, it watches, sharp-eyed, as they walk through the churchyard gates and onto the street.

By the time they get home, the tension of the day has eased. Louisa and Violet prepare tea. Bread and butter, jam, milk in a jug. Rebecca sent a fruitcake earlier, with a note to say she's still feeling sick all the time, but to please save her a piece of cake for later. That makes them chuckle. Louisa and Violet take the dishes into the kitchen to wash and dry. Violet, as usual, is cheerful and talkative. Louisa is pensive, as she always is after these annual cemetery visits.

Sometimes, when she was younger, she used to ponder the "what ifs." What if Jack had stayed with her beautiful, red-haired mother? What if they'd been her family and not Edward and Mary and Rebecca and Amelia? What if she'd been raised by circus folk, and travelled the world in a painted caravan? What a colourful and exciting life that would have been!

Those were childish imaginings. She suspects Violet still has them sometimes, though they hardly fit with Violet's modern woman sympathies. At fifteen, she fairly bubbles over with new ideas, and is always looking optimistically to the future, never to the past. Except once, Louisa remembers, when Violet was about seven. She came to Louisa in tears, confused about whose child she was, who her parents were. Louisa had told her, "Violet, you and I are fortunate, for we have four parents. Most children only have two. We have a little bit of each of them in us, and we can choose which bits we want to make our own."

Louisa and Violet finish in the kitchen and join their parents in the parlour, curling up together in the large chair by the hearth. The afternoon post has come and Edward is sorting the letters. News from people Louisa's heard of, or known, all her life. Mary puts on her glasses and reads the letters aloud. Uncle Thomas in Canada writes of a vast and open land called Ontario, where the air is crisp and clear and it snows every winter without fail. He says they travel by sledge and snowshoes. Rebecca and her husband plan to follow them there next year.

"I'm green with envy," says Violet. "I'm going to go there one day, too."

"Will that be before or after you take Australia, Africa, and India by storm?" says Edward with a chuckle.

Violet rolls her eyes but gives a good-natured smile. "Perhaps all at the same time," she says, "after I've captured the moon."

Mary's old friends, Polly and Martha, have written. Polly has some news that makes Mary and Edward smile. Mrs. Scroggs, she writes, married her silversmith, sold the house, and moved to Brighton. Mrs. Scroggs. Strange name, and one that echoes in Louisa's memory. Mary said she'd been the matchmaker for her and Father.

"Good old Scroggs," says Edward. "She did all right for herself." Louisa and Violet chuckle.

"I'm happy for her," says Mary. "I wish such good fortune had befallen Miss Everett."

"Who was she?" asks Violet.

"I'll tell you some time," says Louisa. She knew that two years ago, Mary had got notification that Miss Everett had died in her asylum, and Mrs. Scroggs had inherited the house in Bedford Court. Their mother is still upset about her friend's fate.

Edward reads from Great-Uncle George's latest missive, holding the letter up to the gaslight to make out his uncle's spidery hand. George is full of complaints about his aches and pains and Great-Aunt Fanny's failing health.

These newsy, letter-reading sessions happen nearly every week. Louisa used to hope that one day there would be some news of Jack, the father she met only once, at Catherine's funeral, but as the years went by, she gave up hope of ever hearing about him. Perhaps he died. She remembered reading a newspaper report of a man found hanging from the neck in a hovel in St. Giles. No one knew who he was. It might have been Jack.

Edward gets up to put the letters away in the bureau. Mary takes out her knitting. Violet nudges Louisa and draws from her pocket a printed leaflet.

"Look at this Louisa," she says, "I've been wanting to show you. It's for a meeting. Isn't it grand?"

Louisa peers at the leaflet. Violet's face is flushed and animated. Louisa puts her cheek against Violet's and smiles. This will be good for Violet, she thinks. It's what a girl like her needs.

Edward, coming back into the parlour, looks towards them. "What are you two girls scheming there with your heads together?"

"Girls' talk, Papa," says Violet. "You know. What I told you before, about what some women are saying down at the community hall."

"What did you tell me before?"

"Well, votes for women, for one thing," Violet says. "Female emancipation."

Edward responds with a puzzled laugh. "Emancipation from what?"

Violet reaches across and ruffles his hair. "You'll find out," she says, with a mischievous grin. She winks at Mary and hands her the leaflet.

Mary reads it, a look of consternation on her face.

"What is this, Violet," says Mary. "I've never heard of such things."

"You will soon, Mama," says Violet. There is a gleam in her eye.

Mary hands the leaflet to Edward. "Can this be true, Edward? What an extraordinary thing."

Edward takes the leaflet, looks at it, and lays it aside. "Dreams," he says. "She's young. She wants to take on the world, and so she should. She ought to have dreams, Mary. It's harmless stuff, and it probably won't amount to anything."

"You may think not, Papa. But there's something in the air for women in England. There are going to be changes, and I want to be part of those changes." Edward smiles indulgently. Violet flushes with anger.

Louisa lays a calming hand on Violet, and seeing Mary's querying face, gives her head a reassuring shake. Rebecca finally arrives with her husband; there are greetings all round. Rebecca goes searching for cake in the kitchen while Edward chats with her husband and Mary goes back to her knitting. Violet lays her head on Louisa's shoulder. The room is warm; the fire has fallen to embers.

Louisa has learnt from her father to read people's lives as maps. For Mary and Edward, the contour lines on the survey map are now almost flat, with few disturbing undulations. The past is theirs and Catherine's and Jack's—the choices they made, and the choices they never had.

The future for Louisa and her sisters is unmapped, but Louisa feels their chosen paths will veer in disparate directions. Rebecca, like her mother, has married a Royal Engineer, a source of pride for Edward. But Rebecca lacks Mary's peaceful soul. Disgruntled and petulant in adulthood as in childhood, Louisa fears Rebecca might find life as a military wife tiresome and lonely. She hopes she will retain the healthy irreverence and dry wit that makes them all laugh and which will help to see her through. She smiles at Rebecca now, who is standing at the kitchen door stuffing cake into her mouth. She gives Louisa a sly wink and Louisa chuckles.

Amelia has inherited Mary's sweet nature. She says midwifery is her calling, which makes Mary weepy with pride. Midwifery is a science now, and the old ways have been discarded. But Louisa has seen how Amelia quietly listens to her mother's gently proffered wisdom. Amelia will blend the old and the new.

And then there is Violet, the unexpected sister. Violet, squished on the chair beside Louisa, leans forward to examine the leaflets on the table. Her hair has fallen from its bun. It curls into tiny burnished corkscrews the way Louisa's does. Louisa recalls a story Mary once told about a child whose soul contained twin birds which formed a heavenly union when they emerged. Perhaps, she has often wondered, the story was really about her and Violet, that they are the twin birds, united as sisters and alike in looks. But unlike twin birds they will fly in different directions. Louisa has already chosen Mary's sober, peacemaking path and is comfortable as Edward's mapmaking inheritor. But Violet, passionate, determined and spirited, has more than a little of Catherine in her. Though Edward's steady love and Mary's patient devotion has tempered her edges, she stands perched like a bird on the brink of a world she is impatient to change. And perhaps she will change it. She and her generation. And it will be for the better.

The unmapped future for Louisa and her sisters may have bumps and hollows, sharp crags, whirlpools, and sheer rockfaces. The contour lines may close up, come apart, close up again. They may lose their way at times. They may weep and rage, laugh and love, question their paths. But then they will only have to look back to where they began and remember Mary, the mapmaker's wife. Louisa looks across fondly at Mary, who is now dozing peacefully, her knitting fallen into her lap. Mary, who made their family whole again; who knew how to soften the sharp contours of their family's map and smooth out the undulations.

As young women at the brink of a new world, their lives will be different from hers. Their paths will fork and branch in new and undiscovered directions. They will have choices she never had. Power and control she could not have dreamed of. Yet still she found a kernel of autonomy, and in her own way she became emancipated. And, in their way, so will her daughters.

~ The End ~

AUTHOR'S NOTE

My mother claimed her great-grandmother was born in Waterford, Ireland and ran away to England with a circus weightlifter. How I wish I'd questioned her further on this, for when, years later, I decided to search the genealogical records for the lady in question, whose surname, according to my mother, was Cavanagh, I could find no trace of her. I did find some Irish ancestors by the name of Joyce; poor weavers and tailors who probably crossed to England in the late 18th century, but I found no one called Cavanagh and no clear connection to Waterford. Nevertheless, the specificity of name and place and the evocativeness of the story, as well as the fact that it survived through generations of an otherwise unremarkable family, leads me to believe Miss Cavanagh and her circus lover did exist. They may both be lost to history, but they provided the model and inspiration for the characters of Catherine Joyce and Jack.

I confess I have taken some liberties with history, for which I beg indulgence from purists. The corps responsible for the survey of Ireland was actually the Royal Sappers and Miners. They were amalgamated in 1856 with the Royal Engineers to create a single unified corps, but for simplicity I refer only to the Royal Engineers.

The military survey work on Ireland was largely completed by 1842. Although the map itself was not finished until 1846, it is unlikely any members of the corps would still have been in Ireland in 1844, when the story opens.

The Royal Engineers (then the Royal Sappers and Miners) were in Stornoway and the western isles during the 1840s and 1850s (my great-grandfather was one of them), but it is unlikely any one sojourn would have been as long as seven years; the long stay was, however, necessary to the plot of the novel.

Astley's Amphitheatre was, as described, a grand building at the south end of Westminster Bridge, but Astley's Royal Circus is fictional, as is Billy Mather's Amazing Circus.

Charles Darwin's theory of evolution, to which Miss Everett refers, was developed over two decades, and although his work was known among his colleagues, it did not become well disseminated to the public until the publication of *On the Origin of Species*.

However, this book was published in 1859, whereas Miss Everett's reference to Darwin's theory of evolution took place in 1857.

St. Giles-in-the-Fields church retains its ancient and impressive graveyard, but it was closed to new burials in 1850, and parishioners transported to another site for burial. Thus, Catherine could not have been buried there in 1858.

Kildean and Woolcot are fictional villages, but all other place names in the novel are real. Although there were several lying-in hospitals catering to the wives of respectable working men and soldiers, I have not found one named the Southwark Lying-In Hospital, so this is likely a fiction.

Although I now live in Canada, I was born and raised in London, England. The narrow, busy streets of Soho with their clatter and babel resound in my memory, revived by several trips to England over the four years it took to write this novel; the London Museum, the Victoria and Albert Museum, and the Royal Engineers Museum in Chatham gave additional insights. A visit to Ireland, including Waterford City, in 2013, and numerous books and online resources on Victorian society, Irish history, the Royal Engineers, the Irish potato famine, and the western isles of Scotland greatly enriched my understanding of how my characters lived and loved and died.

ABOUT THE AUTHOR

 Christine Forth was born and grew up in London, England. She holds three university degrees, in Philosophy, Anthropology, and Social Work, subjects she has found to be an admirable preparation both for creative writing and for life. In 1986, after sojourns of several years in various Southeast Asian countries, she moved to Canada with her husband and two sons, where she settled into a rewarding career in government social policy research until her retirement in 2006. Now she happily pursues the ambition she has had since childhood: to be a writer. She lives in Edmonton, Canada with her husband and two cats. This is her first completed novel.